DEBORAH O'DONOGHUE

SEA OF BONES

Legend Press Ltd, 107-111 Fleet Street, London, EC4A 2AB
info@legend-paperbooks.co.uk | www.legendpress.co.uk

 British Library Cataloguing in Publication Data available.

Print ISBN 978-1-78955-0-023
Ebook ISBN 978-1-78955-0-030
Set in Times. Printing managed by Jellyfish Solutions Ltd
Cover design by Rose Cooper | www.rosecooper.com

Deborah O'Donoghue studied English and French at the University of Sussex, and Performing Arts at the Sorbonne, before teaching for ten years. She has also worked in car body repairs, in the best fish and chip shop in Brighton, and as a gofer in a comedy club. Deborah was born in Plymouth and now lives in Brussels.

Follow Deborah
@thedebodonoghue

CHAPTER ONE

As she runs along the beach, she knows it's the last time she'll see the mudflats at Culbin. She can't bear to look back at the house, to search for wood smoke still unfurling into the sky like a child's drawing. She turns instead to the sea, to this stretch of Moray coast that used to bring her comfort. Ignoring the cold, she takes off her shoes and hurries towards the water's edge.

Where the sand darkens she falters, but the sea surges on, skirting around and behind her as if determined to reach the bands of driftwood and mussel shell middens at the edge of the forest. A few metres away, the waves smack and slap against a natural causeway of sandbars; droplets fling themselves upwards into the salty air, where they hang for a moment, before squirming, finally, across the map of rippled silt below her feet.

She doesn't even notice the sensation of cold water on her toes. Her eyes are fixed now on the Firth beyond: a pewter mass, rising and falling rhythmically against the white-grey sky. She can just see the Hippo, the rock she used to try to swim to as a little girl, four hundred metres out.

He's watching her from the treeline. She hears his voice again, calling her name. She takes a step.

CHAPTER TWO

They find her body on the shore on a summer afternoon.

The air near the forest is fizzing with midges, so the family stay close to the water's edge, their frisbee dipping and soaring on a gentle breeze between father, mother and son. It drifts just over eleven-year-old Jacob's head, and he races backwards, all golden agile limbs over pale, worm-like sand, his eyes on the red disc spinning in slow motion in the air above him.

He almost falls over her.

Later, the pathologist will find wounds on the top and back of her head. But Jacob, thankfully, can't see these, for all his staring.

She has short, dark blonde hair, and is very slight, dressed in a bright green bikini top, orange cotton shorts, and no shoes. Her bikini is askew, so Jacob's dad covers her up with one of their faded stripy beach towels. Apart from his mother's, it's the first time Jacob has ever seen breasts.

The only other signs of injury are on the girl's toes, knuckles, and the front of her wrists – damaged so badly that waxy bones are visible, threading through blackened holes in her skin, like a plant taking root.

CHAPTER THREE

Dominic leaves the office just before ten, two front pages ready to go. After a livid sunset, it's twilight in London, humid. Joggers and lovers and the smell of street food linger on the South Bank. Lights along the bridge reflect faintly from the water, looping like pearls. Dominic sits on a bench to switch the SIM cards in his phone, and calls his father's number.

"Palmer."

"Dad" – he checks himself; his dad hates infantilism at work – "Bernhard. We're breaking the story tomorrow."

"Excellent. No notice?"

"She won't know what's hit her."

"And legal? They've okayed it?"

"They've been all over it. Trust me. It's legit. Public interest."

There's a silence at the other end. Not a silence exactly. A slow, satisfied drawing in of air. Knowing his father, Dominic supposes it's his late-night cigar. Dominic fumbles in his jacket pocket and lights himself a cigarette. He's supposed to be quitting.

"Which networks?"

"Exclusive to our channels for now. They're all running it. Top story, an *Examiner* scoop, of course."

Laughter. "Nice work. I suppose you're allowed that indulgence."

"And we're sure we don't want the focus on Brockwell? On the *Courier*?"

"Oh, yes. Quite sure. I'm not interested in your squabbling with Brockwell and his libtard rag. Focus on Goldman. She needs to learn."

"Fine."

Another slow breath. "You've gone over the timing?"

"You think it's too early?" Dominic has been concerned about this. "Three months?"

"No. It'll run well beyond the election. And we've got kindling. Those old photos from Lyall. Follow with that."

They hang up. The lights on the water seem to perspire into the clammy night. Dominic stands, loosens his collar and hangs his coat over his arm, before heading back to the office.

EXAMINER EXCLUSIVE: FEMINIST LEADER IN SEX FOR FAVOURS SCANDAL

9 June 2018

- **Fiona Goldman, progressive leader, in sex trysts with newspaper chief.**
- **Damning photographs show illicit couple's affair.**

Exposed today in exclusive *Examiner* photographs, Fiona Goldman, radical feminist leader of the Progressive Alliance, is revealed to be having an affair with James Brockwell, married editor-in-chief of the *City Courier*.

Brockwell's wife is television producer Amy Brockwell; the couple have two teenage children. Our photographs (right and centre page) show Brockwell leaving Goldman's Islington apartment in the early hours on over fifteen separate occasions. In one image, the pair share a passionate embrace in a street near Brockwell's family home.

Under Brockwell's tenure, the *City Courier* has openly backed the Progressive Alliance (PA) and its militant programme of infrastructure investment and social reform. Serious questions must now be answered, about both how the paper's support was procured, and Goldman's position at PA's helm. With general elections just months away, PA's members must ask whether a home-wrecker and seller of sex for media favours is the right figurehead for a party campaigning on parental rights in the workplace, and cradle-to-grave mental health services.

Goldman's credibility is already under fire, after recent remarks about the refugee crisis and criticisms of the British arms trade with Saudi Arabia. Goldman chairs the Cross Party Committee on Ethical Financial Strategy. Over twenty CEOs signed an open letter in May, calling for Goldman to resign, condemning the former actress as "a risk to the UK's international standing as a trading partner".

So far, Goldman and Brockwell have declined to comment. Amy Brockwell is not at her home address. A teacher, who did not want to be named, said the Brockwell children were not in school today.

CHAPTER FOUR

Inverness. Three months later.

Election Day. There's nothing more Juliet can do for Fiona or the party. And today, she must bury Beth.

She wakes early, suddenly, after another dream of water. Declan snores gently beside her. She still feels travel sick. The rush from work to catch yesterday's flight north from London, the strain of the sisterly reunion with Erica, have all taken their toll. Juliet is exhausted but knows there'll be no more sleep now. She lies very still, and stares at the ceiling, as she has nearly every morning since first learning that her niece had died.

From the hotel ceiling, cheap downlighters stare blindly back. The sheets feel rough and heavy, too tight. The hotel on the River Ness, booked by her assistant, is a good choice, central, less stressful than staying here in town at Erica's or out at the summerhouse Juliet owns a few miles away on the coast, but she's hardly noticed anything about the place. She pictures Beth as a baby, arms reaching up out of her cradle; today to be laid in the earth. She hears a truck start up in the street five floors below.

Declan stirs and watches her for a few minutes. He draws close and she turns and presses herself to his body. She stretches her palms into the soft, wiry hairs on his chest, fingertips reading his skin, searching out his heartbeat. They make love, tenderly, Declan kissing her face, her eyelids. It's a brief respite. She holds on to him more tightly than usual. Then, he swings his legs out of bed, pads over to the curtains and lets in some sunlight. She squints, crinkling her tired blue eyes, pupils shrinking from the day.

He carries the coffee maker to the bathroom and she hears him letting the tap run for a few seconds first. "Shall I turn on the news?" he calls.

She groans and rubs her face. "Oh, go on then."

He puts it on but mutes the sound. Stock images of voters coming and going from schools and church halls. Racks full of ballot papers. A piece to camera from outside Parliament. About what, for God's sake? It's too soon for any polling data or analysis. Next story: a Greek island; body bags; a mountain of life jackets; a small child's shoe. Juliet reaches for the TV remote and switches the damn thing off. She can't look at that. Not today.

She wonders fleetingly if any press will show up at the service. Some tabloids picked up that the funeral would fall on Election Day, reporting it as a play for the sympathy vote. This is nonsense of course. Juliet has as little sway over the police enquiry or funeral arrangements as she has over the election date. If she's honest though, she wishes more papers had gone with this insane angle; at least it would take the heat off Fiona Goldman's sex scandal.

For weeks, as PA's Chief of Staff, Juliet has been in a numb daze, publicly fire-fighting catastrophic headlines about Fiona and James Brockwell, while trying to cope with her own grief and disbelief about her niece's death and keep it private. The police portrait of Beth, ill and depressive, is at odds with everything Juliet thought she knew, and it haunts her. But today she must try to put aside the last months of doubt and self-recrimination.

Juliet had been alone, working in her shared Portcullis House office even later than usual on the June night when the news about Beth came through. She'd been in full crisis-management mode, poring over the case for slander against Fiona, studying every speech and statement, advising on content, phrasing, legal parameters. Preparation. Preparation is key. Nothing, however, could have prepared her for what she was about to hear.

"Juliet? It's Cathy. Cathy Henderson."

"Cathy. Hello. How are you?" There was no concern. Not yet. Over the years Juliet had taken many of these calls from Cathy, her sister's psychiatrist. She remembers even thinking it was good to hear from her. "How's Erica?"

She'd carried on, methodically making notes in the margin of the paper in front of her. It seems impossible, now, how unalarmed she'd been.

"I'm well, thank you. But I'm not calling about Erica. It's Beth."

Only then did Juliet's pen stop moving, at the cross of a t.

Cathy continued in her soft Highland burr. "I'm sorry to say Beth's disappeared. She's had some sort of episode. It looks as though she destroyed her textiles. Set alight nearly all her university work. She was reported missing earlier today."

Juliet remembers the strange buzzing in her ears; the unprompted show reel of her niece. A little girl in the forest, giggling at Auntie Jet's insistence on wearing beards of moss and speaking only in their moss-voices, shining almond eyes and gap-toothed grin the only features visible through the greenery. A willowy, teenage figure with bobbed caramel hair and a long summer skirt, dancing on the shoreline with her grandfather. The student visiting London, sitting on a high white bar stool, talking excitedly about fabric designs, sipping a cocktail through a straw, cheekbones outlined and eyebrows jauntily raised.

Cathy was still talking. "The police rang me, unfortunately only after they'd already been to inform Erica."

Oh, my God, Erica. Juliet's mind seized on the thought of her twin sister trying to take this all in from a team of uniformed officers. "They stayed with her until I got there. She's in the clinic now. She came voluntarily in the end, and she's named you next of kin. We've had to sedate her."

A flash of a little girl, sucking her thumb, sitting on her mother's knee in a moment of stillness and calm.

"Juliet?"

"Yes. I'm..." She pinched the frown she could feel between her eyebrows. She wanted to ask more about Erica but did a quick mental triage. Erica was safe for now. "How long has Beth been gone? Where was she last seen?"

"Her boyfriend reported her missing late this morning. She was last seen two days ago."

Boyfriend?

"Look, I realise you'll want to come up to Scotland, but I think it's best to limit visits until we know more and can stabilise Erica. She's manic. Blaming you, Alex... everyone."

Juliet stood, walked to the door and looked up and down the corridor. The place was deserted.

"Cathy, are there any signs where Beth might have gone? Do you think she'll come here, to London?"

Cathy was silent for a moment. "I don't think that's likely, no."

"Why do you say that?"

"Nothing's very clear right now, but the police... This is difficult, Juliet. There are some signs she may have tried to... to harm herself."

Juliet stares up through the hotel window, remembering. It's only September but may as well be winter already. The sky is a painful pale blue and the air looks thin. Declan's spoon clinks slightly against the coffee cups as he stirs.

"I wish it were over," she says blankly. She's supposed to read a poem, selected by Erica.

Declan glances at her. "Ah, you'll get through it," he says. "It's just a bit of poetry." *Portry*, he pronounces it. He gets more Irish the more he tries to sound calm. She can feel him downplaying his concern more and more recently. "Besides, you're here for Erica, remember. And nobody's forcing you."

True enough. There was no way that Erica's ex, Alex, always surly and silent, would burst into a eulogy, even for his own daughter. So Juliet had offered to read, despite her own fear of breaking down, anything to soften the despair in Erica's face. The last time she saw Erica like this, brittle, numbed – in and out of episodes – was when their father died three years ago.

Juliet knows she should be thankful that her parents didn't live to bury their granddaughter, but she wishes they were still here. When she was growing up, Inverness had seemed tight-knit, and the MacGillivrays, like many families with twins, had been unusually close, until the onset of Erica's illness, which changed everything. Not long after, Juliet had gone south to university in London, and had never fully returned, physically or emotionally. Creating a life for herself so far away was nothing to do with avoiding Erica's condition, and nobody had ever suggested it was, but Juliet had always had a vague feeling of guilt about it. Especially as it meant Mum and Dad had borne the brunt: supporting Erica's marriage through its crises and, after Beth was born, letting Erica and Alex live with them throughout her childhood.

Now though, that safety net is gone. Juliet is all Erica has left. This trip to Scotland certainly won't be the last.

She meets Declan's eye. "You know if I cry, or even choke up, Erica will lose it? That's what worries me."

"You're not about to cry. It's a dreadful poem." *Porm.* He attempts a gentle smile, but Juliet is already scrabbling on the bedside table for the piece of paper thrown there the night before.

"I mean, the words. Listen, listen." She attempts to straighten a dog-eared corner of the sheet. "'Fair and free... grew strong...' It's Beth, isn't it? Beth all over. Why can't it just be... I don't know, Corinthians or something, like everyone else?"

"Do you want Beth to have a funeral just like everyone else?"

Juliet sinks slightly into the pillows. "I don't want her to have a funeral at all." She can't defend her position again. The burial will mean the investigation's buried too.

"I know." Declan sits on the end of the bed and strokes her toes with his thumb.

Juliet's tried her best to come to terms with the verdict but the facts pointing to a suicide just seem so... shaky. The evidence is abundant; signposts all consistent with Beth drowning herself, but there remains one problem, which apparently only Juliet seems able to see. And that problem is that the girl who supposedly left behind all these clues bears little relation to the niece she knew so well.

In their regular phone calls and messages, Juliet had noticed none of Beth's supposed isolation or strange behaviour. Surely, after years watching for fluctuations in her own twin sister, she would have spotted the signs of depression or anxiety in her niece? Certainly, nothing seemed to suggest Beth was taking Valium, yet a pot of it was discovered among her things. Only Juliet seemed to think it was strange there was no prescription, or indeed any suggestion of where she might have got it from. In fact, nothing even to prove that it was hers.

Every time Juliet has dared to question anything though, she's been made to feel she's being overly defensive, or somehow blind to the truth, as if the suicide is some sort of added family stigma that she's trying to cast off. She feels like screaming out: *Erica's diagnosis was twenty years ago, for God's sake. I'm hardly in denial. I've had quite a while to get used to living with this shit, thank you*. But of course, she hasn't screamed out. If anything, she's bottled everything up more, kept quieter. She's been doing this since she was a teen; this constant moderation of her own behaviour, minimising any impression anyone could form that she was developing the same symptoms as Erica. As the twin of a sufferer, she thought she'd made peace a long time ago with her own supposed risk of being bipolar, but Beth's death has brought it right back to the surface.

Still, her misgivings have nothing to do with shame or denial. They have to do with damn well investigating her niece's death properly, asking the right questions instead of jumping to easy conclusions. She's found it impossible to reconcile herself to details that other people seem to think are straightforward. One of the most upsetting, and supposedly conclusive, was the note left at the family summerhouse. *I can't live like this anymore*. Live like what? Beth had begged Juliet to let her stay in that summerhouse and get away from her divorcing parents and have some adult space of her own. Everyone agreed it was a great idea. She'd been able to spread out with all her designs. She'd even adopted a dog. She'd seemed absolutely in her element. There was nothing about '*living like this*' that she seemed not to enjoy.

That's another thing. The dog. Beth's beloved Bucky. He often looms largest in Juliet's mind, and not just because of her own leaning towards dogs over humans. Bucky was supposedly left on his own in the summerhouse while Beth walked away to drown herself. It just doesn't ring true. *And drowning?* Beth, like Erica and Juliet before her, grew up here on the Moray coast, and loved the water. She was a strong, year-round swimmer who respected the sea.

But after weeks of investigation and the suicide signed off, Erica wants a service, and Juliet's objections are based on nothing but gut.

Declan brings the coffees to bed, treading softly. "You have to accept she's gone, Jet. You're going to read this thing, because that's what you do. You'll do Beth justice, and when it's done, you'll thank yourself."

"Justice? I thought you were just saying how corny it is?"

"Well," he concedes, offering a small smile. "It is corny. But if it's got something of Beth, you'll bring it out. Read like you're reading it to me in the bath. Or in bed, like last night.

I'll be there, in the church. You can say it straight to me. Make it personal."

A few hours later, Juliet applies Declan's advice without fault. Her eyes lock onto his and her voice holds clear. Steady until the very last word.

Fair and free, the Water played,
Whispering of freedom and God's clear seas;
She grew strong and ventured from her glade,
Her song carried sweetly on the breeze.

She entered the valley, she knew the hills
And on she flowed, voice bright and bold.
She faced the darkness, where shadow spills,
And followed undaunted into the cold –

– To find warmth and light on the other side.
Shall they mourn who hear her song no more?
Nay. Hope and Faith shall be their guides.
The Water still sings beyond the shore.

The rest passes in a blur. Prayers. A speech from the white-haired pastor about bearing the loss of one so young. Then the congregation sways out of the church into the chilly sunlight, and everything stands in sharp definition: the silver birches lining the route to the Petty Chapel at Tornagrain, its two small crosses jutting symmetrically into the sky above pretty blush sandstone and white gables at either end of the church roof.

Tornagrain was not Erica's first choice; she'd wanted the Victorian monstrosity in Inverness centre where Beth's grandparents are buried, but Alex dug his heels in. For once, Juliet is grateful to him. To the east of the city, on coastal farmland, Tornagrain is a better spot. Despite being more out of the way, the chapel and churchyard are packed with students and family friends. Unknown crowds. And, as far as Juliet can see, no press.

Erica lets Juliet hold her hand at the graveside. Alex stands back, Bucky's lead wrapped around his wrist. The dog lays very flat with a worried brow, head on his paws. The university's principal and a fellow student speak. Over the coffin, they lay one of Beth's textiles. It's dark blue with grey and silver threads darting through it. Juliet wishes they'd chosen something less… maritime.

Only when the crowds begin to disperse, and Alex walks Bucky away, does Erica fall to pieces.

She wrenches her hand from Juliet's and stumbles to the ground near the open grave. Her sobs fracture the churchyard air, as if she's breathing glass. It's terrible to witness, but Juliet knows she can only wait. She signals to Declan to leave them, which he does reluctantly as she has begun to weep too, tears dripping from her chin. She swipes at them impatiently, clasping her hand to her throat to muffle the strangled noises she can hear herself making. Like ghosts, plumes of mist rise from the hillsides, and steam from the nearby timber plant forms a column in the sky. Gradually, Erica falls quiet. Cathy has a car ready to take her back to the clinic. Juliet helps her sister to her feet. It's like lifting an old woman.

Later, a fog rolls up the River Ness and mercifully obscures the waterfront view from the hotel bar, while Declan plies Juliet with small-batch whiskies. She probes him fearfully. *Did she read the poem like a robot? Spit out the word 'God'?* Declan reassures her repeatedly: neither.

The exit polls are coming in on the television above his head. It's early but they're not pleasant viewing. Juliet studies her whisky; it tastes metallic. Nothing tastes right anymore. She focuses on what needs doing next. The summerhouse and Beth's things will have to be cleared; it's obvious Erica can't manage it. Besides, Juliet wants to do it herself, now, before any clues as to why and how her niece fell apart so suddenly, so inexplicably, are lost.

She sips her drink, and the reflection of the television news wobbles in her glass. She should have spent more time up here in the Highlands; it's not even a two-hour flight from London. She'd been full of good intentions when Dad left her the summerhouse, and Erica the flat, three years ago. She'd imagined little escapes, more family time. Of course, that never materialised. It was never convenient, never the right moment. Letting Beth move into the summerhouse with Bucky had been as much a guilt-alleviation exercise as anything; a proxy for actually being in Scotland herself. Somehow it had been permissible to put off visits. As long as Beth was enjoying the summerhouse, Juliet could keep working.

Even now, already, she's been called back down. A message from head office, from Fiona Goldman herself, came through earlier. The day of Beth's funeral, and still, it's business as usual. *I hope you're okay.* At least Goldman hadn't asked a lackey to write it. *We'll know by four, maybe five in the morning, I'd like to see you as soon after you fly back as you're able.*

Juliet swills the ice around her tumbler. "I think I should go straight to the summerhouse in the morning," she says. "It's twenty miles. I should do it while I'm here." Her mouth sets in an obstinate line. "If Fiona wants to talk, she can call, or come to me." She wonders momentarily when any senior PA figure last visited the Highlands? Perhaps it's an opportunity to… She stops herself.

Declan raises his eyebrows. "You can't make Fiona come here, can you? Not now. Do you know what she wants to talk about?"

"No idea. The post-mortem I suppose."

He looks puzzled. "Really?"

"*Not Beth's.*" Her tone is withering. "The party's." Declan doesn't even flinch. He's taken so much of the brunt of her frustrations and grief. She ploughs on, a clumsy attempt to cover the inexcusable. "I guess she'll want to start planning next steps. An exit strategy, maybe."

Declan shakes his head. She can feel him learning to keep his reactions as neutral as he can. They don't always agree and until recently it was a source of humour and spark between them. But these last few weeks of campaigning have become so personal, so adversarial, and Juliet – normally so calm and wry about it all – has become like a ticking bomb, ready to go off at the slightest breath of dissent. It's wearing for them both and, she knows, not like her usual self at all.

Yet she's not ready to close the discussion down. "You know what? Maybe they should manage without me, just this once? It's the least they can do." Even to her own ears, she's unconvincing. She lays it on thicker. "I've just buried my twenty-two-year-old niece. I should have come up weeks ago. Only I was too busy, dealing with *other peoples' mistakes*."

The spite in her own voice makes her fall silent. She's tried hard not to blame Fiona and the headlines about her affair with Brockwell. Her anger is directed more at herself than anyone else, although she's sure it doesn't always feel like that to Declan. Now that she's here though, her previous absences seem unforgiveable. How can it be that since Beth's death she's managed just one brief and draining overnight trip to see Erica? And even then her work phone didn't stop ringing. After nearly ten years with PA, rising quickly from a junior role to Chief of Staff, Juliet's at the centre of every move the party make. She'd thrived on their dependence. Until now.

During that one miserly visit north, Erica's clinic had sent her away, saying diplomatically it was not all that helpful to have visitors right now. It could have been the perfect opportunity to do some digging of her own, into what the investigation was turning up. But Declan had urged pragmatism, a return to London and routine; her phone had continued to ring. And, of course, she'd given in and flown home. As the plane had sloped into a furious salmon sky, she'd strained to see through its window, trying to locate the summerhouse among the trees along the coast, as if she could extract some clue from it, some sense about Beth's death.

She catches Declan studying her. "You can't just drop everything and disappear up here. Not now, of all times.

They'll need you more than ever. Fiona may be the star, but you're the brain."

Juliet sighs.

The star.

Juliet has never been sure how she'd felt about the correlation between star power and PA's political ascendancy. But she and Fiona Goldman go back a long way. Nearly two decades ago, when Fiona was making tabloid headlines as the thinking man's totty thanks to her provocative role in a trilogy of films exploring sexuality, she came to speak at an LSE event on gender in the film industry. Juliet still often cringes at herself: young and star-struck, she'd managed to ask the panel a question. She'd been flattered when Fiona sought her out to continue discussing the levels of violence against women in the UK, which were among the highest in Europe. A small crowd around them, they'd talked in the Old Building's foyer long after the formal Q&A. By the end of the conversation Fiona had agreed to spearhead a grass-roots campaign Juliet was involved in at the time, to change the way sexual harassment cases were dealt with on campuses. The campaign mushroomed across universities all over the country, and, there's no denying, helped to shoe Juliet into her first press job with Women's Aid.

From there she moved to the Greens, and years later joined a splinter group looking at creating a new party, a political alliance to bring the left together and tap into to a wider electorate. Their priorities seemed to combine everything Juliet cared about: social justice, gender equality, sustainability, not to mention actually being serious enough to get into power to enact change. Not that she was interested in power herself. Juliet was asked to research the leadership frontrunners. She was known for her incisive background papers, and though the contenders had been vetted carefully before even reaching her desk, within forty-eight hours she was sitting with a group of what Declan would call *think tank wankers*, telling them their choices were untenable.

Asked sarcastically if she had a better candidate in mind,

suddenly she knew she did. Fiona had recently retired from show business and had become involved again in a number of high-profile, popular campaigns. She was proving an awe-inspiring debater and emotive orator. "We need Fiona Goldman," Juliet had blurted. The moment she'd uttered the thought out loud, it became an undeniable truth.

It's partly the incest of their connection, what some might see as the… *reciprocity* of it, that bothers Juliet. She can hardly critique Fiona's star power when she piggy-backed on it in the early days, and has played it ruthlessly to PA's advantage. With Fiona at the helm, they won defectors from other parties and disparate independent candidates, delighted to have a face and identity the press could work with. Fiona won support and donations from sources keen to be associated with her new brand of politics, with sufficient money to support some high-profile regional campaigning. A year after her arrival, PA effectively gained six swing constituencies in Wales and fifteen in Holyrood. From there, they continued to gather momentum. Four years later, they took twelve Westminster seats and one in the European Parliament. Post-Brexit though, and with Fiona being portrayed as some kind of scarlet woman in the press, support for PA is wavering.

Declan swirls the whisky in his glass. "You're the Queenmaker," he says, as if he's read her mind. Juliet bristles at the nickname. He backtracks. "You need to help Fiona exit with dignity. You can't just abandon her now."

He sits forward, urgency in his voice. He obviously thinks what he's got to say is worth risking a bad reaction. "Listen to me. If you stay here and go to the summerhouse now – rather than in a couple of weeks – it could be catastrophic for the party, not to mention your career, but it won't change anything for Beth. She's already gone."

"But if I don't do something now, the trail will go even colder."

"The trail?" Declan stares at her and she holds his gaze as

he downs his drink, moderates his voice as best he can. "Juliet, you've got to get a grip. The police have looked at it all. What are you thinking you're going to find?"

Correction. The police claim they've looked at everything, she thinks. It doesn't help that the investigation was run by Karen Sutherland, an old acquaintance from school days whom Juliet doesn't fully trust. To tell the truth, Karen was an ignorant cow at school. A bullying know-all who hated Erica and Juliet because the boys used to say that she was fatter than both of them put together. Adolescent boys can be cruel but Karen made sure she doubled down on the unpleasantness. She barged and tripped Juliet and Erica in corridors, made snide remarks about how freakish twins are, and, long before celebrity portmanteaus became a thing, she coined the nickname Jerrica, or Jerry, for them both. It was a masterstroke of spite, fusing their identities, when it was clear to anyone who cared to look that they were each striving desperately for their own. She stirred up stupid clan rivalries, commenting incessantly about their mother's French background. Most unforgivably, after one incident where Erica ran away, Karen said she ought to be locked up in an asylum. It riles Juliet that a woman like that was responsible for putting Beth's memory to rest.

She looks down into her glass. The whisky is the colour of Beth's hair.

"I think" – she says, as steadily as she can – "I'm going to find that Karen... That they've missed something. I want to talk to Beth's friends, go to the university. Check through her things."

"But look... Meeting with Fiona, hearing whatever she's got to say, waiting until after the results are properly in... None of that will change what's happened. If you can hold it together for a couple of weeks, you take no risks with PA, plus you gain some perspective. We can come back together, and start sorting Beth's things when you're feeling less—"

He stops himself, too late.

"Emotional?" she offers icily.

They make their way up to their room and to bed in silence.

Muffled by booze and exhaustion, their early morning flight back to London passes while Juliet pretends to drowse on Declan's shoulder. The summerhouse will have to wait. The election results are in. The Progressive Alliance has lost. Every seat, every hard-won council, gone.

CHAPTER FIVE

The fallout is shocking and immediate. Fiona's speech is as neat and dignified as she is, acknowledging defeat and congratulating the victors. Obliquely she manages to denounce what she calls the right-wing media's *winnowing of compassion*, while apportioning no blame to the electorate. The only sign of any discomposure is the way her fingers keep fluttering towards her bobbed hair. She leaves the podium while journalists are still calling out questions.

"Ms Goldman, Ms Goldman! What will happen to PA now? Will you step down? Ms Goldman?"

A longer speech in private to campaign headquarters in Brixton follows the next day. Juliet stands in her office doorway, listening from a distance. Fiona still gives no answer to the questions on everyone's lips. If she goes, what will happen to PA and who will lead them? Juliet's name, among others, has been circulating for some time, and she's done nothing to quell nor fuel the rumours. To be honest, Juliet doesn't know how she feels about the idea of being leader. Even in these circumstances, Fiona is a force to be reckoned with. It's intimidating.

A young intern weeps openly in the crowd just a few feet away. In some ways Juliet envies that emotion. The numbness she's felt for weeks drains everything of dimension and colour. Fiona finishes rousingly, expressing gratitude, personal regret, and fighting spirit, but to Juliet it's like watching someone painting a faint wash on a canvas.

Fiona leaves the makeshift stage, and comes to find Juliet, closing the door behind her. The two women eye each other. They are accustomed to working together, but usually with others present. There's a tangible affection, but Juliet is also a little afraid. Fiona would be a formidable woman to fall out with.

Juliet chooses her words carefully. "That was a good speech."

Fiona takes off her neat red jacket and hangs it on a coat stand in the corner. It looks tiny, like a schoolgirl's blazer, next to Juliet's loose trench coat. She steps forward and places her hands on the back of an office chair in front of the desk. "I'm sorry, Juliet."

"You don't have to apologise to me."

"Well, I am sorry. I know what the party means to you."

Juliet remains silent. She doesn't trust herself to speak.

"You've given a lot for many years," says Fiona. "Your intellect, your judgement, your contacts."

"It's part of the job."

"Yes, but you have a talent for it. And a passion."

So this is how it's done? Is Fiona about to cajole her into running as successor? Or maybe the apology and flurry of compliments are a softener before she endorses another candidate? Not for the first time, Juliet wishes there were a set of blinds to pull across the glazed partition wall. Her gaze flickers to the people outside the office, all trying not to look interested in the conversation happening inside. Fiona turns to face them, and they scuttle. Her back to Juliet, she walks over to the glass, and touches it gently with her fingertips.

"You've been under a lot of pressure."

Juliet freezes. *Where is this going*? "Fiona, please. We've all been under pressure with everything that's been going on. Not least you."

"But your niece."

"Beth."

"Yes, Beth." Fiona turns back to face her. "I know she was like a daughter to you. I appreciate you coming back so soon. It must have been a dreadful day. I'm sorry."

"Thank you."

"It's so hard, especially a suicide."

Is Fiona trying to make her grief the story? Put the failure on her in some way? Juliet says nothing for a moment. She moves some papers on her desk and notices her hands are shaking, her nails bitten down.

"I don't see what Beth's death has to do with this."

"Did you know Beth had some kind of connection to Dominic Palmer?"

Juliet shifts back in her chair, blindsided. Dominic Palmer? She's surprised to hear Fiona even mention him. The heir to the Eden Media Group, his name has been dirt in party HQ for some time already. His father, Bernhard, grew EMG's empire years ago off the back of an established newspaper corporation, quickly branching into a record label and television channels. A well-known donor to the political right, he should have long since been put out to pasture, but by all accounts, far from giving up the reins, he has bought up two alt-right social media platforms riddled with racists and Holocaust-deniers.

Most observers agree Dominic is barely given enough space to do his job running the *Examiner*. Desperate to show his father and the Eden shareholders he's got what it takes in a dwindling print news market, he's been sinking to new editorial lows. Anyone left of centre is considered fair game for nonsensical smears. And it was Dominic who broke the story about Fiona's affair and published a set of her old promotional shots, nudes, although his father is probably still in the driver's seat.

Why would Fiona mention Dominic now? Juliet and the PA team looked at legal action; it wasn't clear whether the pictures had been hacked, or more likely, leaked to Eden by Fiona's PR agent from her acting days, Malcolm Lyall.

It would have been child's play to trace a connection from Dominic back to Lyall and Bernhard Palmer – they've thrived off a kind of unholy symbiotic relationship for years – but Fiona hadn't wanted to give any more oxygen to the story.

Fiona sits down opposite her. "I received some information. Before Beth died. There was a suggestion EMG had some kind of interest in her."

"Why on earth would Beth be involved with Eden Media, or Dominic Palmer? She's just… She was just a wee design student."

"Could she have been trying to promote herself somehow? I mean, she wouldn't be the first young woman to go down that route."

They catch each other's eye, and Fiona smiles ruefully. Juliet isn't in the mood for a confessional though. She frowns. "Who told you about this?"

"James."

Juliet marvels that Fiona is able to sit there and mention her lover's name without a trace of shame about the havoc their affair has wrought on the party.

"James Brockwell told you that Beth was in contact with Dominic Palmer?" Juliet shakes her head. "It doesn't make sense. Beth wasn't rich or famous or… There was no reason for her to be involved with a man like that."

"I agree. But he certainly had some sort of interest in her. What we know is that Dominic Palmer…" Fiona pauses, choosing her words carefully. She glances back to the window, but the party faithful are long gone. She pulls her chair further forward. "Palmer had a note about her on his desk."

"About *Beth*? Saying what? And how do you know this?"

"James had someone who gave him information occasionally. Kept him up to date on Eden, ah… projects. The note was just Beth's name, on a piece of paper… alongside your name."

Juliet closes her eyes. "Someone working for James saw this? In Dominic Palmer's office? Christ."

"At the time, we didn't think it was significant."

"We? You and James? Since when were you two running PA together? Why didn't you come to me? Or Head Office?"

"It didn't seem like PA business. And how would I have explained how I knew? James told me because… well, because he cares about me, and he knows I rate you. Despite what everyone wants to believe, I was not abusing him or my position just to gain—" She stops herself. The rare burst of emotion takes Juliet by surprise. It seems to shake Fiona too. She takes a deep breath and continues. "In the grand scheme of things, it seemed like nothing, Juliet. If you remember, we were dealing with the business community after my comments on the Saudis. Then of course James and I hit the press, and there was the impact of all that. By the time Beth died, we'd almost forgotten about the Palmer thing. It seemed petty anyway, and an unnecessary intrusion on your grief."

"And now?"

"Now? I'm not so sure. It keeps playing on my mind. And, well, I thought you ought to know. We're all going to have some time on our hands over the next few weeks. There are some big decisions to make. I think you should get away. You should be with your family. Take time to grieve and…"

"And?"

"Think very carefully about your position in the party. The Palmers are dangerous. If they think taking you down will help destroy PA, they won't hesitate."

EAST COAST HERALD: STUDENT ANGER AFTER LOCAL GIRL'S SUICIDE

12 September 2018

The suicide in June of twenty-two-year-old Beth Winters has led to angry calls for better access to youth mental health services. The young woman's drowning off the Moray coast shocked locals. Students returning after the summer break staged a sit-in at the Elgin campus of the University of the Highlands and Islands on Tuesday. The Principal has promised more resources to combat mental health issues.

Although suicide rates among 15-24-year-olds have fallen in the past decade, they increased for the second year running in Scotland last year.

Beth Winters grew up in the Highlands and studied Fine Art Textiles at the Moray School of Art in Elgin. Jeannie Logan, Lead Textiles Practitioner, described her as "a popular and talented girl, with energy and drive. A great loss".

Winters was the granddaughter of local architect the late Gordon MacGillivray and the niece of Progressive Alliance Chief of Staff Juliet MacGillivray. Beth's mother, Erica Winters, suffers from bipolar disorder.

Fellow graduate student, Georgia Owen, who is raising

money for a counselling service through her Out of the Blue exhibition in the college's gallery, summed up the student community feelings on social media: *Still can't believe Beth killed herself. So sad. She had it all to live for. #RIPBeth #OutoftheBlue*

CHAPTER SIX

The roads are deserted as Juliet advances on the summerhouse, a week later. September is ebbing away, and the summer season is over – what season there's been this year. A death on the coast doesn't do much for tourism. For several miles, the tall pines flickering at the roadside have been her only companions.

She wants to arrive before nightfall but stops just outside Inverness to pee, get some fresh air, escape the gnaw of tyres on tarmac. At the dirty refreshment counter of a small service station, she sips a vending machine coffee that she suspects will reawaken nothing but her bladder. She flicks through a day-old copy of the *East Coast Herald* for the local news, until she sees an article about Beth. She crushes her tiny cup in her fist, crosses the forecourt, and settles back into the car for the last few miles.

The sun setting, she pulls off the A96 and towards Culbin forest, turning finally in among the green-black trees. Her heart begins to race. It's hitting her fully now: all Beth's things will be where she left them. The sea, their old family friend – turned bully – is here too. As she nears the old railway bridge, she diverts these thoughts, forcing her mind onto that trite little *Herald* article. *#RIPBeth*. Do they have no sense of tone? Blatantly plugging that other girl's show is out of place too, even if proceeds are for a good cause.

The last time Juliet drove this route must be nearly eight years ago. She can't remember exactly. Those old family gatherings are not something she looks back on fondly. The only thing that made them bearable, really, was Beth. She provided an excuse to escape the oppressive Sunday lunches and Erica's inevitable arguments with their father. Their mother simply retreated, drying plates and fetching cheeses and coffees and chocolates, while Alex refused Beth permission to get down from the table. It broke Juliet's heart to see her niece looking anxiously at her plate while Erica railed and unravelled. Juliet would ignore Alex, wink at Beth, take the little girl's hand and walk with her.

They'd sit in the family motorboat on the Culbin shore while Juliet rocked it back and forth, making Beth shriek. Beth loved to find words for the noise of the water against the sides.

"*Sploo woomp*!" she'd shout.

"Oh, you think so?"

Beth, giggling, would affirm that she did.*'Sploo WOOMP!'*

"Interesting." Juliet put her head on one side and listened intently, which made Beth laugh harder.

"I'm going to have to disagree,' Juliet would say. 'I think there's more than a wee helping of *ploppity* in there too."

And returning to the summerhouse, Beth repeating *a wee ploppity!*, the tension would be broken, for a while.

Juliet drives under the railway bridge, and on the other side the road is completely over-shadowed by the trees. She feels a mental shift, like a shroud falling.

"Are you sure you'll be okay?" Declan had asked the other day, when she'd finally tied down as many loose ends at work as she could. "By yourself? If you wait a week or two, I can come with you."

She'd not been able to get a flight to Inverness, and had to arrange to hire a car in Edinburgh.

"I'll be fine. I've driven it dozens of times."

"I know. But not with all this going on."

"Declan, are you suggesting I can't steer a car and have thoughts in my head at the same time?"

He didn't push it. Declan understood she needed the time alone. Or at any rate, that's what she told herself. Maybe he was pleased to have some time away from her foul moods.

The unclassified road leading to the house is already riddled with potholes. There must have been some heavy rain. Before she enters the forest proper, she passes the last of the neighbouring houses, a bungalow in a couple of acres. A sorry-looking pony stands with its back to the road. The summer allure of the coast – even the grey seals, squat cottages, and pastel beach huts at Findhorn, their weatherboards in soft greys and blues against the pine trunks' warmth and the wide seascape beyond – is harder to fathom at this time of year. She drives on, passing the empty Forestry Commission car park. About a mile later, the track narrows, and Juliet slows to a brief halt at the old flag post.

Nothing flaps there now but a piece of tattered red tape left behind by the police team. Her parents used to fly a yellow-and-blue sailing pennant. A simple rectangle divided into the two colours. She remembers her dad telling her its meaning: *I wish to communicate with you*. If only she still could.

She drives slowly. She can't help thinking of the place as her parents' still. The old Culbin settlement was buried by sands century ago and the whole area is protected, but Mum and Dad bought a parcel of land just before a conservation order in the sixties. Mum oversaw the build to Dad's design. A young architect at a practice in Inverness city, some twenty-five miles west, Dad had been very proud of the way the summerhouse worked in its surroundings.

What would he think of it now? There's been an attempt to stain the woodwork. She doesn't remember that happening; it must have been Erica's choice.

Typical Erica. Juliet feels immediately guilty thinking it, but it's true. A burst of energy and activity, with no preparation or follow up. Even this paint-job must have been a bodge;

it looks in need of attention again already. There's peeling where the guttering runs, and the decking, wrapped half way around the sides of the building, is rotting in places. A one-storey, low-slung structure, the house seems to nestle in the forest floor, hunkering among the lichen-covered dunes and the blaeberry bushes. The main living space is open-plan, with huge rectangular windows on three sides, blending building with forest.

From outside it's easy to pick out the floral details of the yellow sixties' wallpaper. At night, encircled by darkness, anyone illuminated inside can be seen from a distance into the woods. Try to look out though, and the reflection of the wallpaper on the windows masks what lies beyond the glass.

As she swings onto the hardstanding, the car headlamps cast long floodlights through the trees and the summerhouse lights up briefly, then seems to step back into shadow. Juliet kills the engine and sits in the car, on the driveway, letting the silence and darkness creep around her. She's suddenly afraid of what she'll find inside.

CHAPTER SEVEN

The man called Taj accompanied the young girl from the supported lodging, into Manchester's northern quarter. She wasn't sure where he was taking her. She didn't know what he did at the refuge exactly, but he seemed to work there, seeing as he was there every day, waiting in front of the building at lunchtimes and in the evenings. He was one of the few who spoke her dialect.

At first she didn't say much, but he won a little more of her trust every day, and it was a relief to be able to talk to him. He spoke to her in a way that others didn't. In a way that no one ever had. It reminded her that she existed. She was a person. He asked her about what her home was like before the fighters came, about her favourite foods, films.

She told him about the last film she saw at the cinema. It was also her first, on her seventh birthday. A long time ago. A world away now. It was called *Up*, about a man who attached balloons to his house and flew to South America. She surprised herself by starting to cry when she described it, and Taj put his arms around her. That was when he suggested he could take her to the cinema.

They went a few days later, but she didn't really understand the film, even though he did his best to translate, whispering in her ear all the way through. The sex scenes were embarrassing, but she tried not to show it. She didn't want him to realise she'd never seen a grown-up film before. After that, he kept telling her she looked just like the female lead. That she could become a film star. She smiled shyly. It wasn't true, but she didn't mind too much him saying it.

Quite often he would ask her if she'd ever had a boyfriend, and would laugh when she said no, that her parents would never have allowed it. She was only thirteen after all. Her thoughts would turn to her best friend's brother who used to live on their street at home. He was sixteen and had dark eyes that crinkled sometimes when he smiled secretly at her on the way back from school. His house had orange trees in the garden. Once she tripped over right in front of him, and he helped her to her feet. His breath smelt sweet and fresh, like mint tea.

On the outskirts of Manchester, Taj stopped suddenly outside an old building with huge steps and columns.

"This place used to be a cinema too," he said. "Now it's a famous nightclub. All the stars come here. Footballers. Singers." She peered in through the closed doors and spied a tiled floor. A high octagonal ceiling. It reminded her a little of buildings she used to know.

He made a call on his mobile phone and arranged to meet up with someone. Then they waited in an alley along the street. The concrete was cracked and uneven. A broken diamond wire fence at the end opened onto a building site. Taj smoked a cigarette and laughed when she refused one. He blew smoke rings to impress her, juddering his throat and flicking his tongue grotesquely. Fat white doughnuts wobbled and dissolved in the air, while he funnelled smaller, faster Os inside them.

When Taj's friend arrived, she didn't like the look of him. He was a huge man, his head closely shaven, and pocked with scars. A large pink mole nosed its way through the sparse blond stubble on his rippled skull. She felt like it was watching her.

"This is Paul. It's okay. He works here at the club."

The two men talked quickly in English she didn't understand. Taj said something and Paul laughed. Taj touched her cheek. Then Paul looked at her strangely. He shook his head and raised his voice. Taj reached his arm up and around Paul's shoulder, leading him a few steps away. When they came back, they seemed to have made an arrangement.

"Paul says you're very beautiful. He says he thinks he can get you a job here. You could earn some money. They have important guests. Famous people. They would like you."

She started to get a funny feeling. Her stomach jumped around.

"Well?"

He was waiting for an answer. He glanced at his friend as if she was causing him embarrassment. As if she was wasting their time.

"What is job?" she asked.

He smiled again. A big, warm smile. "You keep important people happy. If you come with us, we can show you. We can explain."

She needed the toilet desperately, so she agreed.

CHAPTER EIGHT

Autumn has chilled the summerhouse. It smells slightly of dog and damp and Juliet does not sleep well. The wood she ordered for the store is dry and she knows the temperament of the old wood burner inside-out, but by the time she's re-made the bed – stripped of its sheets by the police in June – and curled into it, the place has still not warmed through.

She's never been able to sleep with cold feet. Declan hates her habit of inching her toes towards the crook of his knees. "I can feel you sucking the heat out of me," he likes to complain, turning over and pulling her to him. "If you want me to warm you up, let's do it properly, skin on skin."

She smiles to herself in the darkness. It's not often that she misses Declan. Finding each other in their mid-thirties meant their independence was well-established, and they were both self-aware enough to realise they didn't want to live in each other's pockets. His freelance photography entails weeks apart during a shoot, or when she has a lot on. He still has his own place south of the river. Perhaps not living together all the time is the reason why, when she does feel his absence, her longing for him is adolescent, indecent. She once admitted to him that seeing his boxer shorts still shaped in his form on the floor of her room turns her on. He had guffawed.

"And that, ladies and gentlemen, is the Progressive Alliance!"

She'd looked at him, head on one side, disapproving and trying not to laugh. "Believe it or not, Declan," she'd murmured as he traced a finger down her slender neck. "It is possible to be a feminist and actually like men."

"Men. Hmmm." He kissed her. "I don't like that plural. The others are all bastards, remember."

They met a few years ago when Declan had been commissioned to do some portraits for PA. She hated herself in pictures, seeing only lanky limbs, a constant frown and sarcastic jaw, but even she had to admit that Declan's portrait of her was stunning. Colleagues joked that the photographer must be in love with her, but even when they met again at a party, not many people would have placed bets on them pairing up. Friends teased her that he was an adventurer, completely unreconstructed, but Juliet had a knack for getting under people's skin, and before long he'd confided that although he liked to present as a rebel, he was way too cynical and cowardly to really apply himself to a cause. He expressed admiration for her vocation, and spent a large part of the evening mansplaining jazz. Juliet, a life-long jazz fan, growing up with her dad's vast record library and attending the festival in Inverness, had enjoyed letting Declan dig his own way into a pit. He still claims she only took him home with her to humiliate him with her music collection. His face as he stood leaning against the doorframe gawping at it was priceless. That night set the scene for the rest of the relationship in some ways: playful, fiercely protective of each other and of their own minds – nothing taken for granted.

It's an interesting coincidence that Beth's boyfriend was into music too, she thinks now. A musician apparently recording an album in a converted studio somewhere here on the Moray coast. Juliet knows next to nothing about him though. The relationship was barely mentioned in Karen Sutherland's report, as if it had no relevance. And when Juliet had tried to find out more, she was surprised to learn that Erica and Beth had never even had a conversation about the guy.

He didn't attend the funeral either. Once again, Juliet was the only person who seemed to find this odd. She'd tried to persuade herself that maybe it was a just a dalliance for Beth; or perhaps this boy was some shy creative, who kept himself to himself. She'd like to find out more about him though, and his effect on her niece, or at least his view of the situation. That's an avenue. It has occurred to her too, although it seems like a stretch, that he could be the link to the Palmers and Eden Media Group. She knows the music industry is changing but getting signed to a label like EMG would be massive for a young musician, surely?

She shuts her eyes and tries to close down these thoughts. She hasn't told Declan what Fiona said about Dominic Palmer. She's uncomfortable with it, if she's honest. It feels like such a dirty association with her lovely, unsullied niece. Besides, Declan has a commission to finish, and these questions are something she needs to work through for herself.

Every time they talk they end up arguing lately, and she can feel him tiring of having his input rejected. She spent so long as a teen trying to shield Erica and herself from their father's bullish overprotection, that she now tends to give extremely short shrift to any hint of being told what to do. She knows she reacts badly when Declan tries to give advice or voice any criticism, and she'd rather die than admit it's because she wants his unconditional approval.

She pulls a pillow into place beside her where he should be. Its lumpen, feathery shape is a poor substitute.

In the early hours she wakes, convinced she's heard a car. She opens her eyes. If a car were approaching, she should see headlights arcing around the walls, lighting up the shell pattern ceiling, the bookshelf filled with Fleming, the sewing box bedside table that belonged to her mother before Beth.

The room is in darkness. But whether it's the effect of snapping open her lids so suddenly, or not, she's left with the impression that a beam of light has just disappeared from the round mirror with the rosewood frame on the opposite wall. Not for the first time, she wishes Bucky were here, to bark gruffly at uninvited visitors and curl up at the bedroom door.

She listens intently. The sunburst clock on the lounge wall ticks. The fridge, switched back on only that evening, whispers to itself and gives the occasional, reluctant creak, like a man's groan. It takes her a long time to go back to sleep.

She rouses herself mid-morning and unpacks the supplies she's brought, putting coffee on the gas ring and toasting a slice of white service-station bread.

While the oven hums, she walks through the house, wondering where to start. She glances into the small bedroom she and Erica used to share, but stays at the door. It smells musty and clearly hasn't been used for years. The surfaces are covered in dust. *Little bits of you and me*, as Mum used to say. The arguments they used to have in there! Erica sulking about Juliet wanting to read instead of staying up late covertly sipping sickly liqueurs from their parents' cabinet. In their mid-teens, Juliet had found a used condom under Erica's bed. Partly through revulsion, partly through loyalty, partly through the desire to protect both of them from their dad's censure, Juliet had told no one. She'd been somehow appalled at the significance of it; the way it shouted their burgeoning sexuality. And although she knows the science says otherwise, she's sometimes wondered since if they could have stopped Erica spiralling if only she'd spoken up about her sister's promiscuity there and then.

She opens the slim bureau in the hall, and finds a parking ticket from five years ago. A dish containing coins and – for some unearthly reason – an enormous magnifying glass, like the ones the elderly use for reading. Perhaps Beth used it for weaving or sewing? There's an old tide timetable. Two letters from the university enquiring after Beth's well-being. She supposes the police looked at all of this. They found no diaries, a fact they seemed particularly disappointed by.

So instead they built a picture from peripheral details. The retrieval of Beth's shoes left neatly out in the middle of the path leading to the sea. The friends who described her withdrawn behaviour. The pot containing what turned out to be Valium. They added it all up with Erica's medical history, and it was enough for them.

But not for Juliet.

She runs her fingertips over a framed tapestry on the wall showing a wide tree-lined river – a gift for Beth from her grandparents after a holiday to Canada – and Beth's first attempt at needlework. During one of Erica's hospital spells, Mum had spent hours helping her granddaughter use the kit, explaining how the weft threads hide the warp; how the human eye perceives adjacent colours as one. Juliet remembers catching her mum's eye in amusement when, days later, Beth earnestly talked her through the creation, repeating word for word the tips she'd genned from her grandmother. She'd chosen yarns of different textures for different areas: satin and cotton and wool. *Here the water is calm and still, you see, so I've made it silky, shiny like a mirror. But here, it's all churny, rushing over the rapids*. The result was surprisingly good for a beginner. And it was a brilliant distraction from what was happening yet again to Erica. Mum was great at that stuff. If only she were still around.

Juliet sniffs at an old jar of raspberry jam from the fridge. It smells distinctly fizzy. She takes plain buttered toast outside and, wrapped in a chunky blanket, one of Beth's first year designs, sits on a bench on the decking to eat. The wood is old. She can feel rough lichen through the brushed cotton of her pyjamas.

The firepit Dad built seems to cower at the edge of the garden. How can they ever have a summer evening sitting around it again, knowing it was where Beth supposedly set armfuls of her designs on fire before she died? The police found charred scraps of her fabric littering the lawn and the forest. They spent so long analysing them, they didn't find her note and shoes a short way off the path until a few days later, by which time her body had already been washed up. Juliet still has to bite back her anger at that delay.

She runs a hand through her hair, absently tugging out knots at the nape of her neck, and lets the fine golden strands left in her fingers float away across the garden. The bench faces the sea. Through trees, about forty metres away, across dunes and mud flats and the stony, shell-laden shore, is the steel-grey enemy she now must force herself to look at. No movement is apparent through the branches. No glancing sunlight on water. Its rasping murmur, however, is pervasive. *Sea of bones* her father used to say, fascinated by the discoveries of Mesolithic remains – flint tools, traps, roe deer fragments, human burials – rising to the surface around the coast. Under the sands somewhere, is the old fishing village of Culbin, finally buried in a storm centuries ago. She pulls the blanket closer, takes a bite of bread, and stares.

This is the first step. She has to rehabituate herself to the company of that swell of surf, to its voice, and the horror it has come to represent. Even in London, she's been avoiding all water. No jogging around the Hampstead lakes, nor riverside walks with Declan. Her apartment building has a roof terrace with a great view of Camden's canal, but when Declan manages to persuade her to venture up there, she lets him have that vista, while she focuses resolutely on the old telecoms tower. She faces inwards as much as possible. She works all hours. She avoids talking in depth with Declan, not trusting herself, although he hasn't given up and still broaches the subject of Beth gently, trying to bring her out of herself.

One Sunday shortly before the funeral, remains with her. She'd been at Declan's place and had worked on her laptop all morning in bed, emerging onto the metal spiral staircase wearing his shirt as a cover-up just after noon. He stopped her halfway.

"I knew this staircase was going to be the undoing of me,"

he said putting one foot on the bottom rung with a soulful smile. "I thought," he went on, climbing slowly towards her, "I'd fall down it, like a drunken eejit. But now I see," he reached her and began nuzzling her neck, before dropping to his knees. "Now I see, the devil has a different plan for me."

He groaned softly, kissing her inner thighs. "Christ. A body could drown in here."

She tensed. She tried to ignore his choice of word. Tried to relax and be in the moment again. She closed her eyes. But it was too late, after a minute he stopped. He reached his hands up her back and held her gently.

"I've fecked it, have I not?"

They smiled ruefully together, went downstairs, made some brunch. Later, Declan had become desperate to get out, fidgety all afternoon. To cheer her up, he'd put her favourite Esbjörn Svensson album on, forgetting apparently about Svensson's death in a diving accident. She'd promptly turned it off, its rippling broodiness more than she could bear. The more Declan huffed the more she'd dug her heels in and pretended not to notice. Finally, he'd cracked.

"I think I'll go for a stroll. Get some air." He moved her hair and kissed her neck, circling his arms around her while she perused a bookshelf. "We could eat out?"

"No, perhaps another night. I've got an early meeting."

"Juliet… The sunset. Have you looked out the window at all tonight? The light on the water is like oxygen; it'll do you good."

She still hates herself for her venom, the way she'd pulled away. "You can't fucking help yourself, can you? It's not like oxygen to me. Try of a lack of air instead. Try the sea filling Beth's lungs. That's all I think of. Every day. Every minute. Every time I look at the water."

Declan had stayed in after all; made supper with her. But she'd seen the look pass across his face. Concern. Hurt. And fear. Whether it was fear for her, or fear for them as a couple, she didn't know. She'd said nothing, but had already frightened herself.

She knows what the research says. Since Erica's diagnosis all those years ago, some studies around bipolar in identical twins have shown she has a ten-fold risk factor. This thing about water. Her obsessive thoughts about the suicide, the undirected fury that keeps exploding in Declan's face, are all exactly the sort of things that people experience – that Erica goes through – at the start of an episode. But Christ! It's unfair to leap to that. She's grieving, for God's sake. She had determined there and then, that evening: if she's to get through this, if she's ever going to be able to stay in London and have a life there with Declan, she has to learn to cope with her sadness and fear.

She goes inside the summerhouse to get dressed, and find some shoes.

CHAPTER NINE

Juliet heads off on foot a little before midday. Beth's dad sorted out her car, but the little family motorboat should be extracted from the harbour and overwintered on the summerhouse drive. There's no sign of the keys, although she knows that Beth was using it until at least a year ago: last September she'd sent Juliet a postcard describing a trip out to one of her grandfather's favourite haunts, a small island west of Burghead where he used to ferry the family for day-long swimming and picnics. The card still sits on a shelf in Juliet's kitchen in London: a picture of the dustjacket for *Swallows and Amazons*, showing a little dinghy with a red sail.

Auntie Jet! The Swallow *has been exploring again! We went all the way to Kelspie. I took chicken sandwiches and beer. It was bloody freezing but I found some bright red loosestrife which I'm going to use for a new design. Are you coming up next summer? We'd have fun.*

Juliet knows by heart what the postcard says. She's read it over and over since Beth's death, looking for a hint of anything she should have picked up on. But it gives no sign of depression, nothing to contradict the image Beth had always portrayed – that she never stopped loving the summerhouse, the boat, or that stretch of coastline.

She was an unusual teenager. She never grew bored of coming out here from Inverness, year after year, where there was nothing but peace and nature. She pestered to move in to the summerhouse, even though the university had built new accommodation in Elgin. Juliet takes a deep breath and looks up at the sky. It makes her throat catch every time she imagines Beth here, so solitary. Whenever she came to London, she always seemed such a social animal – partying, at a gallery, or trying to persuade Juliet to leave work early and come for a drink. What was it she liked so much up here that made her keep coming?

The jetty is a little under half a mile away by the coastal path, which winds around diminutive bays and pools created by the sandbars, and trails inland through Culbin forest at points. There's only one other summerhouse along the route in that direction – a far more luxurious place than Juliet's – usually rented out these days as a holiday let. It sits up slightly, on a rise at the forest edge, surrounded by a monster hedge, planted in a misguided attempt to stabilise the dunes. On the public side, the hedge grows out wildly, pushing walkers onto the mudflats and the path of the tide, which comes rushing into the reserve at an alarming pace.

Taking this path to the jetty is intentional. Taking awkward strides across the dune tops, Juliet has no choice but to deal with the sea. She tries not to look down at the midden banks left by seabirds, or the rippled sand interspersed with pools of water below. Why is her heart racing? Even if she did accidentally slither down there, she'd cope, especially in deck shoes. After some hesitation this morning, she borrowed Beth's. It had felt wrong at first, touching them; the last thing Beth did supposedly, was leave them out on this path and tuck a note inside them, before swimming away in her shorts and bikini. Sliding her feet inside the soft nubuck, Juliet half expected to feel some sort of deep repulsion or connection... but there was nothing; no bond or comfort or sense of trespass. Just emptiness.

When she can go no further, she unhooks a bramble from her sleeve and slithers almost on her backside down to the flats. A plinking, burping chorus greets her from the damp sand and pebbles and the thoughts she's been pushing away come bubbling back. She's been tortured by the possibility that Beth slipped somewhere just like this and lay unconscious, drowning in shallow water. If she and Declan had just taken the time for a holiday, if it hadn't been election year, they might have been here. They might have found her in time.

At Declan's insistence, she's been over all this with her doctor in London – Edison, an ancient man, with wild, silvery hair – who listened patiently while she choked back tears and described the thoughts bothering her; her numbness and nausea; her guilt; her fear of water. He asked about Declan, about the support she had, and told her he didn't want to prescribe anything. Her feelings were nothing to worry about; they were a perfectly natural part of grief. Hesitantly she'd begun asking him about some of the findings about Beth's death, about the injury on the back of her head, sustained *peri-mortally* according to the examiner's report.

Edison said Beth may have been swept against a rock. In drownings, he'd explained in a kind, quiet voice, investigators often can't tell which wounds happened while the victim was still alive. This is partly because water washes blood away, and partly because – he'd hesitated, did she really want to hear this? – lacerations are often in the same area as damage caused by the way corpses hang upside down in the water. That's how immersed bodies behave apparently. Arms, hands… dangling. Grazing the seabed. Head down. Like a baby ready to be born.

"But what if…" She couldn't even finish the sentence.

Edison smiled gently, and filled the gap. "What if she'd been struck, on the head? What if someone had inflicted the wound?"

"Yes. I read about a diatom test. They can tell whether the heart was still beating in the water, can't they? If algae cells have been pumped around the organs or into the bones?"

"The bone marrow," Edison corrected and nodded. "But it's controversial science." He squinted at her. It was as if he could read her mind. "Would it make it easier?" he asked. "Knowing she was dead when she entered the water? That someone did that to her? That she didn't just wade into the water and do it to herself?"

She took a breath. "I... Yes. In some ways. It just makes me desperate to think she was so unhappy she would do that without talking to anyone. But being sure we had the truth, whatever that is, would make it easier."

"That's the investigators' job. They've looked at the whole picture. I know this goes against the grain, Juliet" – he took off his glasses, and cleaned them with a tissue from the box he'd pushed towards her earlier – "Sometimes there are no absolute answers, and you have to accept the most likely scenario, when you've taken everything into account."

No absolute answers. You'd think, being in politics, she'd be used to that. Accustomed to compromises, negotiation, best fits. But the fact is, she's always found that aspect of the job the most difficult.

Splashing now through shallow puddles, she scans for an opening where she can climb back up the bank. With a jolt of surprise, she sees halfway along the neighbours' boundary a section of hedge is missing. In its place, the sea and shore reflect at her from what appears to be a high, blackened glass gate. Juliet stares. It must have cost a fortune. The neighbours now effectively have their own private route to the beach. This whole area has been protected from development for years. They must have pulled some strings to get permission.

Backing up, she can even see herself mirrored in the gate's smoked glass, a stagey vista of cloud and sea beyond. And – approaching fast across the sands behind her – a young man.

CHAPTER TEN

It's exactly the kind of job that Declan usually enjoys. He met Lotta Morgan years back on an assignment for the Wensleydale Cheese Museum. A popular new TV chef at the time, Lotta was among a group of cooks invited to invent new recipes. Declan had photographed them and their dishes, and all went on display in the gallery at the entrance to the museum's churning rooms.

He'd immediately hit it off with Lotta, a low-slung, rounded woman, whose Welsh and Indian blood seem to lend her a distant eye and darkly humorous take on the world. What's more, when he later introduced her to Juliet, Lotta and she had quickly become close, giggly friends, which surprised Declan. Few people could so easily get beyond Juliet's slight tendency to graveness. Over the years, they'd all spent hours lingering over long meals at each other's places, talking food, love, family, politics. When Lotta needed someone to do the artwork for her new cookbook, focusing on regional foraging, Declan was the natural choice.

Though he's increasingly loath to be away from Juliet, they both know the job will play to Declan's strengths as well as his sensibilities, and if he's honest, Declan needs the work in the current market, where anyone who can press a button thinks they're a photographer. Whether through loyalty or laziness, he stayed for years at the firm he'd trained with, telling himself that weekend weddings and family portraits were not such a bad way to earn a living, but the final straw came a couple of years ago, after an assignment for a wealthy London couple's 25th wedding anniversary, capturing them at breakfast, by the lake, and then at the huge party they threw. The only pictures in which anyone looked relaxed were ones with their family dog. In desperation, he'd made the animal – a lolloping and affectionate poodle as it happened – into a motif through the whole collection. The family loved it. But Declan had had enough. He'd watched his peers win competitions, move into journalism and reportage, and meanwhile clients were ringing his boss asking for the *Poodle Guy*; not a nickname he relished. Shortly after that, he set up on his own, but is under no illusions that serious jobs are hard to come by. In reality, Lotta and her publishers are doing him a massive favour.

He catches the train northwest from London to Liverpool with Lotta on Wednesday, and they spend the evening with Lotta's girlfriend, Sophie, at her place. Lotta and Sophie met two years ago, when Lotta catered a charity event at the Royal Hospital where Sophie works, and they've hardly been apart since, dividing their time between the two cities. Juliet has met Sophie a couple more times than he has, and raves about her. He can now see why. While they all eat together, Sophie gently mines Declan for the lowdown on London, his favourite places and things to do. When he admits he prefers Liverpool, because of its links to Ireland, Lotta kicks him under the table. She's trying to convince Sophie to sell up and come south.

Over coffee, they plan for the following day. Theoretically it's still mushroom season, but pickings are not rich this late in September. It could take a while to find an area where the harvest hasn't been depleted already, and they need to maximise the available light. Sophie has to work, so he and Lotta will find their own way to a ramshackle lead miner's cottage that used to belong to Lotta's mother's family, east of Ruthin in Denbighshire. The idea is to drive down at dawn, spend the morning foraging and photographing, come back, and prepare a late lunch with the spoils.

They rise early and head through the maggoty white innards of the Mersey tunnel and forty miles out into Denbighshire. They leave Lotta's Golf parked at a countryside centre in Loggerheads, before walking for nearly an hour, in sleepy silence at first. They skirt a vast limestone quarry; Lotta is head down and purposeful, so Declan doesn't have time to pause and frame the way its steep terraces eat into and rise above the landscape, a terrifying amphitheatre. They watch their step as they descend a rough limestone staircase, and soon after pass Lotta's cottage.

It's tiny; the last still standing in what was once a small row backed into a cliff. It has a dark stain, perhaps from smoke or damp on the stones above the door, and heavy timber lintels across two small windows. Picturesque, Declan remarks, in the way that derelict buildings are fetishised. They don't go in, but plunge instead deep into woodland populated mainly by ash and beech. Stripes of grey and blue sky and occasional bursts of sunlight penetrate the branches, while their feet crash softly through the knee-height canopy of leaves and fern onto damp earth and moss.

Lotta isn't interested in the *golden hooters*, as she insists on calling the region's prized chanterelles, but is looking for the more prosaic chicken of the woods, or some cep if she can find them. Still, Declan cannot stop himself snapping away at the chanterelles, funnels of extraordinary bright gold burrowed in moss along the woodland paths.

"If you don't hurry up, we'll lose the sun. It's supposed to be clouding over."

Declan points the camera at Lotta, and adjusts the lens.

"You really are a very irritating man. I don't know how Juliet puts up with you. Will you come on?"

"Jet has other things on her mind. I'm the least of her worries." He takes three photographs in quick succession. Lotta, looking up at the sky. Lotta, head on one side. Lotta, smiling crossly, in black wellingtons and a thigh-length green waterproof, holding a basket about a fifth full of fungi.

"Yes. Of course. How is she? You seemed a bit cagey about it last night. She's gone up to Inverness you said?"

"Yup. She's been incredible really. A workaholic as always. But now the election's over, it's all finally hitting her I think."

"And you let her go to Inverness on her own?" Lotta shudders slightly. He knows that even before Beth died there on that stretch of coast, Lotta, who loves city life, had found the idea of the isolated holiday community, and a village buried by sand, a bit creepy.

"Believe me, I tried to make her wait. But if you've ever tried to make JT do anything, you'll know I was on to a losing battle." He captures Lotta peering into the woods at a fork in the path. She has no idea how far in close-up he is. He sees her brow furrow.

"That's not true. She listens to you. You could have cancelled this trip, you know. I'd have understood."

"Oh, come on. She wouldn't hear of it. I was going to tell her *you'd* cancelled, but she'd have seen through that straight away. Once Juliet's decided something, there's not much changing her mind. Anyway, maybe she needs the time to herself. She's been terrified of the water, you know. Some kind of aversion ever since Beth… I think she's got some idea about facing it."

"You should go up to her when we've finished. Surprise her."

"Yeah…" He seems to hesitate. "I just hope she doesn't end up feeling worse."

"What does that mean?"

Declan plays with the lens. "Well. She's going to be sorting through Beth's things. A twenty-two-year-old girl. Jet likes to think they were close but, well… Sometimes it's best to keep the memories we have."

Lotta falls silent. She's found a crop of chicken of the woods, stacked like flamenco petticoats into the side of a beech. She snaps one off at the base and holds it up for Declan to see. There's soil beneath her fingernails. For a few minutes they busy themselves. Lotta reaching and rummaging, filling the basket with these slender treasures, and Declan swapping lenses, loping away from her, and scuttling back to lie down in the vegetation.

When they've collected all they can from the vicinity, Lotta opens her satchel, hands Declan the flask they prepared hours ago, and produces two oversized Eccles cakes, baked the previous evening.

Declan takes a bite before Lotta's even unwrapped hers, and talks with his mouth full. "How many of these have we got? I could eat about a dozen."

"You're welcome, Poodle Boy," she says drily.

They sit side by side on a fallen trunk, and demolish the pastries. Declan wipes his mouth with a dirty hand, and leans back, stretching, looking up at the clouds.

Lotta stares thoughtfully at the basket of mushrooms at her feet. "So. What did you mean, exactly? About Beth? 'Sometimes it's best to keep the memories we have'?"

He turns to her, his mouth half open as if he's about to speak, then looks back up at the sky. "That's the thing about poodles," he says. "Dogs. They're loyal. They never tell secrets."

She's says nothing for a second or too, then replies briskly, "Not true." She rises. "They sniff them out. Then they bark and bark until backup arrives." She brushes crumbs from her coat, careful not to spill them into the mushrooms. "Come on, let's get going. You can help pick too. We need enough for five different recipes."

Declan stretches again.

"Declan," she says.

"Yes?"

"I really hope you know what you're doing." She holds his gaze. "It's easy to poison a perfectly good dish."

CHAPTER ELEVEN

Toby Norton walks the beach at Culbin every day. Sometimes three times a day. He carries his Nagra recorder with him, strapped around his waist, microphone in hand.

He saw Juliet long before she spotted him behind her on the sands. In fact, he saw her set out from the summerhouse. He was up early that morning. He'd had an extra chore: to find out whose car it was on the driveway at Beth's. He would have seen Juliet get dressed inside the summerhouse if he hadn't turned away. He may be a lot of things, but he's not a pervert. Through the trees he watched her eat breakfast though, sitting on that bench where he and Beth used to sit sometimes. He watched her put on Beth's deck shoes.

Toby holds up his hands as if at gunpoint when Juliet turns towards him with a shriek. He nearly made it back without her seeing him. He stays very still, his shotgun mic pointing straight at the sky. He doesn't want to frighten her. He must look pretty strange with his headphones and, after all, he's the one holding what looks like a weapon. She already looks white as a sheet.

"Hey, it's okay!" He smiles, and gives her his best look. "If you're looking for the path. It carries on up there." He points. "You look very cold."

He clips his shotgun mic to his shorts, pulls off his hoodie and hands it to her.

"I'm Toby."

Juliet's heart races. She stares rudely at the boy, and doesn't thank him for the hoodie. *Boy*. He's probably in his early twenties. A little older than Beth maybe. He's wired up with some sort of recording device, and is now left wearing just red floral beach shorts and flip-flops. He shivers lightly. There's the slight drooping puffiness in his torso and nipples of someone who's lost a lot of weight. He gazes at her with a cheeky, searching expression, and shakes her hand as she stands awkwardly on the sand.

More to extract her hand than for any other reason, Juliet gestures vaguely in the direction she has come.

"Juliet. I'm staying along the coast there." Instantly she regrets telling him this. She has no idea who he is, and dreads people making any connection with Beth, expressing condolences. He, however, hardly reacts.

"Well, Juliet, good to meet you." He chats amiably, supporting her elbow and helping her back up the dune. "I'm in this one." He indicates the house Juliet had thought empty, up behind the hedge. "We're recording there actually."

Recording? Since when was the place a recording studio?

She eyes him again. Could she be looking at Beth's boyfriend? When she'd been told Beth was seeing a musician working somewhere here on the coast, she'd had no idea that meant *right next door*, less than half a mile away from the summerhouse.

She tunes in more carefully as he continues to chat and they make it back to the pathway. He chatters on about electronic music, something about using the recorder to capture the infinitely small sounds of the seascape. *Ploppity*, she thinks. Despite herself, she's warming to him. He seems sweet. And she can see exactly why he and Beth might have hit it off.

The jetty is just ahead. Built at the same time as the summerhouses for their joint use, it's the shape of a scythe:

the walkway a handle and the mooring its blade. Made with black alder to resist the marine salts, it's greyed over the years, and a section that once formed a smaller sister jetty has fallen into disrepair, leaving behind a ghostly forest of piles leading nowhere across the water.

Toby turns towards the house, then back. "I'd invite you in, but you never know what state the guys are in," he explains sheepishly. "I'm going to grab a jumper." He runs inside.

Juliet is left alone again, at the foot of the pier.

She treads along the slatted boards, trying not to look at the water below and, at the same time, averting her eyes from the vast petrol blue expanse of the Moray Firth ahead of her. The water slaps comically against the piles. She fixes her gaze on the small motorboat moored before her. Bobbing gently, painted in cream and red, and covered with a jolly, scarlet tarpaulin, it looks exactly like a boat from a children's book, just as her dad must have imagined it would when he named it. *Swallow*.

Shakily, she gets down on her hands and knees alongside the boat, and pops the catches on one corner of the cover. She peers beneath. Odours of wood and musty canvas hit her. In the rouged halo of daylight, a pair of life jackets and a fire extinguisher stuffed under the seats become visible. It all appears dryish. She can't see much else without leaning in precariously.

Sitting back on the jetty, her attention is drawn to the other boat moored at the end of the old pontoon: a medium class sports cruiser, hulking beside Dad's old pride and joy. It's highly unusual for a boat like that to be left here for the cold season. Winters may have been mild recently, but by December both boats would be better out of the water, especially one as grand as this.

Juliet stands and draws closer. The *Favourite Daughter* must be around eighteen metres in length, with a black-and-white fibreglass hull arcing steeply out of the water like a killer whale. The mid-section and stern stretch away in darkness, so

Juliet can only imagine the inside. One of these guys owns this thing? Delta Function he'd said their name was. It does ring a bell. She wonders if Declan's heard of them. They must be doing pretty damn well, not the aspiring young musician she had imagined Beth dating.

Toby re-emerges from the side of the garden and jogs onto the concrete slipway.

She steps lightly away from the cruiser. "Nice ship!"

"Ha! Not mine. Sadly. She belongs to our PR guy."

"Wow. I think you might be paying him too much." Juliet keeps her voice light. She edges back along the jetty to the *Swallow*. "I've had a little look at this one." She gets down on her knees, and fastens the cover back over her. "She's not too bad." She looks up, annoyed that she's kneeling before him, explaining herself. He has an oval tattoo with what looks like tribal figures on his left calf.

"Her battery probably needs charging," he suggests. He hasn't picked up a warm layer while inside. His torso is still naked and begins to ripple with goosebumps as they talk. He seems to notice her looking and as she looks away, he hugs himself, tucking his hands into his armpits.

"It's amazing here, isn't it?" He says. "Know the area well?"

"It's a while since I've been up here. I used to know it very well."

"Strange time of year to come. Have you been here long?"

"No. Yes. Just a chance to get away."

"Some 'you-time'. On your own?"

Juliet nods and could kick herself. There's something about this boy and his guileless blue stare that makes it impossible not to answer him. His tanned, intelligent face and his smile – it's like being in a beam of headlights.

"Well, look, you're welcome to drop in, if you fancy some company. We have a Jacuzzi. It might do you good."

The Jacuzzi! Juliet almost giggles. She'd forgotten all about that thing. Italianate in style, with rococo mouldings and a domed roof, her parents found it in poor taste when the neighbours had it installed, but she'd always secretly quite liked the idea. She and Erica used to take the spare keys left with their parents for safekeeping, sneak through the forest and the hedge, and use it when they thought the place was empty.

"Thank you." She does her best to keep a straight face. "You might be right." She thinks about what her friends would say. It's a running joke among them that she could do with letting her hair down now and then. Lotta and Sophie would fall about laughing at the idea of her hitting the Jacuzzi with this guy.

He looks thoughtful for a moment and drums his fingers on his bare belly. "Seriously, I'm sure no one would mind if you used it, you know, whenever you like. In fact," he pauses briefly, "there's a kind of party tomorrow night. A few people are flying in."

Juliet wonders suddenly about the car she thought she'd heard in the night.

"Nothing wild, just an end of season thing. We're packing up soon. You could come over."

"Listen, Toby, that's very kind, but—"

"Oh, come on. We'd have fun."

We'd have fun. Beth's voice echoes from the postcard.

Juliet hesitates. "What did you say your band was called?"

"Delta Function. You've probably heard of Dirac Delta. Max and Karlo kind of re-branded when I came on board."

She doesn't like to tell him she has no idea what he's talking about. The jetty vibrates. Another man is now approaching. Toby glances over his shoulder and drops his voice.

"It's Karlo," he says. Then switching into a performance, he opens his arms, nervily, it seems to Juliet. He takes in the *Favourite Daughter* and the house. "Max and Karlo and me, this is all ours. For another couple of weeks anyway. Hey, Karlo!" he calls. "I was just inviting this creature tomorrow night."

Creature?

"Hi," Karlo says. He wears a thin moustache and an even thinner smile. He's older than Toby, in his early thirties maybe, with a very lean build and skinny legs. "Yeah. You could come. No problem. The more the merrier." He sports a towel around his narrow waist. His hair is shaven at the sides, the top slicked up into a quiff. He turns stiffly, and walks to the edge of the jetty.

With some horror, Juliet realises he is about to drop his towel. When it falls to the floor though, it reveals a pair of snug yellow swim briefs beneath. Toby, in his baggy shorts, catches Juliet's eye. She purses her lips, trying not to smile.

Karlo stares strangely out at the water.

"We saw you," he says, over his shoulder. At first, it's not clear if he's talking to Juliet or Toby. He gestures towards the flats Juliet has just crossed, in front of the hedge and the glass gateway. "We saw you both on the sand." He strikes a gawky, wobbling pose that Juliet instantly recognises as a mortifying mockery of herself.

"You should come tomorrow," he repeats. He stretches upright and taut, and turns towards the water, fixing the horizon with his gaze. "Relax a bit. Loosen up." He closes his eyes, raises his left hand to pinch his nose between his fingers, and steps neatly off the jetty, disappearing into the water below.

Toby watches the churning spot where Karlo has disappeared for a moment. He glances at Juliet, who's visibly taken aback by the gall of Karlo's last remark. His Adam's apple works up and down once. "Ignore him," he says. "He can be weird sometimes."

She shrugs.

"I'm going in too." He points at the water. Then he too steps to the jetty's edge, gives Juliet a little wave, and dives into the water somewhat clumsily, coming up with a gasp a couple of metres away, and striking up a rapid, try-hard crawl.

Juliet returns to the summerhouse via the main track from where she can glimpse more of the neighbours' place. A couple of expensive-looking cars are parked to the side of the house, looking out of place, their wheel arches splattered in mud. From the front, she sees the entrance has been remodelled. She tries to imagine where they put a recording studio. Is there a basement? There's no reason why she should remember, of course. Is it possible that Erica told her about it, or Dad before he died, and she didn't pay any attention? What really surprises her though is that Beth hadn't mentioned anything.

The last time Juliet spoke to her niece was three weeks before her death. Beth had been staying at the summerhouse as usual where there was little phone signal, and travelling in thirteen miles to the art school in Elgin, from where she sometimes called.

Juliet hates thinking back to the conversation. She'd been working late, preoccupied by the headlines, when the phone rang.

"Auntie Jet. It's me. How are you?" Beth always asked how others were first.

"Well," Juliet hesitated. "Better for hearing your voice to be honest. Work's a nightmare. I suppose you've seen the papers?"

"Aye but… I cannae say I really get it though. I mean, it's no a crime to be bumping uglies, is it?"

Juliet remembers smiling to herself at Beth's soft Highland accent. She all but lost her own in her first year in London.

"No," she agreed. "Not a crime. But an affair with a married man with kids is not something our core voters are going to empathise with. And on top of that, if they can make it look like she's been – well, procuring favours through sex – it's a disaster. And that's not the only thing."

"What else?"

"Tomorrow they're publishing a photo from years ago. You know, a nude. An old publicity shot."

"Oh, Lord, they're such bampots. I mean, nude photos. Who cares? That's her decision, isn't it? Is PA not about women having choices?"

"The point is, it's not Fiona's choice. She doesn't want it to go public. It was taken when she was a young actress, Beth. She was being exploited by her PR guy at the time who was a complete shit. She's never consented to it going public. And the *Examiner* are going to print it. It's a gross invasion of privacy."

"*Examiner*." Beth sounded vehement. "What a dirty rag. Who even reads it these days? Have we no moved on from there? Surely PA voters will see through these lavvy-heads? They shouldn't judge her for it."

"Last week, they may not have judged her for a few photos. They probably would even have sympathised. But it's damning enough just to be a liberal in this climate, and now she'll be painted as a hypocrite too. A feminist who poses for nude shots, steals other women's husbands, and, worst of all, manipulates the press. People hate to feel their trust has been misplaced. The election is in three months. It's a car crash."

"Aye. I suppose."

"Listen, Beth. I've got a meeting. Fiona's going to be door-stepped outside her place and we've got to agree how to handle it."

"Of course."

"I'm sorry, my love. Are you okay? How's things? How's your mum?"

"Aye. No bad. There's a fair bit on. There's some wee things I really need to talk to you about," she pauses, as if waiting for permission to go on. It doesn't come. "But, um, they can wait. You need to work."

"I'll call you, Beth. When's a good time?"

"Anytime. I mean, I'm away out at the summerhouse a lot, but try me. I sometimes get a signal there."

"Okay. Love you. Speak soon."

"Love you too, Auntie Jet."

That was it. Three weeks later, Beth was dead.

I'm away out at the summerhouse a lot. No wonder Beth spent so much time out here. If these are the musicians she'd befriended, she must have been having a fantastic time. *Did they take her out on that cruiser?*

Juliet forces herself to look away in case she's being watched from within. The idea of a group of men sitting and watching her hesitate and flounder makes her cringe. Toby seems sweet enough, but Karlo got to her and she's annoyed.

It's not a new thing: making a foul comment to wrong-foot a woman, get under her skin. It's a crass technique that has been around for years, probably because it works. It makes you unsure of yourself, makes you go back to the guy for affirmation.

The idea that either of them is manipulating her is, however, faintly ridiculous. At forty, she is frequently assumed to be ten years younger, but even so, Karlo is what? Early thirties at most, and Toby – just a boy – barely older than Beth. Declan would stare at her darkly, suspiciously, and say as he always does that she has no idea how men's minds work, but Juliet dismisses this. There's something else going on.

If Toby was Beth's boyfriend – and it's a big if right now – then it's likely he realised pretty quickly she's Beth's aunt. Why he would invite her to the party otherwise is a mystery. Even then, it's bizarre. Why would you want your dead girlfriend's aunt to come and socialise with you?

Juliet sighs. The truth is, she's grasping at straws. She is going to have to go to this shitty party if she wants to figure out where these guys are coming from. She still can't fathom why Beth, a student from a small northern city, would have had anything to do with a creep like Dominic Palmer. This hotshot lot of musicians are the closest she's come to a possible explanation, even if it does seem implausible.

For now though, she has no idea who they are, and no signal on her phone or wifi at the summerhouse to check anything, or to call Declan. And – she almost laughs – nothing to wear.

CHAPTER TWELVE

These days, Toby does not sleep well. He lies in bed, unable to switch off. He hears his own pulse in his ear, like a metronome.

In his teens he'd work on his music until the early hours of the morning and beyond, sometimes crawling into bed, fully clothed, headphones askew, as the Manchester traffic started to brush though the suburbs. Back then he'd sleep almost immediately, the last few ideas floating around his head before he fell into a virtuosic slumber.

But this is different. He's on a cycle of coke and weed just trying to create some rhythm. And as soon as his head hits the pillow, the thoughts start. He often goes to his room early if he can, to get away from the others, find some release.

Of course, it doesn't help – as he prays for his mind to stop – knowing he has to get up and search the beach. With each hour that grovels by, he knows he's got to be out of the house before the others, no matter how little sleep he's had. How the hell is he supposed to stop thinking about Beth, about the last time he saw her face, when she's the reason he's out there, searching morning, noon and night?

Often he gets up in the small hours and goes for a work-out or a steam to try to shake his ideas and wear himself down. That's the one good thing, he supposes, about this house. The gym in the basement; the steam room outside. He can use them at night without disturbing the others.

He ekes out a cardio session on the rowing machine, going

through the alternatives. What if he just stopped? Stopped the beach patrol? It's tempting. He's spent so long now trying to keep a grip on everything. Trying to live up to Max's expectations. Lose the puppy fat; sharpen the image. He grinds his way through the last five hundred metres, trying to keep his pace up. He could just let go. Stop.

The reality is that one of the others would take it on, he guesses. They'd go beachcombing instead, and he'd just wait for them to come back, watching their faces for any news, in the same way that they currently watch his. He doesn't want to rely on them. You can't trust Karlo for a start. He's perfectly capable of lying, of keeping any new information to himself for his own supposed purposes. He's not stupid, but he is selfish and gullible. He could be persuaded to screw them over.

Then there's Max. Toby hasn't forgotten that Max is giving him an almighty leg up. Alright, it's not as if Max is getting nothing out of their arrangement: his career was in the doldrums until Toby came on board. Still, the idea that Max could go patrolling three times a day, every day, in his place is somehow a step too far.

He moves on to another piece of apparatus, sits astride its little bench, arms flexed for a set of bicep curls. Of course, they will never cease to be totally dependent on each other's silence – a sobering thought, to say the least – but it would be almost worth the risk just to be away from them.

It's this train of thought that keeps Toby awake. Does he have to wait for Max to make the break? For Karlo to drop them all in it?

The idea of carving out his own path away from these guys is so magnetic that Toby finds it hard to trust his own judgement on it. The story, he tells himself, is bound to break sooner or later anyway, and in that case, wouldn't it look better if he were long gone? If his involvement with them all had been terminated?

He towels himself down and gulps at iced water from the

fridge, before padding back to his room at quarter to five in the morning. He might get two hours' sleep. He could deny or minimise any knowledge from a safe distance, preferably some way down the years. But what would constitute *a safe distance*? Will he ever actually feel safe again? He's even considered preparing an envelope, an *only-open-in-the-event-of-my-death* package, as some kind of insurance.

Max has tried to convince him that it would all blow over. The more time they put between them and what had happened, he explained, the less it would hurt.

"The less it will hurt, or the less it will hurt our careers?" Toby had asked.

The answer came, after a few too many seconds to be convincing. "Both."

Toby had turned his face away while Max went on about packing up from here soon. They just had to keep their cool, Max said. Get the album out. The tour under way. Then they could put it all behind them.

But now this woman. Juliet. They're going to have to wait for her to leave the coast, just in case. It would be just their fucking luck for it to wash up at her feet. *She needs to be distracted*, Max said. They'll schmooze her tomorrow. Try to give her some closure. Then maybe she'll go.

Toby thinks about her self-possessed face, her features even and thoughtful, despite her surprise. The way she suppressed that childish smile at Karlo's awful swimwear. Her shrewd eyes.

If she doesn't go?

Plan B. Make sure she can't be taken seriously.

CHAPTER THIRTEEN

The next day there's rain in the morning. Juliet wakes early and listens to its soft fall on the forest floor and erratic percussion on the summerhouse roof. Every droplet seems to worm into the cracks in her thinking.

She needs to go into Elgin and buy an outfit for the party tonight. It's the last thing she wants to do. Having had a night to reflect, doubts are setting in. The whole interaction at the jetty yesterday was very odd, but it's a huge leap to assume these Delta guys are somehow the missing link between Beth and the Palmers. Besides, she's only got Fiona's word to go on about Beth crossing paths with Dominic, or that this has anything to do with her death. Juliet's not quite paranoid enough yet to believe Fiona might have simply been manoeuvring her out of London and out of the way of the leadership bids, but the thought has crossed her mind.

While in Elgin with a better signal, she'll check her work emails and just make herself a bit more visible. She can do some research on Delta Function, and get in touch with Declan. She also wants to attend the exhibition by Beth's supposed friend, that Georgia girl. She should contact someone about the *Swallow* too if she has time. Work out how to get a new key. There's a place in Inverness she could drive to. Then, before coming back to get ready, she'll pop in to see Erica, who's expecting her for afternoon coffee.

It doesn't escape Juliet's awareness that Erica is last on her list. Maybe she should call her? They could arrange to go to the Out of the Blue exhibition together. Even as she thinks this though, she knows it's not going to happen. It's possible Erica would be fine, would enjoy the trip out, the distraction. But it could also be disastrous. Erica's doctor, Cathy, has warned Juliet about the current stress factors – the changing season; the divorce; grief – any or all could trigger another episode, just as things are getting back to normal. Best to keep it simple. Visit her at home. Juliet wants to do the digging she needs to do without having to navigate being a carer too.

Beneath it all, she buries the knowledge that all the triggers Cathy spoke of… they could apply to her too.

The route to Elgin is fairly straightforward – much of it A road, through golden forest. She passes a sign for Sueno's Stone at Forres, where local legend says Macbeth's witches are imprisoned. Juliet always felt sorry for them. Now, the poor witches are doubly confined: the stone's knotted carvings encased within a tardis-like, armoured box, to protect them from the elements and graffiti. As for herself, she enjoys the drive. The open roads and countryside feel freeing and make a glorious change from London's clogged streets.

She remembers Beth complaining about parking on campus, so she pulls up by the cathedral, and walks into the centre. Tattered elections posters are still up, and Fiona's face gazes down under the slogan *Equality = A Strong Economy*.

Juliet finds herself heading to a narrow street of boutiques, where Mum used to come shopping for *de jolis tailleurs*. She hasn't been shopping for months in London, let alone anywhere else, and she feels at a complete loss. The fashion outlets she aspired to as a teenager here are probably long-gone and, in any case, wildly inappropriate for her now. To be honest, she isn't convinced she even knows what she should wear.

It is peculiar, now she considers it, that an apparently successful group of young musicians would choose to come to the Scottish Highlands to record and even then, not base themselves in the cultural capital of Inverness, but stay out in a remote place like Culbin. But she's banking this means they're not big on partying. Toby said it would be nothing wild.

It should be fine, she tells herself again. She's not an elected member of PA, and although she wields internal power, she's not instantly recognisable outside of political circles. But her profile is on the rise, and she needs to be careful. She still can't decide what might have motivated Fiona to get her out of London, but it would be extremely embarrassing if, just as she's supposed to be laying low, she was caught by a bunch of journalists looking like she's trying too hard. The whole thought process is taking up mental energy she surely should be applying elsewhere. This is one reason why she's kept out of the spotlight, and never run for office. All this shit.

In a sale, she chooses a charcoal silk dress with a boat neck and discreet studs on its shoulder panels. It falls to the knee. Her low-heeled boots will work. With the dress wrapped and bagged, she heads to the university, intending to visit the exhibition held in Beth's memory, get a feel for the student who organised it, and grab lunch in a café where she can get online and contact Declan.

The plan goes wrong immediately.

A group of about twelve people are assembled in the university foyer. There's a talk on. A young woman with long brown hair and a dark pinafore stands before the crowd. She stammers and falls silent momentarily when she sees Juliet, and the whole gathering turns to see who has entered.

Juliet gives a small smile and a nod, and the girl glances down at her notes and resumes.

"Beth is – was – a casualty of indifference, self-absorption, and a growing obsession with surface appearances. Like a light reflecting on deep water, Beth's talent and beauty blinded us to her distress. In these works we've tried to show that light can penetrate the darkness in surprising ways. All profits from donations and sales will go towards a new fund for a counselling helpline. Thank you for coming."

Juliet forces herself to join in with the uncertain smattering of applause. As the crowd begin to disperse, she makes her way over to the girl, whom she assumes is Georgia Owen.

"Georgia? I'm Juliet MacGillivray, Beth's aunt."

"Yes. I know. Hello." Georgia flushes bright red into the roots of her hair. "Thank you for coming."

Juliet is touched. "I hope I didn't put you off your speech?"

"No. Not at all. It's just, well, you look so much like her. It was a bit of a shock."

Juliet is very used to being an identical twin to Erica but she's never really considered that this must mean she also looks like Beth. She finds herself both comforted and disturbed. Suddenly, Toby's familiarity on the jetty yesterday seems even more bizarre. If he knew Beth, he must recognise her. So why didn't he say anything?

Quickly she asks, "I'd like to see your work. Will you take me round?"

Georgia's eyebrows shoot upwards. "Of course." A small smile lights up her face. "Come with me."

They cross the gallery space, which has the feel of an old chapel hall, with dark wood beams, sectioned with white panels. At one end hangs a sizeable canvas. In the bottom left-hand corner of the deep blue-black square is a minuscule spot of white.

"This is my favourite piece. I was inspired by Breughel. His painting *The Fall of Icarus*? It shows Icarus in a corner, splashing into the sea, but the rest of the world is really the main subject. Everyone's just carrying on as if nothing has happened? They don't notice him, you know? His tragedy?"

"Yes, I think I know it." Her sentences have the millennial upward lilt so often mocked by observers, but Juliet knows it comes from a good place: the desire to communicate and be understood.

"And over there..." Georgia steers Juliet's elbow softly,

and they turn. On the other side of the space is another canvas – the previous one's mirror. It appears completely white – blank – from a distance, but Juliet can discern a tiny spot of blue-black at the top right.

"Yes. I see what you've done. They're rather beautiful."

Georgia blushes again, this time with pleasure. "They're called, *Witness* and *Bystander*."

"Georgia, in your speech just now you talked about being indifferent, and self-absorbed I think it was. Do you really think Beth was those things?"

"Oh, God, no!" She looks horrified. "I wasn't talking about Beth. I meant us. All of us really. We're indifferent to each other so much of the time, but somehow still obsessed with ourselves and how others see us. Social media, you know."

"Yes. Which is why I don't do social media. Ever." She sees Georgia's face, surprised and slightly fearful, and realises how alien this must sound to this girl's generation. How privileged too. She softens her voice. "I mean, I suppose I'm lucky enough to have people at work who take care of all that on our behalf. And of course, I'm not building my profile or career up from scratch, in the way you have to these days." She pauses. "Was Beth very active online then?"

"She had a page where she posted some things... designs and pictures. But not really. She was quite" – Georgia seems to hesitate – "Quite solitary in the last few months. She basically lived out on the coast. We didn't see very much of her."

This ties in with the police report. Juliet still doesn't want to believe it. "What about lectures and so on?"

"Oh, yeah. She came in, worked in the studio. But she... she stopped hanging out with us." Georgia looks out at the river. "I feel so bad that I didn't ask her if everything was okay."

They linger in front of a sculptural piece. Suspended in mid-air a funnel, graduated from teal to black. Inside, small mirrors are dotted.

Georgia seems to hesitate. Then, "It was me who found the work she... damaged."

Peering down the funnel, Juliet catches glimpses of her own face and eyes. She lifts them slowly to Georgia.

"I came in early one morning, and… the textiles she'd been working on, they were all cut up. And other people's work too."

"*Other people's work*?" Juliet had not been told this. She knew that Beth had supposedly suffered some sort of episode. She'd accessed the university building in the early hours of the morning, the day before she was reported missing. She'd trashed some of her work and taken pieces back to the summerhouse, where she threw them into the firepit. Destroying other students' work seems such an act of aggression – quite different from the self-immolation Juliet has tried to get her head around.

She stares at Georgia. "Your work? Was it… affected?"

Georgia reaches out a finger and touches the sculpture dangling before them. It swings almost imperceptibly on invisible wires. "Yes. Experimental pieces. Nothing important. A couple of the other students were much worse off. And really angry. I mean, we'd just had the final show. And Beth just… All their work was gone."

The sculpture quivers. "You were the one who contacted the police?"

"Yeah. I mean, I didn't know what had happened. I didn't know it was Beth who'd done it. And, well, unfortunately I'd already tidied some of it up. I'd put some of the pieces back in Beth's workspace. They photographed it. And interviewed me."

Juliet is unsure how to react.

"I can show you if you like."

Georgia leaves Juliet to look at the other pieces, while she speaks quietly to someone on reception. Then together, they cross the lobby and a small courtyard where a sequence of arched trellises support some roses and raggedy sweet peas, to reach what looks like a temporary hut, near a sign for the nursery and an incinerator. The hut is divided into four workspaces, lined with benches and sewing machines.

A mannequin draped in woven grass stands in the corner. Overhead, an enormous wire framework hangs like a freakish spider's web.

Georgia leads Juliet to the back and pulls a sizeable plastic storage box from beneath a bench.

A disembodied patchwork is jumbled within. Tiny squares and triangles of printed cotton and woven fabrics. Ribbons of denim are stretched across a broken cardboard loom. Frayed edges give the whole a downy, creature-like feel. Juliet lays a hand on the pile and strokes it for a second. She picks up two jagged pieces and tries holding them side by side, like a jigsaw. They don't match.

"Did the police take this away? Did they examine the studio?"

"No. They photographed the pieces. The machine." She gestures towards a terrifying-looking shredder in the corner. "Took fingerprints. But that was before they worked out it was her. The CCTV in the courtyard showed her arriving. They said she must have been in some kind of frenzy. She used scissors and a pen-knife, as well as the shredder, they said."

Juliet's head drops forward onto her chest momentarily. She takes deep breaths. This is the first real evidence she's seen that something might have been very wrong with Beth. She remembers Erica tearing her teenage diaries into shreds. *A confetti of confessions and confidences*, their father had called it when they found the tiny pieces of girlish handwriting scattered all over her room.

"I'm sorry," Georgia says softly.

Juliet places the pieces back into the box, and stands. "Why did she do it, do you think?"

"I really don't know." Georgia swings her legs, rocking. She is sitting up on a workbench, a tiny section of black-and-white kilim weave between her fingers. "It doesn't make sense. She'd been working so hard for months. We all had."

Juliet is impressed with this girl. Any suspicions around her motives for putting on the exhibition to gain attention for her own work, are fading. Georgia seems sensitive and thoughtful.

"It can't have been easy to pull together that show. It's not been that long since Beth died. And I imagine some of the other students might have still felt resentful?"

"Well, I'd already been working on the themes and pieces for my finals, and it seemed right to – to try to do something. We put on shows a lot, so it's not a big deal. I mean," she coughs. "I mean, of course it's a big deal, but— "

"It's okay. I know what you mean. Georgia... Did you know Beth well before all this?"

"I thought I did. You know, we were friends in our first year together here. I even went out to your summerhouse once. But that was a while ago. Three years. She changed a lot, especially last year. I mean, obviously she lost a lot of weight. She was so thin. I wish I'd taken more notice of that."

Juliet's stomach turns. This is news to her. The pathologist had mentioned weight, but she hadn't paid much attention, thinking merely that Beth had always been slender and had no weight to lose.

They make their way back to the courtyard. Before they part, Juliet puts a hand on Georgia's arm. "I don't mean to put you on the spot, but there's a group of musicians staying out near the summerhouse. Did Beth know them? Wasn't she seeing one of them?"

Georgia nods. "I think a couple of people saw her in town with one of them. There have been some rumours about it."

"What kind of rumours?"

Georgia shifts her weight from one foot to the other and swallows. "Drugs. But" – she continues quickly – "I don't know if Beth was, you know, involved in that. I can't imagine it."

It's Juliet's turn to nod, slowly. It takes a lot to shock her. She's suddenly very uncertain about attending the party tonight, but feels the need to be there more urgently than before.

Georgia seems to pick up on Juliet's discomfort. "I'm sorry," she says. "I don't really know much more. I wish I did. I've been over and over it and I just don't understand what happened."

Juliet smiles and tries to reassure her. She'd like to ask so many more questions, but she can feel Georgia backing off, as if she's the root of Juliet's distress. It's inevitable. This is how people react. They start out well, but soon retreat from conversation when faced with raw grief.

After leaving Georgia, she finds a café near the cathedral. The sky has darkened again and the Lossie looks like a river of tar. Juliet shudders, but sits by the window and orders a sourdough sandwich and a coffee. She gets online and searches for Beth's webpage. She must have looked at it a hundred times since Beth's death: a professional-looking, static page with photographs of her various fabrics. The heavy blanket. The maritime weave that they laid on the coffin. It's a beautiful, promising collection. What a waste.

Out of curiosity, she pays a rare visit to the PA social media pages. Even though she's expecting the worst, she's stunned at the degree of vitriol she finds on discussion threads there:

With that media whore Goldman gone, PA will sink like a tampon in a sewer, where it belongs.

All these sluts should be raped until they have enough babies to look after at home.

MacGillivray leader? No way. The crusty old cunt belongs at the bottom of the ocean with her fuckwit niece.

How fucking dare they weaponise Beth's death? What is wrong with people? Hands trembling, she fires off an email to the person who's supposed to be moderating the comments. Why hasn't someone blocked this bile? Is nobody working? She checks her own inbox; it's littered with internal emails, but little of note. The official line is that the alliance is commencing a period of reflection. Fiona and other senior figures are taking time to regroup. Engagements are being cancelled. Even ardent supporters tend to distance themselves from political failure. There's nothing Juliet needs to respond to immediately. She has nowhere to channel her outrage. It's an odd feeling after the workload of the election run-up.

To distract herself, she finds an article on a music website about Toby, and reads with growing incredulity. He's quite the cult star. She saves the page to explore offline in more detail later.

She tries to call Declan. His phone goes straight to voicemail, which she could have predicted since he's probably out in the sticks with Lotta. Partly relieved, she composes a long text to him instead. He'll no doubt be surprised to hear she's going to a party and she feels better able to explain it in writing than in a snatched phone call. Not that she needs to explain to him; they don't have that kind of relationship, but… hating herself for this thought, she knows that she needs to protect her own reputation from any unsavoury aspects of this scene. A written record of her reasons for attending the party might come in useful.

Her fingers hover over her phone: *Walked to the jetty yesterday. Got my feet wet and survived. Met a bunch of musicians recording next-door. Dirac Delta, or Delta Function or something. They've invited me to a party. I need to find out what Beth's involvement was, if any, with these guys, whether they are the link to Palmer, and how they might have affected her over the months before she committed suicide.*

She recalls the conversation with Fiona about the need to be careful. She hasn't yet told Declan what Fiona said. She deletes the reference to Palmer, and hits send.

As she returns to her car at 3pm, the sun, now low in the sky, emerges from the clouds. The ruins of Elgin Cathedral – Lantern of the North – sit directly beside the Lossie, where their doppelganger reflections spill out and tremble gently, like oil. A red glow – visible through the empty rose window and every vaulted arch – make the carcass look consumed by fire. Juliet slides into the car and heads west towards Inverness, and Erica's place.

CRATEDIGGER.COM: HOLD OUT FOR BOLIN – By Phantom Limb

September 02 2018

Another day, another release date slated for Dirac Delta's tenth album, this time for next spring. But is Max Bolin's latest incarnation even worth holding out for?

After rumoured beef between the legendary synth-pioneer and Karlo Southall, his Dirac Delta collaborator, notorious control-freak Bolin has been uncharacteristically humble in interviews, claiming they've found their stride again, thanks to young DJ-producer Toby Norton.

Norton has been heads-down with the duo since Bolin scooped him from the unsigned stage at Manchester's ELX Festival two years ago. Restyling as Delta Function, the newly-formed gang of three have trailed material at secret gigs, switching up Bolin's old-school techno with Norton's out-there glitch-infused dub, to mind-bending effect. Phasers on eleven.

CHAPTER FOURTEEN

Juliet waits outside the large blush sandstone mansion block where her parents used to have a flat. She glances at her phone for any messages. Nothing. She almost presses the buzzer again but forces herself to wait. Erica knew to expect her today. What's taking so long?

The name ticket on the building's roster is yellow with age. *MacGillivray / Winters*. It must have been there since their parents bought the apartment, nine years ago, when Mum declared she could no longer manage the stairs in the old house because of her hip. It's probably too soon to suggest that Erica's ex-husband's surname, Winters, be removed. It was Beth's name as well as Alex's, after all.

Suddenly, Juliet feels sick. She has been imagining a warm chat with Erica, reminiscing about Beth, about what to do with her things, whether there's anything at the summerhouse that Erica wants back. This now seems impossibly unrealistic.

Finally Erica answers. "Juliet?"

Is it just Erica's accent, Juliet wonders, or can she hear something in her sister's voice – excitement? Agitation? She immediately feels guilty for being so late.

"Aye. Yes, Erica." Juliet stumbles, her own accent morphing as usual, in her desperation to communicate some show of loyalty. "Hi. It's me."

The latch release keeps humming long after Juliet has pushed open the heavy door and stepped inside. Erica either wants to make certain that it's opened, or is furious and being heavy-handed. Juliet doesn't wait for the lift, instead running up the stairs to the second floor. Erica stands at the threshold.

Her face looks crumpled, as if she's been asleep, or crying. Juliet kisses her twin's cheek softly and they embrace for a long time. Erica chokes back a sob. She starts talking before they let go, self-protective chatter.

"Thank you for coming. Cathy's been magic. The meds are spot on, I think."

Juliet nods. She told Cathy she was coming to allow time for any adjustments to Erica's prescription. Erica is perfectly aware that Juliet and Cathy take these precautions, dosing information as carefully as drugs, but still, it makes Juliet uncomfortable. It feels like subterfuge. She also knows it's no good overthinking it all, second-guessing Erica's reactions. Seeing the whole situation like this, circling it as if on the outside, is perfectly natural, Cathy says, although Juliet is sometimes afraid it's the sort of paranoia Erica describes.

Erica talks on. "You hungry? I've cookies, or there's fruit. You want a wee coffee?"

"Hey, hey." Juliet touches the silk scarf tied loosely around Erica's neck. It's a pale cream with a sage-green geometric pattern. "Look." She opens her coat and pulls out her own scarf – a mint-and-cream check. Often they used to find themselves accidentally wearing what they referred to as "twin uniform". It's a superficial thing, but makes them feel closer.

Standing face to face, they smile tenderly at each other; Erica slightly heavier set around the cheeks than Juliet, a side effect of her medication; her silvery hair bobbed at the jawline, whereas Juliet's hair is shoulder length and pale gold still. Erica's skin is thinner and fine lines are evident around her mouth and eyes.

They pass through the apartment, Erica waves her hand at the study.

"Ach. Mustn't look in there. It's a midden. I've been trying to recover some holiday pics for a girl at work. Mexico."

Juliet glances in. Their dad's desk is still against the far wall below a group of early sketches he did for the summerhouse, in black and beech frames. In the first days after Beth's death, Erica turned them to face the wall. They've still not been turned back.

A laptop and external drive lay on the green-upholstered chair beside the window that looks out onto the block's managed gardens. Mum's nursing chair. Juliet remembers sitting on Mum's lap, in the old house, the sinewy cushion of maternal shoulder beneath her cheek and the smell of – what was it? – something French. Lancôme, perhaps? As an auntie, she too used to jiggle Beth on her knee in the chair. She has no memory of Erica using the chair herself to nurse Beth. After the birth, Erica's bipolar symptoms had become brutal, with two suicide attempts before Beth's second birthday.

Juliet had hoped her arrival might be a welcome distraction, although anything to do with family and it's all too easy for Erica to slip into dark thoughts. During the last visit, Erica told her she couldn't help feeling aggrieved by all the time Juliet and Beth spent together over the years when she was ill; the closeness they had together. She'd admitted she sometimes felt her place was taken by both of them, that she was doubly usurped, as a mother and a sister. Juliet was shocked and hurt. She puts this out of her mind and follows Erica to the kitchen.

"Coffee? Cookie?"

"I'd love a coffee. Please. But I ate in Elgin." Time to test Erica's reaction. "There's a fundraiser on there."

"Aye, I read about it."

"Do you think you'll go?"

"I'll try. I've been swithering."

Juliet sits on a high stool at the breakfast bar, and carefully describes parts of the show and Georgia Owen. "Do you remember her? She says she visited the summerhouse with Beth in the first year."

Erica pours the coffee and settles opposite. "In truth,

cannae say I do, no. I don't recall a lot from that year. It will have been just before Dad died."

"Yes."

They sip their coffees in a momentary silence, lifting the cups to their lips at the same time.

"So, how's it going?" they both ask, then catch each other's eye. Speaking in sync – another supposed twin thing.

Erica explains she's just started back at work for two days a week. Her programming job at the local council is not particularly challenging, especially since they blocked her from working with the team that supported the other public services – the police, the hospital. Her mental health made her too high risk, according to them, for any access to sensitive or confidential records.

Juliet tries to listen neutrally. She'd been furious about this treatment at first, especially as Erica was one of the only members of the IT team with a proper understanding of coding. But when Erica had talked about quitting, Juliet had ended up encouraging her to stay put. She still feels bad about not being more supportive of a change. But on balance, the council have been a good employer and very understanding about Erica's need for occasional periods off. Once last year, during a reception for visitors from Inverness's twin town in Bavaria, Erica burst in, shook hands with every single guest, introducing herself to them all as Provost of Inverness, and proceeded to give an inspired and quite surreal speech about Scottish-Bavarian relations. The council were brilliant about it and the actual Provost, a portly, bearded man, sent her flowers during her convalescence, addressing them to his "understudy".

At the height of an episode, Erica can talk for hours, but today, she's careful to ask Juliet how she is too, and enquires after Declan as if she's trained herself to stick to conversational norms. Juliet notes this painfully. Most people grieving for a daughter would not be under such pressure to self-regulate, at least not with their own sister. She allows herself to be guided by Erica though. She steers towards work, giving the potted, official version of the post-election regrouping that is taking place. She makes no reference to her own position as possible leader, nor her obsessive thoughts about Beth's suicide. And she certainly can't chance mentioning that she's trying to find out what Beth had to do with Eden Media or the Palmers. If Erica were to think she's treating Beth's death as a public or political event, it would be just the sort of thing to set her off. What's more, she may seem surprisingly together right now, but Erica is capable of blurting out anything to anyone when she's ill.

Erica listens to the political round up, and latches onto this safe topic, launching into a mini-diatribe about the press treatment of Fiona.

"It's unbelievable. Never a good word. Never a serious look at her policies. Ach, but her *sex life?* That gets the microscope. Hounding her. On her doorstep."

Then, she says something that makes Juliet sit up.

"I mean they were even here, asking for a statement about her. Of course, I didn't—"

"Hold on," Juliet interrupts. "Why would they come here?" She realises immediately that she sounds dismissive, which is not what she intended, although it wouldn't be the first time Erica had been utterly convinced of some kind of harassment. She even accused Juliet of trying to take her baby once. But right now she seems completely lucid. There's none of the conspiratorial tone of her more frenetic moments.

"Surely you can imagine it, Jet? Some journo winding me up; make me start havering about Fiona and that editor guy. No doubt they just wanted a reaction. It would make a mighty headline, you know: MacGillivray's Skyrocket Sister Lashes Out at Love Cheat Goldman."

Juliet ponders this. It's not that far-fetched. She'd be lying if she said Erica's illness had never been discussed at senior level. *How much of a liability is she? Would the press make heavy weather of the mental illness in the family?* But these questions had been set aside. A minor risk. She remembers one meeting: it was Fiona who had closed the topic down, declaring they weren't going to indulge themselves in second-guessing the gutter press. The concerns remain though. As a policy-wonk, Juliet's rarely had to worry about being in the headlines herself, but this would undoubtedly change if she became leader. *And how would Erica cope?*

She sips her coffee. "Have you often had journos here then. Journalists?"

"Only twice. The first time after Fiona's adultery came out. Then again, after those old nudes were published. It was before… before Beth died."

Juliet watches Erica, holding herself still, her hands in a diamond shape around her cup. In flashes like this it's plain, to Juliet at least, how practised her twin is at keeping herself together. Packed in tight. Hiding. Managing. She recognises the behaviour in herself, although recently she feels as though her own ability to cope, to be *politic*, is falling away from her, like sand through an hourglass.

Here she is again, thoughts slipping, when Erica needs her.

"I had no idea," she says. "Why didn't you say something? Who was it?"

"Ach, I don't know who it was. Some space slice. She rang me at work. I hung up on her. But she was outside and followed me to my car."

"Did she say which paper she was from?"

"No. No idea. She was… about five foot seven; maybe sixty-five kilos." Erica is useless at faces, but her memory for figures and spatial awareness has always been impressive. "Red hair."

Juliet wracks her brains but cannot think of a political journalist matching this description. It might be a local hack.

"I get hate mail as well, you know," Erica says matter-of-factly.

"What?"

Erica rises and pulls a small bundle of letters from behind the breadbin. She slides them towards Juliet. Some are typed, some are in a scrawled hand: complaints about Juliet's politics and descriptions in no uncertain terms of the violations the writer would subject both MacGillivray twins to, given the chance.

Juliet hardly ever sees this stuff. Now it's twice in one day. Appalled, she asks softly, "Do you think this sort of thing went to Beth as well?"

Is it possible? Harassing a young student just because her aunt's in politics?

"I don't know." Erica blows down lightly on her coffee, though it's lukewarm now.

Juliet reaches out across the table and touches her sister's forearm. "I'm sorry. You shouldn't have to put up with this. Have you told anyone else?"

"It was June," Erica says suddenly, at Juliet's touch. "The journalist. The first time. There was a friendly versus Denmark that night. I watched it in a bar."

Juliet smiles. Football was one of the passions Erica and Alex had once shared. "Have you heard from Alex?"

"No. Not since the funeral row." Alex had wanted Beth to be buried in his family's churchyard in Forres, south of Culbin. It was this disagreement that eventually led to the choice of the Petty Chapel and not Inverness's central church where Mum and Dad are buried. If Beth couldn't be buried with his parents, he didn't want her buried with Erica's either, even though they as good as brought her up.

"Has he no been in touch at all?" Juliet hears herself, slipping into the regional burr. For some reason, it not only happens when she's with Erica, but often when she's annoyed. It sometimes bothers her, this lack of control over her own speech. Not that she deliberately cultivates any accent, but especially in politics, keeping a grip on your delivery and choice of words is key.

"No."

What a pig Alex seems to have become. Juliet refrains from remarking on it. "I expect he's finding it all as difficult as the rest of us," she murmurs instead. *I expect he feels as guilty as fuck*, is what she wants to say.

Well into their old age, Mum and Dad had effectively looked after Alex, as well as taking care of Erica and Beth. But no more than a month after Dad's death, and just a year after Mum's, Alex had filed for divorce. One month, and he'd already had enough, apparently, of dealing with Erica by himself. It would have been too much like responsibility. He'd always taken the easy route. *Selfish bawbag*. It can't have been easy for Beth: the impact of her father walking out, on top of her grandparents dying in such quick succession. Juliet can feel herself starting to seethe. She drinks the dregs of her coffee and goes to the bathroom.

She glances into the study again on her way past. It's an old habit – monitoring Erica's state of mind through the degree of order or chaos on show. In their teens, whenever Erica began turning in on herself, somehow their parents, especially their father, would hold Juliet responsible. She used to carry the dread of his unwarranted disapproval around in the pit of her stomach. But the more she tried to ward off his censure, the more Erica seemed to court it.

The reading lamp arches over the chair. A Sudoku book is butterflied open on the rug, surrounded by notepads. Juliet steps inside the room. *Is Erica still keeping a diary?* She hardly needs to, with a memory like hers. Juliet crouches and – guiltily – turns a few of the creamy pages. They are filled with bulleted lists. Arrows. Boxed-off details.

Better day today. Still wondering where Beth got those pills.

Erica's voice at the door of the room makes Juliet jump. "Not a diary as such, but notes. Thoughts."

Juliet stands up abruptly and backs away from the books. "I'm sorry," she blurts. "I have no right."

Erica talks straight across her. "You're alright. I'm used to people howking around in ma head."

Juliet glances sharply at Erica. They both have a tendency to sound harsh at times, and, let's face it, she would fully deserve it on this occasion. This could go in any direction.

"Aye" – Erica's voice hardens – "I mean, why should I have any privacy really?"

"You're right. I'm so sorry. Of course you can expect privacy."

"So you say, but there's no let up, is there? Cathy, Alex, you... You're always there, watching."

"That's not true. I'm not even here most of the time."

"You say that, but you're always watching. You've always done it. Going through my stuff. Checking up on me. Where I am, who I'm with. You think I don't know. It's like being followed around by my shadow. Constantly. A bloody boring, nagging shadow."

A sudden savagery comes over Juliet. She snarls, her teeth vicious, "And have you never thought that I'm sick of it too? Maybe I'd have kids of ma own? Maybe I wouldn't have to be so fucking boring if there were no a fucking Erica car crash always about to happen!"

Silence. Erica stares at her, shocked. Juliet blinks. Hardly ever has she spoken to anyone like that, let alone Erica.

And suddenly it's flooding out.

"God." Juliet tries to breathe. "I'm... I'm sorry. I think you're doing so, so well. You're very far from being a car crash. I just don't know how you're coping, to be honest. I'm... I just can't stop thinking about it. All the time. What happened to Beth. I just... It feels like nothing will ever be okay again. Nothing's worth it."

Erica's arms are around her, both of their shoulders heaving with sobs. What feel like several minutes pass like that; the two of them locked together, eyes closed, in their own world.

Finally, Erica murmurs. "Whae are you, and what have you done with my sister? I thought I was the one with the temper."

Juliet feels her twin stroking her back, and it's a gesture from long ago, prehistory.

"I'm sorry."

"Wheesht. It's okay." Erica breaks away. "It is worth it, you know. What you do. It's important. And Beth admired it.

Admired you." She picks up a pad. "Maybe you should try writing things down. Helps me anyway, to compartmentalise; get things straight in my head." She puts the pad back on a shelf where there's a rainbow row of them. Then, thinking twice, she selects one – bound in a pretty, pale blue leather – and hands it to Juliet. "Here. It's new. You take it."

She turns off the lamp.

Back in the kitchen, Erica goes to the window and lights a cigarette. The clock on the wall ticks loudly. Juliet weighs things up. Erica seems in a better place than she ever imagined. A much better place than she is. Maybe it's not fair to keep all her questions and feelings to herself?

"Did you know the place next door to the summerhouse has had a load of work done on it?" she asks. "It's a recording studio? Apparently there are some famous guys there. I was wondering if one of them was Beth's fella?"

"I wouldnae know." Erica's cigarette glows in the twilight. "She never told me things like that."

Can she tell Erica she is going to their place, to this party tonight? It doesn't feel right. She's supposed to be at the summerhouse sorting through her dead niece's affairs, not partying with the stars. Besides, there's nothing to tell right now anyway. Is it worth risking Erica's peace of mind?

She hedges. "They're called Dirac Delta, or something."

"Good name." Erica takes a long drag. "Infinite highs, infinite lows."

"What?"

"It's a maths term. Dirac Delta function. It describes a type of distribution on a graph. An infinite spike basically. Or an infinite low. Like an impulse. Maybe a load point of pressure."

Juliet doesn't ask how Erica knows this stuff. She's fully aware that Erica reads prolifically during up times and down. She wonders though what would make a group of DJs choose a name like that? It seems… emotionless.

She and Erica chat a little longer, about clearing the

summerhouse, and how long it will be before Juliet has to go back to London.

"I've probably got two to three weeks. Maximum."

"Will you be running? For leader?"

So, she has been following the news.

"I'm not… I don't know. To be honest, I don't know if I'm the best person for the job or if I want it. Nobody's even broached it with me directly."

The idea of selling the summerhouse hangs in the air – unspoken. Erica inherited the apartment and Juliet the summerhouse, so the summerhouse is her own decision really. Still, it won't be an easy subject to raise. She starts to gather up her things, and strokes the blue notepad with her thumb briefly before putting it in her bag.

"Do you think Beth kept notes? Did they find any?"

"Only to do with her designs. Nothing personal. Some bits and pieces in Mum's old sewing box. Karen didn't think they were significant."

"Ri-iiight." *Karen Sutherland*. Detective Inspector. The most unimaginative person in the world. *Surely Beth's designs were her most personal thing?*

"You're not still bearing a grudge against her? School was a long time ago."

"Course not." Juliet snaps. She changes the subject rapidly. "Have you been to Culbin at all? Is there anything you particularly want me to keep?" She pauses. Everyone has just assumed that Erica can't deal with this herself, which seems way off now. "Do you want to come out there? Go through anything?"

Erica hesitates and for a moment Juliet holds her breath. It's years since she and Erica have done anything so meaningful and intimate.

"To be honest, I just don't think I can – or ought to." Erica's meds give her a distance and clarity which is sometimes surprisingly straightforward. "I'm sorry."

Juliet nods, relieved and filled with guilt, again. Erica at the summerhouse is the last thing she needs, especially tonight.

CHAPTER FIFTEEN

Juliet dresses absent-mindedly. Feeling the new silk fall over her skin should be a pleasure, but she can't stop thinking about the shredded fabrics Georgia showed her. Scissors *and* a pen-knife? Did the police even take any fingerprints? She supposes they must have, but it's another point to follow up. And who was the journalist Erica mentioned, sniffing around Inverness?

Putting on some make-up, mentally she tries to prepare herself for the evening. She will need to find something to make small talk about; try and bring these guys out of themselves.

Toby sounds genuinely intriguing. An article she found said his father was some kind of recording pioneer. Musique concrète. Juliet likes the idea. Art for art's sake; she's all for that. And it's good to be challenged, but surely there must be a limit to how many times anyone can listen to a toilet flushing or a knife scraping a dinner plate?

If you listen carefully enough, if you increase your exposure, your awareness, it can change the whole way you listen to the world, Toby was quoted as saying. *But it's a Pandora's box; you can never go back to perceiving things the way you did before.*

It's strangely like the things she says about inequality.

It's nearly 9pm when she finally takes a torch and makes her way up the main track, a dart of silver through black trunks. As she draws closer, music sighs and throbs through the woods around her, rebounding oddly from tree to tree. If she closed her eyes, she wouldn't know where the sound was coming from. It's a very mild night, for late September. A few more cars than yesterday are parked on the verge. The front door is open and through it an arrowhead of light populated by midges points at her feet. Her boots crunch across the gravel footpath cut pristinely into the lawn. Juliet feels foolish. It's hard not to walk in time with the bassline. She stands at the door and calls out.

Thankfully Toby appears quickly.

"Juliet!" She feels his hand in the curve of her waistline. He kisses her cheek, saying closely into her ear, "I'm so glad you decided to come." She's irritated and, despite herself, amused in equal measure. It's a perfectly suave and very presumptuous greeting, which he layers up straight away. "We don't often get the chance to entertain women of your calibre."

What does that mean? Has he worked out who she is? It would be surprising if a young musician were familiar with PA party insiders. "My calibre?" she repeats.

"Well, what I mean is... You're obviously... I mean, look at you—"

His blue eyes dart back and forth into hers. She feels guilty. It's too easy. He's young. And he's trying to be charming and welcoming. More to the point, she may well need his help to understand what happened to Beth.

She follows him to the kitchen, a granite and high-gloss affair, and Toby pours more ice in the sink. She counts twenty bottles of champagne. "A low-key thing, I think you said?" She raises her eyebrows.

Toby laughs – an appealing, self-deprecating sort of snort. "Champagne. Max says it keeps it simple. And doesn't stain. He can be weirdly hung up about that kind of stuff. There's going to be a couple of guys from the record company. Max's sister. Some friends. We think someone from the Coen brothers' people might come. We know they're in the country. We did a birthday gig for Joel last year in the Hamptons. It was insane. They talked about us submitting a few sample tracks for their new film." He drops his voice. "Max is completely gunning for that." He hands her a drink, pinching the glass carefully by the stem, and invites her to look round while he finishes some preparation.

Trying to picture her niece here, she wanders through the house. Every sip of the champagne feels like a betrayal of Beth, although she and Declan have already talked extensively about this. Enjoying the good things in life is not disloyal to the dead.

In the lounge, she finds two middle-aged men in loose suits, sitting on a low, white sofa, talking too loudly.

"It's tribal, you know. In a way. The rivalries just get bigger and bigger and bigger."

"Yeah. Absolutely."

"Kind of a spontaneous combustion. Centrifugal. Pressurised though, at the centre."

A pile of white powder sits on the table between them. One of the men looks up and nods at her as she glances in. She's adept at networking with all sorts, but this she needs to stay away from.

Finally, she finds a stairway and ventures down. A corridor spotted with small downlighters and carpeted in deep burgundy leads to what must be the recording studio. Two identical square rooms adjoin each other via a glass dividing wall.

A small group of people are gathered around a mixing deck, listening to samples, smoking and chatting. Slow and compulsive, a bassline plays, punctuated by distorted crackles and overlaid with an ethereal vocal. Juliet is offered a spliff and refuses it with a smile and a small shake of the head. At this, the tallest member of the group pauses the conversation by raising his hand almost imperceptibly in the centre of the little crowd.

He is awe-strikingly handsome, a blond man in his late thirties, with grey eyes, and thick, silvery blond stubble on his cheeks and chin. He's immaculately dressed, in close-fitting knitwear, semi-tailored cropped trousers, and expensive sandals. He turns to her, and everyone follows his gaze.

"You must be Juliet," he says, extending his palm. His fingers are strong, tanned and slender.

She shakes his hand, taken aback that he knows her name. "Yes. Ah – Max, I suppose?"

He nods and smiles, his eyes crinkling gently. "Welcome. Toby told me you might come." He speaks to her as if they are entirely alone, and Juliet guesses this is where Toby has learned his eyes-like-headlights trick. Suddenly she knows, with a certainty and repulsion she's rarely felt, that this man is the one Beth would have fallen for. She tries not to let her horror at his age show.

"Let me introduce you," he says smoothly. He turns to the group. "I believe you've already met Karlo – he's the third wheel, I mean, the third cog in the Delta machine." A band of low laughter breezes around the group. Karlo acts put out, then takes a mini-bow.

"And this is Ralf, our encyclopaedia of, well, just about everything; and his girlfriend, Molly, who very kindly lent him to us for the whole summer. Everyone, we're honoured: this is Juliet MacGillivray. Beth's aunt."

A reverential silence falls, just for a moment.

So Toby and Karlo knew all along who she was. And hearing Max say Beth's name, so proprietorially, is like a punch to the gut.

Thirty-five minutes later, Juliet feels lightheaded. It's hot and smoky in the recording studio. She'd like to get some air but Max said he had something to show her. He is, however, otherwise occupied. Several more people have arrived in the basement and for the moment, it appears to be where the party is at. Or where things are being contained. Ralf and Molly have been keeping Juliet's drink topped up and, she gets the impression, keeping an eye on her.

Just as she is about to excuse herself, Max re-appears at her elbow.

"I'm so sorry, Juliet. Forgive me. I was going to show you the artwork. Come with me."

He leads her through to the second studio, which is less fuggy, and closes the adjoining door. They are alone. At the side of the room, propped against the wall, is an A1 portfolio. He grabs a low stool for Juliet and kneels on the floor unzipping the folder, opening it out like a huge book.

Inside are clear plastic sleeves in which a selection of fabrics is displayed. They are unmistakably Beth's work.

Juliet doesn't trust herself to speak. This carefully curated collection is in stark contrast to the box of rags Georgia showed her at the university; a reincarnation. She explores the portfolio slowly, silently. Each plastic jacket gives a little breath as it falls, giving way to the next artwork, similarly sheathed. Every piece is the size of a long-play record sleeve. Some are printed or embroidered on cotton, some are woven, clearly on hand-made looms, and some have been scanned in extraordinary detail to create a photographic replica of the fabric. Juliet lingers over one: a weave using varying shades of dark green and black for the warp yarn, creating a graduated lengthwise grain. A single thread of bright white streaks across the weft line near the top.

"Beth was here with us a lot of the time, when we were recording. We knew what inspiration she took from nature and architecture all around the coast. And I suppose we were trying to do the same, so it was kind of natural to start collaborating. We were planning a run of limited edition record covers, featuring her work, you know, the actual fabric. The rest of them would be these digitally reconstructed versions. Ralf does that."

"They're amazing," Juliet manages.

"Aren't they? We love them. And they're so *her*. I mean, I guess you know she and I were seeing each other? But, if I'm honest, I think all the guys here fell for her in a way."

He's so slick. Saying all the things he must think she wants to hear.

"And yet none of you knew how bad she was feeling?" Juliet says. It sounds aggressive, but she doesn't care. A man of his age and experience should know better.

Max rocks backward slightly.

"No, you're right. I've been over and over it. I mean... she just got us. All of us in a way. Maybe we thought we knew her because she seemed like she understood what we were about. Each sleeve was supposed to represent a different track on the album, so that our fans would have a kind of bespoke version. I mean, I've seen your, erm, father's records at the summerhouse. You must know vinyl is back and people want collectors' items."

He seems to have segued very quickly from eulogising about Beth, to talking about the record industry. *Vinyl is back... Collectors' items...* All the more collectible, perhaps, now the artist is dead? Juliet keeps turning the portfolio's leaves.

Does he sense he's not winning her over? He reaches out and removes one of the fabrics from its sleeve, running his fingers over it lovingly.

"You know, there was something about the way she worked with layers of texture, with colour. It's really similar to how we work with sound. The layering, the patching in. Even the language is the same: spools, bobbins, reels. Toby and Karlo went over to the workshop with her and recorded the sound of one of the looms. We've used it on one of the tracks."

Juliet is surprised to hear this. "How long had you all been collaborating?" she asks. "It sounds like it must have been very exciting for her."

"She didn't tell you?"

Juliet shakes her head.

Max seems relieved. "Well, I guess, we did ask her to keep it under wraps. It sounds, you know, pretentious, but we've got lots of imitators."

"And are you still going ahead?"

"With your permission…" Max pulls a sincere face. "For me, if we could use them, I think I'd get a kind of sense that all is not wasted? In any case, I thought you should see these, and have the final say." Juliet turns the designs back and forth. "I mean, you can take them if you want. They might… they might give you some sort of continuity, or closure? I don't know how long you're planning to stick around while you're sorting everything out, so I wanted to make sure you'd seen these and had a chance to think it over."

Continuity. Closure. Juliet keeps looking at the fabrics, at the white dart of thread. *It sounds like he's trying to hurry her away.*

He pushes again. "We'll credit her fully for the album artwork. And give a percentage of the takings to charity. You name the charity."

"When do you need to know?"

"We need to get it to the plant by the end of next month at the latest. We're aiming for an International Record Store Day release."

"I see."

"It's a big date in the industry calendar. April."

"Yes. I know what it is." Patronising sod. "Let me think about it, Max."

"Of course." He starts packing away the artwork.

Juliet wants to ask him directly about Delta Function's relationship with the media. She wants to demand why Max thinks Beth, *his girlfriend*, committed suicide. Why would she have destroyed her work at the university and thrown half of it on a fire? Why would she have killed herself with a project like this going on? Before she can summon the right words however, the door between the studios opens. A very beautiful, slender woman stands, eyeing Juliet oddly for a moment, then indicates with a slight movement of her hand that Max come upstairs. Max doesn't make any introductions.

"Excuse me, Juliet. I'm going to have to go do some schmoozing."

"Max?"

He's already halfway across the room. "Yes?"

"How did you and Beth meet?"

He pauses, turns back towards Juliet, eyes tracing the bright white dart of thread in the woven square of fabric in front of her. "She was" – his brow furrows – "How can I put it? She'd got into the habit of breaking into the garden here and using the steam room. She thought this place was empty. Toby and I found her in there naked one day just after we arrived. It was quite an introduction."

The woman at the door coughs. Max glances at her and back at Juliet. "I really must get out there and mingle. I apologise."

"Of course."

Juliet watches him go. He seems remarkably together for a man who's lost the girl he loved. The woman at his side is glued to him, murmuring something into his ear as they walk; skin perfectly tanned; her hair slicked back into an elegant bun at the nape of her neck.

As they cross the room next door, Karlo turns suddenly and the two men collide, Karlo's full drink spilling over Max's sleeve and down the front of his fine cashmere top. Max stares at this spreading wet patch then slowly raises his eyes to glare at Karlo, mouthing something petulant and pushing his bandmate in the chest. Ralf steps in and almost pushes Max upstairs.

The smoke from the other room wafts towards Juliet. By now, she feels quite unwell. She's not usually such a lightweight. She needs to get some air. She hurries back along the low-lit corridor to the staircase.

Upstairs, the party has moved to the kitchen, which is crowded with people. Molly, Ralf's girlfriend from downstairs, now sits cross-legged up on the glossy kitchen worktop, plaiting and unplaiting a section of her hair.

And in the middle of the room, holding court, is Malcolm Lyall. Juliet has never met him before but she recognises Fiona's old PR guy instantly. His picture was everywhere after Fiona's nudes appeared in the Eden press. In person, he's shorter than she imagined, and possesses an extraordinary tan, somewhere between mauve and orange. His hair is a peppery silver, curly and longish, almost touching the open collar of his white shirt. He has disconcertingly pale blue eyes, and the appearance of too many too-white teeth for his mouth. He strikes Juliet as strangely familiar, and quite ludicrous.

She hovers unseen at the edge of the room, observing Max near the sink where he's been towelling down his top, his arms now folded across his chest. He looks both bored and quietly thunderous, the muscles in his jaw pulsing as Lyall speaks.

"Almost couldn't make it," Lyall announces, his voice an odd mixture of Highland burr and American. Juliet is puzzled. She didn't know he was Scottish. "I don't know why but the London Film Festival is such a ball-ache. Without fail. Still, I won't bore you with that. We're here to celebrate. It's your night. Karlo slipped me the wink that you were wrapping the album up, and I couldn't let you guys leave without congratulating you. It hasn't been an easy time and it's a phenomenal achievement." He pauses to take a swig of champagne. "When am I going to hear this magnum opus? All so hush hush!" He laughs and turns to Molly. He sidles up to her and drops his voice. "I haven't heard a single track."

Molly smiles uncertainly but says nothing, carrying on with her plait. Lyall suddenly seems fascinated. "How do you do that?" He puts down his glass. "May I?"

He takes the plait gently from her fingers. Her hands stay in the air for a moment, fingers spread. Ralph, on the other side of the room, looks on gormlessly.

"Fascinating!" Lyall exclaims, peering at the plait. "I don't know how you ladies do that. I really don't. And no mirror.

Max could learn a thing or two from you." He laughs, a deep belly laugh, which spreads around the room before reaching Max, where it stops abruptly. Max is not amused.

"Here, you'd better have this back before I muss it up." Lyall hands the tress back to Molly carefully. "So, what do you think?" he asks her. "How many stars do you give the album? The masterpiece?" It's not rhetorical. He waits attentively for her reply.

Molly begins to nod. "Yeah… it's really good." Her eyes dart to the side. There's an awkward silence during which the whole room looks at Molly and Lyall. She shifts uncertainly. "I mean, I've only heard some tracks. Not the whole—"

Lyall chuckles. "Don't worry. It's fine, darling. You don't have to protect my feelings. They always leave me out of the creative side. I'm used to it. I'm just their gofer."

The gritted expression on Max's face hasn't changed. Juliet finds her own jaw grinding too. It's excruciating and a very strange set-up. She frowns. *Surely Lyall works for them?* As far as she knows, Lyall's adept at injecting life into celebrity careers, usually with some kind of hard-luck tale about their backgrounds and setting the scene for an emotional comeback people can rally around. He builds his clients up, and when eventually, inevitably, they're knocked back off their pedestals by a sensationalist press, Lyall is there of course, to restart the wash cycle.

Juliet watches him closely; he certainly has the spadefuls of charm one would expect from a guy whose job it is to create a golden halo around people. Why would Max be keeping him out of the album loop? According to what she's read, and what Toby has said, Max is on the verge of a huge, international revival. Surely Lyall would be an integral part of that?

"By the way," Lyall addresses Max now. "Joel's people were there in London. They're on. Extremely keen. Interested to know where you're taking the new album. Shame, of course, I couldn't tell him."

"You spoke to Joel?" Max asks suddenly.

"Yes, that's what I'm telling you. He's very—"

"But we agreed—"

"We agreed you were interested. Remember? And I had the chance to talk to him. To follow up. Should I have walked away?"

Max smiles now, using only the lower half of his face, and grabs a bottle of champagne from the sink. "Are you okay for a drink, Malcolm?" he asks. He tops up the glasses of those standing near him. "Maybe we should go down to the studio? You're right. We have some catching up to do. Karlo? Could you maybe find Toby? Please, everyone... help yourselves."

Juliet realises Lyall and Max are about to pass through the door where she's standing. She turns her face to one side, and steps back, wondering if she can avoid being seen, but it's too late. Lyall pauses at the doorway.

"My fucking God!" He roars with laughter. "Juliet MacGillivray! Either these guys are going up in the world, or you're... well, coming down." He laughs again. "Bad luck on the election by the way. Fickle punters in politics. Fickle punters."

Juliet doesn't smile.

He laughs again and says for the benefit of the room, "Must be a sore subject." Suddenly he lowers his voice. "Talking of which, your niece. Terrible business. I'm so sorry for your loss. Max was very fond of her."

Juliet still doesn't respond. Max looks at the ceiling and puffs out his cheeks.

"Thank you," she manages finally.

Max puts a hand on Lyall's shoulder as if to guide him away. Lyall stays put.

"I guess you're taking some 'time out'?" He flexes two fingers of each hand in the air around the phrase. "Very wise. Very wise move." He leans into her. She can feel his lips against her ear as he murmurs. "Bit of a risk being here though, isn't it? Just think what a field day the press would have if they knew you'd been at a do like this?"

He nods thoughtfully, sincerely. For a moment Juliet is almost taken in. But how can he stand there, talking about the media circus that surrounds PA when he was probably the one who fed Eden Media all Fiona's old nude shots?

As if he's read her mind, he continues.

"And how's Fiona? She was always a force of nature. Incredible really. She'll bounce back. Christ knows who got into those pictures. That was wrong. I was bloody angry with Bernie for letting Dominic buy them actually. I told him, makes me look bad. But you never know how these things will play in the long-run. Might sex up her image a bit. You feminists can come over a bit, you know, earnest."

Unbelievable.

"Sorry," he goes on. "You'll have to forgive me. But I tell things as I see them. And if I know anything, it's how the public think. Look, here's my card. Bernie won't like me for it, rabid old dog, and I'm sure Fiona wants nothing to do with me, but if I can ever be of any use, to you, or to PA, just call."

"Thanks," Juliet says, taking the card. It glows, like a gold credit card. On an impulse, she mirrors him, leaning her lips towards his ear, matching his volume. "I'll keep it in mind."

Looking her directly in the eye, he squeezes past, muttering profuse apologies. She hopes it's only his belly she can feel rubbing slowly against her.

Juliet is tempted to leave immediately. She edges through the kitchen and finds a door onto the deck and steps down into the garden.

Out here the noise and ringing laughter from the party is immediately muted, the night sky smeared with stars. The temperature has dropped. A yellow Lamborghini – Lyall's presumably – sits on the immense lawn, away from all the other vehicles, looking somehow like a child's toy.

Juliet breathes in the dewy air and crosses the grass towards the tall glass gate she saw from the beach yesterday. She stands looking at the low tide and the low moon, which seem oddly deadened through the blackened glass. It's like seeing the world in greyscale, second-hand, and the sea, unfurling and breaking in the distance over the sandbar, fails to arouse the same visceral response as in the last weeks. Instead of reeling, shuddering, Juliet calculates. How did Beth sneak in and out of this place? If she spent as much time here as Max indicated, she may even have used this gate. She examines the lock, and walks slowly back and forth.

What do these boys know? What is Max, with his vanity and constant stage-management, controlling so tightly that she's failing to understand?

Behind her, the door to the steam room opens. Juliet watches its reflection in the smoked glass, where its classical design appears to float weirdly just above the shoreline. Steam escapes, exaggerating the whole Olympian impression. Then Toby too emerges, wearing a white robe. He pads across the lawn in his flip-flops, leaving the door ajar. Juliet almost calls out, to let him know Karlo is looking for him, but the temple door opens again. A slender ghost of a girl with bobbed caramel hair just skimming the neckline of her white robe, lounges in the doorway. Silhouetted against the soft blue spa lighting and vapour, she lifts her face skywards and exhales a curl of smoke into the night air.

Beth.

CHAPTER SIXTEEN

Taj and Paul led the girl around the corner and into a wide, quiet side street marked *Private Access Only,* on the back side of the grand old place Taj had shown her with all the coloured glass.

On this side were large ceramic panels and balconies with damask drapes hanging mutely behind them. Paul tugged a weighty collection of keys from his pocket and took a moment to find the right one.

Inside, they climbed a wide flight of stairs immediately to the left of the heavy door. She glanced over her shoulder. A large mirror in the hallway reflected black-and-white tiles and a polished, antique console table supported a huge vase of flowers. At the top of the stairs another door and another of Paul's keys took them straight into a sitting room, with a large, low, mink-coloured sofa. Further heavy doors led from this room, and a bay window with a balcony.

"Why don't we have a glass of something?" said Taj.

Paul looked at her. "Have a seat. Make yourself comfortable."

"Bathroom, please?"

Taj grinned at Paul. "She's keen," he said. "Yeah, of course. It's down here."

She followed him along a corridor and through a bedroom with a double bed bigger than her parents', laden with many pillows. Taj stood near the bed.

"While you're here, get changed, yeah?" He said to her, his voice rising in pitch as if talking to a small animal. "Change your clothes?" He smiled and winked, and nodded towards the door.

She didn't understand what he meant. The door he pointed to led to a bathroom which was small, but the cleanest and nicest she had seen in months. She sat on the toilet, her heart racing, and gazed at the walls. They looked like marble. She reached out and touched one. It felt cold.

When she came out, Taj was nowhere to be seen but a small heap of clothing lay on the bed. A uniform? Maybe she was going to be a cleaner? She stepped towards it and noticed its slinky, satiny fabric. Pretty. Lacy. She picked it up and slipped it between her fingers. A peach-coloured set of women's underwear, the type she had seen models wearing in adverts on bus and tram stops, with a bra, knickers and – she didn't know the word – a sort of small dress to go over the top. In the posters, the models would arch their bodies and hitch the top layer up over their hip bone, to show their slim stomachs disappearing into their knickers.

Was she supposed to wear this? Why would she need to?

She stood in the bedroom uncertainly. She could hear the two men speaking English in what she supposed must be the kitchen. Then it sounded like furniture was being shifted around a few rooms away. For a moment, she wondered whether she had time just to creep out, back down the stairs. Then she remembered: Paul had locked each door behind them all.

CHAPTER SEVENTEEN

A chill and a few milliseconds of wonder wash over Juliet. Heart in her mouth, she turns quickly from the gate towards the steam room and stares at the apparition. Her movement draws attention. The girl leans forward, peering into the darkness, then waves and beckons and the spell is broken.

"You can come in if you like," the girl calls out, in a clear, grown-up American voice. "No one'll find you in here."

Stepping forward, Juliet realises the girl must be twelve or thirteen at most, and bears no more than a passing resemblance to Beth. She wishes her mind would stop playing these tricks, conjuring Beth on street corners and trams. It's happened a few times now.

She gathers her wits. "And how do you know I don't want to be found?"

"Well, you're out here in the dark on your own, so call it a wild guess." The girl takes another drag on the cigarette.

"I'm not sure you should be smoking," Juliet finds herself saying. More importantly, she thinks, *What is this child doing out here on her own with Toby?*

Emitting a bored sigh, the girl stubs the cigarette out on the door frame and flicks it into the garden. Juliet is impressed by her own apparent authority.

Behind the girl, Juliet sees the steam room is still hexagonal as it was when the neighbours first installed it, but now has step-like benches forming its sides, rising to about two metres in height. It is fully tiled in a pale blue-and-white Moorish pattern. In the middle lies a sunken Jacuzzi, with a grill around its edge for the run off. The domed ceiling has a sort of trompe l'oeil painting of the sky, dotted with tiny white-blue lights. Near the door, hangs a selection of white guest robes.

The whole place has had a radical revamp since the days when she and Erica used to sneak over here. What were the owners called back then? She hasn't thought about them for years. She and Erica had to drop their breaking-and-entering habit after a nephew of the owners – already a grown man – thought it gave him a licence to grope them. It was never clear if Erica had been encouraging him, but their dad had threatened to call the police. It had caused quite the rift.

"There are spare robes you can put on," the girl says. "They're clean and everything."

The grubby innocence of this remark makes Juliet smile. "I'm sure they are. Are you on your own in there?" She hesitates. "Is Toby coming back?"

"Yes, he's just gone to get some drinks."

Maybe it's the old memory of the groper but for a wild second, Juliet recoils from the idea of Toby getting this child a drink. Something must show on her face because the girl adds, "I'm on Sprite, before you ask."

Juliet nods. "I see. So, you and Toby are… friends?"

The girl shoots Juliet a cripplingly disdainful look. "Uh, no?" Almost instantly, she looks as though she regrets this. "I mean, he's like, twice my age. But you know he's okay. He always gets the job of looking after me. Keeps me away from Karlo."

Karlo? Is he the type youngsters hanker after these days? Juliet ponders this. She suddenly feels sorry for her, stuck here with no friends.

The girl retreats inside, undoes her robe and sits in a red-and-white-striped swimsuit on the far edge of the Jacuzzi, all legs and feet. She stabs a toe repeatedly into the turquoise water, like a bird prodding a snake. Ripples glide towards Juliet. Simply lingering in the heat of the doorway, Juliet feels her hair going lank.

The girl looks up. "You should definitely put a robe on if you're staying. Your dress will get ruined. Won't it, Toby?"

He has re-appeared just behind Juliet, a Sprite in one hand, a champagne bottle in the other. Juliet steps aside for him to come in. He looks speechless.

"We'll look away, won't we, Toby? If you want to get in the water." The girl swings her legs. "Toby's got a huge crush on you, by the way. But he'll look away." She giggles.

Toby closes his eyes in disbelief for several seconds. Juliet stares at him, eyebrows raised, until he opens them again.

"I'm sorry," he mouths at her. He turns and marches on his charge, an incredulous and long-suffering look painted on his face, handing her a can of drink. "You. Are. A. Trouble-maker. Here. Have your Sprite." He hits a switch on the wall, and the Jacuzzi burbles noisily into life, too late to change the course of the conversation. The girl can sense their amusement and has the bit between her teeth now. She talks on in a knowing drawl, enjoying herself.

"I can always tell. He's got a thing about you because you look exactly like that girl. Bess. Toby really liked her, didn't you Toby? But Uncle Max got there first."

Juliet closes the door and supports herself with a hand on the tiled wall, removing her boots and stockings. "I think you mean Beth," she corrects. *So this girl knew Beth too?*

"Yeah, Beth. That's it. Toby was really jealous, weren't you, Tobes? But Uncle Max has to have a girl on every album. He's such a stud."

"Grace, that's enough." Toby snaps.

"What?" Grace is suddenly sullen. "I mean, it's like, sad she drowned but—" She opens her eyes wide. "Oh. My. God. You're not her mom, are you?"

"No. I'm not her mother." Juliet says quietly. She takes a robe, resolutely folds it into a little square, and sits on it, on one of the benches. She flexes her ankles and closes her eyes momentarily with pain-pleasure. When she opens them again, Toby is looking directly at her.

"Well." Grace opens her can. "It's still a shame that happened to her." She swigs as if it were beer.

"Yes, it is..." Juliet pauses. Toby shakes his head apologetically at Juliet, not very subtly.

Grace sees the exchange, and is outraged again. "Uh, why are you looking at each other like that? I'm not three years old for fuck's sake."

"*Grace*?" A woman appears in the doorway of the steam room. It's the same woman who ushered Max away from the studio earlier. "Time's up, honey. We're leaving now. I've been looking for you." She too speaks with a mid-Atlantic twang, but stops suddenly and stares at Juliet. "I'm sorry. Hi. I don't think Max introduced us just now."

"No. He didn't." Juliet stands up. It seems a strange place for formalities.

"I'm Helena. Helena Bolin. Max's sister."

"Juliet. I'm staying next door." They shake hands briefly, Juliet aware how clammy her palms are. She gets the impression Helena would like to wipe her hand afterwards.

"Very pleased to meet you, but I'm afraid we've got to go. We're catching an early flight to London and then New York. Grace wanted to see her Uncle Max before we left Europe."

"New York!" Juliet exclaims. "That's quite a journey."

"Yes. It's not ideal, but frankly if we didn't come to Max, she wouldn't even know what he looks like." She turns quickly to Toby. "Thank you so much for taking Grace under your wing."

"Uh. Yeah. Sure."

Grace is bundled into a robe and ushered away. Cocking her head over her shoulder as she departs, she calls, "So long. See you, Toby. Behave yourself!"

Toby flings the door closed behind her, and a gust of air presses through the room. He throws himself onto one of the nearby benches and puts his head in his hands. "Ahhh. Oh, God. I'm really sorry about that."

"It's fine."

"No no no. It's so… not fine. She's only twelve. But still, you know, old enough to know better."

"Twelve going on twenty?" Juliet smiles, remembering Beth at that age. Naivety blended with crushing hormones. "And it's your job to babysit her, is it? Keep her away from Karlo?"

Toby looks up sharply. "Who told you that?"

Juliet tries not to react to his tone. "Grace did."

Toby shakes his head. "I don't know where she got that. I mean, Karlo…" He blinks rapidly, then pulls down on his eyelid as if trying to get something out of his eye. "Karlo can be a bit… well, he doesn't always think things through." He draws his knees up under his chin, crosses his ankles and wraps his arms around his shins.

Juliet watches him. He's millimetres from opening up about something – and has to hold himself in, hold himself together.

"Do you mind not looking for a moment?" she asks.

She slips out of her dress, hangs it on a hook, shakes out the fluffy robe she's been sitting on and puts it on. Tentatively, she approaches the bench.

CHAPTER EIGHTEEN

Toby won't stop apologising on behalf of Grace, in between swigs of champagne from the bottle. In the end, Juliet has had enough.

"Look, Toby. Please. It really… it doesn't matter. It's a little embarrassing perhaps, which is exactly what Grace intended but—" She considers telling him she's in a very happy relationship, but stops short. She's not sure why.

Toby glances at her.

"And as for what she said about Beth, well, she was absolutely right, wasn't she? There's nothing like hearing it from the mouth of a child to bring it home. Beth is dead. She drowned. That much we do know."

Toby returns his gaze to the floor, where he's tracing the outlines of the tiles with his big toe. "What do you mean, 'that much we do know'? What else is there?"

"Well, you tell me. You're the ones who spent so much time with her in those last months. I really… Actually, it would help me a lot to know what she was thinking. What she was going through."

"Do you think we ever really know what someone's going through?" he asks.

What's that supposed to mean? They both fall silent.

"Pass me that champagne bottle," she says. It may not be wise, but it feels absolutely necessary right now. He shuffles closer along the bench to hand it over. She drinks a mouthful, directly from the bottle too.

His head still hanging, Toby eyes her sidelong. "You should take it easy. That's not a good mix with the heat in here."

"Really?" She swigs again petulantly. Some of the pale golden liquid dribbles down her chin. She snorts slightly, and swipes clumsily at her mouth with the cuff of her robe. Toby looks at her, his eyes sad and tender. He reaches a hand out towards her face and, very deliberately, with a gentle thumb, wipes along her jawline.

Juliet holds very still. She has a sudden urge to take Toby's thumb gently in her mouth. *So wrong*. More and more often recently, she's completely taken unawares by the fluttering hormones in her abdomen. *What would Declan do if the situation were reversed?* It's not as if they're married, or a typical couple even. Declan had a drunken one-night stand two years ago. She sometimes wonders if he was upset that it hadn't been more of an issue. They'd agreed to try to forget it; put it aside. And they'd been pretty successful... she'd thought.

Toby's hand hovers near her face for a second, as if he's about to tuck a strand of her hair behind her ear. Then it's gone.

"Sorry," he says. "I... you had... a thing."

Juliet searches wildly for something to say.

"So. Tell me about your tattoo."

He looks surprised, and pleased. "What do you want to know?"

"I don't know how you decide to do something like that. A permanent mark. Life leaves enough scars, doesn't it?"

Toby turns his calf outward towards Juliet and for a moment they both examine the artwork covering his lower leg.

"It's a noaidi drum," he says.

Juliet nods, although she's not entirely sure what that means. Until now, the tattoo had appeared an abstract oval pattern. At such close quarters though, she can see delicate, sketch-like figures inside the ring drawn on Toby's calf.

"My dad got me into noaidi drums when I was growing up. He used to record and collect, like, everyday sounds? He'd take me out taping with him, then he'd go home and stitch the sounds together. It was incredible. Sometimes it took months. He created this whole new world of… of rhythm and noise, but made up of sounds you kind of recognise. Cars on the overpass. Rain on corrugated plastic."

"Wow, that sounds very interesting." It's not an adequate response. "Very single-minded."

"Yes. He was."

"And so that's what you do? Musique concrète?"

"Yep. Well, no. Not really. I do a lot of recording and sound collation, production, but I'm not a purist. Dad wasn't either, really I guess. But anyway, one day we got talking about how music can be like a mental map of your life and places, and he played me a recording of a noaidi drum. And I remember, I was surprised because it was… actual music. You know, a musical instrument, not something he'd recorded. Anyway, he said it was like beyond an instrument. There are these shamans, and they decorate the drum skins with figures and places, so that the surface is like a… kind of like a symbolic landscape. And then they get a little piece of bone, and it dances on the drum's vibrations as it gets played. And they're able to read meanings from the places where the bones dance."

She watches his eyes flickering, conjuring the memories, as he talks. *Why is he telling her all this?* He seems to be enjoying having someone to talk to but… She suddenly wonders. Where's Max? Is this some sort of distraction?

A trickle of sweat runs from the crease inside Toby's knee and down across the centre of the tattoo. The droplet momentarily magnifies one of the figures: a small stick man, carrying some kind of wand. "There he is." He smiles. "Dad was pretty old when Mum had me. And so when I was a kid, he already had dementia. He would go out recording for hours, and get lost. He nearly died of hypothermia one time. In the end, we had to stop him leaving the house. But his recordings were like a map for him. They would help him to remember times and places. And so, when I got my first royalty cheque, I wanted to… I don't know, make my own map I suppose. Commemorate Dad. So I got inked."

Juliet peers at the tattoo. "What's this?" she asks, pointing to a naïve line drawing of a building with some sort of cupola. Her pale, oval fingernail hovers just above his skin.

"That's the Eden." He rubs the little icon with his thumb, hard, as if he'd like to erase it. "A club in Manchester. I grew up going to the electro festival there every year. That's where Max… discovered me."

"I see." The Eden. As far as she's aware it's some kind of VIP venue. She looks more closely. "And is Max here? Delta Function?"

"No." Toby's voice is suddenly sharp again. "This was before all… all that."

Juliet makes a mental note of his rebuttal of Max. Perhaps Toby notices her awareness. He adjusts his tone. "I mean, I suppose you could say this is a map of how I… how I got to the first track I produced. You know, solo. Max says I should get another tattoo though. He reckons it's the right image."

The right image. The extent of Max's creative control is starting to dawn on Juliet. Did he exert this over Beth too?

"Now that I've lost the weight as well, he said I should get one here." He points at his lower torso, at the V-shaped abdominal muscle disappearing into his swim shorts. He grins.

Juliet looks away. He's a provocative one, this boy.

"I think you look great, just as you are," she manages. "And I'm sorry about your father. The tattoo's a fantastic way to carry him with you."

"Yeah." He nods. "And I'm sorry… about Beth. I guess you carry her with you too, in a way."

"What do you mean?"

"Have you looked in the mirror?" He stares at her. "I mean, I'm sorry but you look *exactly* like her. When I saw you on the beach… you had to be some relation."

Juliet swallows. She's going to have to get used to hearing this. She tries to focus. "It sounds like you were all quite close. How long did you know her for?"

"We were first here last summer. She, uh, came and used the hot tub, and we saw her taking the little boat out a couple of times from the jetty, and it sort of happened from there. She and Max hit it off straight away."

"I'll bet."

Toby looks for a moment as if he is going to say something else, then closes his mouth. Juliet is grateful he doesn't go into detail. She glances around the steam room, trying not to imagine the scene on that first day when Max and Toby walked in on Beth.

"I suppose we didn't realise then how much time she'd been spending on her own before that." This is like a knife to Juliet's heart. "You must have heard all about us, though, from her stepdad?" He smiles sourly. "He didn't like Max much."

"Her stepdad?" Juliet frowns. Beth had no stepdad. Is that how she'd started introducing Alex to people, since the divorce?

"Yeah. He spent quite a lot of time here, early spring. April? Beth tried to get him involved in the PR for the album. There's was a big row. He disapproved."

Juliet is silent. She doesn't know quite what to make of this. She should object to Alex sticking his oar into Beth's business, a father thinking he can tell his grown daughter what to do. But can she blame him? Personally she's nauseated at the thought of Beth and Max together. In her mind too, Beth is still an innocent. Of course, it was a role she probably exaggerated around her Auntie Jet. Max, on the other hand, is so much older than Beth was, and very clearly a worldly man: experienced; creative; relatively sophisticated, certainly compared to the boys she'd have been meeting at university. Not to mention absurdly attractive. There can be something disturbingly appealing about men who ooze entitlement in that way. She can see how easily and hard Beth might have fallen for him. And how Alex might have reacted.

"Did Max…" She feels idiotic asking the question. "Was she happy with him, Toby?"

"Yeah." He answers quickly, nodding vigorously. "As far as I know. They went everywhere together."

He pauses, takes the bottle from her and swigs another draught of it. It's almost as if he's playing at being the unheeded lover, left out in the cold. He leans back against the tiled seat, and raises his eyes to the fake heavens above.

He repeats himself. "Yeah. Really happy. I mean, we went away last winter for some gigs, and came back in the spring to carry on recording. And in the meantime, she'd put together a collection of possible sleeves for us. They were incredible. She'd developed the artwork over the winter and so, I mean, we had no idea there was anything bothering her, you know, anything that wrong with her—"

"Are you telling me she just started doing this artwork for you out of nowhere?"

Toby ignores this and carries on talking. "We had no idea that there might be anything so badly wrong, but looking back…"

Toby waves his hands animatedly while he talks. Juliet watches him closely. He's let something slip. He clearly wants to steer the conversation back to his telling of the story: to his speculation about Beth's depression. Juliet has seen enough politicians scrabbling in interviews to see he's on dodgy territory.

"Just a second," she says. "Going back. Where did she get the idea that she could do the artwork?" Beth hated pushing herself forward into the limelight. She usually had to be cajoled into showing off her work. It seems a pretty big leap for her to think she could just wade in and design Delta Function's artwork. And if Max is such a control freak, maybe he wasn't so delighted by the idea of an unknown fabric designer hijacking their album.

But the answer is not what Juliet expects.

"Um…" Toby hesitates. "I think it was Max and Lyall who suggested it. And she did all this work over the winter…"

Lyall? So Beth had the pleasure of meeting him too. "Hang on. Lyall and Max wanted Beth to be more involved in the band?" Juliet asks sceptically. "That's very generous of them."

Toby looks at her as if she's some kind of savant.

"Yeah. I suppose… I mean…" He clonks the champagne bottle down noisily on the stone tiled floor. It sways from side to side, lumbering precariously at first, then quickening to a vibrato.

Juliet tries to think, but her head is swimming. She can't lose Toby's trust now.

"I'm sorry," she says. "Go on."

But it's not going to be that easy. Toby stands and starts pacing. He runs his hands through what little hair he has. It stands up in wet points on his head. Juliet feels guilty. She's hit some kind of nerve but has no idea how or why.

Finally Toby seems to come to a decision. "I suppose it's fair to say that having Beth around caused a bit of tension a lot of the time. I mean, she and Max had loads of blow-ups and… Max was pretty distracted from the album. I mean, Lyall's a fixer. And he knows what makes people tick. I think his idea was kind of to smooth everything over, for Beth to become more involved sort of creatively. You know, bring everyone closer."

Juliet listens, nodding sagely, as if that all made sense. Perfect sense. Which it would, if Toby had not just said that Max and Beth were ecstatically happy. *They went everywhere together*, he said. So which was it? Were they happy, or was it tense all the time? *Lyall's idea was to smooth everything over,* Toby said. She hates thinking that Beth may have been so slickly manoeuvred by a guy whose job is to fix and manage problems in their clients' lives. What kind of a problem was Beth becoming? What were these blow ups about? Was Max already tiring of her? If Toby's right about Lyall being the one who suggested Beth's creative involvement, maybe Max didn't like his control being usurped.

"Why didn't she come with you, touring?"

"Well, I don't know. I guess she had stuff to do for university. But" – he finally sits back down – "when we came back, after the winter, she just seemed completely into the designs. I mean, we had no idea that she was depressed. But maybe you know, looking back, you can see the signs of…"

There he goes again. Back on to Beth's blues. And he's clearly agitated now. His knees jig up and down. The noaidi tattoo dances. She has a multitude of questions lining up, requiring urgent answers but, in all her years of politics, Juliet has never had to tread so carefully. There is a world of wrongness here and Toby is her only way in.

"When you all came back…" she begins, but he raises the hand that's been resting on his knee, hushing her. The hairs on his legs stand on end and the tattoo is covered in tiny, raised goosebumps. Juliet shivers too. The door to the steam room has opened.

It's Max.

CHAPTER NINETEEN

Even though Juliet can see him trying to hide it, Max is far from impressed that Toby has *gone AWOL* as he laughingly puts it.

"I can't do it all by myself, my friend. There are people arriving to take care of, speak to. This is the nature of the beast." He smiles ruefully and opens his hands slightly, saint-like. His eyes though, are hard. Toby apologises, backing sheepishly towards the door.

After they've gone, Juliet sits for a while and wonders why he didn't defend himself. He had been looking after Max's niece after all. Maybe he's relieved to be removed from her interrogation. She feels strangely soiled as she wriggles back into her dress. There's some sort of chemistry between her and Toby that she can't articulate and it makes her uncomfortable. More than that though, using the chemistry to mine him for information on Max seems unscrupulous. It's not her thing.

She keeps her stockings in her hand, pulls on her boots with some difficulty, and exits the steam room. A long rectangular glow from the kitchen floats above the dark lawns; music and voices reach her. She hears Lyall's distinctive, rumbling laughter. The atmosphere is redolent of her parents' summer parties. She and Erica would dodge all the golf buddies, bank managers and businessmen, scurry along the sea path and sit in the *Swallow*, gossiping.

She makes her way back through the far side of the garden, passing a cut-through to the slipway. She hesitates, shivering, wishing she had a warmer layer. The earlier humid air has gone and been replaced with autumn chills. Suddenly, in that little boat is where she wants to be again. She slips through the cutting.

She's tipsier than she would like. Her heeled boots skid slightly on the wet concrete incline. She crouches to remove them for the second time that evening, and reaches the jetty where the water licks sloppily against greenish algae. She places one bare foot after the other upon the cold, damp boards. Then, spreading her toes, she walks more surely, feeling the ridges of aged wood against her skin.

Crouching and grappling for the *Swallow*, she pulls it towards her. She just wants to get inside; sit there and listen to the water… like she used to do with Beth. To reclaim this place. Her fingers strain and jar against the ties. The cover is fiddly to remove in the darkness, although there's some low light coming from the *Favourite Daughter*. Low lamplight, and low conversation.

Who's in there? Didn't Toby say it belonged to their PR guy – Lyall? But she's just heard him in the kitchen.

Juliet stands and takes a couple of steps towards the cruiser, listening. She can make out voices but no words: Max, wound up, talking fast over the top of… Toby. She can't hear Karlo, but he could be keeping quiet.

Why would they be carrying on some secret congress out here in Lyall's boat while their guests fend for themselves in the house? It doesn't fit Max's strict hosting playbook.

She edges closer, straining to hear, holding her breath, glad she left her boots back at the slipway.

Suddenly Max's voice is raised. "What? What the fuck?"

She freezes.

"She's going to find out sooner or later, so—"

Something inaudible. Juliet takes another couple of careful steps.

Max again. "No. That would be too weird. I want her gone."

There's movement over at the perimeter of the house, facing the sea. The vast glass gate opens, tilting the sea and clouds sideways, and a group of laughing people descends from the garden onto the moonlit shale below. Juliet ducks. If she's spotted out here, eavesdropping…

Toby again. "And how do you suggest I do that?" It's definitely his voice, but with a bitter edge that Juliet hasn't heard before.

The cruiser's hatch opens. Max's voice carries on the wind. "I'm sure we'll think of some means of encouragement."

"But—"

Juliet tries to shift her weight. The jetty creaks and the two men fall silent. Her heart in her mouth, Juliet listens as footsteps pad softly back and forth on the *Favourite Daughter's* rear deck. She crouches as low as possible, hoping she's out of their sightline. What if she's overheard something she wasn't supposed to? *I want her gone*. What the hell does that mean? If Max, or Toby, did have something to do with Beth's death, and they find her aunt out here, snooping around, how will they react?

One of the midnight paddlers across the way shrieks with laughter. A few metres off, the little red *Swallow* rises with the night swell and falls again, slugging against the fenders between it and the jetty. Juliet waits, cowering. Max's fragrance, laundered and sharp and waxy, drifts towards her on the salt air.

CHAPTER TWENTY

Back in the summerhouse, Juliet stands under a hot shower for a long time, letting rivulets run down her face, between her shoulder blades and breasts, and over her stomach. She waits for the steam room's intensity to leave her, along with the clammy sweat and tension of the last hour; her stealth walk back from the jetty into the studio, slipping past the other guests to retrieve Beth's portfolio of designs.

There's no way she was leaving them there.

At nearly 1am, towelling her hair dry, she leafs through the album sleeves again, wondering briefly how Max will react when he discovers she's taken the folder. She finds that she doesn't care. Whatever influence he held over Beth or still holds over the band, he doesn't exert over her.

The dark green design with darts of white remains Juliet's favourite. Many of the others seem too cold, somehow joyless, despite their evident beauty… violent even. There's an abstract patchwork of a building in layers of black, grey and yellow – a balcony, a door – disjointed elements. It's disturbing. In one of the skewed windows, a white, mouthless face seems to stare out.

Another design, a screenprint this time, uses red loosestrife. The spiky leaves are uncanny, feminine somehow, curling in on themselves. But there's a cruelty about it. Between the loosestrife, dots of red, like blood, and – stranger still – fingerprints.

Did Beth really leave no other trace? No explanation? What was it Erica had said? *Nothing personal. Only her designs.*

In the bedroom, Juliet opens the old sewing box that Erica mentioned. It folds outwards, concertinaing away from itself, like a transformer, each layer sliding across to reveal the one beneath. Juliet sits on the bed next to it, running her fingers over the colourful little ranks and reels of cotton, wound so tightly they shine.

On the bottom level of the box, tucked beneath the tray of cottons above, she finds what she was hoping for – a sheaf of miniature sketches and watercolours – Beth's initial ideas for the vinyl covers. They include some small but meticulous illustrations of the wildlife that inspired her. Each is dated. *Red-leaved loosestrife, September, Kelspie,* tallying with the postcard Beth sent after her trip out in her grandfather's boat. He used to talk for hours about the local flora, given the chance. Beth clearly caught his bug. Short cuttings of silken threads and twill are stapled to the roughs: Ostermann Crimson 325; Arkom Rust 960. And a recipe for steeping the loosestrife, turning it into a dye.

Juliet works her way through, cross-referencing the different album covers with the early sketches. Apparently Beth kept this work up, to the end. The last is a wildflower with an uncanny hooded face and angel-wing petals. It's labelled *Eyebright, early flowering, June, Kelspie*. Juliet pauses. Here, the name of the island, Kelspie, is underlined, three times. Another note in Beth's neat print reads, *Eyebright – truth; herbal sight remedy.*

Why would Beth destroy everything, set so much of her work alight, but leave all these intact? And if she were so depressed, why was she still taking day trips out in the boat as late as the month before she died, gathering wildflowers?

Juliet carefully replaces the notes in the sewing box, and curls up on the bed. She should have asked Toby if they had a wifi connection she can make use of. She checks her phone, but there's nothing from Declan. She could do with talking it all through. A young fabric designer putting together a debut portfolio that will catapult her to success with an iconic client… yet who turns around and wreaks havoc on her own work? Georgia is right. *None of it makes sense*. Tomorrow morning she'll pay a visit to Alex. Find out why he disliked the Delta guys as much as Toby seemed to think.

She pulls the covers up and places her hand defensively on her stomach where Lyall rubbed against it. Ridiculous man, telling her to get back to London. But it's not *his* voice that rattles on in her head. It's Max's. *I'm sure we'll think of some means of encouragement*.

She falls asleep with the light on.

CHAPTER TWENTY-ONE

Alex has always been hard to read. Juliet watches him from the door of his workshop. He's wearing ear protection and a face shield. She can't tell whether he's seen her and is ignoring her, or not. Since she arrived a few moments ago, he has chosen a pair of tongs from a blackened, fiendish collection, and lifted from the forge a glowing metal rod, which he is now hitting with a hammer, then turning, then hitting again – drawing it out into a point. The ringing impact hurts Juliet's ears. She wonders where Bucky is. The poor thing must be terrified. She moves impatiently. Alex raises his head, nods almost imperceptibly, and works on.

She waits outside in the car, sitting with the door open to catch a slice of glen sunlight. She doesn't dislike Angasfors, although it's hardly picturesque. South of Inverness, it lies between tributaries to the River Findhorn and Loch Moy, which, along with the gift of all the local charcoal, powered local iron-smelting until industrialisation closed the forges. The town hasn't been cleaned up for tourism, or gentrified with cultural centres, but is losing its identity anyway, as people move away. In the shadow of the glens, dirtied by years of charcoal and coke burning, the village streets are lined with boarded-up garages and empty workshops.

To be fair to him, Alex has persevered. He can turn his hand to decorative metalwork and some bespoke tooling, as well as car repairs. He carried on, throughout his marriage to Erica, making the drive every day from Inverness and the house shared with his parents-in-law, or staying over in Angasfors, sleeping on a makeshift mezzanine that was more just a shelf above the workshop. Juliet used to feel aggrieved, when she rang home, to hear that Alex hadn't been home for a week. Doubtless though, the opportunity for him to take refuge here when Erica had a spell of illness had kept the marriage going, for good or for bad.

Her phone finds a signal and pings through a series of notifications. Juliet gets a little jolt of pleasure to see Declan has replied: *he hopes the party was okay. Yes, he knows Delta Function. Knows them well. In fact, he has a signed album. Can she call him when she has a signal? He really needs to talk to her. He misses her. How is the summerhouse clearance going? How is Erica?*

She thinks back over the conversation with Erica. The hate mail. With little hesitation, she dials Inverness police and leaves a message asking Karen Sutherland to get in touch.

When she hangs up, Alex is still hammering away. The fact that he hasn't contacted Erica, let alone his behaviour over the funeral, sets her teeth on edge. She takes a deep breath. She needs to stay as calm as possible if she is to find out anything useful.

She's about to give Declan a call back when the hammering stops and Alex steps outside, lifting his face mask. As ever, he wears a thick bandito moustache and his hair in a low ponytail, both of which are still dark blonde, though marbled with silver.

"Hello, Juliet." Even in this short greeting, his accent is as strong as ever, his voice gruff.

"Alex." She stands and steps towards him, awkwardly. He doesn't come forward for a hug, or to shake her hand even. "I wonder if it's possible to talk?"

"Nae problem. I was about tae take a break so I was. I'll shout you a coffee." It's as close as he gets to charm.

He disappears inside for several minutes and re-emerges with Bucky on the end of a lead. Spotting Juliet, Bucky ducks and wriggles his whole body with pleasure, yelping strangely, even though she's only met him once before, at the funeral. It's impossible not to smile. Juliet crouches down, rumples the dog's ears and shakes his paw, while Alex resolutely locks the large corrugated doors at the front of the workshop.

"He's taken you for Beth," Alex says over his shoulder.

Juliet doesn't reply. *As if dogs don't know one person from another. More likely, the poor thing's pleased to have some attention*. Bucky shifts his weight and puts out his other paw for her to hold. She looks into his anxious eyes and gives his toes a surreptitious kiss.

All three walk in silence together towards the main street, Bucky decidedly more upbeat than his human companions. Clouds scud across the sun, lighting up then muddying inferior graffiti and *To Let* signs. In the only open shop, a combination of family café and newsagent, Alex orders a sweet drop scone, rather to Juliet's surprise. She's feeling a little queasy after last night's champagne, so shakes her head at the elderly, hopeful-looking owner, and sticks with a black coffee. They take up high perches at a counter in the window, Bucky settling contentedly below. Juliet has to lower her stool so that she can reach the foot rest. She spins the cracked leather seat, searching for a way to open the conversation.

"It must feel good," she tries. "Hammering out your frustrations like that."

"No."

For a moment, Juliet thinks that's all the response she's going to get. She's glad to have the distraction of the stool, and continues winding it down.

Alex blows on his coffee and sips. His fingers have a greyish hue. "That's the last way to do it. You need a clear head to work metal. If you've something on your mind, you'd best leave it. Come back to it later." His brown eyes flicker up the street.

Juliet has always supposed that Alex's silent approach to Erica came about because he had an outlet – a hard, physical job where he could let it all go. She's never considered that the inverse might be true instead: that the focus demanded by his labour might be what gave him the practised discipline to master his emotions.

Suddenly, she remembers him telling her, years ago, that his work was simple really – just heating, holding and hitting. She'd been intrigued. At the time she couldn't help but see a parallel between Alex's work and his relationship with Erica. Something about him had certainly lit Erica up – in the early years at least, their love was fiery, passionate. But he had never been able to hold her, or control her. And as for hitting, to Juliet's knowledge, Alex had not once raised a hand to anyone. On the contrary, he had been a paradigm of self-control. That is until a couple of years ago. The divorce seemed to release something inside him.

She begins again. "I need your help, Alex."

He nods. "What's the problem?"

"I'm clearing the summerhouse and, well, trying to understand what was going on for Beth in those last few months. There are some things… I mean, I know talking about it can't be easy, but there are some things I'm struggling with I suppose, and I need answers."

A low breath of derision comes out of Alex. "Juliet *needs answers*. Aye. Go on then."

Juliet ignores this, finally settles on the stool, and braces herself. "Okay. Did you know Beth went into the university and destroyed her work, before she drowned?"

"Only after the police told me."

"Why do you think she'd do that?"

He shrugs. "Depression?"

Juliet nods and tries not to let her exasperation show. "There's something no right there though, for me. I mean, why was she so down, when she was in love and with such an exciting project to work on? It makes no sense."

"If she were suffering the same as her mother, then why would it make sense? There never was no logic to Erica."

Juliet ponders this statement. It's both true and false. She knows well enough that Erica's episodes are chemical; they sometimes have no sensible root cause. But it's not true to say Erica is not logical. She's one of the most logical people Juliet knows.

She pushes on. "This musician Beth was seeing. Max. You met him. What were they like together? Was she happy with him?"

"I've no met him. What makes you say that?"

"But one of the group told me you went to the place where they're recording. That you met them all?"

"No." Alex is categorical. "I never met him. None of them."

Juliet stares at her ex-brother-in-law. "Well, why would they tell me you did?"

"I don't know. Take it up with them."

Bucky huffs at their feet.

"They said you went out there," Juliet persists. "To the place where they're recording. On Culbin Sands. That you spent time there."

"Look, Juliet, I don't know what to tell you. I've no been out to the summerhouse for years, 'cept tae fetch the dog." He nudges Bucky with his right foot, which makes Juliet want to kick the man back. "I know whether or no I met someone. They must have someone else in mind."

Juliet takes this in. Alex has no reason she can think of to lie about meeting Max, which makes Toby's story a fabrication, or a mistake.

"Right." Back to basics. "So, do you know any reason why Beth would have been depressed?" She hears the edge of judgement creeping into her voice. *Other than the fact that you left her, and her mother, just after her grandfather died.*

Alex sighs. "You don't know about the abortion then. Am I wrong?"

"What?" Juliet's stomach tightens.

The café owner arrives behind them, carrying two plates of drop scones. He sets them down, one for Alex, one for Juliet. Bucky sits up with interest.

Juliet opens her mouth to protest but the owner holds up a hand. "Aye, I know. But you look like you could do wi' one."

"Thank you," she murmurs, attempting to smile.

"On the house, so it is." He smiles and totters away.

Alex pushes Bucky back to the floor and tucks impassively into his plateful. "Beth had an abortion. Last year. They found a small amount of scarring when they did the autopsy. They didn't report it, you know, for her privacy and they were no sure it was relevant, but they think that's when she started taking the Valium. It was another factor the examiners took into consideration."

Juliet's plate has been made into a smiley face, with two pools of oozing blaeberry preserve for eyes, and a smile made of whipped cream. She stares at it in dismay. "And neither you or Erica knew?"

"Erica didnae." He pauses. "Beth told me."

"She told you?" Juliet immediately regrets the incredulity in her voice.

"Aye."

"With no mention of the father?"

"No."

"And the doctor who prescribed the tranquilisers?"

"It were no her usual doctor. She had no prescription for them."

"What? What do you mean?"

He sighs again. "If you must know, we think she may hae stolen Erica's. She had a stash in a wee pot. Her doctor said she knew nothin about it."

"So Beth didn't tell you or Erica, or her doctor, she was feeling like this? I thought… when I saw about the Valium in the report, I thought you would have known she was taking these things?"

"No." Alex wipes a soft fold of drop scone around his plate. "And there's no reason why she'd hae told you either."

"I'm sorry?"

"Ah know what you're at, Juliet. You're making sure your conscience is clear, so you are." He wipes his mouth and moustache with a paper napkin.

"My conscience?" Juliet tries to keep her voice low and neutral.

"Aye, your conscience. You're proving that there was nothing you should hae known about. If her ma and pa knew nothing, then it's all fine and fair that you knew nothing. Is that no how it goes?" Alex is very still, staring through the window straight ahead, not making eye contact with her. "Trouble is, deep down you always thought yous were the important one in Beth's life, am I wrong? Thought she were closest to her Auntie Jet? So, even though she confided nothing in me, and nothing in her ma, there's you thinking if something were up, she'd hae come to you. And she didnae. So now you're after a reason why it was no suicide, something else to pin it to, so you can stop blaming yourself for being unavailable."

Juliet puts her coffee down with a clatter, shaken and angry. "That's no what I think. Not at all."

Alex looks straight at her. "No?" His voice is cold, disturbingly controlled. "Come on. You've always thought it, ever since she were a wee girl. Thought Erica and I were letting her down. And yous, you were the safety net, were you not, Juliet? *Auntie Jet*, with her fancy flat and fancy life in London. *Auntie Jet* with her summerhouse. *Yes, of course you can use it, Beth. Have some independence, Beth*. But where were you, eh? When she needed you?"

It's too much. Juliet can't help herself. "And where in the hell were you? Aside from spending all your time away out here at the workshop? Where were you when her grandfather died? Oh, aye, filing for divorce."

"I promised your father I'd be there, to stand by Erica until Beth was eighteen. I promised. And I kept that promise."

"This was no *contract*," Juliet sputters. "You were her father, for Christ's sake."

"I left when it was time for me to have ma own life back. I'm no Erica's carer. And as for Beth, Beth was a young woman, with a mind and a body all her own, and she was ready to stand on her two feet. There's none of us could hae kept her from what she did. Not Erica. Not you. Not me. But" – he stands suddenly and his stool squeals like an injured dog. Bucky flattens his ears – "at the least now I know what you really think."

"You can leave Bucky with me," says Juliet quietly.

"Ma pleasure. I've work to do," he mutters.

The door swings closed after Alex, and the old café owner smiles again at Juliet and nods encouragingly at the melting mess on her plate. "Don't let it go cold now," he says.

CHAPTER TWENTY-TWO

She stood self-consciously in the middle of the living space in front of the low sofa, where Taj was sitting. Paul was nowhere to be seen. The little petticoat dress didn't fit her properly, even she could tell that. It gaped and drooped at the chest, because she had no breasts to fill it, and that meant it hung too low on her thigh. She twisted the lace on its hem between her fingers.

Facing her was a laptop on a kind of trolley table, but the screen was blank. A thick voice emerged from it.

"Hello," the voice said. "Tell me your name."

She looked across at Taj. He was watching her, his mouth slightly open. It was easier just to turn back to the screen than to seek guidance from him.

"Ishtar."

"Hello, Ishtar. You're very pretty. Has anyone ever told you that? That colour suits you."

Again she glanced at Taj.

"Don't look at him. Look at me. It's okay. Relax." He exhaled softly. "Now, come a bit closer. A bit closer. Good. Yes, you're very beautiful." The man paused, and made an odd noise in the back of his throat, somewhere between a cluck and a sigh. "I'm not surprised you were noticed. I bet all the boys notice you."

She tried not to move.

"You could be a model. Or an actress. Taj tells me you've never had a boyfriend? Am I right?"

She nodded.

"Well, now's your chance to start making the most of what you've got. You must have had a difficult time?"

She nodded again, surprised to find her eyes filling with tears.

"Now, it's okay. It's going to be okay. Do you know we can look after you, very, very well? We can help you earn money. You might even become famous? Would you like that? I bet there are lots of things you would like, aren't there?"

She swallowed and scratched her neck.

"Don't scratch," he said, his voice sharper. She dropped her hand to her side. "It's not nice. It's dirty."

Her hand felt like a lead weight, hanging there, like something that didn't belong to her. Her whole body seemed elsewhere somehow.

"Now, what would you like? Some clothes? A mobile phone?"

"I want… I want study."

The man emitted a laugh. Almost in slow motion, as if the sound were breaking up, a low rolling bellow reached her. "Oh? Oh, well now. To study? That's the best answer I've had in a long time. I'm sure we can help you study. All you have to do is try your best. We can help you if you try. Will you promise you're going to try your best?"

She nodded. She was outside herself. Empty. None of this mattered, she told herself, compared to what she had already been through. *This was nothing*. Why, then, did it feel like everything?

"Good. Well now. The first thing I want you to try to do, is turn around for me. Slowly. Good. Now do it again. Not all the way. That's right. Just face the window. Good. That was easy, wasn't it?" His tone of voice changed terrifyingly. "Will someone close the curtains? I can't see a fucking thing here. It's like watching a ghost."

Taj leapt up. His reaction, as a grown man, to the other's voice was alarming. Still turned to the window, Ishtar watched

Taj fumble with the ties on the heavy drapes. He closed the curtains, making sure to cover a chink of streetlight, then turned on a standard lamp behind the laptop.

"Ah. That's better," came the voice. "Much better. Just stay there, and why don't you… Let's see… Why don't you show me if you can bend over and touch your toes?"

She faltered. Taj smirked as he passed in front of her and sat back on the sofa. If she bent over, she would be showing them both her behind. She was wearing the little knickers that went with the dress thing. She wondered where Paul had gone. Did he know what was going on? It was a mistake to come here.

"Now, you said you would try, Ishtar. You're not even trying. We need to see what you can do."

She swayed slightly, and remained standing.

"Bend over," the man's voice snapped from the screen. Startled, she obeyed almost automatically, as Taj had done. She felt the little dress brushing over the top of her thighs and halfway up her backside. Her knees trembled and she placed her hands on them to steady herself. The sudden fright did not subside. Her belly turned to water and she was afraid she'd have an accident right there in front of them.

"Good. Good." His voice was warm and treacly again. "That's nice." A pause. Her long hair shrouded her head as it hung upside down. At least that was something to be grateful for. They couldn't see her blushes. She glanced upside down across the room. Taj was still sitting on the low sofa, one leg crossed over the other. He kept looking from the screen, to her, and back to the screen, and to her, as if he were a guest on a television chat show.

"Now. I'm going to ask you to stay as you are, exactly as you are. But just… just see if you can pull down those panties for me."

She froze. This was not right. This was very, very wrong.

The screen man sighed, then chuckled. "We need to see how good you are at following instructions, Ishtar. You know, models and actresses, they must do as they are told."

"Please. I not want to," she said.

"Well. Taj can help you." Taj rose from the sofa.

"No!" she said loudly, straightening up and attempting to cover herself, but things moved fast. Taj quickly put a hand on the back of her neck and pushed her over again, pointing her rear end at the laptop. With the other hand, in one swift movement, he pulled her knickers down around her knees. She tried to move but he squeezed her neck so hard she thought she might pass out. He hitched up the little dress so that it hung around her waist and her most private parts were bared.

Taj then patted her on the back and gave her a little nod, as if to say *Just hold on*.

"That's it. Hold it. That's good. That's very good," said the screen man. He made that clucking noise again. "That's it. Let her go."

Taj released her neck and steps away. She stood up immediately, and wrenched up her knickers before turning around. Her eyes flashed angrily at Taj and the screen. "I… I not like this." She bit her lip. "I not want this."

The man sighed.

"I see." The man on screen sounds serious for a moment, thoughtful. "Well, if you're sure. This is a good opportunity… But it's your choice."

She began to feel relief. They would let her go. It would be okay.

But he continued speaking, very slowly to make sure she understood him. "Still, it's such a shame. Such a waste. So, what I'm going to do, is this. I will send Taj the video and the pictures from this little audition. We have been recording you, you see? You understand? Then, because he is your friend and he wants only the best for you, Taj will make sure that all the men at the asylum centre see what you have been doing with us. Okay? That way, everyone will see exactly what you are capable of. The sort of girl you are and the potential that you have."

He paused, to let this sink in. Ishtar started crying softly.

"Now, what do you think about that?"

CHAPTER TWENTY-THREE

Declan's last day in Liverpool doesn't go as planned. He's promised to cook a meal for Lotta and Sophie, but is dreading it. Lotta's been giving him the side-eye ever since their chat in the forest, and if she carries on, he doesn't trust himself not to blurt something out. He knows it's rude, but holes himself up in Sophie's guest room until the afternoon, squinting at Lotta's retouches by the low light of an old Tiffany lamp, waiting for her to leave the apartment.

Finally, she heads off to a radio interview, and he ventures into worsening rain to buy mussels from the market. If he can just make it to tomorrow without a slip up, it'll be fine. He's booked a ticket to fly to Inverness in the morning, and he'll take a taxi east to Juliet in the summerhouse. She may even pick him up at the airport, but he's not counting on it. She hasn't been in touch since she told him she was attending that Delta Function party. He's trying not to read too much into her silence. It doesn't necessarily mean anything. She's got a lot to deal with.

Back at the apartment, he potters in the kitchen, de-bearding mussels and slicing potatoes. He realises he's forgotten bread, and on his way out he crosses paths with a cold and drenched Sophie on her return from a double shift at the hospital. He could swear she gives him a strange look too, but perhaps it's his imagination.

Returning with a stale French stick, he hears the shower running, and tense voices in the bedroom. He tells himself it's not because of him. Probably. He puts a jazz station on, warms the baguette in the oven, and pours himself a large glass of white wine to take the edge off.

By the time they gather around the large kitchen table, he's had two-thirds of the bottle.

"So," Sophie begins. Lotta gives her an intense look across the table – the eyeball equivalent of a kick – which Sophie returns in kind. "Give our love to Juliet, won't you?"

"Course." He plonks three bowls of mussel and bacon soup down, a bit harder than intended.

"Lovely," says Lotta. "Thank you." She pulls in her chair and begins eating keenly. "Mmm. Is that nutmeg? And rosemary?"

Declan is grateful for Lotta's effort, but Sophie has been tenderly protective of Juliet ever since Beth's death. She clearly won't be put off now. She sips her wine and puts the glass down deliberately. Her hair is still wet and her fringe sticks up comically. She presses it down with her palm.

"Look, Declan—"

Here we go, he thinks. She cannot let something go. She's exactly like Juliet.

"We're worried about you," she says. "You know how much we love you guys. And the thing is, I see how bereavement affects people all the time. I've seen so many couples fall apart after an unexpected death in the family."

Declan says nothing. He takes his time chewing a mouthful of potato.

Sophie presses on. "Lotta has told me... look... there's obviously something on your mind and we just think you need to talk to Juliet sooner rather than later."

"Hey!" Declan says sharply. "I know nothing about what happened to Beth."

Sophie raises her eyebrows. "I never said you did."

He swallows a large mouthful of wine, eyes darting between the two women.

"Come on, Declan. Please. You can talk to us." Sophie glances at Lotta. "You might come off better with Juliet if you can say we knew something too."

"Okay then." He clanks his spoon into the bowl. "There is something you can help with." He takes his time, wiping his mouth, gathering his words. "You're a medical professional. Is there a way to tell when someone is taking tranquilisers?"

Sophie leans forward. "What type of tranquilisers?"

"Valium, I think."

"Do you mean be able to tell in blood tests? Or in their behaviour?"

"Behaviour."

Sophie pushes a strand of damp hair behind her ear. "Well, you would need to know what the person's behaviour had been like over time, to see a change. It all depends what the baseline state of the person is normally. I mean, Valium is used to treat all sorts of things: anxiety, agitation, insomnia… So if it was prescribed for any of those, you'd be looking for an improvement in those symptoms."

"So, the only way you'd notice anything would be if you'd seen a change… an improvement?"

"Yes. As long as they're taking it properly and it's been carefully prescribed. It can cause all sorts of issues… suicidal tendencies, liver problems, psychosis."

"Nothing more visible? Would they have changes in their pupils? In their skin?"

"Not usually. Maybe if they had a reaction to the medication. But the prescribing doctor should follow that up."

"Right." He pokes a mussel with the spoon.

Lotta interjects. "Declan. We're talking about Beth, right? The medical examiners found she'd been taking tranquilisers, didn't they?"

"Yep. That's right."

"So, what's this all about?" Sophie asks. "Does Juliet think she should have noticed that Beth was taking them? I mean, she can't blame herself."

Declan picks up his spoon again and rapidly begins eating large mouthfuls.

"Declan?"

"It's juniper and rosemary," he says, mouth full. "The smoked bacon."

"Shit! Yes!" Lotta tastes the soup again. "Rosemary was obvious." She rises from the table and makes a note on a pad on the kitchen worktop, before sitting back down.

Sophie watches Declan eat for a few seconds. He can't meet her eye. She repeats her question, a calm professionalism in her voice. "Is Juliet blaming herself for not noticing that Beth was depressed?"

"Yes," he replies, eventually. "Yes, of course she is. I keep telling her that no one could have seen it. No one." He puts his head in his hands and puffs out his cheeks. "Not even me."

No one speaks. Lotta stands again, her chair scraping on the floor, and opens another bottle of wine, the corkscrew squeaking. She refills the glasses, slowly walking round the table. Standing by the breakfast bar, she asks gently, "Why should you have seen it, Declan?" Her eyes flicker between him and Sophie.

He shakes his head. He opens his mouth but no words come.

"Declan," Lotta's voice is low but persistent. "Why would you have seen it? When? Did you see Beth before she died?"

"I've said too much already." He rises suddenly and pushes his chair firmly back under the table. "I need to talk to Juliet. She should be the first to know."

As he leaves the kitchen, Lotta calls after him. "Declan, the bread!" She opens the oven door and smoke fills the room.

CHAPTER TWENTY-FOUR

Bucky refuses to sit in the front. He can tell Juliet is seething. He jumps neatly between the car seats and arranges himself in the back. She drives towards the summerhouse sheathed in fury, not only at Alex's words but also at the truths they contained. A truck screams past, blasting her with its horn as she pulls out onto the highway. Gripping the steering wheel, and exiting the shadows of the Angasfors valley with relief, she tries to get a handle on herself.

Her instincts are not often wrong. Something is definitely off-kilter about the whole situation, whatever Alex says, but Juliet is finding it increasingly hard to separate each line of enquiry from the other. Everything seems inextricably linked, cloudy. Does Max know about the abortion? Did he pay for it? Was it even his baby?

She doesn't adhere to the school of thought that abortions must always be traumatic events, but neither does she want to dwell too long on how Beth coped, perhaps alone. She wishes she'd asked Alex if they know where it had been performed. Unlikely. He said they didn't even know when. Does Erica know about it now? Is this what her notes about Beth's 'aftercare' were about?

She passes a sign warning of deer in the road. She should have pinned Alex down for more information. She let his quiet aggression distract her, and to be fair, he was not entirely off-the-mark. Yes, she did always believe she had a special relationship with Beth. And yes, she feels guilty. But if she backs off to avoid this kind of scrutiny of her own motives, she'll only be letting Beth down again. She can't let Alex's words kill the trail. And the trail is getting more complex. Going to see Alex has raised rather than answered another question: why the hell did Toby say that Alex had met Max?

She pulls into a lay-by and from her bag, grabs the little notebook Erica gave her. She scrawls her questions down.

Why did B destroy work?
Why did Max/Lyall invite Beth to do designs?
Did Max know about abortion? (Was it his?)
Why did Toby say they met Alex?
Why don't they want me here?
What's the significance of Kelspie Island?

Bucky whimpers and starts panting as she starts the engine again and pulls back onto the forest road. He sits up to look through the window as they wind through the trees. On the track in front of the summerhouse, sits a police car.

"*Shit*," Juliet says under her breath. She parks on the hardstanding, opens the door and Bucky clambers right across her, digging his doggy claws into her thighs and running into the woods. Juliet leaves her things in the car and chases him towards the back of the house.

She hears Karen Sutherland before she sees her. Although they haven't spoken since a school reunion in their twenties, the foghorn drone of her voice is unmistakeable. She's explaining something to the officer with her. Juliet had forgotten about Karen's tendency to speak unbearably slowly when she doesn't need to, and too quickly when a decent explanation is required. And either way, in monotone.

Bucky lollops delightedly over and sniffs around Karen's not inconsiderable calves.

Karen turns and ignores the dog. "Ahh. Juliet." They face

each other across the firepit and Juliet sees that Karen, still overweight, is a lot burlier than she used to be, as if she's been working out. Her hair had been mousy before, but highlighted blonde waves now swoop back from her broad forehead and cheeks. "How are you?"

"So-so," says Juliet.

"Juliet, I got your message about Erica. I wanted to check you're okay and find out more." She nods at the house and they start walking towards the door. Her voice changes immediately to a low, slow, sympathetic drone. "Also, I should say on a personal level, how very sorry I am about Beth. I didn't get a chance to speak to you at the funeral, and I think it was my colleague Andrew Turner, who asked you some questions during the investigation."

Juliet hears the car click as it cools.

She nods. "Yes, that's right."

"And now you're here to pack up Beth's things?"

"Yes. I—"

An electronic notepad appears from Karen's pocket. Writing on it with a stylus, she works her tongue over her lips. In out. In out. A habit she's had since school.

She looks up expectantly, her head tilted to one side. "Do go on."

"Well. Nothing really…" Juliet is nonplussed. "I've been here a couple of days."

"Do you mind if we go inside?" Karen asks. She glances at her colleague and gives him a signal to go back to the car.

Karen inspects the summerhouse as they enter, nodding to herself. She stands at the window looking out into the forest. Juliet wonders if she feels at home, after all the time she must have spent here during the investigation.

"Would you like a drink?"

"No, thank you."

Juliet puts down a water bowl for Bucky, then takes a seat at the table. "So, let me explain," she says, spreading her fingers on the tabletop. "I visited Erica yesterday and she showed me a number of hate letters she's received. Violent threats."

"I see. Do you have any of the letters?"

"No. They're at Erica's.

"And Erica knows you've contacted us?"

"No."

"I see." Karen says again. She stops writing. "Usually we can only act on a report of this nature if it comes from the person affected."

"Well, the letters mentioned me too." Juliet tries to keep the exasperation from her voice. "And they're making threats to my twin. So perhaps you could consider this a report from someone affected?"

Karen nods. "And do you have any idea who might have sent them?"

"No." Juliet's mind flicks briefly to Alex, but dismisses this.

"Has anyone ever made any other threats, verbal or otherwise?"

"Well," Juliet pauses. "Letters sometimes come to headquarters in London. But I'm lucky in that they rarely make it to my desk. It's something you get used to in my line of work I suppose, but" – she recalls the comment thread on the PA website – "there have been some increasingly foul things posted online, and one comment actually mentioned Beth. So, I did wonder if there was any value in digging a bit deeper."

Karen looks up. "Value?"

"In relation to Beth."

Karen's stylus hovers over the notepad. Her tongue darts in and out. "Juliet. The investigation into Beth's death is closed."

"But would this hate mail not count as new information?"

"I can look into it certainly, see if there are any links worth following, but we found no hate mail addressed to Beth during the enquiry. I suppose I'm trying to avoid you getting your hopes up."

"My hopes?"

A bird sings outside. There's no sound in the living room other than the tick of the sunburst clock and Bucky's tongue chasing his empty water bowl across the kitchen floor. Juliet gets up and refills it. Alex probably kept him thirsty to reduce the need for walks.

When she comes back to the table, she decides to try a new tack.

"I've read the report, Karen. And I know I've asked a lot of questions already in the past months, but… can you tell me, why was there nothing in the report about Beth's abortion; or her relationship with these guys from Dirac Delta?"

"Delta Function," Karen corrects. "Look, I'm sure you realise, police reports are public documents." It's as if she's reciting the rulebook. "If we can't establish the relevance of… certain information, especially medical records or personal details, we're obliged to disregard it for the purposes of the public record. People have a right to privacy."

"But surely the fact that she was in a relationship would have a bearing on her mental state? I mean, we're not talking about just any relationship either."

Karen plays innocent now. "What are you implying?"

"Oh, come on. These guys are pretty famous. Beth was just a young girl from a small city."

"So, being famous, having a glamourous lifestyle, that makes you fair game for suspicion, does it? No right to privacy?"

Juliet glances at her sharply. Was that some kind of jibe? But Karen's face is entirely neutral. Ever the professional.

"Of course not." Juliet is tiring of this. "But isn't it possible that…" The politeness. The circling. "Oh, I don't know, Karen. Shouldn't it be you who investigates the implications?"

Karen puts her stylus down.

"It's interesting that you should say that," she says. "Because, surprising as you might find it, Juliet, we did conduct an investigation. A very thorough one. Over one hundred hours of interviews. We did a fingertip search of the entire scene." Her head is on the other side now.

The two women hold eye contact. *You didn't look at Beth's designs*, Juliet thinks. *You didn't invest them with any possible meaning*.

"Well. Perhaps you missed something," she says matter-of-factly.

"Perhaps." Karen gives this about as much credence as she would a member of the flat earth society. She looks through the windows up at the treetops and says nothing for a few moments.

"Juliet, we can speak frankly, can't we? When something happens to a well-known local family, as yours is, do you have any idea what happens to an investigation? People feel like they knew your father. Their homes, their workplaces, the fabric of the town, so much of it was built by Gordon MacGillivray. He had old friends on the council. And you – your politics, your role in PA – people feel like you're public property, a daughter of Inverness. Now," she continues, "can you imagine how many questions, how many interested parties there were, making sure we got the investigation right? That it was all tied up?"

Juliet stares at Karen, taken aback.

"Who? Who was asking?"

"All sorts of people, Juliet. More people care than you think. Old clients of your father, councillors. Your sister's doctor. The band."

"The band? Like who? Toby? Max?"

"Among others."

Juliet realises she's grinding her teeth.

"And?" Juliet manages not to jab her finger at Karen. "Did it not occur to you to wonder why they would have been paying such close attention to the case?"

"A lot of people were affected by the case. I assumed Toby was showing an interest on behalf of his grieving friend."

Juliet doesn't lose her temper often, but when she does, it's spectacular. She tries to weigh her words before she speaks, but they're spilling out of her, like hot, uncatchable shards.

"Assumed? My God, Karen, I already had doubts about how this whole investigation has been conducted, and what you've just said implies you were pressured to tie things up nice and fucking neatly. Get the bloody job done and to hell with whether it was done properly. And I think there's at least an element here of… of some kind of institutionalised discrimination. Just because there's a history of mental fucking illness in the family, you all jumped to a bunch of facile conclusions about Beth."

Karen nods slowly, carefully. "There are always things we can learn and improve. But you must understand the note… the suicide note made it very hard to justify continuing the investigation."

Juliet sits back rigidly. This half-baked acknowledgement, not quite an admission, does nothing to dilute her anger. It's a politician's answer, crafted. Learning something from this case is all very well, but will not undo whatever happened to Beth. The more Karen sits there, calm, listening, patronising, the more Juliet's head thumps with rage. She must control herself, otherwise she'll look hysterical and it will play into Karen's hands, into the very assumptions she's just called out.

She breathes deeply. Bucky wanders over and puts his head on her knee. She strokes the dent between his brows with her thumb. She runs the next sentences around in her head, trying them out before uttering them.

The band. Delta Function. They were arguing last night. I overheard them. I think Max is behaving strangely. I think they want me gone from here.

It already sounds absurd; the sort of thing Erica would be convinced people were saying about her. Perhaps she should never have gone to the party. Just having been there frays at the edges of her credibility.

And Alex. Why did he deny meeting Max? Why would Beth have told him about her abortion and not her mother?

Karen is watching her, head tilted again.

Juliet can feel the paranoia rising by the minute. And she knows: feeling paranoid feeds itself. She's already paranoid about becoming paranoid, and this will worsen if she's not careful, like a winter cyclone. She resolves to say nothing to Karen about last night and about Alex. Not yet.

As soon as Karen drives away, Juliet heads through the woods towards the recording studio with Bucky darting between the trees in front. If Karen can't do her job, then *she* will ask the questions. She's not going to hide in the bloody shadows. She's going to dig again about their supposed dealings with Alex. Find out what Max knew about the abortion. About Beth's last trips out to Kelspie. And if Lyall's there, she'll damn well ask him why his friend Bernhard Palmer was keeping notes about Beth on his desk.

Underfoot, pine needles and mud muffle her footfall. The air is cool, odd, skittish: humid clouds are harried by sudden gusts of wind. Her anger is suddenly pierced through with doubt. She remembers Fiona's parting shot: Lyall is dangerous. This is not a game, or a political in-fight. The last twenty-four hours have thrown up more questions than answers but she is more certain than ever: she does not believe Beth committed suicide. At the very least, she was driven to it.

Bucky halts at the studio's garden path and sits with a glum expression, refusing to come any further. The place looks empty. Not abandoned – there are still cars outside and a box of empty champagne bottles under the porch – but it's closed up and has that deadened feel of a waiting house. The Lamborghini has gone. She has no idea how long the party continued last night but is astonished they've all managed to get themselves up and out by – she looks at her watch – nearly three.

She presses the electronic bell, already suspecting she won't get a reply. She's turning to go when she realises she can hear a low whine coming from inside. A vacuum cleaner. She hammers on the door. The whine ceases.

A woman in her sixties opens the door. She re-ties a dark headscarf and mops her face with a tissue. Juliet asks when the *gentlemen* will be back.

"They out."

"Yes. When – What time they return?" Juliet hates herself for her lilting tone and precise syllables, but doesn't know what else to do. She points to her watch. "When will they be home?"

"They out."

"Yes. I see."

"You leave message?"

"Yes! Yes, please."

"Wait." The cleaner disappears towards the kitchen. The vacuum crouches at the head of the stairs leading to the basement. Two large half-full black bin liners slump against the wall below a piece of abstract art. Juliet doesn't envy the woman's task. She wonders how long she's been in the UK; what her story is.

A small key cupboard clings to the hall wall. Its door is ajar.

Juliet steps inside, glancing around. Before she knows what she's doing, she's peering into the cupboard.

There, among about twelve different keys and car fobs, is the key to the *Swallow*. She would recognise it anywhere, with its worn red plastic cover and painted wooden keyring in the shape of a red-and-blue Dala horse.

When the cleaner returns, Juliet has already gone.

CHAPTER TWENTY-FIVE

Juliet rips off the *Swallow*'s red cover. She remembers what Toby said about the battery needing a charge. Was he trying to tell her something? Why would the key even be at the recording studio, anyway? Have they been using the boat? She calculates. Sitting there, unused, it might lose, what? Ten percent of its charge per month? It's been at the jetty since July. It's not October yet. She gives it a try. Nothing.

And again. Nothing.

She swears loudly, and her voice volleys away into the small harbour. Surely the goddamn boat isn't going to thwart her now?

How could Karen patronise her like that? And Alex? Is this really what people think of her? Somehow pathetic and controlling and superior all at once? It's one thing, having these thoughts about oneself, secretly worrying, but to have them confirmed by others… After all, they do realise she's actually quite a competent person? That she fucking runs a political party? She catches herself, and almost laughs. *Do they not know who I am*?

She'll take the boat is what she'll do, and she'll damn well go to Kelspie, and explore. See if there's anything unusual. If not, she can cross it off the list. She doesn't need to answer to anyone.

On the third attempt, the outboard motor rattles noisily into life. Bucky, who's been scrabbling up and down beside her on the jetty, realises what she's doing, leaps into the boat and sits importantly at the helm, looking pleased with himself. She pulls on a lifejacket, making a conscious effort to take long, calm breaths. The harbour looks glassy. There shouldn't be anything to be afraid of, but her knees shake. Not so long ago, this would have been like second nature, even if it's been years since she took a boat out by herself. She can't remember the last occasion, but her lifetime trips must run into the hundreds. Hopefully, it's like riding a bike.

From the water, the sky seems wider and flatter; the clouds – which look fleecy overhead – seem to clot and jostle against the horizon. Kelspie Island is about fifteen minutes away. A quarter of an hour, out on the sea, by herself. Declan would be impressed with her progress. The email that came through in Angasfors said he might be able to fly in tomorrow.

She motors further, towards Findhorn, standing up and carefully taking the darker channels between sandbars and avoiding the Hipporockamus, as Beth liked to call their old swimming marker, the water deepens and she feels a now-familiar hollowing in the base of her spine. The surf is choppier out of the small bay, and a sense of water-induced vertigo is still with her. She does her best to ignore it. No matter what Karen said, those designs must have some sort of significance. If there's a reason why Beth underlined the name Kelspie Island, Juliet is going to get at least one answer today.

The forested shore at Culbin shrinks to a dark grey-green line in the distance. Juliet's hair lifts and writhes around her face; the salt spray nipping at her cheeks and eyes. Bucky's ears flap. Motor keening, the little red boat bumps over leaden waves, and a gull clips along just above them. Strangely, now that she's at the centre of her worst fear, Juliet begins to feel calm.

Kelspie is small, no more than four hundred metres across at its widest point, and already bleak at this time of year, stunted pines barely showing their tips above low slabs of risen bedrock. Juliet navigates to the point where her dad used to moor up when he brought the family out. About fifty metres from land, she drops the grapnel anchor from the stern and lulls the motor. The anchor plunges through the dark, brackish water and scrapes the rocky shoal at the sea bottom, seeking a hold, while she slowly motors as close as she can to the shoreline. She rolls up her jeans until they tighten around her knees, and throws her shoes to land. Bucky doesn't wait. He splashes into the water and runs ashore, before shaking spectacularly. Juliet follows him awkwardly into the water with a gasp, carrying a line that she ties around a largish boulder. Her feet are the colour of scrubbed bone.

With the boat secure, she stands, hands grasping fruitlessly at her hair to ram it into a vastly underqualified clip and stop it whipping around her eyes. She surveys the island. The first impression is of nothingness. She makes an effort to correct herself, to see through her father's or Erica's eyes. Or Beth's, more importantly. Is there anything here of significance? The terrain rises dully to a maximum height of perhaps three metres above sea level, sloping and shelving and carved with channels and ridges. There are scattered clusters of forlorn almost bonsai-sized pines. The shore is stippled with tufts of tawny seagrasses. She re-ties her shoes, whistles for Bucky, and begins to walk.

Scrabbling over the rocks and pausing to scrutinise the surroundings, it takes them just under thirty minutes to lap the island. Juliet's damp, salty toes become sore, rubbing inside her shoes. There are clutches of eyebright foliage, no flowers. The wind picks up. They arrive back at the natural harbour point, Juliet's cheeks pinched and eyes watering, chilled hands shoved into her pockets. Spots of rain hit her light jacket with unsettling clout. She pulls the hood up and strides towards a smooth, concave slab of stone rising above the beach with a slight overhanging lip.

The Sith's Mouth.

Dad used to tell them that if they sat there and thought hard enough, the island sith would sing for them. She and Erica, and later Beth, would jostle backwards into the natural seat, close their eyes, and listen in solemn silence. The sea's echo, hissing and booming, rolled off the rock, right through their bodies. Despite the cold, she smiles. This was Dad's way of getting them to wait quietly while he prepared for departure.

She just fits into the hollow space and is thankful for the immediate wind cover. Bucky sits a few metres in front of her on the beach, looking nobly out to sea, blinking in the rain. More layers of clothes would have been advisable. It will have to be a short-lived reprieve. The sky is darkening and she should get back as soon as possible. She's seen nothing out of the ordinary and it was foolish to come here with no preparation. The *Swallow* rises and falls impatiently. Juliet watches and listens. What song can Kelspie sing her?

Then she sees it, in her eyeline, as if by design. On the bluff about thirty metres away at the other side of the cove, obscured and revealed in turns by the *Swallow*'s agitated prow, is a pile of stones. It's not a natural phenomenon. The stones have been corralled in order of size to form a miniature cairn.

Juliet extracts herself from the sith's mouth, and scrambles across the beach, Bucky following a little less enthusiastically now. Gordon taught his twin girls how to make these little stone monuments. The beaches they visited would be littered with them by the end of the day. Over time, they learned how to make them more and more elaborate, how to create little windows and flat stone layers, if they had the patience to seek out the right pebbles. One summer they all built one together, with a bridge. It's one of her favourite childhood memories.

The waves bash the small cove with bullying force as Juliet runs and stumbles. Those summers out here seemed such an integral part of growing up, the long days on the coast. She remembers one year, visiting at midsummer, being amazed and saddened to discover that Beth had never built a cairn, and she promptly passed the skill on. Gordon had stood on the beach at Culbin watching them – an odd look on his face, as if he'd forgotten the whole exercise.

Juliet reaches the cairn, cold wind robbing her of breath. Three sticks protrude from the centre of the squat, sturdy little structure – jammed in between the tightly-packed stones. She strips them out and starts dismantling the pile, grazing her knuckles as she pulls it apart. Bucky takes one of the sticks in his mouth.

Buried in the middle of the mound is an army-issue green tin container, about the size of a large Bible. Juliet lifts it onto her knees and glances around like a thieving child. It's light, possibly even empty. She prises at the lid, which doesn't budge. There's a small lock on the front. She gives the tin a shake and catches a paperish rattle from the inside. It begins to rain now in earnest.

She removes her hairclip and bends it apart to form a hook, which she twists and worms into the lock. Her fingers slip awkwardly. She curses and stands up to look for a rock.

From the bluff, she can now see the waves hitting the north shore of the island. Their power has swollen even in the last few minutes. A crack of lightening streaks through the dark sky and onto the mountains to the north west. There is little hope of getting back to shore in these conditions. The sensible thing to do would be to try to secure the boat and wait the storm out.

She picks the tin up and runs with it tucked under her ribcage beneath suddenly torrential rain. She leaves it in the sith's mouth, and Bucky stands on the beach. He's sensibly made up his mind not to get back on the boat. She doesn't bother rolling up her jeans or taking off her shoes, but wades into the sea. She hauls herself onto the *Swallow*'s prow, knees first, and retrieves the second anchor on its heavy chain from under the seat. Thunder explodes around her. The boat lurches as she lumps the anchor as far as she can over the side. She nearly goes with it.

Back on shore, armed with the boat's tarpaulin cover, she

creates a makeshift shelter. The sky lights up again. She hauls and drapes the tarp over the lip of the sith's mouth. It flaps furiously as she weighs it down top and bottom with stones. She pats the cold surface inside and makes encouraging noises, until Bucky clambers into the hollow, and then she squeezes in too. The world goes blood-red.

Hunched cross-legged in the dark space, Juliet takes the tin and examines it again as her eyes adjust. Its green powder-coating is chipped and flayed. The rounded rim and hinges are rough with rust. She finds scratched into the underneath the initials, *G.M.* Gordon MacGillivray. She vaguely recollects her father using a tin like this to keep receipts in.

She turns and smashes it down onto the rock beneath her. Bucky whimpers.

"Sorry, boy," she says.

In these confines, she can only lift the tin to about eye level, and the rock surface below is hollowed away unhelpfully. She inflicts barely a dent. She repeats the exercise, her hands useless, frozen claws. Taking it outside and smashing the lock with a rock would probably do the trick, but that would be foolhardy right now. Her jeans are soaked through from the knee down, and her jumper and canvas jacket are not much better. Wind and rain batter the tarp violently. She needs to be patient until the storm wears itself out. Using the tin as the world's most uncomfortable headrest, she curls up, one arm over the dog. The tin's small handle presses stonily into her temple. It's going to be a miserable and painful wait.

Two hours later an almighty crash wakes her suddenly from fitful drowsing. Bucky has gone. She's so cold she's been shivering in her sleep and it takes her a moment to work out where she is. Another slam. It's not thunder. She lifts herself awkwardly. Her left arm and leg are numb. She shuffles to the edge of the sith's mouth and peers out from behind the tarpaulin. Icy rain spikes her face and at first she struggles to make out what she's seeing.

Fuck.

The *Swallow* has been thrown ashore. The wind is rocking her violently and with every gust, the little boat is thrown against the ridge that has stopped her path up the beach. If there's not a tear in the hull now, there will be very soon. Bucky is nowhere to be seen. Juliet tries to call him, but her voice is carried away by the wind.

She can't think. She's so cold. Could she roll the tarpaulin up and use it as a buffer between the boat and the rock? *Stupid idea*. It's way too small and, besides, she needs to prioritise shelter.

If only she could cry. No sound or tears will come. She's too angry with herself. Her first thoughts are how distressed her father would have been to see the boat wrecked. How Beth, too, had loved the *Swallow* – and now that's another line to her niece, lost.

Why the hell didn't she check the forecast before setting off? Why didn't she wait for Declan to fly in? She hears the echo of her own earlier thoughts, and shudders: *they do realise she's actually quite a competent person?* It's only as she inches back into foetal position inside the lip of rock that she considers the deadly implication of her actions. There's a possibility she will never get off Kelspie now. No one even knows she's here.

An hour later, night has fallen and the storm has eased a little. Glacial rain is still falling steadily but the wind is less biting. Juliet crawls outside and gets stiffly to her feet, the blood rushing painfully back into her left side. She limps across the beach, and, under intermittent slits of moonlight, inspects the boat. A gash about half a metre wide has been riven through the hull.

She breathes heavily, and forces herself to look away. The sea is still incensed, the whole Firth a churning mass of white. Even if it were calm, what could she do? It's four miles back to Culbin. The last time she swam any distance was years ago, trying with Erica to make it out to the Hippo. Neither ever made it. They always turned back, usually Juliet first. Four hundred metres may have been feasible on a good day, maybe in a pool, but in open water it was too testing, and there was nowhere to rest and recover before the swim back. The only one who ever succeeded was Beth.

In sudden fury, Juliet strides to the sith's mouth and grabs the tin. She launches it against the ridge. It glances and clangs away at an angle. She picks it up and throws it again. And again. The hinges give way before the lock, finally rupturing after about twenty throws. She can spy the edge of a small bundle of shiny paper inside.

She retreats behind the tarpaulin again, pulling it back a little, to let in some silvery light. After wiping her hands on her damp jeans she prises the tin's dented lid off. What's inside stops the breath in her throat.

The papers are photographs. About sixteen of them. Black and white. Professional standard. Declan's watermark is printed across most of them. Rights Reserved.

They are all of Beth.

Beth, topless, stretching on tiptoes towards the sky, waving one of her own fabrics like a flag. Beth reclining on a low sofa, eyes darting left at a scantily clad girl, a man snorting cocaine at her side. Beth, naked, on a bed Juliet doesn't recognise, the same fabric draped over her slender waist and hips.

CHAPTER TWENTY-SIX

Declan's flight is delayed by adverse weather. He lands in Inverness an hour later than expected. Still, he's surprised Juliet hasn't met him at the airport. It's unlike her, and doesn't bode well. He tries not to read too much into it, though. Maybe something's come up. Maybe she's with Erica.

The taxi driver raises his eyebrows and huffs when Declan asks to go to the summerhouse. It's a longish drive to the small holiday community, and it will be difficult to find a return fare and make the trip worthwhile.

"Forget to close the place up?" The driver asks as they join the A96. "Nasty storm last night. Autumn's arrived."

Declan nods, and mumbles agreement. He had lain awake in Liverpool listening to rain all night too, rehearsing what he was going to tell Juliet.

Breakfast with Sophie and Lotta was fearsome and overly jolly. Lotta was up early and made cinnamon buns, loading him up with them, like Little Red Riding Hood.

She held on to him warmly, saying goodbye. "Make sure you save some buns for Juliet."

"Good luck, Declan," Sophie murmured in his ear when he left. "You take care."

For all their affection, Declan hates himself so much that their words might as well have been a death wish.

The cab journey costs a fortune, and Declan's irritated to see

Juliet's car sitting idle on the summerhouse drive when they pull up. He fumbles for the cash, aware of the driver staring at the police tape still strung between the trees. She could have taken that down at least. The guy doesn't stick around to inspect the tip Declan hands him, he's in such a rush to drive away.

Last night's rain has made the decking treacherous. Declan tentatively approaches the front door and tries the handle. It's locked.

"Juliet?" He calls. "JT?" There's no answer. The spare key lies in its usual hiding place, in the tray of a wooden bird box to the left of the door. He lets himself in.

He dumps his bag in the hall and looks around, checks the bedroom. The bed is unmade; the sewing box splayed open. Papers are scattered on the floor. It doesn't look like Juliet has made that much progress in packing things up. Well, that's something. He might have the chance to speak to her before she finds out for herself. He shivers. Back in the lounge, he opens the little ironwork door of the wood burner; the ashes inside are stone cold.

He steps back outside and walks around the garden, breathing in the briny, pine cone-scented air. It smells very different to the last time he was here, springtime, when the days were lengthening and warming up.

"Juliet?"

The woodshed door is unlocked as ever and has been blown wide open. It must have been quite some storm. The dirt and sawdust floor is wet for about a metre inside, but luckily the rain hasn't reached the woodpile. Declan collects an armful of logs and shoulders the door closed behind him. As he turns towards the house, he nearly drops them all. At the edge of the path, a great grey owl is perched in a tall pine. Its pale disc face swivels in his direction and stares at him reproachfully, through bilious eyes. Declan wishes he had his camera on him. He pads quickly back inside and the bird's citrine gaze follows him, but by the time he returns to the doorway, camera in hand, it has flown.

The wood burner lit, Declan puts some leftover coffee on the hob. While it warms through, he wanders back to the bedroom, makes the bed, and tidies the pile of papers beside it. Juliet has always had the habit of night-time reading until the material drops out of her hand. Beth's designs. He flicks through them. They're as beautiful as she was.

He goes to fold away the sewing box, and spots the other papers on its lowest shelf. His stomach cramps nervously while he checks through them. Why didn't he tell Beth to destroy everything? It was stupid to let Juliet come here alone. She might have found anything by now.

He riffles through shoe boxes in the back of the wardrobe, through the bureau in the hall. The bookshelves. He looks under the armchair cushions, and through the magazine rack – there are some ancient gems in there. He tries not to get distracted by the old photography. He can't find a thing. He sits by the wood burner, sips the burnt coffee and waits. Either Juliet has already found out, or he's got a chance to explain first.

For a late lunch, he heats a can of soup. He chops potatoes into it; warms some bread. Juliet will be cold, and probably hungry, when she gets in. It's raining hard again, icy sheets splattering against the windows. *What the hell is she doing?*

By four o'clock, with dark clouds still in the sky, it's more like twilight. There's still no sign of her. He goes outside for what must be the eighth time. The wind has dropped but the trees are still shivering. He's been telling himself all day that she can't have gone far without a car. He looks around the driveway; peers in the car windows. There's a dog lead, and something else on the passenger seat. Writing. He tries the door. Locked. He squints. He can just make out some of the words.

destroy
Max
Kelspie

Has she gone to speak to the Delta guys? He doesn't really fancy going over to their place, but can't sit around any longer.

The forest floor is sodden. His shoes clog up quickly and weigh him down like mud shackles. He's kicking them grumpily against the side of the band's house when Toby answers the door.

Toby looks blank for a moment, as if he's trying to place Declan's face. Music pumps up the stairs from the studio, along with a waft of pungent smoke, and a low ring of laughter.

"Oh. Hi. It's... ah... Sorry I've forgotten your name?"

"Declan. We met in the spring."

"Oh, of course. The photographer. You're Beth's stepdad."

Declan snorts. "Is that what she told you?" He kicks the wall again.

"Um. Yeah?" Toby looks over his shoulder for a second and turns back. "She also said you didn't like us much. In fact, I think she said you called us 'a bunch of poisonous hipsters'." He folds his arms and smirks. "So, uh, how exactly can I help you?"

"I'm looking for Juliet." A clump of mud flies off Declan's boot and hits him in the face just below the eye. He claws it off, leaving four dirty streaks down his cheek. "Juliet MacGillivray? Beth's aunt. I understand she was here the other night? I'm her partner."

Toby's eyes widen involuntarily. "Right." He leans casually against the doorframe. "Well, she's not here I'm afraid. Just us hipsters."

"Look – Toby, isn't it? I'm worried about her. Her car's on the drive. She's not been in all day."

Toby laughs. "Wow. Don't let her hear you say that. A whole day? Call the police! Woman on the loose."

Declan's had it with this. Not knowing where Juliet is. Not knowing what she has found out. And now this... *fucking moron*. He steps forward, backing Toby against the door. "Listen, you cocky little—" His face is so close to the younger man's that he can smell Toby's skin. "She knew I was coming. She should be home."

Toby says nothing. He simply raises his eyebrows. The rain starts up again, pitter-pattering against the porch.

"Christ." Declan retreats a step and runs his hand through his wet hair. "I'm sorry. But… I've hardly slept. I flew in this morning. I don't think she's been in all night. She's hardly out for a walk in this weather, is she? I'm worried."

Toby stares into the distance, into the woods. He seems to consider for a moment. "Do you want to come in?" he asks.

As they pass through the hall, Toby closes the door leading down to the studio, from where faint voices and laughter are rising. He leads the way to the kitchen, and pours Declan a coffee.

"No, thanks," says Declan taking the cup anyway. He doesn't know what he wants, apart from Juliet, home. "Thanks. I suppose you haven't seen her then?"

"No."

The kitchen window looks down over the jetty. Declan peers out into the dusky scene, at the ghostly trail of piles leading nowhere beside the walkway.

"Ah. She's moved the *Swallow*, though?"

Toby follows his gaze. "*Shit*."

"What?"

"She must have taken… Hang on." Toby strides back out into the hallway and checks the key cupboard. He shakes his head. "Someone's taken the key. It was here." He points at the empty space where the Dala horse keyring had been until a couple of days ago. He turns to Declan. "Beth always left it here. She left loads of stuff here."

Declan stares at the empty hook. He tries to keep his voice calm. "You didn't notice the boat was gone today?"

"No. We've hardly looked outside. Have you seen the weather? We've been down in the studio nearly all day."

Declan bangs his coffee cup down onto a slim, glossy

sideboard. "I'm going to need you to come with me. Can we take the other boat? Is Lyall here?"

Toby's jaw hangs open uselessly for a moment, then he seems to make up his mind. "Er – yeah. Yes. We can take the boat. I think. I mean. No, he's not here. But I've seen how it works." He searches among the keys. "Er—"

"It's this one." Declan snatches a keychain. He can tell a key for a boat like that anywhere. "I'll meet you down there in five minutes. You'll need some warm clothes." He's already half way through the door. "Have you got a torch? A powerful one. A flask? Can you bring something hot? Some coffee or something?"

Toby looks stricken. "Uh. Yeah. I don't know about a torch. Declan?" He calls out, "Where are we going? Where do you think she went?"

"Not sure, but I'm guessing Kelspie."

Declan runs all the way back to the summerhouse, bursts in and shakes his travel bag empty onto the floor. Right there in the hall, he strips and changes into his warmest clothes. He throws open the kitchen cupboards so violently that they swing back on the hinges and almost break. He pushes packets of pasta and cans from side to side, and pockets a bar of cooking chocolate. He finds a heavy metal torch in a drawer, and throws it into the bag with a thump as loud as the blood in his temple. Snatching up the duvet from the bed, he rolls a thick jumper from the cupboard and a pair of joggers up inside it, before shoving the lot inside his holdall. He yanks the door behind him, and not waiting to see if it closes, runs back to the jetty.

Toby is waiting, his fringe flattened damply against his forehead beneath a grey woollen hat. He gestures to a large bag.

"I grabbed some things," he says. "Beth's old jacket and stuff. In case Juliet hasn't got anything."

"Yep," Declan nods. "Good thinking. Thanks."

They cautiously motor out of the small harbour, trying

to follow the channel. Toby has only seen others do this, and Declan has only done it twice: once with Juliet about seven years ago; once with Beth last spring when they went down the coast. Both times he was in the *Swallow*, a much smaller vessel.

They pick up speed further out. The light fails fast at this time of year. Declan calculates: they've got under an hour.

CHAPTER TWENTY-SEVEN

About two hundred metres from Kelspie, Declan and Toby can just about make out the small hulk of the *Swallow* and her red tarpaulin, draped further up the shore, like a discarded dress. Declan's torch is no use from this distance. It lights up only a ring of moisture in the air, and some buttery froth on the sea's surface a few metres away. They've hardly said a word, except one or two shouted instructions. Either Toby is terrified or a complete novice on the water.

As they approach the shore in the tender, they hear a dog barking. Declan waits until he can see the outline of stones on the shore, slowing to a chug. Over the quieter motor, he shouts.

"Juliet!" He scans the shore. "JT!" The anchor bites, and they secure the boat. Declan clambers off first and runs up the beach. Bucky, yelping with relief and delight, races towards him, before bowing his head and attempting to wrap himself around Declan's legs. Declan yells again. "Juliet!"

Reaching the *Swallow*, he sees the gaping hole in her side. He looks around again, shining his torch left and right. Toby arrives breathless beside him. He points at the tarp and follows behind as Declan races towards it.

Declan pulls back the sheet. Juliet is lying semi-conscious on the narrow lip of rock. She's completely naked.

"Jesus. Fuck." Declan drops to his knees beside her. "Juliet?"

She doesn't reply.

His heart thundering, Declan reaches in, cradles her face. Her skin looks a healthy colour, but she's ice-cold. He lifts her eyelids with his thumb. She surfaces briefly, struggling to focus on him.

Thank God. "Juliet. Your clothes. What's happened? It's so cold. Come on."

She murmurs something, sounding drunk.

"It's okay. Come on." He tries to ease her from the space. She curls up tighter.

"Wet. Too cold. I took them off."

"Shhh. Shh now. Come on. Come with me."

She opens her eyes wider, blinks, and begins to moan, as if she's in pain. "No, no, no, no, no, no. Get away. You get away from me!" Her voice gathers into a weak scream. "You GET AWAY! GET AWAY! DON'T TOUCH ME!"

"What the? Hey, hey. It's okay. JT. Calm down. Stay calm. It's okay. It's me, Declan."

"NO! DON'T!"

By now, Toby is at Declan's side, a down-filled jacket in his arms. He tucks it tenderly around her.

She cackles strangely. Then her arms, like a child's, reach up for his. "Toby." She begins to cry. "Toby. Please. Get him away from me. GET HIM AWAY!"

Declan steps back, futile hands on his head, feeling possessive and helpless and terrified. Toby lifts Juliet out. Her arms slip against his wet skin, falling from his neck, and she flops backwards, like a rug. He staggers slightly, then straightens. Meanwhile, Declan spots the broken tin still lying in the hollow. He pulls it out. Inside, a photo of semi-clad Beth winking at the camera.

Toby is already halfway down the beach, shouting something inaudible. It's Declan's turn to follow. He charges across the stones. Bucky, who had been bounding after Toby, stops dead and skulks at the shoreline. He won't put a paw in the water.

Declan heaves him into his arms and splashes clumsily into the water towards the boat. Bucky lets out a disgruntled growl.

On board, Toby fishes Juliet's hands through the jacket's arms and zips it up to her neck. He tries to dress her lower half from the bundle of clothes Declan has brought, but can't. Her legs are heavy and stiff, and he's too shy. He wraps her in the duvet, and puts his own hat on her head. Bucky watches anxiously.

Declan steers back towards the pale spotlights of Findhorn. "Give her some of the coffee," he calls from the helm.

"I don't think you're supposed to give hot drinks straight away."

"What do you mean? She's fucking freezing."

Toby edges towards Declan and lowers his voice. "I think she's got hypothermia," he says. "You have to warm them up slowly. Did you bring any food?"

Declan pulls the chocolate from his pocket and holds it out with one arm.

Checking that she can swallow without choking, Toby pokes tiny, glossy shards of the dark chocolate between Juliet's lips. Something cheaper would have been better, with a higher sugar content. She passes out with a lump of it still in her mouth. Awkwardly, gently, he delves it out with his index finger, and lays her in the recovery position.

He appears again at Declan's side. "She's either asleep, or unconscious. But she's breathing."

"You'd better get back down there and keep her warm." Declan coughs slightly. "Lie next to her."

Toby hesitates. "What was that about, back there, on the beach? What was she trying to say, Declan?"

"I don't know. She's delirious."

Toby sees Declan's Adam's apple rise and fall against the steely moonlight. He glances at the tin box on the seat. Its lid is rammed shut.

CHAPTER TWENTY-EIGHT

Juliet wakes in a hospital room. She hears a *shush shushing*. It's very restful. She opens her eyes. Pale green walls and white paintwork. Someone is slowly sweeping the floor of the corridor. Erica is sitting by her side, doing a Sudoku.

Juliet tries to raise her arm, which is pierced by a cannula and attached to a drip. She wonders if she's been tied to the bed, it's so hard to lift her limbs. Or maybe she's paralysed. Can anyone even tell that she's awake? For a groggy moment, she considers what life would be like, *shut-in*. A prisoner of her body. At the mercy of fluids coming and going, chemicals. That's how some women are treated every day, of course. Is that how Erica feels sometimes?

Erica completes the puzzle and turns the page, glancing up.

"Juliet!" She leans forwards, grabs Juliet's hand. "Hey."

Juliet tries to speak and emits nothing but a rasp.

Erica pours a tumbler of water and holds it out to her twin's lips. "Welcome back to the World," she says.

Juliet clears her throat, points a weak finger at the walls. "I don't think much of what you've done with the place."

Erica smiles and looks around. "No. Pissy, isn't it? Green is supposed to be healing, calming or something. Not this shade though; it's so cold."

A nurse enters. He smiles at them both. "Nice of you to join us," he says to Juliet. He takes her temperature, sticking a small plastic bud in her ear. "We've been having quite the party here; guzzling hot chocolate all night and dealing puzzle books to the other patients." He checks Juliet's drip and reads her notes. "That was quite a fright you gave us. They considered a bypass."

"A bypass?" she croaks.

"Yep. They take the blood out and warm it up. Then put it back in."

Juliet processes this. "A lot of people might say I should have had that done a long time ago."

The nurse laughs. "You'll be fine. You're doing just fine." He bustles out of the room, still chuckling.

Erica searches Juliet's eyes. "I'm not used to being on this side of the equation. It's usually me between the sheets."

Remembrance flickers across Juliet's gaze. It's not Erica's exploits she's thinking of though. *Between the sheets*. Declan and Beth.

As if Erica can read her mind, she says, "Declan's outside. He's told me everything, Juliet. The photos you found? He can explain."

"How can he—"

"Shhh. It's okay." She rests her hand lightly over Juliet's. "I think you should see him. Let him tell you what happened." She gets up and goes to the door.

Juliet tries to sit up and fails. She lies on her back, looking at the sky. Gossamer clouds, like steam, drift impassively past the window. Maybe they're smoke, from the hospital chimney. *Little bits of you and me*. There's a tap on the door and Declan opens it a small way.

"Can I come in?" he asks.

Juliet moves her head on the pillow and looks straight at him.

There's a shiny padded chair just to the right of the door. He gestures to it. "I could just sit here. Talk from here?"

"Yes." Juliet's eyes well up. "Stay over there." She glances towards the window again, blinking. She would give almost anything to have him closer. Have him touch her.

He arranges his coat over the back of the chair. She notes the grey skin under his eyes. The stubble. He looks exhausted. She suddenly wonders how long she's been here, how long he's been waiting. He takes a deep breath.

"How are you feeling?"

"Fantastic."

"Okay. Stupid question."

"Yes."

"The pictures you found—"

"Your pictures. Of Beth."

"Yes… Pictures I'd taken. Of Beth. I'm sorry I didn't tell you about them. I can explain everything." He waits again. No permission comes. He plunges on.

"Look, in the spring, Beth emailed me. It was when I was in Reykjavik. She said she had some exciting news. She'd met these guys in a band, Delta Function. They wanted her to design record covers for them. For their new album. And they were playing around with how to promote it. How to make the most of Beth's designs. Their PR guy wanted photographs for magazines, promos – of Beth – and she asked him if I could take them. For some reason he agreed."

He leans back, head against the wall, doesn't meet Juliet's steely gaze.

"She was so excited. She wanted it to be a big surprise. I changed my flight home. Came to Inverness. I was excited too, if I'm honest. It was potentially a big job for me." He leans forwards now, bracing his arms across his knees.

"She introduced me to them, and they – they just seemed like a normal bunch of musicians. I mean, as normal as spoiled, rich boys get. I kind of pitched to them about the way I usually work, and that's when things got strange. First, they wanted to control all the fly-on-the-wall stuff. I tried to explain, that's not how fly-on-the-wall works, like you don't plan it too much, but they clearly thought I was trying to stitch them up or something. Their PR guy got stuck in—"

"Malcolm Lyall."

"Yes." Declan looks at her. "Lyall started making noises about me not being up to their vision for the shoot. Beth was an asset, he said. It should be mainly about her. He wanted a full portfolio to suit all different platforms. So, I planned shots of her at work on her designs, plus some... well, more candid shots, some more arty shots, a kind of Bohemian, ingénue look. But Lyall was always there."

Juliet closes her eyes.

"He was constantly hanging around, being crass. He kept saying that sex sells and stuff like that. It was pretty fecking foul. And he acted like I was in on it."

Juliet snaps her eyes open again.

"And the photographs with the cocaine? No wonder he thought you were colluding with them. What the hell were you thinking?"

"Look, I didn't take those. You must have seen those pictures didn't have my watermark. I don't know where they were taken... where they came from."

Juliet glares at him.

"I promise you, Juliet. I did not take those pictures. The only time I spent with her, with them, was here, at the coast."

"Go on."

"Beth was getting uncomfortable with Lyall. So, I took Max, the—"

"I know who Max is."

"I took him to one side one day, and explained the problem. We both tried to talk to Lyall. Max was like... He didn't want her doing anything she wasn't okay with. But, and I'll never forget this, Lyall said, *It's all or nothing. It's not a free ride*."

Juliet pulls herself up a little. "How did Max react?"

"They were both weird to be honest. I don't know, some kind of power play between them. I could see Beth didn't really want to do the candid shots, but it was like she was beholden to them.

"I didn't really handle it well. I lost my temper and told them to get another photographer. And then Beth begged me to carry on. She said she wouldn't be comfortable with anyone else. But it still felt all wrong. I tried to speak to the other guys, and they just, kind of, laughed it off. I think they were coked up most of the time. They didn't want to see the problem.

"In the end, I blew up with Beth." He rubs his hands over his face, remembering. "I called them a bunch of cocks. Said she should stay clear of them. I didn't like the atmosphere. It wasn't healthy. I thought they were taking advantage of her. But she seemed anxious to have something to show from the sessions, to show Max. So… I gave her the best pictures I had, but told her they were for her eyes only. I didn't want anything more to do with it."

"Declan." Juliet's voice is low and gravelly. "Why didn't you tell me any of this before? Beth died in the summer. You took these in the spring. You've had months."

"I don't know." Declan hangs his head, examines the lino floor. "I felt bad enough as it was. You had so much on and you weren't dealing with the grief, and I didn't want to feed into that."

"So, let me get this straight." Juliet studies the ceiling. "You were perfectly aware I had doubts, that I was struggling to make sense of it, and, instead of telling me what you knew, you chose to treat me as if I were insane."

Declan's eyes dart at her. "It's not as if I knew anything really. I didn't realise how down Beth was. How much she was struggling. I had no idea she was on Valium. If I'd added it all up, of course I would have said something. But I didn't know any of that. The only sign anything was really up was the way she cried when I said I wasn't going to do it. I've thought about that a lot."

He bites his lip and breathes heavily. His voice wobbles.

"She cried, and said I was probably right. She was ashamed,

said she felt stupid, and she begged me not to tell anyone. Especially not you. I think… I assumed she just wanted so much to make a success of it, you know. Make people proud. Make you proud."

He hesitates. He knows how upsetting this must be to hear. Juliet's face is crumpling.

"I didn't lay a finger on her, Juliet. You know that. Surely? I mean, those pictures were wrong. I should never have taken them. But" – he hangs his head for a moment, then lifts it – "I actually thought it could become, like, a great thing all round. Beth's designs were fantastic. She seemed so happy at first. It looked like she was going to have this… this incredible opportunity. And I wanted to help with that. Be a part of it." He clears his throat. "It's difficult you know, being a part of your family."

She turns now, livid. "What the fuck is that supposed to mean?"

"You and Erica. You're so close. I know that she'll always be higher up the list of priorities—"

"Oh, don't give me that bullshit." Juliet heaves herself up now in bed. "There is no list of priorities." Her voice cracks. "Why do some men think there's always a fucking hierarchy? It's not a zero-sum game. Love is not a burning building. We don't have to choose who we're going to save."

She stares at him, then turns away suddenly and bites her thumbnail, looking intently back through the window. "Sorry," she mutters. She so often takes things out on him. But how dare he try and blame his lack of judgement on her and Erica? "What I mean is" – why is she now the one explaining? – "there's enough love to go around for everyone."

Declan falls silent.

The previous night, when Juliet was rushed into intensive care and the doctors had been looking at the case for cardiopulmonary treatment, the consultant had come to find him outside in the waiting area. She'd asked if he knew Juliet was pregnant. Only seven weeks. There was a high likelihood the baby would miscarry, she'd said.

He shook his head. He'd had no idea. "Does she know?" he'd asked.

The consultant blinked. "She doesn't know much about anything right now." She'd continued quickly. "But whatever you did before you got here helped to stop her going into a severe hypothermic state. Cardiopulmonary bypass is not indicated in mild cases, which increases both of their chances. She's been very lucky, but, I'm afraid to say, the foetus remains at some risk."

Lucky. Declan had tried to imagine how Juliet would feel, having all this discussed without her.

Now, Juliet looks away as he walks slowly over and sits on the bed. He gazes tenderly at her profile. Hair thick with salt. Skin dry and pale. She lifts her chin slightly towards the sunny window, and closes her eyes.

"I love you, Juliet," he says simply. "You're the woman I want to spend my life with. I should have told you what happened with Beth, and I didn't. I was a shit and a coward." She turns now, and he swallows, searching for the right words. "We should be able to tell each other everything."

He takes her hand, and she lets him hold it.

CHAPTER TWENTY-NINE

On the morning of Juliet's discharge, two days later, she sits on the side of her hospital bed, her hands folded over her belly, in a ray of queasy sunlight. She's dressed, but not in her own clothes which were left on the island. She arrived only in Beth's deck shoes and the jacket Toby wrapped her in. Declan brought in her laptop and phone and Erica supplied a pair of soft tweeds and a chunky jumper. They hang a little loosely, as if she's shrunk. Surely she should be thickening out? She finds it impossible to believe there's another human inside her.

She hadn't even noticed the missed bleed at first and certainly hadn't put two and two together when the strangeness started. She began to feel permanently heightened or angry and blamed it on grief and stress. Her appetite shifted; she was tired all the time and craved coffee, only to find it tasted odd; she'd assumed it was something to do with the menopause, and had been surprised to feel not regret, but relief. The burden of choosing to be childless had weighed heavily in recent years. Throughout her thirties people asked relentlessly when she'd have a baby, and seemed to think it was fine to tell her that she needed to hurry up.

She feels annoyed again now, thinking about it. Yes, she's great with children, as she's always having to acknowledge. Yes, she loves babies, as she's bloody explained so many times, but the notion of having one to look after, twenty-four-seven, for the next… well, for the rest of her life. It's almost unimaginable.

She can picture individual moments. Of course she can. She's not an idiot. She can imagine things, like feeding. Tiredness. Changing a nappy. Going to the park. First words. First steps. First day at school. She had a lot of experience of all these while Beth was growing up. But parenthood is not made of moments. It's the day-to-day that has always troubled her. The constant responsibility. She may have spent a lot of her working life advocating for maternity and paternity rights, but the truth is, she has no idea how she would be expected to do her job – which she has worked hard at, loves, and finds rewarding – as well as care effectively for the every need of another tiny human. Politics doesn't exactly stop while you have maternity leave.

You'd manage, people tell her. Other people do it, and she would too. You just get on it with it. But why should she… when she has never wanted to?

She wishes she could talk it over with Declan, gain a better sense of his views. He's never even mentioned children to her, although she has caught him occasionally, making silly faces at babies in cafés and staring at prams.

They really should discuss exactly what they want for the future. They should have done so before now. She suddenly feels they've been improvising for seven years, riffing with each other, with no plan, no script or score. Until now it seemed fun.

But his lack of judgement over Beth, his failure to tell her what he knew. It's not that he was irresponsible as such, or lacking in discernment. After all, he was shrewd enough to see Beth's situation was unhealthy, and tell Beth so in no uncertain terms. But why didn't he say anything to *her*?

She's mustering the energy to bend and pull on the battered deck shoes, when her phone starts to vibrate and shimmy across the white table beside the bed.

Fiona Goldman. Juliet's heart sinks. Was it too much to believe that she might be left alone to recover?

Fiona's voice is warm but businesslike. "Juliet. Hello. Now, I'm not really calling. I know you need to rest. I won't take much of your time. How are you?"

Juliet considers lying, and sighs. "I'm exhausted, to be honest. All over the place."

"I can imagine," Fiona makes a sympathetic noise. "I just wanted to let you know we're all thinking about you. And we're looking forward to having you back fighting fit."

A hospital orderly puts his head around the door and withdraws it sharply on seeing Juliet on a call.

Fiona continues. "You are coming back."

Was that a question?

"Yes," Juliet says. "I mean, I don't know when. There's a lot to sort out still."

"You're sorely missed here, Juliet, for what it's worth. In more ways than one." She pauses. "Everybody is assuming you're going for the leadership. It's getting to the point where we need to know."

Juliet takes a deep breath. "I'm undecided. What about you?"

"I'm dead meat."

Fiona has always been blunt, Juliet thinks. So self-effacing, despite her celebrity status.

As if Fiona can follow her thoughts, she suddenly asks, "Any light on the Dominic Palmer thing? Why he was so interested in you and Beth?"

Her tone is casual, but hardly anything Fiona says is casual. Juliet moves the phone to her other ear.

"I don't know that Dominic Palmer was that interested in Beth, to be honest. It turns out Beth was involved with a group of musicians, Delta Function." She pauses. "Brace yourself."

"I'm listening."

"Their PR is Lyall, believe it or not."

Juliet can almost hear Fiona rolling her eyes.

"Beth had been dating one of them. They were recording up here. But it seems like she was a bit of a distraction, and Lyall tried to fix it by getting her involved in some work for them, album designs. I think Bernhard Palmer must have got the tip-off from Lyall too, his old pal. Lyall worked out the connection to me and probably thought there was an angle to play. But I don't think Palmer the younger was that interested. Maybe he was just humouring his father, pretending to follow up some lead. I mean, there's not really any story there."

She suddenly recalls Lyall's behaviour at the party, offering his services and advice to PA.

"Lyall's constantly working an angle, isn't he? As soon as he saw me, he started on about your image. Said you were a force of nature."

It's Fiona's turn to sigh. "Don't be taken in. He'll say anything to anyone. Lyall's an egotist. Obsessed by the idea he can always make things play to his advantage."

You never know how these things will play in the long-run. Juliet's mind slides to the photos, and Declan's account of Lyall and Max both trying to control his shoot with Beth.

"There's some kind of alpha rutting going on between him and these Delta guys, but I don't understand why they don't just shrug him off. I mean, he's an experienced PR, but... he's so old-school, he came across as an embarrassment. Especially to Max, this guy Beth was seeing, who – by the way – is a huge control freak."

Things seem to take shape in her mind. "To be honest, I'm less concerned by Dominic or Bernhard Palmer, than by how Max might have messed with Beth's head."

She stops herself. Fiona may have rung on the pretext of Juliet's health and plans, but PA's future is her real concern – and until recently, it would have been Juliet's entire focus too.

"Look," Juliet says. "Next steps for the Alliance aren't solely dependent on me. There are plenty of people, in the ranks and out, who'd like to see me gone. The strategy, the campaign – they were largely down to me. Some would say I should fall on my sword."

"No. We need to be clear on this, Juliet. People are asking which candidate I'm going to endorse. And it's not only me who'd like it to be you. But we need to think extremely carefully. For one thing, I could damage you. Those focus groups you commissioned? They show our losses were about me. People were anti-me. Not the Alliance, not party policies."

"People were anti the image of you created by Palmer and his attack dogs."

"Perhaps, but the damage is done. And I wouldn't want to harm you by association."

Juliet allows herself to wonder about her own image, and – for just a split second – how it might be affected by her pregnancy. She hates herself for it immediately. "The focus groups. What were my ratings?"

"You're scoring well. People like the fact you're not a celebrity playing at politics. They like your commitment to family."

"I don't really have much of a family." *Yet.*

"They're sympathetic—" Fiona breaks off.

Juliet fills in the gaps. *Sympathetic to my grief. My sister's mental health.*

"Well, that's something," she says wryly.

"I would like to be able to endorse you—"

"Thank you, Fiona. I'm grateful and I know it looks like I'm stalling—"

"But I'm afraid I can't."

Juliet falters. "I see."

"Not until we know for sure what Palmer's connection to Beth was, and how that might link back to you. I'm afraid I don't buy that Lyall was just cooking up a PR stunt. Bernhard Palmer and Lyall go back a long way. It's more likely Palmer was mining Lyall for information, something he could use against us."

Fiona is beginning to sound as paranoid as Erica. As paranoid as Juliet has been feeling.

"It's not personal, Juliet. I cannot overstate how much Palmer would get off on bringing us down. He only needs the barest excuse. Our kinds of policies threaten oil and development in the occupied territories. Arms manufacturing. All his major interests. He's been donating to the right-wing for years to protect himself. You don't make that kind of investment without following through when you have the opportunity. The simple truth is, PA can't risk a whiff of any scandal. If we elected another toxic leader, he'd use it to destroy us."

Juliet glances at the tinful of pictures of her niece. Declan's pictures. The cocaine.

"I'm not toxic." Her voice wobbles slightly. "And neither was Beth."

"I hope not. I really hope not. But we can't rely on hope. We need to be sure. If you can prove Palmer has nothing, you'll be unstoppable."

NORTHERN HERALD: HISTORIC CINEMA GETS MILLENIAL MAKEOVER

20 May 1997

The iconic Eden Building in Manchester is to be given a new lease of life for the new millennium – as an exclusive nightspot.

Developers have won more than £2 million in EU funds to restore the Art Nouveau gem to its former glory. Work will include complete restoration of the famous cupola, tiling and friezes.

Three years ago, Manchester city took legal action when ceramic panels fell into the street below. "We're delighted," said a city spokesperson. "The Eden is a unique part of our cultural offer which will now be preserved for future generations."

The building dominates an entire block in the northern quarter and has a chequered history. Privately built in 1879 by the landowning Palmer dynasty to rival the nearby Free Trade Hall, it started life as a concert hall, and later housed a cinema and print works. It allegedly escaped German bombs because Hitler admired its elegance.

Critics argue wealthy proprietors should not benefit from public funds, highlighting that membership of the new Eden Club will be exclusive. However, the Palmer family have promised publicly available tickets for some events, and have pledged to support the city's growing electronic music festival. EU heritage funding is not restricted to buildings intended for public use.

Well-known celebrity publicist, Malcolm Lyall, close friend to Bernhard Palmer, brushed off the negative coverage, stating, "Bernie is doing a great thing preserving this place, but you can't please the cynics. They'd all love membership if they could afford it. It's sour grapes." Lyall claims to be one of the first to sign up for membership. "It's very exciting," he said. "My membership card says number three. Bernie has number one. I can't tell you who got number two, or I'd have to kill you."

CHAPTER THIRTY

Juliet is still surfing through archive newspaper articles about the Palmers on her laptop, waiting in her room for Declan, when she hears the door handle turning.

She looks up to see the face of a woman, surrounded by a nimbus of fine curly red hair, poking around the door.

"I'm so sorry," says the woman. "I don't want to disturb you, but I… I wanted to express my condolences."

The woman steps inside the room. She's wearing jeans and a blue-and-white-striped jacket and carrying a large bag.

"I realise this is a private time, but my daughter is in the oncology ward, and… I saw your name on the chart outside and I've been dithering all morning wondering if it would be totally out of order for me to come in and pass on my condolences. My daughter knew Beth. And she tells me she thought an awful lot of her."

She takes a few steps and pulls the chair by the door a metre or so closer to Juliet. She sits with her hands clasped reverently on her knees. "We're both so very sorry about her death."

Juliet swallows. "Well, that's very kind. Thank you."

"And you're quite well?"

"I'm sorry?"

"It looks like you're all packed and leaving. That's good. Are you better? You've been ill?"

"Well, yes… A bit of a fright."

"A fright? Gosh."

"Yes," Juliet reaches for one of the shoes. She sits there with it – Beth's deck shoe – in her lap. There's something not right. For a moment her mind clouds. She shakes her head and smiles ruefully. "It was my own stupid fault. But – there we are. Your daughter… I'm sorry you didn't tell me your name?"

"Oh, she's called Jennie. I don't expect Beth will have mentioned her. I mean, do they ever tell us much about anything? Jennie's so uptight with me. Sometimes I only know how she's feeling when I catch a glimpse of her Facebook page." She looks piercingly at Juliet. "It's difficult, isn't it? Did Beth confide in you?"

Juliet sinks back and breathes out slowly. "Not more recently, I suppose. No."

The woman nods sagely. "Did you try to get her to talk? Try to help her?" She leans in.

Juliet looks down at Beth's deck shoes again. She wishes Declan would hurry up and take her back to the summerhouse.

The woman presses on. "I mean, I just wish it could be me instead of Jennie. Did you have that feeling? You don't have children, do you?"

Juliet glances up sharply now. "No. I don't. But, I'm sorry, what did you say your name was?"

"You must think me so rude. But there are so few people who really understand. When Jennie first was diagnosed, I…"

She fishes for a tissue from her large tote bag. Juliet sees a MacBook inside. The woman dabs at her eyes.

Juliet stares at the woman's red hair. Is it possible? She hesitates, not trusting herself. If she causes a scene, calls security for a poor woman who really does have a daughter with cancer…

"I don't suppose I could ask you to pour me a glass of water?" she says.

The red-head looks briefly taken aback, then rises swiftly.

"Of course. Yes, of course." She busies herself with the

jug and the plastic cup, while Juliet observes her. "I mean, you understand what I'm going through." She's slow with the water. "What went through your mind when you first heard about Beth?"

The woman is about 170 centimetres. Juliet tries to think how much she herself weighs, to make a comparison. Yes, perhaps 65 kilos. Red hair.

"Actually I'm feeling rather tired. I think I'm going to have to ask you to leave," she says evenly. "Please give Jennie my best wishes."

The woman pretends she hasn't heard. "We both think you're amazing. What you do. Politics. How do you keep going, when you've lost so much?"

"Please could you leave?" says Juliet. "Now."

She's furious but her voice is breaking up.

"I'd like you to leave now."

"Of course. You must have so much to think about. Will you be running for leader?"

That's it. This has to be the hack Erica talked about. Juliet reaches for the call button next to the bed, but before she can push it, the door is opened again. She's almost relieved to see it's not Declan, but Karen Sutherland. Karen stares at the red-head, and plants her feet and muscular calves firmly, slightly apart, blocking the path to the door.

"YOU," Karen says loudly. "How did you get in here?" She calls over her shoulder, out into the corridor. "Security! Please! Here! NOW!"

Some sort of scramble happens outside, but the woman doesn't budge for a moment. She stands and glares at Juliet. "People have a right to know what state you're in."

"NOW!" roars Karen. A nurse bursts into the room, flanked by a woman and a man in dark blue uniforms. They seize the woman by the arms and lead her away.

"Don't let her go. I want to speak to her!" Karen calls after them. She turns. "Juliet, are you okay?"

Juliet backed into a corner of the room, breathes heavily.

"Yes, yes," she shakily pulls herself upright. "I'm fine. Who is she?"

"She's from the *Examiner*. Janine Rap. At least that's what she writes under."

Juliet watches Karen put the chair back to the side of the room and stand, crisply, almost to attention.

"Why are you here?" Juliet asks, only just aware of how rude this sounds. "Have you been guarding my room? I didn't ask for that. What's going on?"

"No. Juliet. There was no one guarding your room. Obviously." Karen sighs. "I'm here because I was hoping to speak to you, very briefly. I didn't want to bother you once you'd gone home to rest, and I thought I could catch you… But now perhaps isn't a good time."

"No, it's fine." Juliet speaks quickly. "What do you need?"

"Are you sure?"

"Unless you ask me now, I'll go home worrying about what you want, and that won't help me."

Karen nods. She looks over her shoulder, then asks, "You went out to an island?"

Great. So Karen knows. Juliet looks back down at Beth's shoes. She frowns.

"Juliet?"

"Yes. Yes, I went to Kelspie."

"Can I ask why?"

"I thought I might find something there. Beth used to go there."

"And did you? Find something?"

Juliet fights the urge to look at the green army tin on the table next to the bed. She should tell Karen, but… those pictures. Taken by Declan. She feels protective of Beth, and of herself. But there's something else. She feels ashamed.

"No."

Karen licks her lips. "I see." After a few seconds, she moves towards the door, where she lingers, her hand on the door knob. She turns back. “I know you don’t trust the investigation, Juliet.”

No response.

“I know you have questions of your own. And last time we spoke, it was a difficult conversation.”

Juliet folds her arms across her chest, trying to prop herself up. “Questions?” She rocks slightly. “Karen, they’re only the same questions anyone with any interest in actually finding out what happened would ask. I want to know why everyone made up their mind so quickly that my niece was suicidal. I want to know why nobody close to her knew she was depressed. I want to know why she might have been driven to destroy her work. Who was making her feel like that? Has any of that even been looked at?”

Karen nods. “I understand, Juliet. But you’ve read the report. The note—”

“Yes. You’ve already told me how conclusive you found the note. Left with the shoes off the path, so that they weren’t found for days, even when people were looking for her. Strange isn’t it?” Juliet’s voice is rising. “I also want to know why nobody paid any attention to the science, the diatoms.”

“Diatom tests are unreliable.”

Juliet presses her fingertips to her eyes. Little juddering dots and tadpoles swim in the darkness behind her eyelids. “Some people don’t think so. They were only in her lungs. I’ve done the reading, Karen. If she’d drowned, if she’d been swallowing water while… while her heart was still beating, they’d have been pumped through her system.”

“Not necessarily. That research is very controversial. In some cases, the larynx goes into spasm, or there’s a heart attack before drowning, so you don’t always see diatoms pumped around. The diatom test says nothing about the absence of a beating heart. It means nothing, I’m afraid.”

Silence. *The absence of a beating heart*. Juliet moves her fingertips to her forehead now, her eyebrows, her cheeks. It feels like they are being melted, contorted, by acid. She presses harder, trying to keep everything in place, trying to stop herself dissolving. *Is she rambling? She feels as though she's rambling*. She must sound like Erica. She makes an effort to keep her voice low and steady.

"It means something to me, Karen. Beth's heart means something to me, every day. Every second. And it means something to me to know whether her heart was beating when she entered the water."

"Juliet, you're upset. I think we should—"

"No, no. Let's not stop now. There's something else." She bends to pick up one of the shoes. "These. Left on the path. Why do they fit me?"

"I'm sorry?"

She shakes the shoe. "These are Beth's. The ones you all said she'd left on the path, with her note. I've been wearing them. But I wasn't the same shoe size as Beth." As Juliet speaks, the fog in her head starts to clear. "The label says they're a forty, but Beth always wore a man's shoe fitting. She had wide feet. Like flippers my dad used to say. I'm telling you, any shoes of hers would be way too big for me. These cannot be hers."

She catches her breath. Karen has picked up the other shoe and holds it lightly across her palm.

"Why haven't you investigated that?" Juliet presses the point. "Who put these out on the path? Who put that note out?"

"Okay, okay," Karen says, suddenly. "Let's suppose you're right, and someone else put them on the path." She's riled, but it's towards herself. Juliet can recognise anger aimed inwards, all too well. "How do you suggest I go about investigating that?" Karen waits, eyebrows raised. "You admit yourself, you've been wearing them. Down to the sea perhaps? You've worn them inside and outside the summerhouse, I suppose? Therefore, they're contaminated. You've contaminated them. I can't send them to forensics. Shoes stretch and shrink with use. Do you want us to dig Beth's corpse up to see if they fit?"

As soon as Karen says the words, she knows she's gone too far.

There's a long pause, while Juliet focuses on the shadows chasing across the green walls, trying not to see a group of white-coats wedging Beth's swollen, damaged feet into the shoes, like some kind of zombie Cinderella. She fills her lungs again. And again.

That was monumentally unprofessional. Yet it's somehow refreshing to hear someone else react with some feeling rather than simply delivering a stock response. Juliet's so tired of being *managed*. Her breath comes freer and faster than it has for months. For the first time, she actually feels as if she's had a proper conversation about Beth's death. She's heard somebody else thinking it through and it's strangely liberating.

Karen holds the shoe awkwardly, in one hand. She flicks the other hand across her face, as if swiping away a fly. "I'm sorry," she says. It's grossly inadequate, but somehow enough.

"I just want you to stay open to the possibility that it wasn't suicide," Juliet says, finally. She reaches for Beth's jacket.

"Where did you get that?" Karen asks. "Is it yours?"

"No," Juliet looks surprised. "It's... I don't know. I think Declan said Toby wrapped me up in it when they came to find me."

Karen pulls on a pair of latex gloves from her pocket. "May I?" She takes the jacket from Juliet's hands, and, turning it over, examines the hood. She holds it close to her nose, not quite touching, and sniffs. "Do you mind if I take this, Juliet? It looks like... I think this is the jacket Beth wore when she went to the university that night. When she destroyed her work. On the CCTV footage from the courtyard, she's wearing a jacket like this."

"Of course," Juliet replies. "Take it."

"We weren't able to find it before, when we searched the summerhouse." She reaches into a pocket inside the jacket, and mutters to herself. "Bingo." She holds up a piece of paper with four numbers written on it and catches Juliet's eye. "Did you say Toby brought this out to the island? From their place?"

Juliet stares at the down-filled jacket. "I think so. But why would it be there? Wouldn't that mean… Beth went back to theirs after going to the campus?"

"Possibly," says Karen. "Or someone removed it from the summerhouse and took it to the studio for some reason. Or… I don't know, I'll have to run some tests. Although this will be contaminated too."

Juliet nods.

"Juliet," Karen starts. "You realise, I shouldn't really even be here, talking to you? There would have to be significant new evidence to re-open the case. This is not protocol. I could be suspended. I could be investigated myself." Wind buffets the branches beyond the window pane. "But I will keep an open mind, and you must share any information you think is relevant."

Does Juliet imagine her glancing at the army tin?

Her free hand is on the door now. "Anything at all."

CHAPTER THIRTY-ONE

Later that day Declan drives Juliet back to the summerhouse. The silver birches along the highway have turned, and many are already losing their yellowed leaves. In a few weeks, the fruiting catkins left on the branches will release their seeds and the trees will be bare.

Sitting by the living room window bundled up in Beth's blanket, Bucky at her feet, the notebook with its list of questions in her hand, Juliet doesn't speak a word about the baby, nor about Fiona's phone call. She doesn't have the energy to explain that Fiona won't endorse her until Beth's involvement with the Palmers, whatever it was, is accounted for. Declan will only be indignant on her behalf, they'll have to launch into whether or not she even wants the leadership, and that will lead to discussing the baby. She knows she can't avoid it forever, but right now she can't face it..

Together, they start to wrap things, write on labels. They stick to practicalities; discuss the *Swallow*, how much it will cost to try to repair her, retrieve her from the island.

"We should definitely look into it," Declan says. Juliet can almost feel him steering away from the word *irreparable*.

At around three in the afternoon, there's a light knock on the door. Juliet emerges from the bedroom, aching all over, wrapping her dad's old dressing gown around herself. A half-sliced loaf sits on the breadboard in the kitchen. Toby is framed in the front door, standing awkwardly, hands shoved low into his pockets. Declan, at the threshold, still has the breadknife in his hand.

"Toby," Juliet says, peering past Declan. "What's going on?"

"I'm sorry to disturb," Toby says. "I just wanted to check how you were; see if you guys needed anything."

Declan puts his arm against the doorframe casually, blocking it. "We're fine," he says. "Thanks." He doesn't move.

Juliet tries not to roll her eyes. She can see exactly what Declan's up to. He'll have a vested interest, now that he's told her the story behind the photographs, in maintaining that tale – that Toby and the Delta guys were the irresponsible ones, lacking in judgement. He can hardly act as if they're best friends, just because Toby helped on the island the other night.

And, she reflects, Declan's not entirely wrong to want them at arm's length. She hasn't forgotten the argument she overheard Max and Toby having on the boat.

What's more, it's not Max, not Beth's boyfriend, who's coming over all concerned to check if she's okay. But being so hostile is hardly going to help unravel what really happened to Beth.

She smiles for the first time in two days. And it's genuine. This boy makes her smile, despite everything. "That's kind," she says. "I was napping."

Declan turns from the door as Juliet runs her fingers through her hair self-consciously. He drops his voice. "Are you not going to get dressed?"

Juliet ignores this, folds away a few papers and pulls an upright armchair towards the wood burner. "I understand it was you who carried me, Toby. To the boat." She clears her throat. "I was in quite a state. I'm sorry."

"Yeah." He pauses. He looks from under Declan's arm at her; smiles crookedly. "You were like a baby."

Her abdomen flip-flops.

"Come in, Toby," she says. Declan sets his jaw, and steps

aside. He closes the door a little noisily and returns to the kitchen.

Juliet watches Toby take in the room. Boxes are stacked at the side. Some shelves are empty. He walks over to the old record player and hunkers, flipping through the EPs on the shelf below, scanning their covers. She can just see the edge of his tattoo.

He puts out a finger and pulls forward the first pressing of a 1979 Georgio Moroder track. He seems pretty comfortable, as if he knows his way around.

"By the way," he says, rotating the record in the tips of his fingers and examining the label. "Max was wondering if you'd thought about the album designs? He says you took them the other night?"

"Yes." She doesn't feel inclined to explain herself.

"I don't blame you. Max will get over it if you decide it's not what you want. Personally, I reckon they're too good not to see the light of day. But it's your call."

She rearranges the blanket around her, weighing her words. If what Declan has told her is true, then there's nothing to hide, is there? "I also came across some photos Declan had taken for you guys. They were pretty eye-opening."

"Oh. Yeah." He screws up his eyes. "The ones from the spring. That was a disaster. Beth told us Declan was being over-protective. I could have sworn she said he was her stepdad."

An image of Declan as a father flashes into Juliet's mind, a newborn in his arms.

"Well, maybe she was trying to save face."

Toby joins her now, near the fire. He opens the burner's little ironwork door and pokes and rearranges the embers.

"I actually only ever saw one or two of the pictures. But whatever you think about the, er, style of them, Declan's good at what he does."

For a moment, she considers fetching the tin from the

bedroom and showing the images to him, but it's too much of a violation. Beth hid them for a reason.

"Yes," she says. "He is."

The fire crackles. Toby prods at a log, turning it to a better angle. Glowing tendrils of fire wriggle along its charred edge. The way he makes himself at home should be annoying. Taking liberties. But at least he seems in a mood for confiding. She wonders how many more arguments there have been since the one she overheard on the boat.

"Max is very driven, isn't he?" she remarks.

The warmth fades from Toby's gaze. He turns slowly to look at her, the poker in his right hand. "What makes you say that?"

The poker in his hand trembles. It's just how he reacted in the steam room, as if he can't help projecting his emotions directly outwards. Maybe that's what makes him a good DJ. It's unnerving.

"Just, you know. His attention to detail."

"Yeah." Toby nods slowly and takes a couple of steps towards the door. "Talking of which, if there's nothing I can help you guys with, I should be getting back," he says. "But there was one other thing, I just wondered if you got that jacket. The one we wrapped you in. I think Max wants it back. You know. Before you guys go."

Declan re-enters, a tea towel over his shoulder. "I thought you said it was Beth's jacket?" he says.

"Yeah. Actually, it belonged to Helen. Max's sister. She left it behind when she came last year."

"Yes, of course." Juliet half rises, trying to keep her face neutral. "Is it not there, hanging up?"

Toby shakes his head.

"Well, it must be here somewhere," she lies. "Unless Erica has it?" She gestures at the chaos and piles of books. "Maybe she took it from the hospital. To dry clean."

Toby's jaw pulses. He lingers in the hallway, looking at the coats hanging there, then lets himself out.

Juliet heads back into bed, with the tin of photographs. She lies on her side, flipping through the images quickly, over and over, like a pack of cards. Sky. Flag. Bed. Balcony. Sofa. Cocaine. Sky. Flag.

What's the deal with the jacket? She turns to the only picture featuring Toby. It's not one of Declan's. She falls asleep with it in her hand.

She's woken much later by Declan coming to bed, bringing her some of the hot milk recommended by the hospital. He doesn't seem to realise it makes her gag. He stands looking at the photos all over the bed for several seconds, and clocks the one of Toby on her pillow.

He mutters under his breath, "For fuck's sake," before starting to gather the pictures up.

She sits up. "Pardon?"

"I said, for fuck's sake," he repeats loudly. "What are you doing?"

"I'm looking—"

"Yes, I can see you're looking at the fucking pictures. Again. Are you never going to let this drop?"

She turns sharply. "Don't speak to me like that. If I want to look at pictures of my niece, I'll look at them as much as I want. Have you not figured out that this isn't about you?"

"I never said it was about me. This is about you. Torturing yourself."

"I am not—"

"And have you not figured out that Beth didn't want people looking at those? Otherwise she wouldn't have hidden them in a locked tin, beneath a pile of rocks, on an island in the middle of fucking nowhere. I'm surprised she didn't fucking throw them on the fire with everything else in her life."

Juliet closes her eyes. The idea of Beth burning her life away on that last night is heart-breaking enough, without it being weaponised by Declan to make a point. She lowers her head onto her chest, swallowing.

"I'm sorry," Declan says. His hands drop uselessly to his sides. "I shouldn't..."

She tries to keep her voice even. "No. You're right. But the thing is, she didn't burn them, did she? She didn't burn everything. Her notes, the sewing box. She kept those. And these..." Juliet looks at him and shakes her head. "I don't know."

Declan sits heavily on the bed. "I told her they were for her eyes only. I said to keep them safe. But it's crazy to think she would take that so far." He sighs. "They're not even all my pictures."

Juliet picks up the black-and-white stills of Beth. On their backs, a handwritten phrase: *FOR THE ATTENTION OF BETH WINTERS*.

Beth is seated on a deep, curved sofa. Heavy drapes hang behind her, in front of a tall window with a balcony. There's some sort of figure in its ironwork. A man hunches over a low table, hands to his face. He's snorting cocaine. Beth is looking at him with a strange expression.

"Does it look like it's been set up?" Juliet asks. "Like a fashion shoot or something?"

"Hmm. Not really. Worst fashion shoot I've ever seen. Anyway, look how bad the images are. Really low quality. It's like they've been taken by a security camera."

"Beth doesn't look happy, does she?" Juliet says.

In the next photograph, Karlo sits beside Beth, laughing, a semi-clad girl on his knee. Another girl stands behind the sofa. Juliet and Declan study the images in silence.

"Where the hell is she?" Juliet murmurs. "It's weird. Look at those other girls. What are they? Strippers? Dancers?"

They compare the two images side by side.

"What's that?" Juliet asks abruptly. "Behind her?"

Declan's already seen it. At the edge of the first frame, beyond Beth on the sofa, through an open door, a blurred presence. For a few moments, neither Juliet nor Declan say a word.

Finally, Declan clears his throat. "Well. I'd say it's someone getting a blow job. In any case, I think we can safely say they're not showgirls."

Juliet pushes back the covers and gets out of bed.

"Put your dressing gown on," Declan urges. It's late now, past eleven, and cold. He stopped feeding the fire a little while ago.

"Please, Declan, stop fussing."

She exits the bedroom and rummages at the bureau in the hall. Her feet, unslippered, pad back towards Declan and she re-enters the bedroom holding a magnifying glass.

"Jesus," Declan says. "You weren't joking about following a trail, were you?"

She climbs back into bed, holds the magnifying glass up to her eye and moves the picture towards her. The figures in the background remain out-of-focus, but there's no doubting what's going on.

She lowers the lens slowly. "Declan. That looks like a child," she says.

Declan grabs the lens and looks himself. "Or a very small adolescent."

"*Toby keeps me away from Karlo*," Juliet mutters.

"What?"

"At the party. It's what Max's niece told me. She said Toby had to babysit her to keep her away from Karlo. I didn't think..." She thrashes angrily against the pillows. "There was me thinking *she* was the problem. Grace. You know, teenage girl, pestering the celebrity."

"Hang on. What? You're not saying that's Max's niece in the picture?"

"No." She grips the edge of the picture. "But these are young girls. I think that's what this picture shows. Very young girls. And Beth with them."

Declan stares at her, and looks again at the photograph. After a few seconds, he leans back. "She'd never have been able to stomach that."

"Precisely. See the look on her face?" They both lean over the picture. Beth's face is anguished. Disbelieving. On closer inspection, there appear to be runs of mascara down her cheeks.

"What the hell was she doing there?" Juliet is incredulous. "Why isn't Max with her?"

"Why don't you just ask Toby about it? He's very friendly." Declan makes an effort to keeps his voice level.

She ignores this remark. "He's hardly going to tell me. Even if he wanted to, Max runs a tight ship." She looks again through the magnifying glass. "This writing on the back. *FOR THE ATTENTION OF*... She obviously didn't write it, did she? Does it sound like a threat to you?"

Declan slips into bed beside her. He just manages to refrain from sliding his hand possessively into the curve of her hip.

"Look." His leg briefly grazes hers. "I don't know where you're going with this, but if that picture shows what you think it does," he pauses. "Karlo with young girls? Is that what you're suggesting? And Beth receiving these, why? To keep her quiet? Some kind of coercion? Then, it's not going to be easy to prove anything. This is way bigger than..."

It's too late. Juliet is already connecting the dots. "We should be able to find out where this is," she interrupts. "That ironwork on the balcony. That devil's head thing. I've seen it somewhere. It's distinctive enough, isn't it? Do you think Alex or Erica would recognise it?"

"Possibly. We could google it, if we had a bloody connection. Or... are there any of your dad's old books around?"

They both get up this time, and go back out to the living room. Declan gives the embers in the wood burner a poke. Juliet stands on tiptoe at the bookcase. Moving back and forth, she pulls out an armful of tomes: among them, a tall, thick encyclopaedia of English architecture, a guide to architectural styles in Europe, and an understated-looking volume called, *Hidden Gems: Ten UK Cities*.

They sit at the dining table, looking through the indexes, flicking through pictures. It's thankless. They pull out more and more, ranging from coffee table collections of famous buildings, to detailed architectural plans from across the decades. After fifteen minutes, Declan's had enough and Juliet's teeth are chattering.

"I think we should get to bed. You're getting cold. This isn't good for you."

"I know I've seen that ironwork somewhere though. Recently." She closes *An Architectural Atlas*. "This is useless. I need to remember."

Pregnancy brain, she almost says. She's been reading up on how hormones and tiredness affect expectant women. She bites her tongue.

Declan fetches Beth's blanket and puts it around Juliet's shoulders. She runs her fingers over its thick knit. "Hang on," she says suddenly. "Hang on."

The album designs. She weaves through the house and brings the record sleeve swatches back with her. Impatiently now, she swipes each plastic jacket to one side. Until: there. A patchwork building in abstract layers; a door, a domed roof, the balcony. And looking out, a distorted child's face.

"Christ!" says Declan. "Dark."

"The roof," says Juliet. "Look at the dome. It's the same as Toby's tattoo. It's the Eden Club."

She pulls the encyclopaedia towards her, and examines the index.

"Look." She shoves the open book towards Declan. "Manchester."

He reads aloud, "In the northern quarter is an imposing building conceived as a rival to the Free Trade Hall. The Eden Building's conservative owner was so incensed by the repeal of the Corn Laws that he commissioned a series of lively ceramic panels depicting bucolic English scenes in the Art Nouveau style, all ruled over by the devil in various guises including well-known Whigs and industrialists. The observant visitor will spot the devil motif raising its horned head on plasterwork, on balconies, doorknobs, and drain covers..."

A yellowed newspaper cutting from 1997 about works on the Utopia cinema falls from between the pages.

Under the low-hanging light over the table, the shadow of Juliet's finger comes up to meet her from the page. "Toby's from Manchester originally," she says. "He got his big break with Max – in a club there."

"Yep. That makes sense." Declan rubs his eyes. "The Eden supports an electronic music festival every year. The rest of the time it's hard to get in. You have to be on the guest list. It's always in the gossip magazines. VIPs. Who's been spotted with who? Who's cheating on their girlfriend? That kind of thing."

Juliet rests her chin on her hand. "I bet Max is precisely the kind of guy who likes to show off by getting people in though. Ego trip. And Beth would have been excited if they took her there."

Declan nods. "And not very impressed with whatever it was she found."

"Not very impressed," Juliet repeats. "Or terrified."

It's the longest conversation they've had since the hospital, but now they both fall silent. Outside, the trees whisper between themselves. An owl hoots. They both hear it. Juliet pushes her chair away from the table, and Declan follows her back to the bedroom. Her dad's tartan dressing gown is enormous on her, the cord wrapped double around her waist.

In bed, Declan stares at the shell pattern on the ceiling. Juliet leans over and switches out the light.

"I could probably get in there," Declan says. "The Eden Club."

She turns towards him again, pulling her pillow further beneath her cheek. "How?"

What is he trying to prove? In some ways, Declan is her dad's mirror image, she thinks. For all his macho reputation, when it comes down to it, she has hardly ever seen Declan lose his temper. She tries to imagine his confrontation with Max, with Malcolm Lyall during the shoot.

"I know some guys in Manchester," he says. "Celebrity chasers."

In the darkness, she wonders who these shadow people are, in the corners of Declan's life; who Declan even is. And, with the lights out, she wonders whether to say something about the shadow within her.

That was how it looked on the ultrasound. They had inserted something, they explained at the hospital, while she was unconscious. An intra-vaginal baton. It was *normal procedure*, apparently, after her bloods had indicated that she was pregnant, to check for a foetal heartbeat. And there it was: a grey print-out thrust towards her. She wasn't even sure she was looking at the right thing: a black and white moonscape at Mach 3.

The hospital staff had looked shocked, shifty even, when she'd told them that neither she nor Declan had known. It's possible that they'd already told him, she supposes. But if so, why hasn't he said a word?

She remembers a flicker passed across the consultant's face when she'd first reacted, unable to hide her consternation, her doubts. She'd attempted to disguise these feelings and hurriedly asked about all the champagne she'd drunk. All the coffee. But it wasn't fooling anyone. The consultant gave her a look, of pity possibly, but also annoyance, as if they'd gone to all this trouble to save her life, save the baby, and if only they'd know she didn't want it, they needn't have bothered so much. In that moment, she felt her life's value dwindle a little bit, in the consultant's esteem. She would have been angry, if she'd had the energy.

Declan lies on his back, still talking about Manchester. She can almost feel his desperation to do something. "I'll get in touch with a couple of them. I promise. See what they know. What they can sort out."

She breathes, "Do you think it's safe? And, even if these contacts had some information – I mean, we're talking abuse, aren't we? Some sort of exploitation? – would they tell you anything?"

"I can do some digging." He slides his hand into the curve of her waist. "Secrets always have a way of coming out."

NORTHERN HERALD: GIRL'S BODY FOUND ON WASTELAND

September 16 2018

Media sources are reporting that the body of a teenage girl found in an area of northern Manchester could be that of an unaccompanied 14-year-old asylum seeker who arrived in England a year ago.

The remains were found on Tuesday when a jogger spotted a body part on wasteland near the Ashton canal. Police have launched a murder investigation.

The girl has not yet been formally identified but news outlets reported on Wednesday that she is understood to be a young female migrant, who went missing from her hostel on 20 June. She had been seeking asylum from war-torn Syria.

The *Examiner* cites unnamed sources who say police are investigating honour motives for the killing among the refugee community.

Refugee charity Hope for Survivors released figures last month showing a rise in offences committed against asylum seekers across the country. They warn the risk is increasing as some turn to the sex trade for income. They also suggest the real figure could be much higher, with cultural beliefs preventing some victims coming forward.

Police teams have so far refused to comment on the ongoing enquiry.

CHAPTER THIRTY-TWO

A flight of semicircular steps rises ceremoniously to the arched entrance of the one-time Eden Cinema in Manchester. Behind Art Nouveau glasswork lies a grand foyer; an octagonal light-well high in the ceiling; decorative floor tiles underfoot. In the gods, private boxes and back-to-back projection rooms now furnish the state-of-the-art club with intimate VIP areas. Artful sepia photographs hang in winding corridors and keep the newly famous in their place, conjuring instead sheen-haired golden-era patrons in perpetual kisses and handshakes, white gowns and gloves, bow-ties and velveteen jackets.

Two days after his promise to Juliet, Declan passes the building with barely a glance, his hood up and his head down. He spotted the security camera high above the street from fifty metres and doesn't want to take any chances. After a few calls to contacts and his old boss, he's on his way to meet Marcus, an old drinking buddy, in Hemming's – a dive bar a few streets away – and decided to take a detour past the club, for a little reconnaissance. He doesn't want to come across as wet behind the ears.

He's tried not to get excited about the baby, that would be stupid with such a high risk of miscarriage, but he's dying to tell someone about it, to talk to someone who won't question why he and Juliet haven't discussed it yet, someone who'll understand their relationship. But given that Juliet's trust is at an all-time low, perhaps chatting to a journalist about her biological rights is not the best move. Besides, he has no idea really what Marcus has been up to, whether he's settled down at all, has a partner, kids of his own. You can hardly just launch into these conversations. He hasn't clapped eyes on Marcus since their apprentice days and, he wonders if they'll even recognise each other.

He needn't have worried. It's the bruising that gives Marcus away. Sitting in an orange-hued booth at the back of the place, well away from the window, he frowns at a laptop, nursing a curvy glass mug of Irish coffee, and a black eye.

He flinches, even in Declan's loose embrace.

"Marcus! Christ, what happened to you?" Declan grimaces. It looks like someone has implanted an aubergine deep into Marcus's eye socket and cut a vegetable slit for him to see out of.

"Angry lover." With a wry smile, Marcus twitches his face away, and sits back down. "They get like that."

"Indeed they do." Declan cringes silently at his own glibness. He slides across the fake leather into the booth opposite him. "That you could inspire such passion though, now that surprises me."

"Just a sec. I need to save this."

Marcus orders them both an Irish coffee, shouting at the bar maid, hardly looking up from his laptop. Declan catches the young woman's eye apologetically. She gives him a small smile and tosses her pony tail as she turns heel.

"So, to what do we owe this honour?" Marcus says finally, closing the device. "You mentioned the Eden Building?"

"Yeah. I'm after coming into town for a few days, and I wondered what you knew about the place. How easy it is, you know, to get in there? I'm thinking about working something up on Art Nouveau iconography."

Marcus stares at him. "You always were a terrible liar," he shakes his head. "That's why you were never going to make it as a hack. Here's a tip. The long words. They're a red flag."

Declan smiles but adds nothing.

"Well, look," Marcus shrugs. "If that's really what you're after, there's nothing stopping you from taking photographs from outside. Plenty of tourists do it. You can get the glass inlays. The devil heads in the balconies."

"And inside?"

"No chance. I mean, not on a club night. At a push in daytime. They might even give you a tour if they think they'll get some decent publicity. But security is tight on club nights. They have their own cameras, their own photographers. No phones. No devices. You have to leave everything in the cloakroom."

"Wow. Are they paranoid much?"

"Smoke and mirrors."

"What?"

The bar girl brings the coffees to the counter. Marcus gets up to fetch them. He takes a large swig of the froth on the top of his glass. The girl hands him a paper napkin before walking away.

He sits back down. "You limit press access to the club, right? To create an illusion of exclusivity. And at the same time you publish the advance guest list to your selected paparazzi. It guarantees some sort of feeding frenzy almost every night." He dabs at the milky moustache on his upper lip.

"And? I still don't get where the smoke and mirrors come in?"

Marcus grapples in his jacket pocket and pulls out a hip flask. He holds it out over Declan's drink, eyebrows raised.

"Ah, go on. Just a dash."

Marcus splashes some extra whisky into Declan's glass and then pours at least a double measure into his own.

Declan eyes his old friend. "Thanks. You ought to take it easy."

"Please. Too much caffeine'll kill you. Best to dilute it. Besides" – he touches the bruising on his cheekbone – "beverages are the least of my worries."

Declan wonders if the story about the jealous lover is true. Marcus is always in some sort of trouble. Even back in their apprentice days, he permanently operated far south of most people's moral compass. That's what made him a useful choice of contact under the current set of circumstances. It's also what makes him a risk.

"Look, why are you so interested in the Eden? You do realise you can't just go sniffing around this place?"

"Just curious. Thought I might be able to get on the guest list. Have a little look."

"Well, if I were you, I wouldn't be going anywhere near it. At all. I'd go back to snapping poodles. Dobermans, fighting dogs maybe. Less chance of losing your fingers." Marcus retrieves some rolling tobacco from his jacket pocket. "If you can avoid it, these are not people you want to mess with, my friend."

If you can avoid it. Declan ponders briefly what that means, but Marcus is still talking.

"Do you remember Harry Bamford?"

Declan starts to shake his head, but has a bolt-like recollection. "Hang on, wasn't he the guy from that kids' TV show in the eighties? Ah. What was it called?"

"*Waterworks*." Marcus evens the tobacco out along an undyed rolling paper.

"That's it! There's a blast from the past."

"Yeah. Well, he was a regular at the Eden, until he disappeared last year. Turned up a few months ago, during some drainage work in the harbour."

Declan stares. He vaguely remembers the story in the news – some kind of accident to do with the construction site supposedly. His stomach starts to turn.

Marcus continues, almost enjoying himself now. "Rumour has it, he jumped in the water but forgot to take off his cement trainers." He licks methodically along the cigarette adhesive. "It's the ankles that rot away first. Your feet come off. Then your hands. Then your head. How's that for waterworks?"

"Christ." Declan is thankful Juliet is not listening to this. "That's grotesque. Poor guy."

"Poor guy, my arse."

"But… You're not saying the club was behind that? Why would they do that to someone?"

Marcus drops his voice. "You realise who we're dealing with here?" He swallows.

Declan tries to follow him. "It's an Eden Media venue isn't it? So, Bernhard Palmer? The club belongs to him, doesn't it?"

"Yes. But Palmer's not just your average billionnaire tycoon. He is fucking ruthless. He owns the news. He owns the press. Television. Media. He owns his own son."

"What? Ah what's his name? Dominic Palmer? Yeah, but come on—"

"No, listen to me. He's a ruthless bastard, his son, Dominic, is a ruthless bastard, and they come from a long line of ruthless bastards. Ruthless bastardry is all they know." Marcus lights up his cigarette, inside the café, and takes a long drag.

"But I thought Palmer married in? You know, to the Eden dynasty? He's not bloodline."

"Ha, yeah. That's a story in itself. The Edens built the Eden Building. Mortimer Eden was the father-in-law. He was the one who took it from a cinema into an infotainment empire. It became the place to be seen. Politicians. Businessmen. I mean, he must have been some kind of genius. The place was on the edge of the old red-light district, right? He brought the 'whores indoors'. All of a sudden you had film stars pictured with beautiful, dancing girls. He generated his very own gossip, titillation – blackmail, some said – and it all went in the bloody cinema pamphlet. And everyone played along, because, you know, no such thing as bad publicity. And circulation grew, and the stories got more outrageous, but no one would hold him to account because they all depended on him for coverage."

"So, Eden… what? Invented the gossip column?"

"No." Marcus raises a nicotine-stained finger. "More than that. He invented the modern tabloid."

Declan sips his coffee. "Sounds like he's a hero of yours."

"No way. Not a hero, but fuck man, you've got to admit... It was clever."

They fall quiet for a moment and Declan watches Marcus smoke with some envy and – beneath that – something he doesn't quite want to recognise. Pity. Back in the day they would spend hours between assignments in a pool hall in Stoke Newington, smoking, drinking beer and soaking it up with grilled sandwiches. Marcus would complain. Photography wasn't what he'd been expecting. He hated feeling like a bystander, a witness. When he got a job as a junior reporter and went to Manchester, Declan was envious of his change of direction. His drive. So how has he ended up as a jobbing paparazzo?

The bar girl comes over, plucks Marcus's cigarette straight out of his fingers, and stalks away with it.

"Shit," he says wistfully. "You used to be able to smoke in here." He looks forlorn for a moment. He shouts at her back, "Hey! Can we get two grilled sandwiches? Cheese."

He nods at Declan. "Just like the old days. Plus," he winks, then winces with pain in his bad eye. "It'll keep her busy." He starts rolling another cigarette, and continues his tale. "It gets more interesting though. I mean, everyone knows the rumours about Eden in the war, right?"

"What, the stuff about Hitler wanting the building for his HQ?"

"Yeah, yeah, yeah. But that's all bullshit. What people don't so often talk about is the thirties, about what was going on with the newspaper. Column inches devoted to whether England should get in bed with Hitler. Complaining about all the Jews fleeing to England."

"Okay, okay. Keep your voice down." Declan darts a look out of their booth. The place is nearly empty, apart from an old guy at the bar. "But how did they—"

"Get away with it? Every now and then they ran an editorial calling for less appeasement. Being tougher on Hitler. All of that."

"What, so they couldn't be accused of leaning one way or the other?"

"Exactly. But what it actually meant was they had no editorial policy, no" – he laughs a high-pitched, incredulous laugh at the prospect of even uttering the next words – "journalistic integrity, except to voice the most popular fucking view on any story. The Edens turned the war years into an opportunity. You know there was print rationing during the war?"

"No."

"Well, there was. Papers were allowed to print something like sixty percent of their prewar tonnage. Some papers went down to four pages. But old man Eden had somehow increased his tonnage just before the war, so he still had enough room for the stuff people wanted. Gossip. Titillation. Escape. He just" – Marcus swoops his hand through the air like a hawk – "manoeuvred into the space left behind. By the sixties when Bernhard married in, the Eden empire had already gone from one small Manchester pamphlet to a national group of seven papers. Nice." Marcus finishes rolling his new fag triumphantly.

"But why did Palmer inherit the lot, and not one of the Edens? I mean, the building. The Eden brand runs through it like a golden thread. The decoration in the glasswork? The tiles? It's like, the garden of Eden isn't it? Like some kind of Utopia. Ears of corn. Fields of gold."

"Ha! Fields of gold is not wrong. All Eden cared about was his fortune. He did everything in his power to ensure his own son, who was seen as weak-minded, didn't inherit. The poor sod committed suicide in the end."

"Christ. And the daughter?"

"Don't be stupid. In those days, girls didn't run businesses. The only option was for her to marry someone Eden approved of. And Bernhard Palmer was that guy. I mean, can you imagine what sort of man Palmer must be, if he was the approved heir of a fucking Nazi-loving, blackmailing, warmongering…"

Marcus almost lights his cigarette again, then makes a face like a disappointed child.

"Look." Declan runs his hands through his hair. "Can we go outside? I need one of those as well."

Marcus carries his laptop under his arm protectively. Declan wonders what's on it. They stand outside, huddled against the bins near the kitchen. The smell of grilled cheese mingles with stale beer, coffee grinds and rotting lettuce. Declan attempts to roll a fag so clumsily that Marcus hands him his own, and starts rolling yet again.

"Sorry," Declan mutters. "I'm out of practice." He groans with relief at his first drag. "Right, let me get this straight. Bernhard Palmer built Eden Media off the back of his unscrupulous, if genius, piece-of-shit father-in-law. And Dominic's going to repeat the whole shebang."

"Yep. Don't underestimate them. They get worse with each generation… Or better, maybe," he muses. "Depending on how you look at it. You could say Bernhard took it to the next level. After the war, he made sure they got involved in consultations about the television networks. Expansion. Bernie knew how to diversify, you see. Created subsidiaries. Production companies. Film. TV. Now Dominic has picked up the flame and they're fully international. Digital."

"Sounds like fields of fucking gold is right."

"Which is why you don't cross the Palmers. They own *everyone*. Anyone who's anyone needs them. Last week, Bernhard – and bear in mind he's over eighty – was at a private reception at the White House. Last month, he attended a polo tournament in Beijing."

"Beijing?"

"Bearing in mind the Chinese were falling over themselves to pay over two hundred thousand just to get near the guy. His rags and channels hold so much sway over public opinion in so many different countries, he's courted like fucking royalty."

"I still don't get what this has got to do with a sad old-timer like Bamford? How was he a threat to them?"

"Ahh. Now you're asking." Marcus looks up and down the alley. "Bernhard Palmer only has one weakness. He and his circle of friends. Friends like Bamford. They all have one thing in common." As if this explains everything, he raises his eyebrows.

"What are you talking about?"

"You've never heard the rumours about Bamford?"

Declan shakes his head.

"Young kids. Girls. Boys."

Declan takes a sharp draw on the fag, staring at the greying brickwork in the wall behind the bins. He tries to exhale slowly and keep his voice down. "They can't be doing that, right there in the club?"

Marcus shakes his head. "Not in the club. Remember, smoke and mirrors; Bernhard Palmer has his own private apartments at the back of the building. Exclusive access for his very special friends. Inner circle."

"Jesus Christ. Who are these people? How many of them?"

"Not sure." Marcus grinds his fag butt into the concrete. "The Eden Club has always been Bernie's special palace. He's all sentimental about it allegedly. Except it's hardly anything to do with sentiment. He's driven by power. Imagine the hard-on he gets with all those A-listers and celebrities partying in the club. Red carpet treatment. Meanwhile, right next door, he and his friends are raping kids."

It's the first time Marcus's mask has slipped. Declan is relieved to see his friend's anger. They stand in silence now, taking in smoke and the implications of what's been said. The kitchen's extractor fan next to them starts up suddenly, making Declan jump out of his skin. A bell sounds inside. He stubs out his cigarette on the wall.

The grilled sandwiches are already plated up and on their

table as they re-enter. They edge back along the seats, into the same little orange booth, but to Declan it feels different: the surfaces harder.

Declan gives Marcus a side glance. "How in the hell do you know all this? You're not telling me you've been in there?"

"No. Course not. They don't let plebs like me in. I'm just a pap."

It's Declan's turn to look disbelieving. "What was it you said about *me* being a terrible liar? You have a lot of information for someone who says it's not wise to be sniffing round?"

"And you're mighty persistent for someone who's just curious?" Marcus looks at him uneasily, his voice low. "Look. I shouldn't have told you this stuff. I know a couple of the security guys. One of the drivers. They gossip sometimes."

"Gossip? This is a bit fucking beyond gossip. Are you honestly telling me these people know all this and haven't, you know, reported it?

"Not everyone's got the same outlook as you, Declan. The same sweet moral purpose."

"Outlook? This is abuse, Marcus." He leans forward, his finger jabbing at the table top. "It's abominable. How old are these kids they're—"

"Okay, okay, mate. You need to calm the fuck down. But you've got to promise me…" He clears his throat and glances around. "The truth is, I've been working on this story for two years. It's not easy. They have… threats. Archives. No one wants to talk."

Declan sits back, and whistles softly between his teeth. The pallor of Marcus's skin, the pouches beneath his eyes, suddenly take on a different hue. This is the guy Declan thought he knew.

"Archives?"

"They keep images of the back-room clientele, recordings. You know. Leverage."

Declan shifts back in the squashy old banquette thinking of the grainy photos of Beth and the band.

"Seriously, this is not something you want to get into lightly," Marcus tells him. "I can't go on the record about any of this. I've got an international interested in an exclusive. You said it was personal, not work. This is two years of my life."

A tram fills the café window for a few seconds with a blur of ice-cream colours. Declan watches its passage, his eyes flicking left to right.

"It is personal," he says. "Juliet's niece. I don't know if you saw but she committed suicide at the start of the summer. And Juliet's convinced she was caught up in something bad. What we do know is she was hanging out with a band, who are managed by Malcolm Lyall. Now, he's a friend of Palmer, isn't he? What's Lyall's involvement in the..." Declan can't bring himself to say it. "Is he...?"

Marcus picks up a triangle of sandwich. The cheese has melted into strings, which divide and dangle between his mouth and the crisp bread. "Could be." Marcus chews. "I'd say he's inner circle."

"Ah, shite. I was frightened you'd say that."

"Frightened is good. Frightened is what you should be. What part of *people are getting killed* do you not understand?"

Declan puts his head in his hands. "Just hang on. Bamford... Jesus... He must have been what, in his seventies? And Bernie Palmer's eighty something, right? And they're still raping these young kids? What made Bernie give Bamford the concrete foot spa? He was one of them, was he not?"

"Bamford had dementia."

Declan shakes his head. "I don't get it."

"Too much of a risk. He started babbling. And who knows? Could have been Dominic who organised it."

"Holy fuck."

"I told you. Ruthless." Marcus picks a bit of cheese from his teeth.

"But it must be possible to... I mean, the police—"

"I'm telling you. The Palmers own them."

"What?"

"Bernhard Palmer has invested shitloads in the city, for years. They've sold off half the northern quarter to him for regeneration. Their economic strategy relies on a media and culture boom. The night-time economy. And if he pulls out of the projects he's bankrolling, they're fucked. Manchester – Event City, right? Where do you think the donations come from? If they lost that money, you know how it would play with the voters?"

"But they can't be like, what? Instructing the police to disregard—"

"No, no, no. That's not how it works. The cops have a team for that part of town. It's always been an edgy area, I told you, used to be red-light. You walk down the street and you see urban coffeehouses in old warehouses. Go round the back, you'll still find crackheads in the stairwells. So, the police focus on anti-social behaviour. Any whiff of anything – complaints, noise, whatever – they go straight in. Smooth things over. Of course, they know there's prostitution at the club, but that's no different to what's going on at events all over the place. Just think of the Presidents' Club thing. They pretty much turn a blind eye to it, all the while making a show of keeping the neighbourhood safe."

"Safe? But these are kids we're talking about?"

"Ah, but there are kids and *kids*. Middle-class kids out getting drunk and being sick and fighting and stabbing each other. That's one thing. You get a nice high profile when you tackle them and reduce the stats. But what about the invisible kids? The ones no one even sees, let alone complains about? Who's going to report one of them missing?"

You? thinks Declan. He's brought up short. *Me?*

Marcus is still talking. "And they're hardly about to go to the police and turn themselves in, are they? The kids?"

"Whyever not? They must have families? I mean, where do they—"

"Come on, Declan. *Think*. Vulnerable kids are not in short supply. I mean, there's an asylum centre about half a mile from the club." He breathes deeply and his gaze glides off to the side, as if he's weighing something up. "Look, it's taken me six months, but I've got a girl who's talking. She's already identified three men she says have raped her."

"Jesus Christ." Declan can still taste the burn of tobacco. "And Lyall? What's his role exactly?"

"Not sure. I've got nothing on Lyall, other than he goes way back with Palmer. But that doesn't mean he's involved. Doesn't mean he's clean either. To be honest I've been focused on nailing Palmer. That family have got away with just about every criminal fucking thing they've ever done, but I'll die before I see him worm his way out of this."

He bites his thumbnail.

"But going after Lyall would be interesting. Palmer bought Lyall out of his precious record company years back. Paid peanuts for it, and now it's worth a fortune. You'd think Lyall would have a chip on his shoulder about that, wouldn't you?"

"What're you getting at now?"

"Palmer can buy politicians. He can shape the world in his own image. And that must kill Lyall. I'm willing to bet if we could get to Lyall, he'd hang Palmer out to dry, just to get himself off the hook." He smiles now.

"What do you have in mind?"

"I…" Marcus eyeballs Declan strangely. "Look. I could do with some help, as it goes. When you got in touch, I was trying to figure something out. It's risky. But if you're interested…"

"Go on."

"This girl who's talking, she's agreed to try and get some proof of what's happening next time she's called in."

"Called in? That's a nice choice of phrase."

"I know. But – get this – she's agreed to try and capture something on film."

The tobacco bile rises in Declan's throat. He swallows. "But wouldn't that be putting this kid at massive risk? I mean, can you not go to the police with what you have already? Or go public?"

Marcus shakes his head slowly, gazing through the window. "Look, how many other scandals like this have there been? They do the groundwork and evidence disappears. Witnesses are discredited. The whole thing loses water faster than an Indian reservation. I'm not letting that happen. This girl, she's the ballsiest kid I've ever met. One of her friends disappeared a few months back, and her body was found in the park. And now, well, it's like this kid's on a mission. She's identified people through pictures I've shown her. But that won't be enough. It won't stand up. It's her word against theirs. We need hard evidence."

"I am not liking the sounds of this."

"I've got her a pen camera."

"Shite alive."

"I know. It's not great but it can't be something she's wearing, for obvious reasons. She's going to take in a little bag and the pen will be fixed inside. Pin hole through the bag. Bingo."

"And have you tested all this out? Does it work in low lighting? For how long will it record?"

"Yeah, yeah, yeah. I've been over all that. It works. Lasts an hour."

"And so what do you need me for?"

"I need help to document her getting picked up, taken there. Just in case she messes it up. I mean, she's just a kid. She'll be afraid, and she might forget something or keep looking over at the bag. And I want images from inside the club as well. The escorts they use in there. I want to bring down the whole fucking show."

"I thought you said there was no way to get in?"

"Yeah, but surely you and Juliet know someone on the circuit? The circles you mix in. Juliet must have to shake all sorts of hands."

Declan shakes his head. "Not the kind of people who go to the Eden Club. She's a politician, not a porn star."

"Ha. You say that," says Marcus.

Of course, Declan thinks, Goldman was an actress, but she's the last person they can approach to get involved in this.

If only they could ask Toby. According to Juliet, he's a hero in Manchester, his hometown, and the Eden's electronic festival kick-started his career. But that only makes it more unlikely he would betray the place. He's beholden to it, and to Max, Karlo and Lyall.

"So, you've never been inside even?" he asks Marcus.

"No."

They sit in silence while Marcus tamps down the tobacco in another rollie, tapping the cigarette against the melamine. "I'm going for another smoke," he says, shuffling along the leather banquette. "But listen, if you do manage to find someone who can get on the list and get you in, they'll need to have balls of steel."

Declan sits very still. He seems transfixed by the laminated pub menu. As Marcus gets up, Declan turns to him.

"Would a celebrity chef do the trick?" he asks.

THE STANDARD: SOUL-SEARCHING FOR THE PROGRESSIVE ALLIANCE – WHO ARE THE LEADERSHIP FRONTRUNNERS?

20 September 2018

- *Following dramatic defeat in this month's elections, Progressive Alliance enters inevitable period of introspection and recriminations.*
- *Outgoing leader Fiona Goldman yet to step down, but sources say it's just a matter of timing.*

Every day this week, political editor, Sarah Hausman, gives her angle on the five main contenders for PA's top job. Today's focus: Juliet MacGillivray.

Former Legal Advisor and now Chief of Staff, Juliet MacGillivray could be mistaken for an anonymous alliance mandarin. Her experience is in internal matters, not public office. But make no mistake, she is one of the few heavyweights to have thrived during the cleansing of the Goldman era. How did she do it? And can she make the transition to centre stage?

Unelected status has camouflaged her influence, and certainly contributed to her longevity. She rarely appears on camera or talks to the press. But the MacGillivray stamp is on every policy and speech. Insiders say she was crucial to Goldman's 2011 selection, which took the party to new heights of popularity.

However, MacGillivray and Goldman's closeness, personally and politically, could now be a liability. To what extent MacGillivray will now be damaged by her association with the outgoing leader, remains to be seen.

And that's not the only question mark over MacGillivray. Rumour has it she still edits all major speeches, and personally vets all party candidates. A control freak, some aides say. Her ability to step out of management and truly lead is in doubt.

Yet a bigger thorn in the MacGillivray camp's side could be MacGillivray herself. Critics remain sceptical about her public image and degree of personal ambition. Her career has centred on promoting and protecting others.

Childless MacGillivray's family life is a similar picture and, some might say, a liability. A bipolar twin sister, the recent suicide of her young niece, and the departure of long-term ally Goldman could all serve to kerb MacGillivray's appetite for the leadership fray. In fact, just when her campaign should be hotting up, she has retreated to a summerhouse she owns on an exclusive stretch of coast east of Inverness, where her neighbours currently include the likes of celebrity DJ Max Bolin – hardly proof of her common touch.

CHAPTER THIRTY-THREE

Toby is on his usual evening patrol along the beach. There was no sun today, just flat goose-coloured clouds. Now what little light there was is draining from the sky. He wanders easily among the mudflats and pebbles, half listening to the scuffle of his own feet, hardly having to look where he puts them. There's a tell-tale hiss away in the distance at the mouth of the inlet. The sea will be rushing inwards soon. He used to find that sound interesting; he recorded it once or twice, and it's on the album, but he hates it now. He hates this job.

He scans the darkening shore but nothing has turned up, just as there has been nothing on any other day, apart from the occasional lump of driftwood. During the storms of the previous weekend, the waves dumped an entire section of tree at the water's edge, where it stayed for three days before mysteriously disappearing. It made him shudder. Its freshness. The scaly golden bark and cloven branches were like something unholy.

As he approaches Juliet's summerhouse, he slows. He can see the light inside; the yellow wallpaper creates a warm glow.

Suddenly, on the bend of the track as it stretches beyond the house, he glimpses a parked car, one he hasn't noticed here before. A small 4x4. It looks like a rental maybe. What's it doing there? There's no house in that direction for a few hundred metres.

He slips among the trees and draws nearer, keeping an eye on the house. Juliet crosses the living room and sits at the table. She props her chin on her hand. She appears to be alone. Toby can't see the newspapers strewn over the dining table.

***

Juliet hasn't been anywhere since Declan left for Manchester. She's tense and restless. This must be what they mean by cabin fever. The only person she's spoken to is the property agent who came out to visit the summerhouse.

The sample details he left are strewn on the table, alongside post-election newspapers Declan picked up from the hospital, all keyed up with rumours about PA. Is this the end for the party? For Goldman? *The Standard* carries an analysis with mini-bios of Goldman's possible successors – Juliet among them. At first, she was staggered to see this, and furious. She re-read the article four times. You'd imagine some of it at least would be flattering, confidence-boosting, but its assessments are crude and intrusively personal. The journalist also all but leaked her whereabouts. It would be easy for any hack to come and find her here. The sooner she can sell up and go the better.

A chill slithers between her shoulder blades when she imagines losing her connection to Moray, to her childhood and roots. It seems ungrateful after Dad left her the place. Selling up is not, however, an entirely unpleasant thought. As well as the sense of loss, there's a lightness and freedom too – a kind of *becoming*. Is this what Beth felt about moving out of her grandparent's flat, leaving her childhood and mother behind? It may have only been fifteen miles away, but living out here must have been a world apart from the strain of living with Erica.

Erica. Of course, she would still be living in Inverness. Selling the summerhouse would mean Juliet had no base of her own up here; nowhere to get away to if Erica had a crisis. It would either throw them together in that respect, or be a cutting off, of sorts. A transformation. Alex's words still ring now and then like hammers in her ears: *Auntie Jet with her fancy flat and fancy life in London*. If only he knew. That life is about to change irrevocably very soon, no matter the choice she makes. To stand for leader. To have her baby. Do neither?

Talking to Declan about any future they have together is more and more pressing. She should just drive to a phone signal and see if there's any word from him, find out whether he's managed to meet his friend Marcus yet. Find out too if PA have been in touch. The political wheels are spinning, with or without her. Given the news coverage, the articles, somebody must be briefing in her favour despite her absence. Who?

She hears the thump of feet on the decking. It startles her and Bucky, who lets out a low grumble and then barks sharply, twice. She looks up, at one window, then another. She sees no one; nothing but the floral walls reflected in the glass.

CHAPTER THIRTY-FOUR

Lotta flies straight from recording in London into Manchester the next day. It's Friday, rush hour. Declan meets her at the airport, and they sit in a taxi in heavy traffic on the way back to the hotel. They keep their voices low in the back, while the cab radio plays drivetime tunes.

"Well, fancy seeing you again so soon," says Lotta. "This is nice. I'm looking forward to wearing my little black number and heels in this weather."

"The weather is the least of it," Declan says. "Are you sure you're going to be okay with this?"

"Declan, would I be here if I wasn't up for it?"

As far as Lotta is concerned, the hard part was the flight. She hates flying, and has to do enough of it already, between Liverpool and London. Neither she nor Sophie really like London, but it looks increasingly likely they'll have to get a place there together. The commute isn't sustainable. It means Sophie giving up her work and research in Liverpool and starting again.

Lotta continues, "I've told you, I'll help in any way I can. Although, I still don't understand why Juliet doesn't just go to the police."

"There's nothing to go to the police with. What's she going to say?" He drops his voice. "'Oh, excuse me, I've heard a rumour that there's some nasty business going on, that Bernhard Palmer and Malcolm Lyall are grooming young kids for sex? Oh, and I've got no proof and I can't tell you who told me.' Besides, if what Marcus says is true, the police aren't exactly overzealous in that regard. According to him, Palmer has them where he wants them."

"What about the newspapers?"

"Yes. Marcus has someone interested. An editor. He's been setting this up for two years. It's a big deal for him. We absolutely cannot fuck this up."

"Which editor? Brockwell?"

"Don't know. Brockwell's gone to ground. Some kind of sabbatical since the story about him and Goldman broke."

"So, what's the link to these DJ guys? And Beth?"

"In among the photos Juliet found" – he avoids Lotta's eye as he speaks of Juliet's discovery – "there were a couple of other pictures. We think they must have been taken in Palmer's private apartments, at the back of the club. There's something not right about them. I mean, Beth hid them away for starters, and they're… well… they're fair compromising. The look on Beth's face says it all. There's a half-naked kid in one of them."

Lotta's eyes widen. "With Beth?"

"No… with the band guys."

"What the hell? How did she even get this picture? Why would she have it?"

"We think someone must have sent it to her. Using it to keep her quiet." He drops his voice even lower. "This is not a fucking game. Beth's not the only victim. Marcus has got some hairy stories. If you want out, you just have to say."

Lotta leans her head against the cool taxi window. What Declan's not admitting, she guesses, is his own desire for redemption. She may have had her suspicions since their chat in the forest, but when he'd explained to her over the phone about his photos of Beth, she'd been astonished Juliet hadn't already killed him.

"You're definitely on the guest list?" he asks again.

"Yes, definitely. My agent nearly fell through the floor when I asked her if she could pull any strings. I mean, she knows it's not exactly my customary haunt." She laughs, and not for the first time, Declan is grateful for Lotta's stoic sense of the absurd. "She probably thinks I'm having a mid-life crisis."

"How is Sophie? Is she okay with it?"

There's a pause. "We don't have a permission-based relationship," Lotta replies cryptically.

Declan wonders if Sophie thinks badly of him; of the secret he kept from Juliet. He imagines Lotta and Sophie arguing about whether she should come to Manchester to help. "So you've basically ignored Sophie's objections?"

Lotta says nothing. Declan scrutinises her profile. Her set jaw, and dark eyebrows. The lustre of raindrops on the cab window gives her a timeless quality somehow.

They arrive at their hotel, an anonymous mid-range place near the stadium, with a coffee machine in the reception area and trendy lime-green circles painted on the walls.

Lotta naps, then takes a long bath and attempts to replicate a hairstyle she likes; one the television make-up team sometimes use on her. She's marginally successful. Finally, glancing self-consciously up and down the quiet corridor, she exits her room wearing the most glamourous items she owns: a simple vintage Chloe dress, and chunky silver necklace that was a birthday gift from Sophie. She knocks on Declan's door.

They sit on the bed and down a couple of mini-bar vodkas, while Declan shows her the tiny camera he's taking in. She exclaims over how dinky it is, like a car key fob. Declan hopes it will go unnoticed. He doesn't tell her about the wire Marcus has given him to wear, figuring she'll act more naturally and they'll both be safer the less she knows. He explains the plan, to get a feel for the place. See what the access arrangements to the private areas are. And, if he can, get some evidence of the sex workers.

He gives her Marcus's number. "If anything goes wrong, go and fetch your phone from the cloakroom, and call Marcus."

"I wish you'd stop talking like that. It's only a club. How bad can it be?"

Before Declan can answer, a call comes up from reception that their car has arrived. They take the lift down and find a black Audi, with dark windows waiting. With ill-disguised distaste, their driver escorts Lotta the few metres from the cheap hotel to the kerb with an umbrella.

"You really have spared no expense," she murmurs as Declan slides into the leather seat beside her. "It even *smells* expensive."

"I thought it might help. You know, look the part."

It's a short drive to the northern quarter. They pass cafés and restaurants. A CCTV police van is parked on a pedestrianised square. The students are well and truly back in town and out enjoying themselves tonight.

When they pull up outside the Eden Club, there are two crowds of people outside: a long queue of shivering hopefuls lining the cobbled street to the left of the door; and a much smaller, more assured group flowing up the red-carpet on the steps to the right. Loops of gold silken rope, strung between brass posts, separate the two worlds. Three hulking doormen monitor the entrance. Declan asks the driver if he'll wait for them, and tips him a suitably encouraging amount, trying to keep the pained expression from his face. He slides his wallet inside his jacket.

They join the little huddle of beautiful people to the right. A slim blond man glances briefly over his shoulder at them, and doesn't take a second look. Although the idea was to slip into the club as unnoticed as possible, the utter dismissal of it gives Declan an adolescent pang. He dubiously examines the waiting crowd on the left; mostly young women in pairs, tottering in enormous platform heels, or groups of lads in untucked, shiny shirts. They all look frozen but are laughing. Is it just a punt for them? Do they expect to get in? As he watches, a stunning girl unravels herself from the back of a cab, all legs and incredible heels. The doorman on the left beckons her, and she strides straight by the waiting crowd.

Lotta nudges him in the ribs. They've reached the front of the right-hand queue. Before Declan is even able to compose himself, the doorman greets them and waves them through.

"Good evening, Ms Morgan. Good evening, sir."

Lotta emits a peal of nervous laughter, as they pass into the atrium. They can suddenly hear bass throbbing from what sounds like every wall of the building. Declan doesn't crack a smile.

"Right. Well, that was too easy," he mutters.

"It's fine. You were ice cool."

"Try shitting yourself. It helps keep a poker face."

"What can be so bad?" Lotta takes his arm. "It's a club. We're surrounded by people. What's the worst that can happen?"

Declan hasn't mentioned Marcus's story about Bamford's cement foot treatment. He's so grateful Lotta's here but terrified for them both. He should have been more specific with her about the risks. She's still chattering, oblivious to the wire he's wearing. "I'm hoping for narcotics. A bit of S and M?" She laughs again and then says through gritted teeth. "Seriously, relax your shoulders."

Declan stretches his neck from side to side, trying to ease the tension. He glances up at the light-well and takes in the two flights of stairs leading up from the foyer.

"Where to?" Lotta asks.

Marcus has told Declan what he can about the venue, but it's mainly information pulled from websites. Straight ahead, on the ground floor, lies Amphi One, where an aspiring top-tier DJ will be attempting to push the envelope of mainstream dance; to the right a half-flight of stairs leads to the old theatre's mezzanine bar, now a chill-out lounge. To the left, a wide, elegant staircase disappears upwards to the Dress Circle. There, a VIP bar with its own decks overlooks Amphi

One, the former loges have been converted into VIP boxes, where, according to Marcus, the lapdancers and escorts do most of their work. Beyond that, the Upper Circle and Gods are off-limits, transformed into a gym, swimming pool, and connecting to the high-end apartments on the back of the building.

The security is ubiquitous, discreet, but everywhere – flat, neutral faces and dark suits. One of them, biceps rebelling against his jacket, holds open the door to Amphi One. For a second, Declan wonders if his wire will interfere with the security headsets. But they pass through.

It's like walking straight into a force field. Declan's trousers and entrails reverberate in sync with the bass and the glistening body parts before them: writhing arms and spread fingers reaching into an immense web of green and white lasers, splayed across the vast dry-ice-filled dance floor; emanating from, and converging at, some central point above the stage, like a Hollywood version of a future holocaust. It's hypnotic.

Despite himself, Declan grins.

"Find a bar?" Lotta shouts. She begins to steer through the crowd. She's so tiny, Declan is impressed how easily she rebuffs the swaying tide of flesh.

"Are you doing alright?" he yells.

"I'm fine. I've got a low centre of gravity."

Finally, towards the back of the room they order champagne cocktails. Declan leans back against the zinc and squints up into the veil of smoke and lasers above them. He can just make out some former private loges overhead, draped in velvet.

"We need to get up there," he nods towards the Gods. "Private areas."

They gaze upwards. Slender figures drift at the glass of the VIP bar, looking down on the main space. As they watch, one of the set of drapes shielding a private box is partially drawn back. From their vantage point, it's impossible to see who is standing in the shadowy opening. It's unnerving. Despite the heat, Lotta shudders.

"Shall we go together? Or split up? I could check out the Mezzanine?"

He nods. As he turns, Lotta grabs his arm. He bends his ear towards her.

"Good luck, Declan." She sips her drink and adds, "One hour only, then I'm leaving. This is terrible champagne."

"Yep. Meet in the foyer?"

Lotta nods, and Declan smiles a tense, flat-lipped smile, which is more of a grimace. He puts one hand in his jacket's inner pocket and checks for the camera. She watches his shoulders disappear into the dancefloor's mass.

CHAPTER THIRTY-FIVE

Juliet stands on the decking, framed in the doorway. The air is cold and the moon just a pale watermark somewhere low behind the trees. She shivers. Bucky stands warily beside her for a couple of moments, before sniffing his way out onto the decking and then into the grass, where he cocks his leg. The sea sounds quieter than it usually does at night. There's a threshing though, among the branches. Juliet strains her eyes into the veiled darkness. Bucky looks up and stands, ears cocked, staring. He emits another low growl.

It's always been one of Juliet's little nightmares; leaving the summerhouse at night. She's never enjoyed the sudden awareness it brings of how alone, how isolated you are. In high season, when light is still in the sky and people are still out walking, it's different. But in the dark, quitting the glow and safety of the house, and stepping outside…

As a girl, she dreaded autumn evening errands to the woodshed. She would dash there and back, even with arms full of heavy logs. Sometimes Erica would offer to go in her place, but as often as not, she'd want payback – usually a joint run to the sea for moonlit skinny-dipping. Erica loved trying to swim to the Hippo, which was intimidating enough to attempt in daylight, let alone in the dark, when even the mildest of lapping waves became amplified. They rarely even made it a quarter of the way before Juliet would concede.

She remembers one occasion in particular though, when Erica disappeared about forty metres out.

Treading water and turning like a spinning top, Juliet had scanned the dark surface of the swell, looking for the brisk, glistening chop of her sister's pale arms. She'd called out – more in warning than anything else – expecting to be splashed in the face or pulled under. One of the usual pranks. She'd waited. Nothing. She called Erica's name again and again and again, until finally the rising terror in her voice must have triggered some sort of compassion: she heard a voice from the shore, and saw Erica standing there. Safe. Waving. Juliet arrived, breathless and furious, back on the beach, ready for a fight. But Erica hadn't laughed at her.

"I wanted to see how far you'd go," she'd said simply.

Juliet turns now and reaches for a coat, and pulls it on awkwardly over her thick jumper. She rummages for some rubber boots. She grabs Bucky's lead, and calls him to her, fumbling for the ring on his collar. He's not used to being restrained out here, and looks sad.

"It's not because I don't trust you, boy," she says, crouching, holding his muzzle in her hands and stroking his dark cheeks with her thumbs. "Just stay close."

She leaves the lights on, takes a torch and locks the door. At the forest's edge, she pauses. Bucky slinks ahead until he reaches the lead's limit, and looks around at her reproachfully.

"Hello?" she calls.

She sweeps the torch beam into the murk. Its light makes hideous looming shapes of the boughs and her own shadow. Of course the sensible thing would have been to stay put, locked inside, she thinks, as she strides slowly, grimly further into the trees. Bucky pulls keenly until she relents, reeling him in towards her, before fumbling with the little hook to let him off the lead.

He charges around, greeting every tree with assiduous sniffing and snuffling, while Juliet peers between the trunks around her. She dislikes the feeling of the darkness at her back. Every now and then she swings around and shines the torch behind her, on the pretext of calling Bucky softly – even though he's never far off.

Suddenly she hears movement a few metres away. Bucky hears it too. Something like a twig breaking, although the ground is soft and cushiony with needles. *You could lie low here*, she thinks. *You could lie down and hide*. The whole forest feels feathery and muffled. *You could scream and not be heard*.

"Who's there?" she says sharply and Bucky looks up at her with surprised respect. It's her shonky emotional wiring again; fear making her angry. She stands still and listens intently. She can hear her own breath, as well as Bucky's panting.

"Good boy," she says loudly. "Go on. Find the rabbit!" Bucky's eyes widen madly, showing the whites, and he's off, crashing into the undergrowth, rootling in a wide circle through the trees. She turns this way and that; the spindle to his thread. He chases back to her for a quick check of his approval rating, then stands with ears on full alert, before making another tour of duty.

Neither he nor Juliet find anyone.

She returns to the summerhouse, trying to calm herself, holding the torch firmly and following its wavering cone of light. She stands next to the wood-store for a few moments, at the property's edge, staring at the place in darkness. She thought she left the house lights on, but must have imagined it. In the moonlight, she can see all the way through the lounge, for once, to the trees at the front. Neither she nor Bucky see Toby though, just on the other side of the main track, his black hoodie up, hands in his pockets.

She lets herself back in. Bucky slaps his tongue noisily at the water in the dish in the kitchen and settles in front of the wood burner. He, at least, is very pleased by their excursion. Juliet heaves off her boots and jeans, and pulls the heavy jumper over her head. Her hair floats, electrified around her face. She should look over the few lines of the candidacy announcement she began working on earlier; have a further think about answers to the criticisms the newspapers made. If she wants to answer them, that is.

The papers aren't on the table where she left them. The pile of her dad's books is there, and the green tin too, but no papers. No draft. She stands perplexed in the middle of the room. She riffles through the catch-light pile next to the wood basket. Nothing.

Where the hell are they?

She picks up the poker and, slowly, walks to the bedroom, as quietly as she can. She stands in the doorway, and pushes the door so that it swings right back against the wall. She pushes it again, to make sure there's no one hiding in the space behind it. She switches the light on and steps inside and pulls the wardrobe open. The hangers jitter. She checks beneath the bed.

Bucky growls from the living room. She holds very still.

"Bucky?" she whispers.

The dog comes pattering into the bedroom, and offers her his paw as she kneels on the floor. She could cry. With Bucky at her side, she repeats the process in every room, all the while wondering if she locked the door when they came back in. Should she have done? Would it be better if she had? To be locked in with an intruder?

When all the lights are blazing, and every room is checked, she secures the door. She finds her papers on the hallway table. This place is like a bloody, black hole. It swallows everything up – feelings, objects, sensible fucking thought processes – and compresses them into something so dense and dark that there's no getting through it.

She brushes her teeth, peering at herself in the veined mirror in the bathroom. Perhaps it would be a relief to be going insane. Nearly killing herself on the trip out to Kelspie. Searching the woods for ghouls. Sending Declan off devil-hunting to some club in Manchester. These are not the actions of an okay person.

She opens the small bathroom cabinet. Beth's toiletries. A pot of face cream. Some mascara. Even a large old bottle of some old eau de cologne of her dad's, a pale absinthe green. She remembers Beth saying she liked to wear it sometimes. She unscrews the top and takes a sniff: a whisper of lemon and leather, and instantly she falls through the rabbit warren of years to her parents' Friday evening homemade cocktails at the house in Inverness, and fundraising socials at the golf club.

What is she doing? She should be boxing this stuff up, finishing the packing. She's hardly gone beyond the small stack of boxes she and Declan did together in the days after she left the hospital. Instead, clothes and papers and crockery and bric-a-brac she's removed from shelves and backs of cupboards just keep multiplying in totemic piles. She must get on top of it. Tomorrow.

She reaches for the tartan dressing gown on the back of the bathroom door. It's not there. She must have left it in the bedroom. She switches off the lights and hurries naked through the moonlit summerhouse to the bedroom.

Outside, Toby turns away. The 4x4 is still there. Unoccupied.

CHAPTER THIRTY-SIX

Back in the early days of his career when he would do weddings nearly every weekend, Declan developed the habit of sweeping venues. He would charge up and down stairs, seeking the lie of the land, the best vistas and angles. Now, he does the same as he makes his way back through the main foyer, eyeing different doorways. Some are marked as fire escapes. Others have security on duty.

He follows signs for the cloakrooms and pads quickly down into the basement where a plush carpet spreads underfoot, and the walls are painted almost black, directly over brickwork. Two men in their fifties exit an unmarked door, painted the same colour as the walls.

"I'll fucking drag her there by her hair if she doesn't like it," he hears one of them say. Declan stops in his tracks, stoops to tie his shoelace, and watches them walk away. *Which part of the building did they come from?* A security guy, shoulders as wide as the door itself, repositions himself as it slowly closes.

Declan had forgotten how hard it is to loiter anywhere without a mobile phone for occupation. He goes to the bathroom and washes his hands, drying them on thick linen disposable towels. He emerges. He re-ties the other shoe, and grasps at the tiny camera in his jacket. It's still there. No more movement at the door. The bouncer hasn't budged.

Back in the foyer, Declan heads for the main staircase. With their names on the guest list thanks to Lotta's agent, he should be able to access the VIP bar. On his way up, he nods at another security guy, who blinks impassively. Declan takes the steps two at a time, pulsing drums rising with him.

The Dress Circle bar has low, blue lighting, and its own DJ playing Balearic anthems from a central booth. A smallish off-set dancefloor is currently empty, apart from wafts of dry ice. Declan strolls to the far end of the room, where the floor-to-ceiling window overlooks the main space, like an airport in fog. One or two dark alcoves with tables and seats fringing the room are occupied, but it's almost impossible to see anyone's face. It looks like table service only and a waitress or hostess or whatever is already making her way across the room to him. There's not much exploring by yourself, that's clear. He smiles and makes a small, apologetic gesture to the girl as he strolls back out into the corridor, at a loss where to try next.

Saloon-style double doors seal the private boxes from the corridor. A middle-aged couple push through them. She has bouffant blonde hair and he is a jowly, greying non-entity. *A couple*. For some reason, Declan had never imagined that. He'd thought sexual deviance would be a solitary activity. A dirty secret. Not something to be enjoyed among friends. How naïve. *Of course, they share. Showing off must be part of the pleasure*.

Declan makes a decision, and walks at them, greeting them warmly.

"Long time no see," he says, reaching out to the man, who looks flustered and shakes Declan's hand in an automatic response.

Why not go the whole hog? Declan kisses the woman's cheek, one eye on the door and the doorman.

"Looking stunning as always," he says smiling ingratiatingly, as he turns and now backs away from them towards the door. "I love what you've done with your hair."

The doorman touches a finger to his earpiece, listening

intently to some new instruction. His eyes flicker towards Declan, who grabs the edge of the closing door just before it swings shut, and squeezes through, heart hammering. He expects a hand on his shoulder at any second. It doesn't come.

Ahead lies a carpeted corridor with dim wall lighting. The music is finally muffled, but only just. The building wasn't designed for hardcore sound systems, and even here in the club's old arteries, the music is a washing constant; a happy coincidence, Declan suspects, stifling the sound of other sins. Further along, he can make out a bank of thick, red velvet curtains hung across what he assumes are the entrances to the old loges: the private boxes.

Reaching again for the camera in his pocket, he feels slightly sick. He tries to pull himself together, summoning the courage Marcus's girl will exercise in a few night's time. He's a grown man for Christ's sake. If she can step up, after what she's been through, so can he.

He checks the corridor again. No one. What looks like a smoke detector is fixed to the ceiling about a metre away. *A camera?* On the wall facing him, a sepia photograph of Sophie Loren and Cathy Bergman on the set of *Indiscreet*. He edges grimly towards the red curtains.

With one finger, he pulls the drapes back. Behind, there's a small alcove and another narrow swing door, which he nudges ajar with his elbow. The music throbs, louder again now. He darts his head quickly into a becurtained private loge high above the main auditorium, in semi-darkness. Seated in a wide love-seat facing Declan, is a man, groaning profusely, his trousers around his ankles, and a butt-naked girl riding on his lap. The professionalism of her gyrations makes Declan think it's unlikely she's his girlfriend.

The guy digs his fingers deep into the flesh of the girl's arse. She tries to move his hands, and he slaps her across the face so hard that even Declan can see the shadow left on her cheek. She almost falls from his lap. He pulls her back into position and she continues gyrating.

Declan sharply withdraws, and trying not to think about what he's about do, readies the tiny fob camera. He pushes the door again, just enough to get his hand and wrist through at what he estimates to be a good height, and takes two shots. He's adjusting his position to take a third when his arm is grabbed, and he's yanked through the door.

The man, bald and short but fast as it turns out – especially with his trousers still half down – slams Declan around the face now, with a fully open palm and unrestrained force.

"Cunt! What the fuck are you doing?" he shrieks. He strikes Declan again, harder. "Eh?" Three. "You fuck!" Four times, until Declan, ear ringing, lifts an arm to block the next blow.

The incensed client goes for the windpipe next, grinding his elbow into the soft dent below Declan's ribs. All Declan can think about is his assailant's naked genitals rubbing against his suit. He twists, doubling over, and blow after blow to his kidneys follow. Such pent-up aggression. *Jesus. Imagine having to have sex with this fucker.* Finally, the attack relents, but only long enough for the short man to, at last, pull up his dark trousers and fasten them around his barrel-waist. Slowly, deliberately, he buttons the middle and removes his belt, winding it around his wrist, leaving the buckle end dangling. Declan buries his head beneath his arms, awaiting the inevitable.

But nothing comes.

The girl is on her feet, standing directly behind her client. It takes Declan a second to work out that she's snatched hold of the other end of the belt. The guy now returns his attention to her. He yanks the strip of leather from her hands, and she stumbles. He raises his arm and brings the belt and buckle down across her body. She cries out. He raises his arm and whips the belt through the air again. This time the buckle catches her across the temple, and she falls.

Declan stands, unsteadily. He's never been good in a fight, so he does the only thing he can think of: charges the guy, shoulder-barging him across the closeted space. Together, they clatter into a small round table laden with champagne; the flutes and bottle crash to the floor along with both men. Even though Declan chose the move, the bald guy recovers faster and is quickly on his feet, now armed with a broken champagne glass, which he waves at Declan's face like a burning torch.

Holding out his hands in what's supposed to be a calming gesture, Declan tries to edge away, but he's backed up against the love-seat just in front of the balcony. Taking tiny side-steps, he keeps an eye on the girl behind them. She's on her knees, crawling, blood trickling down her temple. She'll get out if she's got any sense.

But it's a mistake to look over at her. During the lapse, the guy lunges, and Declan just manages to dodge the broken glass as it streaks past his cheekbone. He gets a glimpse over the balcony as he turns, and is shocked to discover that there's no safety rail. The client seizes the advantage and forces Declan backwards, half over the balcony's edge, holding the tip of the broken flute about two centimetres from Declan's eyeball.

There's no physical way out. It's over the edge, or lose an eye. Diplomacy seems like a long-shot right now, but Declan opens his mouth, just as the bald guy collapses on top of him, and slithers to the floor of the loge.

The girl is a metre away, swaying gently, the champagne bottle she used to club her client around the head hanging loosely in her hand. Declan and the girl stare at him, waiting for him to move. He doesn't.

The girl snaps into action now, pulling on a kind of high-cut, shiny, black leather leotard. She wriggles into it and turns, and Declan realises she's waiting for him to zip it up. With shaking hands, he obliges.

"Thanks," she mutters, her hand already on her hair, patting any stray strands.

"Are you alright?" he asks. "I didn't—"

She speaks over him. "We should go."

"What should we do about him?"

The girl kneels beside her former client and checks his neck for a pulse. She nods, and clambers to her feet, still wobbly. She can be no more than eighteen. "Okay." She puffs out her cheeks. "Okay."

"Are you… Is there someone you can…?" As soon he forms the question, Declan begins to doubt: *she isn't going to follow the same channels as any regular person*. And in a sudden unravelling, he has another realisation. *He's in this with her now.*

"Follow me."

Cautiously they exit the box, letting the swing door thump to a close behind them. Declan, head swimming, struggles to keep up as she hurries along the corridor, away from the VIP bar. She stumbles just once and as she rounds the corner, her bottom bowls from side to side in its tight black wrapping. It's anything but erotic.

They reach a door with an entry pad, and she keys in a code. A stairwell drops ahead, lit coldly by strip lights. She beckons. Declan descends with her, listening for approaching steps. At the bottom, another set of double doors, with an emergency exit sign above. Declan can feel a draught of fresh air coming through them. In the opposite direction, another narrow corridor. Dull red and green lights glimmer deep within, as if someone is watching television.

"Come on," she says.

Exhaling adrenaline like petrol fumes, Declan sidles along the passage. How is he going to explain what he was doing in that private box? What the hell is going to happen to this girl? She just knocked out her client. That's probably not what most clients request.

They near an old-fashioned janitor's office with a round port-hole window. Voices sound from within. The girl hammers on the door. Declan glances back. There's no way out other than the way they arrived. His heart surges. He tries to step back into the shadow, fingering the camera in his jacket pocket, just as the door opens.

***

Lotta checks her watch. It's been fifty-five minutes. She sits as demurely as she can muster, legs crossed on a bar stool in the jazz lounge, finishing her second drink. The sax sounds as mutinous as she feels. There's been no sign of Declan returning yet. Good to her word, she decides to give him another five minutes, and waits, sipping her drink, trying not to swing her leg impatiently.

After twenty minutes, irritable, a bit drunk, and worried now, she slips from the stool and heads for the exit. Perhaps Declan thought they were going to meet outside? She collects her phone from the cloakroom. The bouncers drizzle polite remarks over her at the door.

"Good bye, Ms Morgan. Please join us again soon."

She emerges with a mixture of relief and anxiety into the misty Manchester street. In the last hour, the queue of prospective young club-goers has grown, and a small group of paparazzi has gathered. The two groups cast glances in her direction, a mix of envy and pity as she leaves. She looks up and down the road, searching for their waiting car. The area isn't well-lit; it's too sombre to see clearly. Eventually she thinks she spots the Audi, about three hundred metres away.

As she begins walking though, she notices something else: two men half-dragging, half-carrying a form along the street. It takes her a second to realise that what they are dragging is a man. She squints, slowing her steps. Is it Declan? He has dark trousers. His head lolls backwards, like a cabbage.

One of them opens a side entrance and they place him carefully on the floor of a corridor inside the club, each inspecting their hands before closing the door behind them.

It's male laughter that wakes Declan. He has no idea where he is. The lights are dim and his eyes are puffy; he can just make out a polished sidetable with a lamp, and expensive-looking drapes.

He tracks back, trying to recall how he got here. He remembers standing in a corner of the basement office, while the girl explained to security what had happened. They'd poured her a whisky. One for him too. Meanwhile, she gave an account in which Declan came to her rescue when the client got out of hand. She was so convincing he had to wonder if that's what she really believed.

"We'll sort it," they kept saying, comms crackling on headsets, as information came in from teams in various locations around the club. The basement guys switched between cameras on the huge wall of CCTV. Declan cringed as his own image flashed up: a hand on the semi-clad lap-dancer's shoulder; eyes on her arse. That alone would look bad enough, but it was the least of his worries. If they find the camera and wire he will be screwed. Perhaps they sensed his agitation. They poured him more whisky.

At least, it tasted like whisky.

He just about remembers climbing the stairs to the Eden apartments, via the guts of the building and a curving staircase in the Gods – a vertigo-inducing ascent above the crowd in Amphi One – while he hung onto the bannister on one side and a suited bouncer on the other. As they reached the top, there was an arc of blue light. A taser?

After that, blank.

They've tied him to an upright armchair. Fine. Not moving is probably the best policy anyway given the acute pain pretty much everywhere. Christ. *What have they done to him?* Did he have a fit? Did he fall down those stairs in the Gods? Could it just be the aftermath of the beating he took from Angry Bald Guy? His head, face, nose, sinuses – everything throbs. He can feel how swollen his eyes are, like he's wearing some kind of fat mask. As a precaution, he keeps his eyelids closed, listening to his surroundings. There's a groaning noise from somewhere.

He wonders how long he's been in here. Where's Lotta? With any luck she's gone, taken herself far away from this fucking hole.

His mind leaps to Juliet. Lotta will call her no doubt. She'll be insane with worry. She may not have gotten over what happened with Beth and the photographs, but she hasn't fallen out of love with him overnight. Okay, so she may not be ready to tell him about the baby. Will she even tell him if she loses it? he suddenly wonders. And now, all this extra anxiety… It won't be good.

He shifts slightly, and nearly lets out a shriek of agony. His fucking ribs. He tries to huff through the pain like a woman in labour, but that just makes it worse. It's like a bad, old joke. Something that Marcus would say. *It only hurts when I breathe*.

Lotta paces up and down beneath the dripping lime trees, waiting for Marcus to pick up his phone. She's been watching the side door where the bouncers took the unconscious guy. There's been no further action.

"Hello?"

"Marcus," she drops her voice. "It's Lotta. Declan's friend. He gave me your number."

There's some scuffling and a long silence. She begins to wonder if he's hung up. Finally, he gathers his wits. "Where are you now? Can anyone hear you?"

"I'm outside the club. In the street. Listen. Declan didn't come back to the rendezvous on time. I think the security may have him. I've just seen them carry someone through a kind of side door."

"Fuck."

"What?"

"That's not good."

"What shall I do? Call the police? An ambulance?"

"Are you fucking mental?" Marcus's voice goes up an octave. "The Palmers practically own the city."

Lotta listens with a sinking sensation.

"Do they know who you both are?" Marcus asks suddenly.

"Yes."

"They saw you arrive together, I guess?"

"Yep."

"And you're sure they've got him? A side door, you said?"

"Well… Pretty sure. Yes."

"Then the most important thing you need to do is get yourself out of there. They'll be looking for you next."

Marcus seems to be focusing on an aspect of the problem that Lotta hasn't considered. She glances over her shoulder. The queue at the entrance to the club has grown again. She can't see the doormen.

"What about Declan?"

Marcus is silent again for several seconds.

"Hello?"

"He's good at talking himself out of a hole."

"And that's it?"

"Believe me, it would be suicidal to try to cause a fuss. They know who you are, and if they've worked out what Declan's doing, they will come after you. They've got too much at stake."

"But—"

"But nothing. They know who you are. You need to leave. Now." He hangs up.

Lotta shakily pockets her phone and starts walking, eyes still on the side exit near a closed-up café. She quickens her footsteps, which echo metallically as she passes, as if she's near some kind of pit. She shudders and runs the last few metres towards the Audi.

She tries the car door, with no luck. The driver, tilted back in his chair, eyes closed, doesn't even jump as she taps on the glass. He opens his eyes slowly and looks at her, heavy-lidded, with complete contempt. She signals urgently for him to wind down the window, which, with some reluctance, he does.

"Could you open the door please? I'd like to get in."

Inside, she catches her breath for a few seconds. The driver starts up the engine, as if this is all a perfectly normal night's work. The wipers swish disconcertingly in automatic response to the tiny pinpoints of moisture from the air gathering on the windscreen.

"Back to the hotel?" he asks.

Decision time. Can she really just drive off and abandon Declan in that place? What did he find? And what did Marcus mean? *They know who you are. You need to leave.*

"No. Could you wait, please. I need to..." she trails off. What does she need to do exactly? Wait for Declan? She sees the chauffeur eyeing her in the rear-view mirror. A little pink pine tree air freshener dangles oddly in the centre of her vision of the street.

She calls Sophie.

"Hello?" Sophie's voice is thick with sleep. Thank God she didn't switch her phone off, or take an extra shift.

"Soph. It's me. I... I've got a problem."

She hears Sophie shifting in bed, propping herself up on her elbows, plumping the pillows noisily, the way she does when she's called in to the hospital at night. Usually it's infuriating but right now Lotta finds it strangely reassuring.

"Go on."

"Declan's... The bouncers have him. I think he's hurt. I don't know what's going on. He went off, to explore the club..." It sounds stupid as she describes it. Juvenile.

"Where are you, now?"

"I'm outside. In the car." There's a silence. She knows what Sophie will be thinking, weighing up.

"How badly hurt is he?"

Lotta doesn't want to spook the driver. "It looked bad," she murmurs. "Unconscious. His head was just dragging along the street."

"Can you call the police? An ambulance?"

"I don't think so. I've been warned off. Declan's friend told me to get away."

Another silence.

Then – "You can't just leave him."

That's more like it. Sophie has always been like this. The voice of conscience.

"You arrived together right?"

"Yes."

"So. You've got two options." Ever logical. "Tell the security on the door you're waiting for him. See what they say. Maybe if they know someone's waiting they'll think twice about… well, about hurting him anymore."

"Yep. Okay." *That's not going to happen*. "What's the other option?"

"Are there any press? You make a big fuss… Maybe the security will decide it's not worth the attention, and let him out."

Let him out? Lotta is starting to feel sick. "I'm not sure the press photographers are interested in Declan and me. They haven't taken any notice of us. We're not exactly celebrity gold."

"So, make yourself interesting."

"What? How?"

"I don't know. Do what celebrities do for attention. Announce you've just got engaged. Or that you've just split up. Get blindingly drunk. Have a wardrobe malfunction."

Lotta would laugh if she didn't feel so anxious.

"Yep. Sounds like a plan," she says. "Except" – she hesitates – "you realise, even being associated with him… if he's on the wrong side of them… These people are dangerous."

She can hear Sophie breathing, soft and low, and wishes to God she were beside her in bed. What Sophie won't say, what she'll never say, is *I told you so*.

"Just take it one step at a time," she says finally. "Try and get him out in one piece and take it from there. Your best friends right now are the press outside the club. They could expose anything. These guys must know that. Daylight is a great disinfectant. Cause a fuss, get him out, then, if necessary, we'll go to the authorities."

The authorities. Working at the hospital, with the

emergency teams and the police, gives Sophie a faith in the right channels that is pretty unshakeable. And completely misplaced.

Declan keeps his eyes closed for as long as he can without passing out. He's no idea how much time has passed. Probably only a few minutes. He wonders absently if it's brain tissue he can feel blocking his nose. He's heard of that. Well, if that's the case, let it hurry. Let all his brain ooze out quickly. Get it over and done with.

Suddenly worrying where his camera is, he forces his eyelids apart. Have the bastards taken it? His jacket is hanging over a plush chair on the other side of the room. His shirt is intact. They don't appear to have found his wire. But glancing around the darkened room, he realises he recognises it from the grainy photographs in Beth's tin: it's the lounge where Beth was photographed with someone snorting cocaine. The place with the kid.

Finally, through his one good ear, he hears the door open. In gold-embroidered slippers, slinking before him across the thick carpet and tucking an open-necked white shirt into his trousers, is Malcolm Lyall.

Declan squints beyond Lyall through the still half-open door into the adjoining suite. In the darkness, he can see a huge, projected screen plastered with the image of a young girl. She's naked except for a dog collar around her neck attached to a lead, which a man behind her is tugging exultantly. Declan forces himself to look at her face. It's expressionless, dead-looking, her eyes glazed. She looks about thirteen.

As he takes this in, Declan realises with a shock: somebody is seated there in the other room, in front of the screen. But before he can see who it is, Lyall closes the door quietly. It actually eases Declan's nerves a bit. He'd had visions of being forced to watch that filth. Of being filmed watching it even. Although that would at least mean they intend to keep him alive long enough to blackmail him.

Lyall takes a seat. "Mr Byrne. We owe you a debt of gratitude, I believe."

"I'm sorry?" His lips feel thick and unworkable.

"You were quite the hero to a rather distressed young woman tonight." He pauses. "We have the footage."

Declan swallows. "I'm not sure—"

"Oh, yes. Quite the hero." He leans forward. "It seems you make a habit of coming to the aid of young women in distress. You were very keen to help your niece, weren't you? Last spring? With her publicity? And now here you are again. Quite snap happy."

He holds the fob camera delicately out in the palm of his hand. "I'm afraid it seems you damaged this during your… exploits."

Declan says nothing. He holds Lyall's stare.

"To be honest, I'm disappointed. I would've expected more of you. I know, I know. You're the photographer after all, as you were always so keen to tell me. So why you would feel the need to bring" – he drops the camera on the floor, stands and puts his foot on it – "a piece of equipment like this…" He grinds the camera under his heel. Declan hears its plastic case cracking apart. "Why you would bring it to our club…"

Declan resists the temptation to correct him. It's Bernhard Palmer's club. Lyall's stake is small. This is not the time to be a smart-mouth though.

"… when you know we have strict policies here, to protect our client's privacy. Clients such as your new *date*, Lotta Morgan, for example." He pauses. "Why would you breach our trust in this way?"

"Lotta has nothing to do with this."

"No. I'm sure."

The derision in Lyall's voice sets Declan's teeth on edge. He tries to keep calm and think fast. "Look," he says. "I was doing someone a favour." *No long words*. "A friend, who thinks her husband is messing around, so—"

"Oh, no, no, no. Come now, Mr Byrne. Can I call you Declan?"

Declan doesn't reply.

"Declan." Lyall smiles. "Now, that's a very amusing story, but I don't know anyone in your line of work who would have recourse to kit like that." He reaches into his pocket. "Or this." He pulls out the Nagra wire that Marcus gave Declan to wear.

Shit.

"I don't know who you're working for Declan, but they've put you in a very, very difficult position. You'll have to return empty-handed, of course."

Lyall rises, and pads back and forth, adjusting a laptop on a stand, switching on a lamp. A soft glow fills the room and Declan's stomach lurches – there's a girl sitting in a chair about four metres away. How long has she been there?

She looks into Declan's eyes, and a moment of unguarded despair passes across her face. It is immediately replaced, however, by a sultry pout. And with that, Declan has a terrible realisation.

He's not going to be made to watch the show. He's going to be the show.

"Now. I'm sorry to tell you Ms Morgan has given up looking for you downstairs. She has left the building. But I'm sure Juliet would love to know what you've been up to tonight."

Is Lyall just testing the water? Or does he really think Juliet doesn't know he's here?

"In fact, it seems you have females dotted all over the place. Jodee, for example. She's been waiting while we finish our little talk."

For the first time, Declan strains at the ties around his wrists and ankles.

"You see, Declan, we have a standard insurance policy here. I'm sure you understand how these things work. So, in a few moments, I'll make myself scarce, and I'll let Jodee take you through the ins and outs of it."

Lyall reaches forward, tilts and swivels the laptop slightly, checking that Declan is positioned centre-screen. As if this is a cue, the girl crosses the space between them, and sits on Declan's knee. She's petite, but even her small weight against his ribcage nearly sends him through the ceiling.

Declan's lips feel like they're crusted together. He wishes to God they were.

***

Lotta sits in the back of the car, drumming her fingers on her knees. She needs something to go back to the doormen with, something to draw the attention of the press.

A wardrobe malfunction? She looks down at her lovely Chloe dress. It's so simply cut there's no way she could bust out of it inappropriately without it looking like an obvious play for attention. Besides, it's too ludicrous. She can't be posing outside with a tit hanging out while Declan is beaten to within an inch of his life.

Could she rip it, or maybe say that Declan ripped it? That he assaulted her? Demand that Declan be arrested? That would be one way to guarantee the security guys release him, surely? Bring the police down on the place. But after what Marcus said about the police and the club being tight, that's maybe not such a good idea. Besides, she can't harm Declan's reputation in that way. A sex scandal? That kind of stink never goes away.

The windscreen wiper chunters to itself. She turns and looks through the rear windscreen at the club, the view divided by the lines of the demister conductors embedded into the glass, like a musical score. A car pulls up outside the club's entrance and a group of young people spill out. There's some yelling from the paps, and flash photography. It looks like lightening going off.

Perhaps she should do as Sophie suggested and announce she and Declan are getting married? *I'm waiting for my fiancé. He'll be coming soon. I'm not leaving without him.* Could work. Maybe. It feels wrong though, in any number of ways. Not least that she and Sophie have never got around to it. They're both always so busy; living and working in two separate cities; practical obstacles that seem so stupid now. Worse though, Lotta has not yet come out publicly, something that Sophie has found hurtful and frustrating.

"You're frightened," she sometimes says. "Of what people would say. 'Dyke in the kitchen. What does she know about cooking for a family?'"

Lotta has always insisted *private life means private life*. And here she is contemplating a fake engagement to one of her best male friends? Of course, she and Declan *wouldn't actually be getting married*. It would just be a story. An immediate fix to get them out of trouble. Why does she feel so uneasy about it then? As if it's a jinx on her future?

She takes a deep breath and leans forward to the driver. "I don't think… I think we probably don't need you anymore. Thank you. Sorry for making you wait."

She lets herself out of the car and straightens her dress. Behind her, she hears the driver start the engine and close his window with an almost undetectable electric whir. If any sound represents indifference, Lotta thinks, that's it. The sound of an electric window closing on the world.

She starts rehearsing in her head. *My friend. My fiancé. He's disappeared. I think he's hurt. Call an ambulance. He's been hurt, in the club. He's unconscious…*

She passes the closed-up café, its chairs chained together at the edge of a terrace. In the gutter is a smattering of broken glass. She eyes a shard – a piece of bottle, with one slightly thickened, rounded edge.

She did a butchery course once, up in Norrland. She was doing a series on foraging in other countries. She hunted moose on foot in the snow all day, with a man who made her want to howl with laughter every time he blew long notes on his large bugle to mimic an ululating female. He did not appreciate her sense of humour. They learned how to skin and butcher the thing, right there in the wilderness: slicing down its back bone like a zip, to the fluffy nodule at the hip; peeling back the skin. The more she tried to make light of the situation the more deadly serious the guide became. He was creepily insistent on one thing: the quality of the knives. Obsessed, in fact, with sharpening techniques, spare blades and alternative tools.

"People don't realise how good a glass tool is," he'd said, eyes gleaming. "If you don't have a knife to hand, broken glass is more than adequate."

He eulogised about how glass is usually double-edged, and how the point, for making a clean enough cut to please your taxidermist, is often "exquisitely sharp, better than a scalpel; you don't want to have to hack and dig at the flesh, and risk puncturing an organ." His exact words had stuck in Lotta's mind for a long time. "You want clean incisions, so you don't taint the meat."

She picks up the shard.

She focuses on the glass under the streetlight. She wishes it were clean. Gritting her teeth, trying to think of her thigh as a piece of animal, she punctures her stockings and skin and lets out a long, low moan. She pushes the point in further, braces herself, and manages to flick it upwards and out.

The blood rises and spills onto her hand. Good. She drops the glass shard down a drain, and wipes her hand down her face and neck. She needs to look savage. She sucks air as slowly as she can into her lungs and blows it out again, just as slowly. *I've been hurt*, she'll say. *I need my friend. He's still in the club. Declan Byrne. Please find Declan.*

In her mind, Declan emerges from some restricted area, propped up between two thwarted, muscle-bound brutes, who will help him on with his jacket and dust down his shoulders. He'll turn to her, grin and say… something… something self-deprecating and witty.

Bleeding thick and fast now, she begins limping towards the flashing lights and the queue.

The door opens suddenly and Jodee, kneeling between Declan's legs while he desperately wriggles away from her, trying to prevent her accessing his fly, scrambles to her feet. Two men are already in the room, wearing dark shirts and earsets. She grabs a cushion and covers herself, while the men wrench the ties from Declan's hands and feet.

They take no care to be gentle. Declan tries his hardest not to scream.

They work in complete silence, hauling him up. His head thunders, and he almost passes out again. He fumbles with his trousers. One of the men shoves him towards the door.

"What are you doing? Where are we going?"

On the corner of a side table by the door, Declan sees the recording fob confiscated by Lyall earlier, a cracked black disc.

"What about her?" he asks the men, dipping his head at the girl standing in the other corner, still clutching her cushion.

They turn, glancing at the girl and at each other. In that split second, Declan swipes the pieces of broken fob up in his hand and pockets them.

Insurance.

As the guys' eyes swivel back to him, he staggers into the side table, knocking over a lamp. He grabs the table edge as if to steady it and himself.

"I'm not feeling good," he mumbles.

"Don't worry," one of them says. "It'll be over soon."

CHAPTER THIRTY-SEVEN

During the night, Juliet wakes to a feeling that something is wrong. It's not the habitual remembering, the grief that sinks like cold air into her during the first seconds after opening her eyes. She's used to that by now. No, it's something else. Something physical. The room is filled with the musk of her sleep and breath, the slight raw choke of the wood fire, and something else. Something tangy, like metal.

Her first instinct is to touch her fingertips between her legs, to check for blood. Since the dire warnings about her age and health at the hospital, she's been expecting to lose the baby, a feeling that's thickened into a sort of resignation. It's not the first time she's felt as though she's watching herself – from the outside – watching to see how she'll react when it happens: relief or disappointment? She doesn't know why it feels like she has a binary choice between just those two emotions, or why these feel like emotions outside herself that she must somehow wear, like a hat or a scarf. She reaches under the covers, holding her breath, and her fingers come up clean.

On her way to the toilet, she notices an odd glow in the hallway, coming from the windows in the lounge. She opens the door of the summerhouse on the latch. What looks like mist or fog, floating in horizontal bands, moves across the visible slice of garden. The smell is more acrid here. She opens the door wider.

Smoke.

Fifteen metres from the house, the wood shed is alight. Horror laces through Juliet. It's hard to tell how long it's been burning but the doorway is already just a smouldering black hole, and one of the old corrugated roof panels is tilting inwards. Flames are building along the side where the wood is stacked, flashing up into the air above.

The wind blows glimmering dust and ash towards her and the house. She tries not to breathe in the choke, but her heart rebels, pounding, willing her to fill her lungs. She takes fast, shallow breaths, and quickly turns left and right, trying to stay calm, checking that the house isn't ablaze as well. They've always kept a bucket of dousing sand next to the fire pit, although they've never had call for it, and it's uncertain what a bucket of sand will accomplish here: the fire is vigorous already. How the hell did it catch? Logs like those don't go up this quickly without some kind of fuel. Juliet runs across the decking and down onto the lawn in bare feet. When she reaches the sand bucket, it's empty. It hasn't been refilled since Beth supposedly used it to douse the flames they say she started.

Juliet races back to the house and unreels the old, yellow garden hose attached to the tap on the outside of the kitchen. The faucet has seized. It's so stiff and cold that it releases hardly a trickle. Her cheeks and forehead hot, face manic in the firelight, she heaves the dribbling hose around the shed, onto the path and grass, as close to the woodpile as she can. At this rate it will take hours to damp everything properly, which will only ruin the wood. Either way, the store is going to be a write-off. The rapidity and violence of the destruction is shocking.

Who the fuck has done this? And where are they now? Are they watching her? Watching her reaction?

Helpless, and frightened someone is about to approach, Juliet edges back against the side wall of the summerhouse, a hand held protectively over her abdomen. Even if she drives to the road for a phone signal to call 999, the shed will be mostly destroyed by the time anyone arrives.

She tries to think rationally. How great is the risk that the flames will spread to the house, or into the forest? Slim, surely? Her father ensured the outhouse was at a suitable firebreak from its surroundings. In the rural Highlands, people know they won't be reached quickly in a blaze.

Yet, this is what Beth supposedly stood and did, three months ago. Here, in this garden, she not only watched, *but fed* a burning pit, fed it with work she'd spent years perfecting, and that of others. Such bleak callousness. *So out of character.*

This is why they talk about a *roaring fire*; the noise is terrifying. The whole thing creaks and groans, but more than that, it roars, artlessly, sucking great gusts of vapour and oxygen from its surroundings. Beth stood and listened to something like this, watched the flames, heard their bellow, then walked impassively into the sea for a final time. But... before she did, stopping to pour sand over the embers?

Why would she do that? If she were in such a destructive mood, why would she give a shit whether the house burnt down and everything in it?

CHAPTER THIRTY-EIGHT

"So, let me get this straight."

Marcus puts his hands on the tiny table between Declan and him. It looks like he's been biting the skin around his thumb nail. They're sitting in a caravan belonging to one of Marcus's contacts, on a surburban Manchester driveway, north of Altrincham and south of Sale. Its owners are away. Marcus texted him the address and told him where they keep the key. After being discharged from Accident and Emergency, Declan spent the night here curled in a bunk with nothing but a child's sleeping bag for cover. Freezing.

"I said, be discreet." Marcus says.

Declan hangs his head, a mistake which is immediately punished with another debilitating episode of nose-throbbing. A day and a half ago, at the hospital, while Lotta received twenty-two sutures, a specialist had distracted Declan with questions, all the while gently feeling his way around Declan's face. With a brusque warning, he'd yanked Declan's nose to the left. Declan's feet had flown into the air. The specialist scolded him. *Keep still.* One more wrench to the left, then a hoik up and into Declan's face. Within seconds, the agony receded, leaving him with souvenir bruising across his cheeks and eye sockets to rival Marcus.

Declan holds out his plastic cup. Marcus stares at him

reprovingly but fetches the hip flask from his pocket, like a child feeding treats to a naughty dog.

"'Don't draw too much attention to yourselves,' I said. And what do you do? Let me see now" – Marcus counts on his fingers – "Bust into all the private areas, get caught on camera with a murderous prostitute, get tasered by Eden thugs, get threatened by Lyall himself, Lotta stabs herself, and you both get papped staggering into an ambulance, looking like the... the Bride of bloody Frankenstein."

Declan shudders, and expedites the drink. He keeps wondering what happened to the bald guy. A horrible little fuck of a man, admittedly, but a person. Dead, possibly. Lotta told him about the man she saw being dragged along the street and dumped in the cellars. He's been over it, and over it. The girl checked the guy's pulse and nodded. He thought that meant... He keeps trying to remember the bald guy's face, but it's gone, overwritten for the moment with the blank look of the girl in Lyall's antechamber; with the numbing shock of it all. The quantity of blood Lotta managed to draw was hellish, glazing her clothes and hands, coalescing the whole night into a surreal, blackened nightmare.

"And you told the police you fell down the stairs."

"Yes," Declan nods, very slowly. Very gently. "Yes. That is correct."

In fact, Marcus is the only person he's told about the bald guy and his time upstairs with Lyall. It's not the sort of thing he was about to describe in his voice messages to Juliet. He left her a series of them from the hospital while the nurse was stitching Lotta up, but he'd been distracted and his main aim had been to pre-empt what she would see in the papers. He hasn't been able to charge his phone since, and to be honest he's in no hurry, but he knows he must speak to her soon, or face the risk that she'll get on a plane to Manchester herself.

Marcus frowns as he looks again at the newspaper in front of them. Emblazoned on the front page, a picture of Declan exiting the Eden Club flanked by solicitous security, looking for all the world like one of Palmer and Lyall's cronies.

Declan knows what Marcus is thinking. Even if they had any footage, those cosy front page pictures give them a credibility problem now. He reaches into his pocket and holds out the broken camera fob. "All is not lost," he says. "Might still be something on there."

Receiving the device in the palm of his hand, Marcus looks at it as if it were a piece of used gum. "Declan..." Marcus hesitates. "What exactly happened up there?"

"I..." Declan closes his eyes. "Like I said, they were trying to film me with a girl. Leverage, I guess. Make sure I would keep quiet."

"And?"

Declan pauses a second too long before replying, "Lotta pulled a blinder, didn't she? They put everything on pause. Dusted me down. Escorted me out like royalty."

Declan doesn't want to admit it, but the fact that Lyall's thugs let him go has been eating away at him. They must have got the footage they wanted, needed, or they wouldn't have released him, would they? Lotta could have bled out and it wouldn't have stopped them. They have footage of him with that lapdancer, as well as the younger girl. She might not have got very far, but whatever they have, they think it will be enough to make him back off, to ruin him.

And they're right. It would ruin him, and Juliet. He'd lose Juliet and she'd lose her career if any of it came out. He suddenly knows what Beth must have been going through. Those photos. She must have been terrified they'd be made public.

But terror has different effects on different people.

Do these fucking shites think he's just going to crawl away? Persuade Marcus and Juliet to give it all up and go back to life as normal? For a start, they don't know Juliet. If he tried to persuade her to forget it all now, he'd lose her anyway. And they don't know him. Nothing enrages him more than people assuming they know how he'll react.

"Oh. Thanks, by the way." He raises his eyebrows. "Lotta told me all about your help."

Marcus ignores this crack. He turns the fob over in his hand. "So we know Lyall's in town," he says. "But the proof was on this thing?"

Declan nods. "And there was definitely someone else there. Sitting in the other room. Watching… something filthy."

"Who?"

"I don't know." Tentatively Declan bends his neck, snuffling at particles of whisky. "Do you still have to send that girl in?" he asks. "To film?"

"*Send her in*." Marcus snorts. "I'd like to see you try and stop her."

CHAPTER THIRTY-NINE

The next afternoon, Declan takes the train and bus out to Lyme Park, an hour outside of Manchester. He's supposed to meet Marcus and the girl there. It's a long walk from the bus stop up the main drive of the country house, and his aching body and ribs force him to take it slowly. He looks over his shoulder every time a car passes. The house is spectacular, but – in the way of manicured country estates – leaves Declan unmoved. It's hypocritical for a photographer, he knows, but he hates it when someone has already carved up the scenery into vistas, deciding for him where he should look.

Wide gravel pathways undulate across overfed lawns and between Lego-like trees. The house itself rises, huge in glowing sandstone against the landscaping. Declan lingers near the main entrance and watches an elderly couple help each other up the steps, and two mothers chasing polka-dot-booted toddlers off the sloping grass. None of them look like they work for Eden.

Marcus arrives after about fifteen minutes, accompanied by the girl. She's wearing trainers, black jeans, a thick grey jumper, and a loose black headscarf. Dark rings encircle her darting eyes and she looks undernourished. Marcus said she was fourteen. She seems younger than that, and yet older. Jaundiced-looking skin stretches over her prominent cheekbones. She repeatedly tucks a stray wave of long dark hair back under her scarf. Perhaps she hasn't had a haircut for a while. Perhaps she's nervous.

"Declan, this is Ishtar. Ishtar, my friend Declan." She picks at a seam of dry skin on her lip and keeps her forehead tilted down.

Declan tries to give her a reassuring smile, but, to tell the truth, his own nerves are not faring well. He's hardly slept since the last visit to the club; he's not looking forward to the idea of putting himself back within Palmer or Lyall's clutches. At least he managed to bundle a bandaged Lotta safely back to Liverpool. But there are no bandages for the images in his mind. He leaves his phone charging in Marcus's car and they make their way inside.

The three of them attract some attention from the middle-aged woman on the ticket desk. It's hard to tell what bothers her more: two grown men covered in injuries, with a young, foreign girl; or the fact that it's a school day. After a series of furtive stares though, she looks away. It's starting to dawn on Declan just how easy it must be for Lyall and his cronies to do whatever they like. In general, people are too polite to ask questions when they see something odd, like the arrangement Marcus has with the girl, for instance. Even Declan found it hard to get his head around. Marcus took a job working part-time in the canteen at the asylum centre. Over six months, he somehow got her talking. The idea of the old cynic being able to win the trust of a broken, teenaged girl had Declan baffled, until now. Seeing them side by side, it's clear. The brokenness. They have it in common.

They start to make their way across the gardens, gravel crunching and glinting like snow. Ishtar seems to know where she's going. She walks ahead at first until they reach the more open lawns, then drops back between them. Declan keeps at her shoulder, trying to give her a friendly sign. She doesn't meet his eye.

Finally, he mutters to Marcus, "If you can take her out for the day, can't you get her out of that place?"

"So now you're suggesting I abscond with a registered asylum seeker? A minor?"

"No, but surely you could have already reported what she told you? I mean, isn't there any kind of safeguarding?"

"Very little, it seems. It's an open hostel. They can come and go. And it means almost anyone can get in. There are all sorts of people just hanging around. To be honest, it's amazing there aren't more problems. Her friend – the one I told you about, who was found dead? – before she disappeared, she ran away and lived rough. She was picked up by the police and she told them what had been happening to her. Guess what? They brought her straight back to the accommodation."

"Please. I speak," Ishtar's voice comes as a surprise. It's soft, low, resonant somehow, like strings. "I ask Marcus not say anything anyone. Is shame for me. I am… is much danger for me, if people know."

Declan stands still in the middle of the path, listening intently and with growing concern as she speaks. "But you do know he's a journalist? He wants to publish your story?"

"He will to hide my name."

Declan darts a look at Marcus.

"Yes," Marcus looks shifty. "If I can."

"Is danger now for me. So. We stop them. I film them. We make them pay." She makes it sound so simple. "This not good life. I am nothing. I understand now. So. Is all the same."

They start walking again. Marcus coughs, "Those are her words, by the way. Not mine."

"I don't like this," Declan says.

"Do you think she does?"

"You get a story out of it. What does she get? Your editor, or whoever, are they going to guarantee her safety?"

"No," Marcus looks grim. "That's not how it works. But with the public's attention on her… on her case, she'll be a lot safer. There'll be people watching how it works out. With her story out there, a benefactor will probably get her a scholarship somewhere."

Ahead, looming glass elevations reflect and bend the hazy September sky into the elegant form of a nineteenth-century orangery. A smile begins to play on Ishtar's lips.

The heat and scent of camellia and fig greet them before they've even gone through the door. It's like being smothered by a giant airline serviette, hot and clean and comforting. Ishtar gazes up and down the tiled walkway. She closes her eyes and breathes in. Her face takes on a kind of dewy sheen.

Keeping their voices down, they wander between a tiered fountain and lush fragrant foliage, and go over the plan again. Ishtar will receive a text telling her where to wait and when. Usually, she's picked up from the same spot, a couple of blocks away from the asylum centre. Marcus and Declan will tail the driver who takes her to the apartments on the back of the club. Marcus wants Declan to photograph the whole pick-up process.

"We'll follow you there and back," he says to Ishtar. "Like I've done before. We'll be there just in case. Then we'll follow you back to the drop off. You give us the bag with the camera. Job done."

When they exit the glasshouse, the air outside feels suddenly colder in their throats and noses, as if the season has turned somehow while they were inside. Clouds of their own breath gather before them as they walk back across the lawns.

They sit in Marcus's car in the near dusk. Ishtar leans forward between the front seats, and quickly picks up what she needs to do. The camera is not difficult to use. It looks exactly like a pen, dark blue and gold, but contains a USB stick, mic and high definition digital video recorder.

As Marcus unscrews it to show Ishtar the switch that turns it from camera to video, Declan wonders what she must be thinking, going undercover to record men… what they do to her. She seems so calm, but his own mind races. He thinks of Jodee, the girl in Palmer and Lyall's den, and his skin burns with shame.

He should call Juliet again. It's strange that she hasn't

called back, but he's almost relieved because, when he does speak to her, he'll have to tell her everything. Wouldn't it be better if she didn't know just yet? As soon as she does, she'll want to go straight to the authorities. Can he keep another secret from her? For a day or two?

He tries to refocus on what Marcus is saying. On the camera pen. He hopes it works. It's hard for him to believe this kind of kit is available on the open market for anyone to purchase. Not so long ago this was the stuff of espionage films. Ishtar, however, doesn't look impressed. Compared even to her battered mobile phone, the pen looks impossibly antiquated. *A pen, for fuck's sake! What kid would even have one of these in her bag?* For a moment, Declan has a panic that the whole plan is just going to fall apart. He's had several of these already.

"You just need to ensure this switch is flicked here," Marcus is saying. "To the right."

"Yes," she says.

"It will record an hour. You're sure that's enough?"

"Yes."

"So. Don't switch it on until you're sure you can capture… you know."

Declan thinks of the blank-faced girl on the film he saw. He feels sick. Ishtar doesn't bat an eyelid.

"Yes."

"You need to lay it down in this direction. So, this little hole is facing what you want to record."

She nods.

"And it still works as a pen. Look. If someone tries to take it out of your bag and use it, it will still be fine. They won't notice. But you'll have to try to position it back in the right place again."

She takes and attaches it inside her little woven bag. They inspect the result from the outside. It's good. The hole they've created to film through is minuscule. It shouldn't be seen.

"We'll have a camera outside, on the car and the apartment. Everything. So if anything happens, we'll be right there."

Right there. To do what exactly? Witness the carnage?

Marcus needs to drop Ishtar back. He hands Declan's phone over and makes him take public transport again, saying it's better to avoid them being seen together anywhere near the refuge. The fourteen-mile return to Manchester seems longer to Declan than the way there. He looks out into people's back gardens, and children doing homework at warm kitchen tables. Then, he's on a tram jangling through rush-hour traffic. His nose begins to throb again. Reflections of brake lamps and headlights elongate and festoon the shop fronts like Christmas baubles.

Four missed calls from Juliet. He hesitates, then calls her. He's relieved when it goes straight to voicemail. She must be at Culbin with no signal. Unless she's now ignoring him. He leaves a brief message.

"Hi, Juliet. I hope you're okay? I don't know if you've had my messages? I expect you've seen the papers now. Like I said, it's nothing to worry about. I wanted to let you know, I'm fine. Lotta's fine. I've met up with an old friend. He's got a lead on the Eden Club..." He pauses. "Look. I can't say much right now but if anything, it's worse, much worse, than anything we thought."

He hesitates. He doesn't want to frighten her, but the idea of her being alone in the forest is too much for him. If the Palmers decide to go after her, she'll be a sitting duck. "I wonder... I'm thinking you should move into town. Go and stay with Erica? I'd be able to call you more easily."

The tram driver rings the bell and swears loudly at someone running across the track. A woman rushes along the pavement in high heels and catches one of them between the paving slabs. Declan closes his bruised eyes. "I love you. I'll call as soon as I can say more."

The trip is not delivering as he'd envisaged. There's no easy redemption here.

CHAPTER FORTY

"What do you have for me, Frank?"

Karen's cheek burns as she holds the phone to it. She likes to think of Frank in his lab at the forensic unit. He took her under his wing in the early days of her career when she was on a forensics placement. She sometimes wishes she'd opted for that. She knows all too well that the public-facing bit of her job is not her strong point. Right now she could be there, somewhere at the end of all those white corridors, calibrating, instrument to instrument, at her side Frank and his moustache. White moustache it is now. Occasional court appearances. Process. Detail. Prints appearing like magic in fumigators.

Frank scolds her. She can hear something scratchy on the line as he speaks. She wonders if it's his whiskers. "It would've been quicker if you'd told me what I was dealing with," he says.

"Now you're just trying to catch me out." She smiles, remembering the way he'd drilled it into her years ago, *They don't tell you what to look for. You tell them what you've found.*

"Burnt fibres matching those found at the Beth Winters fire. The girl who drowned at midsummer."

"And?"

"A jumble of partial prints. It's not easy on a jacket like this. A lot of unknowns. But four sets of DNA. Beth's. Probably a relative of Beth's. And matches for two of the guys I think you eliminated from the investigation. Karlo Southall and, er, Toby Norton."

"What about the bit of paper from the pocket? The numbers?"

"Just him."

"Sorry?"

"Just Karlo," his voice squeaks a little, as it does when he's excited or agitated. "It's interesting, isn't it?"

Karen says nothing.

"Sorry, but that's it."

Her tongue works along her lower lip. "No. It's okay. It's what I suspected."

"What are the numbers?" he asks.

"I was hoping you'd tell me."

"Bank card pin code?" he suggests. "Mobile phone security code?"

"Yep. Those were my guesses."

She thanks him and hangs up. She stares at her own hand holding the phone for a few moments before opening her laptop and clicking into a video file.

From a static camera, a dark courtyard with rows of arched trellises. In the background, a tall incinerator chimney. A counter in the corner of the screen reads *1.26AM*. A slender figure appears, wearing skinny jeans and the down puffa jacket that Frank now has in his lab. Head held low. A quick glance left and right before exiting the shot. A few moments later, the flicker of a striplight in the temporary hut at the right of the shot. She watches it again. And again.

Karen closes her eyes, hesitates, then dials another number.

"Nick. If I were to need an extra patrol on the A96, between Inverness and Elgin, and up to the coast at Culbin, who've we got?"

"There's a game this weekend. You wannae take a car out of the city?"

"No. I said extra. Not redeployed."

"But with the match—"

"I'll answer for it."

"Alrighty then. No harm in asking, I suppose. Night patrols only?"

Karen's tongue flickers over her lips. How hard would a twenty-four-hour presence out there be to justify? Every recent decision seems to attract such scrutiny. "Let's ask for two six-hour shifts. From 2100 hours until to 0900. Until further notice."

"Very nice. That'll make tidy overtime for some lucky bastards."

"And during daylight I want a regular sweep down there. A passing patrol every ninety minutes."

She hears Nick whistle between his teeth. "What are we looking for?"

***

With only Bucky for company, Juliet takes the risk of leaving the smouldering woodpile and driving to the passing point beyond the railway bridge towards the A96, where she has a signal. First, she listens again to the disturbingly cryptic set of voicemails from Declan in Liverpool, and immediately tries his phone again, only to get the same response she's had for the last forty-eight hours. *The mobile phone you are calling is switched off*. Her worry is morphing into infuriation.

She calls Karen, and gets through to a colleague. This is it, she thinks; she's finally losing her mind. Did she somehow set the shed alight herself? What was it she heard out in the woods? She tries not to garble the information down the line.

When she hangs up, five other messages ping into her phone in quick succession from London – PA headquarters, Fiona. *How are you getting on? Any progress?* Fiona asks.

Returning home, Bucky races around the smouldering shed, frantic and curious. Juliet goes indoors and puts some coffee on. Fuck it. She deserves a coffee and technically one cup is allowed. It's only since she's been trying to give it up that she's noticed how much she wants it. She stands at the lounge window, staring, sipping coffee as black as the charred wood.

Karen arrives less than an hour later, having left the office almost as soon as she heard about the fire. She finds Juliet inside the summerhouse, in a small city of boxes; labels and Post-It notes like bunting, everywhere.

As Karen glances around, Juliet sees it all through her eyes: the unfinished packing; stacks of linen on top of books on top of paperwork. And outside, she can't help but feel that Karen only half inspects the scene, making all the appropriate noises, and taking a few photographs. They stand together for a few moments, watching the bristling aftermath of destruction. A fire is a compelling thing.

Back indoors, they clear a space at the dining table where, just the other night, Juliet and Declan sat together poring over her dad's books.

"So," Karen begins. "Tell me again what exactly happened."

"I woke up. There was a smell. The shed was on fire. I couldn't put it out."

"How did it catch alight?"

Juliet tries not to sigh. "I don't know, Karen. That's why I called you. It would've taken fuel to make it go up like that though."

"I'm sorry, Juliet, but I have to ask. An examination of the scene, will be… well, costly, difficult to justify. People may say…"

"What? That I did it myself? Why would I do that?" She frowns. "Oh. I see."

Because people think I'm just as crazy as my sister and my niece. And that I'm getting special treatment.

Karen changes tack. "What motives do you think anyone else might have to do this?"

"I…" Juliet hesitates. She has to admit, it sounds truly insane. "To scare me?"

"And Declan's not here with you?"

“No,” Juliet pauses.

She’s wasting Karen’s time. Is this what the police have to put up with? Grieving relatives making a fuss of pathetic details, grasping at reasons, anything, to explain the tragedy that’s befallen them? Should she explain why Declan’s gone to Manchester? If that’s where he still is. She doesn’t even know. Won’t it just make them both sound, well even more nuts? *Worse than we thought* is what Declan said in his message. She’s aware of Karen watching her.

“He was called away,” she says finally.

“And have you been… feeling better? Since the… island?”

“Yes. Thank you. I was lucky. It was foolhardy.”

Karen nods. For all the career risks Karen says she’s taking, Juliet can’t fault her professionalism. And it’s hardly fair questioning Karen, and all the while going off on her own tangents, sharing no information about the photographs, or her suspicions about Palmer with this woman she’s been all but accusing of not investigating Beth’s death properly. The green army tin is sitting there, in the bedroom. A box of secrets.

“Karen. Would you… wait a second?”

Juliet fetches the tin and places it purposefully on the table. “I found this,” she says firmly. More firm than she feels. She’s ashamed and afraid and still angry with Declan for taking the damn pictures in the first place; and worst of all, she feels mortified for Beth.

Her voice shakes slightly. “You asked in the hospital whether I’d found anything when I went to Kelspie. I found this. It belonged… well, originally to my father, and then Beth.” She takes a deep breath. *Is there any going back from here?* “She’d hidden it.”

“Hidden it? Why?”

“I’m not sure, but…” *Is there a way to sift out the coked-up images in the Eden Club?* Juliet opens the battered tin, and begins carefully sliding them across to Karen, with a running commentary that, once started, she can’t seem to halt.

“Declan took these, in the spring. Beth was doing some

work on album designs for the band." *A black-and-white shot of Beth, topless, her back to the camera, facing the sea.* "And these were supposed to be publicity shots." *Beth, lying on a bed.* "They were… well, it didn't work out. In the end Declan gave a few proofs to Beth but he didn't feel comfortable with the way the shoot was going."

Karen takes her time looking at each image, long enough that Juliet is able to deal them out, one by one, onto a little pile in front of her. She keeps the final two back, the most compromising – the unknown man snorting cocaine, and the girl on her knees.

Karen spreads the pictures out over the table. "Did you know Declan had worked here?"

"No. And I was..." –what's the point in mincing her words?– "I was shocked. Very upset. Apparently, Beth didn't tell anyone, and she asked Declan not to either."

"You found these on the island, you say?" Karen looks at the tin.

"Yes. You know, those little cairns people build on beaches? The tin was buried inside. I can't work out why."

"And how did you think to go searching out there?"

"Kelspie? Well, she'd been out there, collecting plants. It was in her design notes. I—"

"And you didn't tell Declan you were going out there?"

"No." Juliet clears her throat. "There's something else. In with Declan's photographs, we found these." She places the two mystery images on the table next to the others. "We don't know who took them. It wasn't Declan. We think it might be in Manchester. The Eden Club? Look at this girl. And look at what's written on the back." Juliet turns one of the pictures over. She rises from the table. "And Beth designed a really disturbing album cover for them… well, take a look for yourself."

She lays the large portfolio out and cycles through it, to the pale face in the patchwork window.

Karen is silent for a long time. It's interesting stuff, but there's very little here she can work with here.

"Is this where Declan has gone? To Manchester?"

Juliet hesitates. "Yes."

Karen puts away her notepad. "I can see that it looks as though Beth was involved in something very unsavoury. And I agree, it does raise questions." She purses her lips. "But you understand that I can't re-open an investigation based on this? Some substance abuse? A decontextualised picture? A piece of artwork?"

Hearing these doubts spoken out loud makes Juliet's heart and lungs deflate.

"And, to be honest, Juliet," she says, slowly, deliberately. "In the immediate, I have other concerns. I'm coming to the strong conclusion that it's possible..."

Here it comes.

Yes. It's entirely possible. I'm losing my mind.

Karen retrieves her tablet from her bag, and starts to login. "I want you to see something too. I'm starting to agree that... if someone wanted you gone from here, urgently, if someone was trying to make you leave, then destroying your wood store so you've no way to heat this place might be a start."

Watching her own movements, Juliet picks up the coffee pot and refills Karen's cup, then her own. She brings the mug to her lips, and blows across its surface. That was not what she was expecting Karen to say.

She's saved from answering by a thump at the door. Karen turns the tablet's screen off, and sits back in her chair, arms folded, while Juliet rises to answer.

Toby crosses the threshold, ducking deferentially as he pulls an outsized pair of headphones from his ears, and tidies them into a satchel. He's slightly out of breath. He gazes open-mouthed straight at Karen, then around the room, as if to check who else is there.

"I'm sorry. Ahh. You're okay. I won't stay long. I just..." He looks at Juliet. "I was wondering if you were alright? I... I saw the police car outside."

Juliet smiles. "Yes, I'm fine. You know Karen Sutherland,

I think." Karen doesn't seem impressed at the interruption. She gives Toby a piercing stare, which he returns with a smile.

"Yes. Yes, of course." He walks over to the table and shakes Karen's hand. "I was a bit concerned about Jet."

Listening, Juliet goes to the kitchen and fetches him a cup. *Jet? Did he pick that up from Beth?*

He continues. "You know, she hasn't been well. And being here by herself..." He sits awkwardly at the table, glancing at the photographs laid out in rows. "Ahh. Declan's famous pictures."

Karen gathers them up and raps them smartly against the table. She raises her eyebrows. "Famous?"

Toby laughs. "Well, infamous maybe." He looks suddenly reflective. "Is Declan alright?" he asks.

"Why do you ask?"

"Well..." He digs in his satchel and pulls out a redtop newspaper, which he opens and hands to Juliet. "Because of this."

Declan and Lotta are emblazoned across the middle pages.

> Celebrity chef Lotta Morgan in wild meltdown at Manchester's legendary Eden Club with Declan Byrne, previous squeeze of Progressive Alliance leadership candidate, Juliet MacGillivray.

Juliet knows Karen's eyes are on her. She scans the article, and tries to brush it off.

"Oh"– she smacks the paper down harder than intended on the table – "Those two. They're a terrible influence on each other."

Toby hasn't finished yet though. "I didn't have you guys down as clubbing types. I mean, I was telling Jet how uptight Declan seemed when he took those photos. It was quite funny in a way. Beth even told us he was her stepdad."

Karen clears her throat. "But at the funeral you all met her real father, I suppose?"

Toby glances sharply at her, then at Juliet. "Well, I… We didn't go to the funeral. Max… We didn't want to hijack anything. I mean, we wondered if it would cause press coverage, us being there, and it didn't seem fair on her family."

"Well, that was very thoughtful of you all." Karen licks her lower lip. "And I expect it would've been a bit of a dampener on your whole scene. Wouldn't exactly lend a feel-good factor to the album release, would it?" She smiles inscrutably.

Toby's eyes dart uneasily between the two women.

Juliet feels a little sorry for him. And impressed by Karen. *What's she driving at?*

"I'd say the album was the last thing on our mind," he finally says, evenly. "Max wasn't in a good place."

"Of course."

There's a long silence. Juliet is acutely conscious of the odd rapport she and Toby have. And suddenly she feels things begin to shift. *Has Toby been working her, manipulating all along?* Karen sips her coffee, eyes on Toby.

Juliet pushes her chair back suddenly. "Toby was the one who helped find me, actually, out there on the island. With Declan." Her voice sounds too loud, as if she's trying to convince herself. She laughs. "Toby saved me."

A ghost of a look passes across Toby's face, so brief that Juliet wonders if she's imagined it. And then he's smiling, turning on the headlights.

"I should get going. Let you two carry on, but Juliet, I'm glad you're feeling better. You know where we are if… if you need us before you go."

He winks at her. *Winks?* What the hell is he doing?

"I tell you what though," he says, as if it's an afterthought. "Did you find that jacket?"

"Oh," Juliet says. "Yes. Of course. I…" She tries not to look at Karen. "Let me… I can find it." Her face flushes. In the hallway, she pretends to fight her way through the jumble of coats draped on pegs by the door.

"Is it an important jacket?" Karen asks. She's clearly better at dissimulation than Juliet.

"No," Toby says quickly. "Seriously," he calls into the hall, "it doesn't matter. It's not a big deal."

Juliet shows him out, murmuring apologies. She could happily kick him in the backside as he saunters away. Karen is opening the tablet again when Juliet returns to the dining room.

Juliet glances out the window, checking Toby's gone. "Any news on the jacket?" she asks.

"Some prints," Karen says. "A mix of DNA. From you. Those guys. Burnt fibres from the firepit. And the piece of paper only has Karlo's prints, which is weird. It could be a phone or bank code. Trouble is, we have nothing conclusive forensically. But I want to show you something."

She navigates through some files and turns the tablet in Juliet's direction. Before she plays the clip from Elgin campus courtyard, she pauses, and looks Juliet in the eye.

"Brace yourself. This is the footage of the courtyard, the night all the designs were destroyed at the university."

Juliet stiffens and watches the screen. It's the first time she's seen this: some of the last moments before Beth died. It ends, and she swallows, her finger hovering over the play button.

"Do you mind if I…?" Her voice is hoarse.

Karen nods and Juliet watches the clip again.

"So there's Beth and there's the famous jacket," Karen mutters.

Juliet squints at the screen and presses pause. She closes her eyes and lets her mind wander back to Georgia Owen, leading her across the same yard, pausing at the door of the temporary hut.

"Could the numbers be a door code?" she asks. "That door. The student studios?"

"But why would Beth need them written down?" Karen asks.

"Perhaps she didn't write them down. You said the paper had Karlo's prints, not Beth's."

They look at each other and watch the footage again.

Karen drums her fingers on the table and leans forward. "Juliet, do you mind if I ask: when are you planning to return to London?"

"I don't know. I need to do some more here. I mean..." She gestures weakly at the room.

"And when is Declan due back?"

"Erm. I'm not sure actually."

"Well, you may think I'm overstepping the mark, but could Erica come out to be with you? Or you stay with her, in Inverness? You could come back as needed, to work on packing up. I'm concerned about you being here alone."

Christ. Is this another diagnosis by Karen Sutherland?

"Thank you, Karen. But as I've said before, I'm fine. I'll be done in a few days. As you can imagine, it's been rather difficult for all of us. But" – suddenly it's extremely clear what she has to do – "the summerhouse is going on the market, and we'll start to put it all behind us."

Karen turns and gazes through the window towards the sea. "I see. Well, I'm going to give you my direct number. I want you to call me if anything else unusual happens. Anything at all." She seems to hesitate. "I don't want to make promises, because it's not really my area, but given your situation, I've tried to put into place some extra... patrols."

Situation?

Karen continues, "I imagine you're preparing for your return to PA. To London." She pauses. "If that's what you're intending to do. Of course, I don't expect you to tell me. But you are a national figure now, as far as the media are concerned. And you're vulnerable out here, Juliet. Many people in your position would have security."

Juliet blinks. Unable to speak, she nods slowly in acquiescence. She should be grateful, but the reality of Karen's words overrides any sense of good grace or manners. Declan had said the same in his message. *She shouldn't be out here alone.*

CHAPTER FORTY-ONE

At dusk, Juliet drives out to the railway bridge and calls Declan for the seventh time since the clusterfuck at the Eden Club. She finally gets through. He sounds physically in a bad way, his voice is tight and adenoidal, and yet somehow they end up arguing again, this time about him playing things down, getting Lotta involved. About Juliet's reluctance to involve anyone, or ever ask for help.

"That's no true," she says. "I've told Karen. Pretty much everything. It's called using the proper channels. Not running around like a kid trying to prove my masculinity."

"For Christ's sake," Declan clears his throat. "That's not the proper channels. What the hell can Karen do anyway?"

"Don't. I was wrong about her. She's putting herself on the line."

"Oh, surprise, surprise. Another U-turn on who you trust. Another person you value more than me."

She sits in the car after he's hung up and cries properly, huge aching sobs, for the first time since Beth's funeral. Once the tears have passed, she stares expressionlessly at the red-brick bridge as night falls and it turns the colour of dried blood. She picks up the phone and calls Declan back. He answers straightaway but says nothing.

"Declan," she begins. "I'm sorry. I... Maybe we should just get back to London?" Her voice cracks. "This is madness."

For a moment, he doesn't reply and her stomach turns with her old fear of her father's disapproval, of male disapprobation.

Then – "Is that what you want?" Before she has a chance to respond Declan continues, "Is it? Look, you were right about these sick bastards. Marcus is onto something foul here, and he's relying on me. And besides… After what I've seen, been through, I'm not letting it go."

"In that case, I'm coming there, to you."

His voice rises. "You can't come here, Jet. I'm holed up in a fucking caravan. It's freezing, and you're… recovering still." His tone softens. "Anyway, my ribs wouldn't take the excitement."

Juliet laughs for the first time in a long time.

"Don't worry," she murmurs. "I can be gentle."

The signal bars on her mobile screen flicker. A moment of silent tenderness and desire pulses between them.

"Please be careful," she says finally.

"Don't worry about me, just take care of yourself. Pack up and get things sorted there. Listen to what Karen said. Go to Erica's."

She knows it's good advice and later takes Bucky and a small crate of Beth's things with her to Erica's on the pretext of going through it together. On the almost deserted A96, a dark car pulls out of the lay-by and tails her at a steady distance as she glances repeatedly in the rear-view mirror with growing alarm. It's not until she reaches her exit and the car peels away, that she recalls Karen's promise of extra patrols. She came good then.

It's past ten when she arrives, and she and Erica sit up into the early hours going through treasures and reminiscing. Erica has read the papers and Juliet has to lie to her about what Declan and Lotta were doing in Manchester. She makes up a story about promotion for Lotta's book, strings out one small glass of wine, and tries her best to dodge Erica's questioning glances.

***

Early next morning, she lies in a hormonal funk on the sofa, Bucky on the floor beside her, and listens to Erica stirring and grumbling to herself about going to work. Reeds of late September sun begin to filter through the blinds and in the civilisation of the waking suburbs, things seem clearer, more sensible already, her questions, her priorities.

Digging into Max and Delta Function is not something that has to be done at all costs from up here on the north coast, and she's not about to let those pricks screw up her life with Declan. She should focus on answering any questions she can right now, and then head back to London to her job, her life.

Erica leaves for the office, and shortly afterwards Juliet showers, dresses and visits the medical section in the public library, where she checks what their take on the diatom test is. Infuriatingly, Karen's right. The science is much contested.

She searches in town for something to put on Beth's grave. A florist suggests a dried autumnal arrangement. They are fairly uninspiring, but she chooses one with little purple berries and sprayed coppery leaves.

The tears flow again for the second time in twenty-four hours as she crouches in front of Beth's headstone in the Petty Chapel yard and places the tribute carefully. She tries to talk to Beth – to that slender body in the cold earth below – but grief wells up in her throat and lungs and drowns the words. She sits on a bench with Bucky flat at her feet, until the cold makes her clenched teeth hurt.

She makes her way back to Inverness for a late lunch, caving to a sudden urge for meat and salt. At a café on the river, she sets up her laptop and, waiting for her burger and chips, drafts some crib notes for party activists. It's a relief to think about work. She spends some time personalising thank-you emails for messages of support, many from backbenchers and veterans jostling for influence and – presumably – position, should she become leader. There are a few event invitations from lobbyists, businesses and public bodies. One stands out. She blinks.

It's a Home Office email, from the Minister of State for Policing and the Fire Services.

He's new in post, aware of her activism on women and the criminal justice system. Juliet ponders. He's a potentially useful ally. His portfolio includes national police resources and reform, the independent police complaints commission, crime statistics and transparency.

He will be attending an event near Inverness, and wonders if it's an opportunity for them to meet. Today.

She looks at her watch.

CHAPTER FORTY-TWO

Ishtar waits at Cemetery Road tram stop, two streets away from the asylum centre.

Declan and Marcus drive by slowly. She makes no acknowledgement of them. "She's seen us," Marcus says.

They park on the other side of the road, about sixty metres away among parking spaces below a large block of flats. Declan attaches a large lens to his Canon, and prepares a shot of her against the plastic half-seats, her head covered, bent against the neon of the tram shelter. She's wearing a dark red headscarf, a long black skirt, trainers and a denim jacket. Her small woven bag hangs over her shoulder.

After about five minutes, a black Mercedes with dark windows pulls up into the stop. Ishtar gets in. Declan takes a burst of shots.

They follow the Merc as it covers the short distance to the northern quarter, rumbling through a cobbled, tree-lined square where the pubs are rammed with students.

Declan is surprised that the route heads directly past the steps of the Eden. It seems brazen somehow.

"Shit," murmurs Marcus.

A taxi stops ahead, blocking the road directly in front of the club, and although Marcus slows to a crawl he can't avoid pulling up directly behind the Mercedes. The crowd outside is even larger tonight. Finally, the cab pulls off, and so do they again. One of the doormen, a brick-shouldered, shaven-headed guy, seems to stare fixedly at their car as they pass. Declan looks hurriedly away.

The Eden Building fills the whole block. At the corner, the Mercedes takes a left. They follow. The Mercedes turns left again, into a smaller road at the back of the club where the private apartments are.

"That's it," Marcus murmurs. "We can't go down there. It's a private street. Can you get anything from here?" He pulls up on the right, on the main road.

Declan has to clamber over the seats into the back, but can see the Mercedes's brake lights. He quickly adjusts the shot and manages to capture Ishtar exiting the vehicle and disappearing between the pillared entrance of the apartment block.

Now they wait.

"Who the fuck *are* the guys they find to pick up these kids and bring them here?" Declan mutters. "How do they live with themselves?"

Marcus, still at the wheel, starts fiddling with the radio.

"I don't know. I guess some of them don't care. They need a job, money." The bluish light from the head unit catches the side of his face. "Maybe they do one or two errands, then before they know it, they're in. They find themselves one day so steeped in blood, they can't turn around and go back." He finds a soft rock station, and sits back, satisfied. "Maybe they know too much? If they make a move like they want to get out, they'll be next."

Declan nods. He'd forgotten how well Marcus understands people whose lives are way beyond the dirty fringes of the acceptable. He seems to have an affinity with them, without ever compromising himself.

"I think some of them even imagine they're somehow… some kind of protection. Ishtar says there's one who likes to talk to her. One of the drivers. He asks her if she's okay, holds her hand. That kind of stuff. Talks about how he could take her away."

"She's fourteen! He can't fucking take her away. He's as bad as them."

"Believe me. I don't think he's as bad as them. What they do to these kids..." He trails off. The soft rock track ends and another, sounding exactly the same to Declan, begins. Marcus taps his hand on his knee.

"And these *punters*, will they be there already? Or will we get the chance to catch one arriving?"

"We might. If we're lucky. Ishtar said it depends. Sometimes she arrives first, and there's a woman who greets—"

"A woman?"

"Oh, yeah. You don't think we men have the monopoly on being pigs do you?" Marcus starts fishing for his tobacco. "Sometimes there's already someone here when she arrives, or a group of them. And they're not punters by the way. Not Ishtar's punters. She might get the odd gift if she behaves herself, but she's not a prostitute. Her main mode of payment is not to end up in a ditch somewhere, like her friend."

Mist has begun falling around them. The streetlamps jut like matchsticks into the white vapour, appearing to prop up the heavy sky, like curtains in a strange theatre. Declan watches uneasily. Conditions like this won't make his job easy.

Marcus smokes.

"How long does it... will she be in there?" Declan asks.

"Can be quick. Half an hour sometimes, then they want rid. It's not as if they're going to have great conversation afterwards is it? Once she was nearly three hours."

"Oh, my fucking Lord in heaven."

"I don't think he's got much to do with it... for once."

Declan leans through the gap in the seat, and grips the radio dial.

"Sorry," he says. "but if there's any chance we're going to be here for that long, I'm not listening to this shite."

CHAPTER FORTY-THREE

Peter Blythe seems an unlikely person to reach out to PA on women's justice. But as an advocate of bipartisan working, Juliet must take the invitation at face value. After the stress of the last couple of days, it's a relief to think of work. She drives through Inverness and heads nine miles east on local roads to Finlochy.

On the way, she runs through everything she knows about Blythe. He may be new at the Home Office, but is far from a young dynamo. More a grandee. She remembers first hearing his name in the nineties when he helped to push through draconian welfare reforms.

Following that, he infamously left the government for a directorship in the private sector, before working in public prosecutions for a stretch, and later... she's not sure. He made a comeback in a safe Tory seat and at the outset of the refugee crisis, was all over the media, vocally criticising the border control failures. He landed his new job just a few weeks ago after the election. She wonders what he'll want to talk about, especially now that PA are weakened.

The car park is empty as she pulls up at the old hydro-electric station where the event is supposed to be taking place. She digs her phone out to check the address and date given in Blythe's email. This is definitely the right place. He said he'd be here addressing a twilight conference on policing and vulnerable groups.

The plant was decommissioned years ago, and since then, as far as Juliet knew, had been an Energy Museum, but there are pallets strewn around and the forecourt is surrounded by hoarding.

When she climbs out of the car she looks up, searching the sky for the plane that must be flying overhead, before realising the roar she hears is the river pounding through the old barriers. It's deafening.

She shivers, gives Bucky's ears a ruffle and locks up the car. Laptop bag over her shoulder, she walks over to the temporary fence and peers into the site.

About two hundred metres away, on the other side of a mound of grass, she can see a large main building, and further back, a clutch of old red-and-white clad structures and halos of light. Perhaps she's at the wrong entrance? She steps over the concrete footing of the metal fence and squeezes through the gap between two panels.

But, crossing the grass, she realises the lights she spotted are merely security lights on the other side of the building. She glances around apprehensively. The whole site is deserted and dark is falling and it's unnerving, not to mention how embarrassing it would be to default on the invitation now that she's replied to say she's on her way. Blythe is renowned for his urbane, old-school approach, and is reportedly impatient with poor manners.

To the right, the dam's rickety wooden platforms and concrete buttresses straddle a section of the Beauly; the water high and glassy on one side; pouring violently through disused sluices on the other. On her left, giant leadlight windows stare at her blankly from the main stone building. Studding its façade, the great iron wheels that once controlled the water flow to the turbines are now motionless.

Behind her, a car swings into the entrance, and parks across it, blocking it. Juliet watches, her racing heart punching her ribs. *What the hell is going on?*

Blythe exits from the rear. He straightens his jacket and lifts his head. Catching sight of Juliet standing on the rising ground near the river, he turns and says something to his chauffeur, then strides towards her. He's tall and thin, in his late fifties, and elegantly dressed in a tailored pin-stripe suit and expensive-looking ox-blood shoes.

Juliet has a sudden impulse to run, but where would she go?

"Juliet. How do you do? How very nice to meet you. Peter Blythe."

They shake hands. Blythe runs his fingers through his thin, wavy blond hair. His face is pale and freckled.

"I'm so sorry about the mix-up. There are two other hydro plants on the Beauly. My assistant… It doesn't matter. Anyway, I'm very glad I've found you. I thought it would be worth just checking if you were here. I appreciate you waiting around."

"No, of course. I've just arrived."

"Shall we explore?" He runs a finger around his collar but doesn't remove his tie. "I'd rather like to look at the water. I've been stuck in cars and an overheated conference room most of the day."

Juliet just about hides her reluctance. "Sure."

Side by side they stroll towards a footbridge on stilts over a section of the dam. Rusty reinforcing rods jut out from broken concrete slabs at its base. Alongside them, an aged cast-iron manufacturer's plaque glints dully: Carrick & Quick.

Blythe sashays surprisingly jauntily up the steps and emits a loud exhalation at the top before filling his lungs through his nose. Juliet hesitates slightly, before gritting her teeth and following him. The river churns noisily below her, visible through gaps in the iron steps.

Blythe leans back on the guardrail which rocks disconcertingly, but he doesn't seem to notice. "I expect you're wondering about my request to meet, so let's get straight to the point. Juliet, I've followed your career with interest, and I'd like to ask you to head up an independent review of women's experiences of the justice system."

Juliet raises her eyebrows.

It's a totally unexpected proposition, to say the least. She thinks fast. It would be a solid public platform at a time when PA desperately needs a credibility boost. But it would also be a vast distraction from the task of rebuilding the party.

She hedges. "You're talking about a huge remit. I'm not sure I'm qualified. And I'm certainly not independent."

"Nonsense. I can't think of anyone fitter for the job. Anyway, you wouldn't be working alone, you'd be pulling together a team."

Juliet turns to face the dammed side of the Beauly, her hand lightly seeking out the wobbly rail. The water near the far bank, polished and green, reflects the dusky trees above – a fringe of two-headed pines, like purulent cotton buds.

Something isn't right. Why would Blythe have sought her out?

"I wasn't aware there was a review in the offing," she says. "Isn't there an approval process?"

"Ah. Nominations," he says dismissively. "It's all perfectly straightforward."

"Isn't this a parliamentary matter?"

"Of course, but" – he bristles momentarily. A spike of ego – "I am perfectly at liberty to commission work as well."

Then the civility returns. "Listen, I know your interest in women's justice goes beyond party lines, Juliet. It's time to come out of your ghetto, if you don't mind me saying. I've seen too many good minds go rancid, raking away at conspiracy theories and personal interests."

"I'm not sure I follow you."

"Oh, come on now. Look, this is sensitive, I realise, but I'm a straight-talker, and well, it's come to my attention that resources are being diverted back into the enquiry around your niece's death." He pauses. "A closed enquiry."

A straight-talker. Juliet watches a bird circling above the treeline. In her experience, people who claim to be straight-talkers are the most slippery. How has Blythe found out about the minuscule bit of digging Karen's been doing, and why would he care? He has oversight of national police operations and resources. He can't possibly be able to swoop down on such localised activity, can he? There's no need for her to defend herself or Karen quite yet though; the man's still talking.

"… all of which I have no objection to of course, but some people might look at it rather askance. The political classes can't be seen to be giving each other's private agendas too much credence or special treatment, I'm sure you understand. That would be damaging – and more for you than for us, I have to say. That is, of course, if it were to come to light."

What a complete shit. Who's sent him here to lean on her? Juliet murmurs something non-committal.

"Just before we go on," he says. "May I ask: are you out here alone?"

Juliet frowns at him. "Why?"

He wears an innocuous, smiling mask. "It's just that I'm aware the local beat has been providing some additional security for you, which again is somewhat, how shall I say, irregular? You're not an elected official after all. You're here in Inverness as a private citizen, aren't you? Visiting family?"

"Yes."

"You can see how all this would look, I'm sure." He shakes his head. "The press can turn the most well intentioned among us into pariahs."

Turning around now to face the water, he puts almost his full weight into the railing. The walkway shudders as he shifts. He chuckles and grabs and shakes the balustrade.

"This thing really is quite a safety hazard, isn't it? They should cordon it off. But then I shouldn't imagine for a second that they're expecting anyone to be out here on site. It's hardly the sort of place where you get passers-by."

It's a masterclass in intimidation. Juliet edges away from him and stands squarely in the middle of the platform. Blythe looks out at the water. His tone becomes harder.

"Do you know what I learned today? I learned they had problems out here from the get-go. Wrong location. The water becomes supercooled this low in the stream. You get slush or slurry or something. All it takes is one little impurity, one little grain of contamination somewhere and the whole system grinds to a standstill. You'd think they'd have done their homework, wouldn't you?" He stares at the far verge, then swivels towards where the cars are parked. He raises a long arm and waves. "But I expect you know all this already, being a local girl." Behind them the river continues coursing, spewing through the sluice gates. "I'm a big fan of doing my homework, Juliet."

She doesn't reply. He offers her his hand again. She looks at it, a sinewy, liver-spotted wedge of flesh.

He smiles and withdraws the gesture. "I should get going I'm afraid. I'd rather hoped I could persuade you. Such a shame to waste political talent like yours."

She braces as he pats her on the shoulder. "I shouldn't spend too long out here. I expect it attracts some rather unsavoury types at night."

He quickly descends the steps and crosses the grass, glancing left and right. Juliet stands on the bridge and peers over to the hydroplant car park. As Blythe retreats, a man, dressed in a black tracksuit, exits the car. The two exchange a few words and the tracksuit seems to glance up at her.

Juliet looks over her shoulder. A jagged hole in the bridge's ironwork about seven metres behind her prohibits fleeing to the other side.

She flies back down the steps, but, reaching the bottom, turns right away from the cars, her footsteps accelerating into a run. She doesn't stop to look back.

CHAPTER FORTY-FOUR

After an hour, the fog has worsened. Declan and Marcus can still see just about four car lengths ahead, but further than that is a struggle.

"This isn't good," Declan says, repeatedly. "I can't see this being any good." He fidgets with his camera settings, and the air conditioning in Marcus's car, anxious to ensure a clean line of sight. "This really isn't good."

"For fuck's sake!" Marcus eventually blurts out. "Have you never had to wait for anything before?"

"Alright, keep your hair on," Declan replies. He eyes Marcus. "Sorry, but… I'm not going to be able to get a shot from here. It's useless. We might as well not be here."

"We're staying. When she comes out of there, Ishtar will be looking for our car. We're not going anywhere."

"No. I'm not suggesting that. But I could get out. Get nearer. I could get a shot from down the street. Look, no one's going to see me in this weather, are they? I'll hide between two cars or something."

"Mmm," Marcus is unconvinced. He hesitates, clenches and unclenches his fists. "*Shit*. Okay. Go for it. But get back here as soon as you've got the shot." Declan opens the car door. "And, Declan?" Marcus hisses. "Don't get seen."

Declan crouches awkwardly with the camera dangling heavily around his neck. He holds it against his chest and runs, keeping low, across the road to the private street where the Eden building apartments are. For a moment, a thrill goes through him; it's like being immersed in a boyhood fantasy. He could be a spy or a war photographer. There's a shallow kerb and private parking along one side of the bricked road, and a line of trees on the other. Cold damp particles cling to his forehead. It's not a fantasy, of course, but… it feels meaningful. More significant than his other work. No offence to Lotta, but taking photographs of cooked cheese is not why he left his cosy job with his old boss.

He stands beneath a sodden tree about twenty-five metres from the door Ishtar entered. There's a spot across the road, between two cars – a massive Audi and what looks like a Tesla – which he runs for, and crouches, panting, the Audi's number plate pressing into his back.

After twenty minutes of shifting position, Declan lies prostrate in the gutter in front of the Tesla, behind the Audi's rear tyre. His shirt jacket and the front of his trousers are soaked through, but at least he has a clean frame of the apartment.

The door opens. A woman in her late fifties opens it and pokes her head out. Declan is ready. He gets her face. The car waiting in front of the apartment starts its engine. The woman opens an umbrella and holds it out. Ishtar steps beneath it. Declan lets out a snuff of breath. *A fucking umbrella. Is she supposed to feel cared for?* He takes three shots.

Ishtar gets in the car which pulls out of its space, does a three-point turn and heads back up the street. Declan stays put. He checks the apartment door has closed, before stumbling back, in his amateur commando style, to Marcus, who has the engine running.

"Done," he says breathlessly. "I got it. I got the bitch's face."

Marcus nods. He looks more stressed than pleased. "Let's just hope Ishtar's got the goods too."

"Yeah," Declan says, still on a high. "But at least we've got something, right? I mean, this is evidence," he taps the camera. "Right here."

Marcus keeps a safe distance behind the Mercedes. Its brake lights fan out in the damp air, like starbursts. "It's the time stamps that are really important," he says. "The time stamps on her footage, combining with your pictures. That's what proves what happened to her tonight. In a sequence. What year it is. How old she is. Everything."

Declan applies his mind to these dry technicalities. At least someone is focused. Not playing at heroics. He reminds himself: *Marcus has been working at this for months. Don't fuck it up.*

It seems to be going to plan though. As expected, the Mercedes almost seems to coast the short distance back to Cemetery Road where Ishtar was collected earlier.

"Right," Marcus says, "She's going to get out of the car, go to the tram stop and wait. Once the driver's pulled away, I go across and she hands over the bag. I want you to get it on camera: Ishtar getting out, the handover. How close do you need to be?"

Declan considers.

"Twenty metres?"

"Really?"

"Yep."

"Okay. I'll see how close I can get. You might have to improvise. We shouldn't have to wait too long. Unless it's the driver who likes to chat with her."

Declan frowns. "Bit of a risk? Just handing over the bag in the tram stop?"

"It's a quiet road. Look, Ishtar can't carry it around, or take it back to the centre. That would be worse."

By this time, they're on Cemetery Road. The tram stop is four hundred metres ahead, occupying the central reservation. Marcus pulls right, into a park-and-ride lane off the main drag, crawling past a never-ending fleet of cars, below the back of an office block. There are no spaces. Declan glances up at the building. Most of the windows are empty and black, or glimmering with the faint blue of forgotten computer monitors.

Marcus slows to avoid driving alongside the Mercedes. They are separated only by the row of parked cars. Finally, he pulls into a free space and lets out a scratchy breath. He kills the engine and the headlights. "Right. Okay?"

"Yup, fine." Declan mutters. In fact, it couldn't be any better. The Merc pulls up about twenty metres away. Its rear passenger door opens and Ishtar's foot emerges. She stands, and glances up and down the street.

"She's looking for us," Marcus says. "She doesn't know if we're here."

Declan takes a test shot, and adjusts a setting, keeping his head down. Ishtar's face is shadowed by the red scarf still. he takes a burst, the camera impossibly loud to his ears. He zooms in on the little woven bag hanging over her shoulder. She walks to the bus stop, and perches on the seat.

The Mercedes doesn't move.

"What's he doing? Why doesn't he go?" Declan mutters, but there's no reply from Marcus. He's already out of the car and walking towards the bus stop. Afterwards, Declan realises he didn't even hear the car door closing.

The Mercedes still has not driven away. Is the driver watching them? Declan's heart quickens as Marcus approaches the shelter. *At least sit a couple of seats away from her. Or, better still, stand. Just stand.* But Marcus sits down right next to Ishtar. She stares straight ahead.

The Mercedes driver opens his car door, and emerges from the car, drawing himself up to his full height. The impossible mass of him stands, silhouetted, almost blotting out the envelope of light cast from a street lamp to the ground. He's already taken two steps before Declan sees he's holding a long, narrow object. A baseball bat perhaps? An iron bar? Declan takes a picture, and a kind of fascination comes over him. The guy doesn't smack the thing repeatedly into his palm like a film villain straining at the edge of self-control.

He has the confidence of someone who knows this is going to be uncomplicated.

For a second, he seems almost to stare straight at Declan. With his free hand, he reaches into a belt pack and retrieves a smaller piece, which he appears to check… and arm. Declan takes another picture, camera on the dash to keep it steady in the low light. He can't use a flash. He hardly dares breathe. Should he start up the engine? *Get out of there, Marcus. Get up and start walking. Now.*

Ishtar rises. She looks at the driver, and starts walking, quickly, but not too hurriedly, down the street. She still has the bag. She hasn't given it to Marcus. *What the fuck is going on? Has she sold them out?*

The guy walks towards the shelter where Marcus has, at last, got to his feet. It's a saunter… a slow, purposeful stroll with the most brutal intent. Good. Slow movement is better. Declan takes another photograph. He expects the driver to shout, to order Marcus to stay where he is, but apparently, such courtesies are in short supply.

Only now does Marcus start walking, but he doesn't head back towards Declan and the waiting car. *Is he trying to lead the guy away? Going after Ishtar?* She's already a hundred and fifty meters off.

Marcus breaks into a little run, and his shoes slip on the slick tarmac. The guy is on him before he's had the chance to pick himself up. There's no chance to call out. Declan flinches and involuntarily emits a whimper as the driver raises his arm and delivers a catastrophic crack to the back of Marcus's skull.

The car door handle is right there, next to Declan's hand. He should get out. He should shout. He should at least try – but he doesn't. He doesn't move a finger, except quite literally, to keep taking pictures. He breathes hard, taking shot after shot.

Marcus's knees surrender, putting him at the perfect height for the next blow, across his face this time. Fluids from Marcus's nose and mouth jettison into the air, dotted with

– yes, those are teeth – two teeth. The attack is relentless. Marcus rolls up on his side, arms over his head. Finally, the guy puts his foot on Marcus's face, grinding it into the ground, and – at this, at last – Declan opens his passenger door.

He keeps his head low, placing the camera back around his neck as he squats between their car and the one next to it. He's too far away to hear the full sickening crunch and suck of Marcus's elbow being broken as it's twisted behind him. He does hear a scream though. He pokes his head up above the car's bonnet and takes another volley of frames.

At this point, Declan is still capable of noting that he's been witnessing this from a place just beside himself, like the viewfinder on his old camera which showed an image a few millimetres shy of the real thing. You hear on the news about people being beaten unconscious. He's sometimes wondered what special kind of motivation it takes to do that to another human? The world is shifting now – he's moving inside the true lens – and the answer is just a few metres away.

It won't take long, and unconsciousness is not the endgame, not for these people. This guy is going to kill Marcus. If he hasn't already.

Another scream. Declan cringes pathetically. He glances at the black hole of the offices above. If anyone is still inside working, they'll be glued to their screens, earphones in, seeing and hearing nothing. It's up to him. If he doesn't do something…

The driver kicks Marcus's head like a locked door. Declan pumps three deep breaths into his lungs and pulls himself shakily up to his full height. But something tugs at his jacket, from behind, yanking him back down. He turns, instinctively ducking behind his wrists for protection, expecting another Eden thug.

It's Ishtar.

CHAPTER FORTY-FIVE

Ishtar still has the bag, with the recording inside. She must have doubled back around the block. Crouched on the damp ground between the cars, she hisses at Declan.

"We go. We need to go."

Declan nods, glancing back across the car bonnet, to the crumpled shape of Marcus writhing near the tram shelter, just as another salvo of kicks comes his way. How is he even still moving? Declan remembers the weapon he thought he saw earlier.

"Does that guy have a gun?" he whispers.

"Yes," Ishtar glares at him. "We go. I have video."

Declan nods again. He knows she's right, but her clear-headedness is disturbing.

"Go and wait around the corner. Far away." he says to Ishtar.

"No, please. Please." He can hear her voice catching with emotion.

"I will come and get you, but if that guy comes over here… He mustn't see you. You understand?"

She slides her hand into his. Her skin is strangely warm and dry. She's trembling. "Please. You take me. I come with you. If something happen to you, I dead. Please."

Fuck.

He darts another look towards the shelter, and imagines

driving straight over, mounting the small strip of pavement, crossing the Cemetery Road tram tracks, and ploughing the brute down. It would be the only way. The guy's as big as a moose.

He nudges Marcus now with his foot, enjoying the fruits of his labour no doubt. And as Declan squints to see Marcus's response, a coldness comes over him, an emptiness in the base of his spine that he knows will never go away.

The guy is waiting for Marcus die.

The fog is thinning now and a kind of coagulation, a pale dense form, appears in the middle distance. A familiar jangling rings out, and a large oblong comes into sight: blue and cream, and possibly the most gladdening thing Declan has ever laid eyes on. The tram.

Thank Christ. This idiot won't shoot Marcus in plain sight of the driver and the passengers. Will he?

Marcus lies inert. The guy bends and checks his pulse, then drops his wrist and, inexplicably gently, reaches under his armpits and begins dragging him across the ground. He stops after just a few metres and stands back.

Declan frowns, puzzling. His jeans scuff against grit and chewing gum as he shuffles closer, and suddenly it hits him: bait. The guy is using Marcus as bait. He's dumped him across the tram tracks. If Declan tries to get over there before the tram crushes Marcus, he'll give himself away; give both him and the girl up.

In those few seconds of distraction, the Merc driver has crossed the street towards them and disappeared. Declan edges past Ishtar on his hands and knees, and peers around the exhaust pipe, along the series of parked cars. About 100 metres away – with leisurely, deliberate footsteps – the guy walks the row, pausing to inspect each vehicle, making his way nearer. There's a dark object in his right hand.

"Declan," Ishtar whispers, and suddenly he can hear Juliet's voice too. *Focus. Think it through.*

Juliet alone in the summerhouse. He wishes he'd told her he knew about the baby before he left.

Think it through.

This decision: it will be the worst thing he has ever done. The tram is close now.

Focus.

He tries to visualise where the car's ignition is. It's electric. He hopes the keys are still in the car. If not, if the keys are in Marcus's pocket across the street, the car won't start. And they won't be able to lock themselves in either. Plus, they're on the passenger side. He's going to have to clamber across the front seat.

The guy's footsteps are audible now.

Make a choice.

The night's mist is vanishing up through thin trapezoids created by the tramline's catenary wire. He wonders whether Marcus can hear the trolley-car descending; whether he sees the same partitioned sky. And suddenly it's too late; not making a choice has become a choice, and taking no action has become an action, and the tram smashes into Marcus's body and erupts into a clattering, squawking of brakes, drowning out everything apart from the imperative to move.

Under cover of the chaos, Declan speaks. "Get in."

Ishtar doesn't hesitate. They open the front and rear passenger doors simultaneously. Declan hauls himself into the driver's seat and presses the electric ignition. The engine whirs almost noiselessly into life, and the doors lock with an anodyne click. *Fucking hybrid. What they need is a monster truck, not this yoghurt pot*. That guy could probably punch his way through these doors in seconds. Declan engages reverse and, hardly looking, accelerates backwards, hoping he hits the fuck.

They reach the junction where the park-and-ride meets the main road, the tram's alarm wailing into the damp air, uniting now with passengers' shouts and cries. People spill out of the tram; a man runs to the side of the road to vomit. Declan's eyes fill with tears.

"We go," Ishtar repeats urgently.

The Merc driver is sprinting towards them, arms like huge pistons at his side. His enormous face looms in the rear window, and the tips of his fingers grapple at the door handle. Ishtar screams. Declan puts his foot to the floor, and drives.

CHAPTER FORTY-SIX

Juliet hides, her back to the wall of the old pump house. She's pretty sure Blythe left some time ago; she heard a car start up and sweep away, but the other guy in the tracksuit? She has no idea where he is, and she's not voluntarily about to find out.

She listens intently and hears nothing but the wind playing through the old hydroplant like an instrument.

She needs to make it to her car, but every time she considers doubling back, she changes her mind. If she were trying to accost someone, the car's exactly where she'd wait.

She could try to slip through the woods to the road. Walk back to Inverness. But it would mean nine miles on foot, along dark back routes, at risk of being lit up like a cruise ship if she's caught in headlights. It would make an unusual and tragic end.

MACGILLIVRAY THROWS HERSELF UNDER CAR ON LONE NIGHT WALK.

In the first weeks after Beth's death, she read hundreds of articles about suicides and unexplained deaths. The spy who was deemed to have committed suicide zipped inside a sports bag. The weapons expert who went out into the woods to slash his wrists. If cases like that can be labelled suicide, anything can. She knows now, if something happens to her, if she's silenced out here, it will be filed away as a tragic inability to cope with her recent political losses, her grief over Beth and Erica's illness.

Maybe even something to do with the pregnancy.

Her stomach is killing her. She was gripped by vice-like cramps almost as soon as Blythe led the way onto that bridge.

She reaches into her bag and checks her phone for a signal. It's feeble. She keeps hoping she'll be able to call someone, anyone, Declan, Karen, Toby. For the dozenth time, she makes sure the device is silenced and not about to betray her. Before long, its battery will be out anyway.

CHAPTER FORTY-SEVEN

"I had the plate checked," Paul says. It's nearly 2am. He stands before Bernhard Palmer's large oak desk in the office at the back of the Eden apartments, crossing and uncrossing his massive, bloodied knuckles behind his back. "The car was registered to Marcus Keyes. A journalist, independent, registered with the NUJ."

Palmer's double chin and left jowl overlap flabbily on his strangely smooth fist. He lifts his eyes and, from beneath massive grey-blond eyebrows, studies Paul.

Drivers. Security. Imbeciles most of them, and this one appears no different. Used to be uniform before… a death in custody, wasn't it? Still. Police contacts, and a nasty temper. Not an unhelpful combination. But where the hell is this moron's initiative, when there are guests downstairs and Drappier on ice? Palmer swivels his chair and looks onto the neat illuminated shrubs in the courtyard below.

Paul tries on the room like an uncomfortable outfit, watched over by a portrait of a heavy-lidded old man; Palmer's father-in-law. The green light from the garden catches on Palmer's bulbous nose, improving his complexion momentarily.

"He'd been spotted a couple of times, sir. Talking to her. We thought he worked at the Centre. He drank at

Hemming's. We were keeping an eye on him. And then tonight he followed us—"

"Stop." Palmer doesn't turn. Paul notes how he keeps his voice low, measured. "I don't need a fucking dissertation. You took care of him, didn't you?"

"Yes. He's out of the picture."

That's something at least.

"But the point is, sir," Paul coughs. "Where is she? They took her."

Palmer lays his pudgy hands one over the other now, and stares at Paul.

"Oh. That's the point, is it?"

Does this klutz have some kind of crush? An attachment to the girl? Palmer examines his fingernails, ignoring Paul's agitation, however amusing it is. "You're sure she was in the car?"

"Yeah, it was her. She's gone. She's not been back to the Centre. We know that much. Taj is there covering it."

"And?" *Christ, it's like spoon-feeding a baby*. This guy came highly recommended by Blythe, wasn't it? But this is embarrassing. "Who was at the wheel then? If Keyes is dead? She wasn't fucking driving herself, I imagine?"

Paul shifts slightly from one foot to the other. "There was another guy. We've seen him with Keyes twice in the last week. Looked in a bad way. The girl in Hemming's said he's called Declan."

Palmer lowers his voice further. "What did you say?"

"The bar girl in Hemming's. She said Keyes called him Declan. That's all we've got."

A glass ashtray, heavy and ovate, edges curved and fluted obscenely to receive a fat cigar, sits to the right of the puce leather desktop. Palmer absently runs his fingers over it. He picks it up, weighing it in his hand.

"Are you telling me it was Declan Byrne, the same guy Lyall had here the other night? Came in with that cookery lesbian bitch?"

Paul looks stunned and puzzled for a second. “I wasn’t here that night, sir.”

Palmer slams the ashtray down onto the desk so hard that its corner leaves a crescent moon groove in the leather. He opens a cigar case, takes one, and runs it slowly under his nose to calm himself. Cohiba. Sun-cooked earth, cocoa and tarmac.

Palmer goes over it again. *There’s no way this is all just a set of chance happenings*. Morgan and this Byrne in the club. Now, Byrne stalking around town, *with a fucking journalist*.

A dead journalist.

They should have seen to Byrne too, while they had the chance. *Christ. Lyall let him go*. Thought it was enough to put the shits up him. He’s always been a soft negotiator.

“They were heading south out of the city, you said?”

“Looked like it. The number plate has been tracked on the M56.”

Palmer opens the desk drawer, looking for a cigar cutter. He finds his double-blade guillotine next to a pad and a pile of receipts. He speaks very slowly.

“Paul, that’s your name, isn’t it? If you were Byrne and you suddenly landed yourself responsible for a young girl, what would you do?”

Paul blushes. He looks at his feet. “I don’t know. Head to the nearest safe place? A woman’s house?”

“A woman’s house,” Palmer repeats. He raises his thick eyebrows. “Byrne’s friend Morgan has an apartment in Liverpool, doesn’t she?”

Paul shrugs. ‘I’m not sure, sir.’

“Okay. Here’s what you’re going to do, Paul. Follow them. I’ll get you the address.”

“I can put the word out. I’ll find them. I’ll find her.”

“Yes,” says Palmer. “I was told I could trust you.” He eyes the guillotine. He’s too old for histrionics. Despises them. He takes a different tack. “You’re divorced, aren’t you, Paul?”

Paul nods, blinking. “When I lost my job.”

"And how's your boy?"

Paul shakes his head, but the truth comes spilling out of his mouth. "She doesn't let me see him."

"Well, we can arrange to put that right for you. Make her reconsider." Palmer moves the guillotine suggestively, a few millimetres are enough.

Paul nods. "Thank you, sir."

He doesn't sound all that grateful. Perhaps it's better just to double up. Be sure. He knows Paul prefers working alone. "Pick up Taj, will you?" he says. "Take him with you."

Paul stares straight ahead. "What do you want us to do when we find them?"

"Make it look like an accident. A fire, a car crash. Don't take any chances on anyone. We don't know what Byrne's got or who he's told."

"A robbery gone wrong?"

"That sounds lovely," Palmer replies. He picks up the guillotine, slides the cap end of the Cohiba into it and makes a clean cut.

CHAPTER FORTY-EIGHT

Crossing the Mersey Gateway, Ishtar leans forward and lifts her eyes to the tall, semi-fan stay-cables rising above the structure. The bridge feels like a lodestone, suspended in the air, searching the compass. A mile or so later, Declan pulls off the main road and finds a service station.

The night air at the suburban roadside smells of ice and fuel. He fills the car up. Then he taps on the passenger window and Ishtar winds it down.

"I'm going to make a call," he says, gesturing to his phone. "I've got friends we can go to." He walks to the edge of the forecourt, and dials Lotta's number, glancing up and down the dark road. There's a boarded-up pub on the other side called The Good Companion. Billows of freezing fog from the river are the only sign of movement for now.

There's no answer for several rings. He imagines Lotta hobbling with her bandaged thigh to the big kitchen table in Sophie's apartment, where she's probably left her phone. Or maybe she's avoiding contact with him. She was quiet when Sophie came to collect her from the hospital. He'd assumed it was because her leg was hurting as much as his head and ribs. She was probably cursing him for getting her into this whole nightmare.

Finally, she picks up.

"Hello, Declan."

"Lotta. I… Are you okay?"

"Yes. I'm fine. I was asleep. It's two-thirty. What's going on?"

His voice is shakier than he would like. "I need to come to yours. There's been… I've got… one of the girls is with me. I don't know what to do. Can we—"

Lotta interrupts. "Where's Marcus? I suppose he's dumped you in it again?"

"Marcus is dead."

Lotta is silent for a few seconds. He thinks he hears her swallow. "How?"

"I can't… Listen, I can't tell you now. No time. I'm sorry I got you into this. I don't know what else to do. I've got this girl with me. She's run away from them. I just got in the car and drove. If we can just come to yours…"

"Where are you now?"

"Not far. We've just crossed the Mersey at Widnes."

"Are you being followed?"

"No. Not right now. I don't think so. I don't know."

"Go to the cottage."

"What?"

"Don't come here. They know who we both are. Marcus was crystal clear with me. You can't come here. Go to the cottage. Follow the signs to Ruthin."

Declan looks back at the car. Ishtar is watching him.

"Can you remember how to get there?"

Declan hesitates. "I think so."

"Have you got a satnav? I'll send you the coordinates. It's the A494. Hang on, let me check." He hears her fumbling and swiping, looking at a map on her phone. "Yes. You should recognise the pub at Loggerheads. There's a key under the stone on the step of the hut. I'll come out to you. I'll probably be there before you with any luck. I'll light a fire. And bring food. Does she need clothes? Do you need anything?"

Thank God for Lotta.

"Yes. No. Don't worry about me." His whole body is quaking now. "Just food, yes. That would be good."

"Okay. Drive safely."

"Lotta?"

"Yes?"

"Thank you."

He glances across the forecourt at Ishtar in the passenger seat of the car, who's twisting, looking back at the main road. He turns and follows her gaze. Was that a car? Headlights rounding a corner? Lotta's words hang in the cold air. *They know who we both are. You can't come here.*

He thinks about Juliet in the summerhouse. Eden's thugs are bound to go there now, aren't they? He's got no way of speaking to her if she's still stuck there, and any message he leaves at this stage is going to be terrifying. But he's got to try.

He goes straight through to voicemail.

"Juliet." He pauses. What the fuck is he going to say? That Marcus is dead? He's driving through the night taking an abuse victim to a safe house? "I'm… I want you to know I'm okay, but… listen to me, it's not safe. I'm getting out of the city and I'll call you again soon. You need to understand. It's not safe. Do you hear me? You shouldn't be at the summerhouse by yourself. Get to Erica's if you haven't already. And… I don't know… keep the dog with you."

He hangs up. Going to Inverness, to the city, will be safer, won't it? Yet it's the opposite of his current plan.

He can hear an approaching car now. It's surprising how quiet a suburban night can be; there are no other sounds other than the keen susurration of wheels on tarmac. He runs to Marcus's Toyota, starts the engine, and without turning on the lights, drives it forward a few metres, to the side of the service building where it's partially hidden from the road.

Ishtar looks at him, worried. "I need to go bathroom," she says.

"Right. I don't think you can here. They'll be locked up."

"Is okay. I go outside."

"Just wait," Declan says desperately. She can't get out of the car now. "Hang on two seconds."

The car sweeps by, and Declan breathes again. Ishtar opens the door and makes her way into the bushes at the back of the pub on the other side of the road. This is madness. There has to be a better way than this insanity. How long before the next set of headlights are upon them? And even when they get to the hut, what then? What next? Are they all going to stay in hiding forever?

Ishtar seems to take a long time. He searches the dark hedge for movement but there's none. He's about to open the car door and shout her name, when she reappears, walking calmly, brushing her hands on her jeans.

She's been living this life, of transition, no stability or security, since she left home… since before then. He thinks about the last hour they've spent together, side by side in silence, in the car. He knows nothing about her, and he hasn't asked her a thing about herself, her family or background… her hopes for the future. He's acted as if this experience – living in that Centre, the abuse – defines her.

She climbs back into the car. "We go?" she asks.

Her favourite question.

CHAPTER FORTY-NINE

Twice Juliet has heard him, patrolling, looking for her.

Crouching in a small hole beneath the level of the path, where a sunken window gives daylight to the hydroplant's basement, she makes up her mind to make a call before she or her battery dies. She cautiously raises her head to check she has no company, and heaves herself out of the space.

Earlier, running from the bridge, she'd passed an ancient service ladder to the roof. If she can get up there, she may improve her chances of a signal, and she'll have an overview of the terrain. High ground. She might even be able to use the keys to the car to create a distraction. Get Bucky barking.

But she'll be trapped if anyone follows her up there.

Leaving her bag, but taking her phone and car keys, she creeps around the side of the building, staying in the shadows, and quickly finds the ladder. It runs fifteen metres up the three-storey building, and has a hooped cage around it to stop anyone toppling backwards if they miss their footing.

It's rusty and she wonders briefly how old it is, how secure its bolts and rivets are. It wobbles when tugged and produces a faint metallic ringing sound. She's going to have to remove her shoes to avoid being heard. Another pair of shoes left, like a breadcrumb trail.

She prises off her boots, hides them in the shadows, and starts climbing.

She usually has a head for heights but it's not long before she feels giddy, unable to look down, yet desperate to check no one is watching. She focuses on each hand, moving each foot – slick with nylon – in time as she grips the cold rungs. The trick is a steady rhythm but, as she ascends, the ladder begins to vibrate; to her ears it must clamour her presence. She tries to slow down, painfully placing each foot as gently as she can on the ironwork. It seems to take for ever.

At the top, she scrambles breathlessly on her knees onto flat, rough concrete. There's no moonlight. It takes a while for Juliet's eyes to adjust. The roof is a dull grey, littered with a discarded roll of barbed wire, a huge bitumen tin, cans and bottles – the remnants of industry and trespassing kids and the homeless.

She gets to her feet, ducking as low as she can behind the squat parapet, and makes her way to the other edge, avoiding a giant hole in the roof's surface that drops directly into the floor below. Her car is alone, in darkness. Bucky, inside, is invisible at this distance.

Her phone has hardly any charge, but just enough signal for a message alert to have appeared. *Declan*. Treading carefully, peering at the surroundings below, she listens to the fear and shock in his voice, hardly hearing his actual words.

But before Declan finishes, a harsh ringing sounds out in the night. Someone is climbing the ladder, heavily, rapidly, and they don't care if she knows it.

She looks quickly around, backing away, towards the roll of wire. There's nowhere to hide.

She reaches for her keys and grips their metal shafts between her fingers like some kind of Kubotan, all the while the footsteps nearing the top of the ladder.

She sees a shadow first.

"What do you want?" she calls out. He looks young. Maybe it's just the way he's dressed. The hoodie. The trainers. "Whatever you've you been told, you don't have to do it. There's always a choice."

No reply. He glances sharply left and right, then simply charges straight at her.

She grabs for the wire, and attempts to haul it between them. The roll is heavier than she thought and its barbs tear at her skin, catching at her fingers, still entwined in the keys. The car, down in the car park, beeps and flashes, locking and unlocking. She hears Bucky barking faintly.

Whether it's any one of those things that seizes his concentration just in those milliseconds, Juliet will never know, but he fails to see the pit in the rooftop before him. Too late he tries to leap it, and with a single gasped expletive, disappears, legs first, the back of his head smacking loudly against the jagged concrete edge on the way down.

CHAPTER FIFTY

By the time she's completed her paperwork in the corner of the staff room, a familiar, dizzying sensation sets into Sophie's neck and scalp. She reaches over her shoulders and grips each one in turn, as if she's hanging onto the edge of a building, squeezing to release the tension. Before she leaves, she checks one last time on a late-stage muscular dystrophy patient who defied expectations and made it through the night.

The sky is still dark when she exits the building, but Sophie enjoys the quiet sheen of her post-shift walk home, and today is no exception. In fact, that sense of otherworldliness is heightened this morning, because it looks like snow. The freezing mist and fog of the last few days have gone and there's a muted yellowness about the lamp-lit clouds above.

She knocks lightly on the back door of the small baker's on the corner. He won't open to the public for hours, but, since the day she passed him on his cigarette break outside – when he commented on how bleary-eyed she looked, and handed her a dark, dense fruit loaf – they have a little ritual. A cloud of steam, rich with yeast and sugar, hits her as he opens the door.

"*Hola, doctora*," he says. Since he found they have a common passion for languages, he likes to test her out.

"*Buenos dias*," she replies, smiling broadly. "Euuh. *Podrias darme… dos… pasteles con canela*?"

"*Por supuesto. Que rico*." Humming to himself, he

disappears among the tall metal shelves and orderly trays crowding the kitchen. It's not unlike the storeroom at the hospital, Sophie reflects, except filled with soft, baked wonders, not chemicals and surgical instruments.

This exchange over, Sophie thanks the baker and hurries to her flat, looking forward to a hot drink and her pyjamas and climbing into bed beside Lotta. She wonders if Lotta remembered to change the dressing on her thigh last night. No lights are on in the block. She closes the main door as quietly as she can and takes the stairs, not the clanking lift, to avoid disturbing the sleeping neighbours.

When she reaches the front door, it's already slightly ajar.

She frowns and pushes it open and stands outside, looking into the long hallway.

The coat stand has been knocked, and is leaning precariously into the corner. Coats have slithered to the floor and hats and scarves are strewn all over the place, like the aftermath of a child's dressing-up game. She takes a step inside, her stomach fluttering.

"Hello?" She takes another step. "Lotta?"

At the end of the hall, the bedroom door is open. Hardly breathing, she approaches, and pushes it gently. It swings in a slow, wide arc. The bed is unmade, their soft grey duvet thrown aside. Sophie places a hand on the sheet. Cold.

In the lounge an armchair has been turned over, drawers from the sideboard have been pulled out, and all the books have been swept from the bookshelves. They lie variously: open; broken-backed; dust-sleeves bent. She notices her treasured first edition of *The Box of Delights*, pages butterflied down on the floor; on its cover, a series of vignettes of dancing bears and thieves and Punch and Judy stalls and mermaids. The stuff of danger in a child's imagination. It must be worth a thousand at least but whoever broke in has missed it. Unless... they haven't finished?

She stands still, and listens. Nothing.

"Lotta?"

There's no reply.

On the counter in the kitchen, she finds a hastily scribbled note next to the coffee pot.

I've gone to the cottage. Declan needs somewhere to lay low. I'm taking supplies. I'll be back soon. Be careful. I love you.

There's no time on the note, so Sophie has no idea how long ago Lotta left. She walks slowly from room to room, eyeing the trashed apartment, but this is not the work of someone who's packing supplies in a hurry. It's a break-in. Presumably it happened after Lotta had already gone. Hopefully.

Sophie riffles in her handbag for her phone. Five missed calls. Standing in the kitchen, she calls Lotta's number.

***

Just as Sophie finishes her shift at the hospital, Declan is arriving at Loggerheads. He passes right through the hamlet, its pub and countryside centre still sleepily closed. He has to turn around and come back before he spots two giant yellow excavators – bowed and silent at the roadside – and finally recognises the works site opposite the rutted track leading to the quarry and Lotta's cottage. He's not sure Marcus's car will cope with the potholes, but he doesn't want to risk leaving it on the main road, visible to curious eyes. Besides, Ishtar is sleeping, and he can't bear the thought of waking her to this freezing, still dark morning and making her walk the couple of miles to the hut. She'll wake soon enough.

His headlights pick out tree trunks that deepen into dim rows at their side. And, as he figured, by the time the car has bumped and threaded along the track, Ishtar is alert again, sitting forward, shivering and pulling her scarf closer around her. Lotta's 4x4 is already parked at the quarry edge, and at the bottom of the old limestone steps, a thin column of smoke trails weakly upwards from the cottage's ancient chimney.

Lotta opens the door as they exit the car, and ushers them quickly inside, leading Ishtar to the fire and installing her on a low stool with a faded rug folded over it. She turns to Declan, eyes darting anxiously across his face, and he suddenly cannot hold himself together anymore. She has to reach up on tiptoes to put her arms around his shaking shoulders. He slumps and holds on to her, sobbing uncontrollably.

Ishtar watches them for a moment, her hands clasped, then lowers her eyes to the bare floorboards.

"Come on," Lotta says. She rubs his shoulders. "Come on, let's get something warm inside you two." She opens a flask of coffee and pours it into enamel cups. Porridge heats in another pot. Her movements have the brisk quality of someone who has a coping plan and is sticking to it.

She hands a bowl of sweetened porridge to Ishtar, who peers into the pale gold gloop and sniffs doubtfully. Lotta smiles encouragingly. "It's good," she says. "Try it."

Declan tucks in, making appreciative noises. The heat seeps up through the roof of his mouth and radiates through his bruised nose. "Oh, God. Mmn."

Ishtar moves her spoon. It stands almost upright, then starts sinking slowly. She picks up a lump of porridge and lets it plop back into the bowl.

Lotta lowers her voice. "Are you both okay? What happened to Marcus?"

Declan shakes his head. "One of Palmer's guys." He blinks rapidly. "He just… he just destroyed him. Laid him on the tram line."

Lotta stares, horror all over her face. Declan swallows another mouthful with difficulty. She doesn't ask any more questions and he's quietly grateful. There's no way he can describe last night's events right now, much less justify his own role. He keeps replaying the moments before the tram struck Marcus, trying to will a different outcome or solution into existence.

It's not working.

Lotta pours herself a coffee from the flask and walks outside the cottage's thick walls. The birds are beginning to stir. Sophie should be home by now and will have found her note. Sure enough, there's a long voice message from her, left about ten minutes ago. Lotta lifts the phone to her ear and listens. There's some grey fluttering between the trees and a hooded crow lands on the roof of the cabin, noisily *kraaa-ing*.

"Lotta." Sophie's voice sounds like something's wrong. Lotta frowns at the crow, trying to ignore its racket. "I hope you're okay? And Declan's okay? I've seen your note. Listen, I don't want you to worry but we've had a break-in. I just wanted to check that… that you weren't here when…" She pauses, then whispers, "Shit" softly. Sophie hardly ever swears. "There's someone—"

The phone crackles and there's a series of violent thumps at the other end. Sophie cries out, and so does Lotta. The hooded crow flaps off, startled. At the other end, there's a noise like the phone scuttering across the floor. Lotta clasps her hand to her own mouth, although any sound she makes will have no effect. She's stands uselessly on the narrow track listening to the recording. Declan has come to the door of the cabin and is watching her.

A man's voice now, with a lilting accent. "Tell me where they've gone."

Sophie sounds further away, as if she's backing off. "I don't know. I don't know."

She's lying. The fine, dark hairs on Lotta's arms and neck stand on end as an electric shiver of fear and adrenaline goes through her.

"Yes, you fucking do. You cunt." Another clunk. A scuffle of paper. "This note. Where's the cottage?"

"I don't know."

"Don't fucking lie."

The metallic zing of something being unsheathed. Lotta recognises it straightaway. It's a knife being drawn from her kitchen block.

"You're going to tell us where they've gone. Do you understand?"

Us? How many of them are there?

"No. Please. I don't know. I hardly ever drive. I don't know how to get there."

"We'll drive. You can take us there."

"No." A different note to Sophie's voice now.

"Then you're no use to us, are you? Fucking dyke." A snort of laughter.

Whimpering.

A different voice chips in, higher pitched. "Cunt. Maybe she'd enjoy one last proper man inside her, eh?"

The sounds of a mammoth struggle now. Chairs scrape across the kitchen tiles. Something crashes over. A series of thuds and screams – at first loud and persistent. Then muffled.

And then silence. A long silence.

Lotta closes her eyes. She curls over herself and sinks to the cold gritty earth, with a long, low wail. Declan starts walking towards her, and then he's running, running across the track to her. He plucks the phone from her limp hand.

Lotta shakes her head violently. "It's a recording. It's—" She retches and throws up thin, coffee-dark puke into the gravel.

Declan listens to the crackle at the end of the voicemail. Finally, after another thirty seconds, a cautious male voice can be heard, as if in another room.

"Hello?"

Slow footsteps.

"Hello…? Sophie…? Lotta?"

Stillness. No response.

"Oh, my God. Oh, my God." Scuffling now. "Oh, God. ROSLYN! ROSLYN! Call an ambulance. Call an ambulance NOW!"

***

Declan paces back and forth in the cottage. Every footstep makes the wooden floor and a set of shelves in the corner, filled with old bottles and baskets, vibrate. Ishtar watches him nervously. It's taken him a quarter of an hour to get Lotta off the ground and back inside.

"I've got to go back," Lotta says, sitting at the small table. Her voice is clogged and squeaky from crying. She blows her nose on an old tea towel.

Declan takes his head in his hands, rubbing his face over and over, pressing his fingers into his temples. He's so tired. The greasy tension of his own skin and scalp is his only reality check right now.

"We should call the hospital first," he says.

"Declan, I'm going back. I've got to see Sophie. We need to talk to the police."

She's tried Sophie's mobile repeatedly but there's no answer. She's been all through her phone but has no numbers for any of their Liverpool neighbours. She was always too busy pushing for the move to London to bother putting down too many roots there.

"If that was Juliet"– her face crumples again – "what would you do? You'd be on your way to her already."

Declan kneads little circles on his skull with his fingertips. She's right. But he can't let her go back there.

"Lotta, last night I watched one of my oldest friends get killed, and I… I did nothing. I know you want to go to Sophie, of course you do, and I can't stop you if that's what you decide, but… for God's sake, just listen to me a second. If you go back now, that's exactly what they'll be expecting. Whoever did that to her will be there, waiting for you. Do you think that's what Sophie wanted? Why she lied and protected you? So you could just go walking straight back into the lion's den?"

"We can tell the police everything. The police will—"

"We've got no idea who we can trust and who we can't right now. Marcus said this goes way up."

"So what? We're just going to sit here?" She stares at him. "Wait for them to come for us?" Her eyes are like fire and ice. "Let them come then. What have we got to lose?"

Declan glances at Ishtar. "We've got a lot to lose still. And we're not the only ones."

Lotta falls silent. Her eyes well up. She picks up her phone. "I'm trying the hospital again."

Ishtar coughs gently and begins speaking. "When we leave Syria, it night-time. We living close near fighting. Al-Hasakah. They make everybody say who they supporting. President, YPG, rebel, Daesh. But we not want follow no one. My cousin die already and my mother very afraid for us. My brother eighteen and now he told go in army, so we make escape. My mother, father, my brother, we pack and we go at night. Not take our stuff."

She says all this without really looking at Declan or Lotta. Now she turns to them though. Her face is flushed.

"My father is teacher. He say we go England because they allow stay together and be family. But he not well. He not walk well. We pay to Turkey. Truck to Istanbul. Long time in truck with not breath air. My brother he make hole for breathe.

"After that they make we put boat in water. No room for everybody. My mother and myself only we go. But the water it come in boat. All panic. Try swim. My mother disappear. Italians guard come in boat. And after I take train to France. It very cold. I sleep on street and go Calais. It take three month."

Declan and Lotta stare at Ishtar.

"Marcus, he say me when everybody find out what happening, I be safe. I will have help find my family and bring to England."

Declan clears his throat. "Ishtar, I'm not sure—"

Her voice becomes more insistent. "We must to try. We have Marcus computer. We have film I make. We take story to someone. News. Police."

"But it's not safe—"

"You know safe person," she says. Her dark eyes seem to fill her entire face. "Marcus tell me. Your wife, she very strong lady. She not accept this. She fight. She know people."

Declan tries to catch Lotta's eye but her gaze slides away.

He clears his throat. "I'll… I'll call first thing in the morning. I think we should all get some rest if we can."

They need someone to get into Marcus's laptop. They need someone in the police they can trust. And Juliet has access to both. Whether they like it or not, he knows Ishtar is right. What he doesn't know is where the hell Juliet is.

CHAPTER FIFTY-ONE

Juliet crawls to the edge of the pit, torn hands on broken concrete, knees rebelling. She peers in and a sour smell of piss and mould rises from the darkness. Four metres below, Blythe's foot soldier lies completely still. His hood has fallen away from his face. His eyes seem open, staring blankly. A broken sportswear mannequin.

She clenches her jaw, feeling herself about to cry with shock, relief, and something else, something between contempt and pity.

"Hello?" she calls to him. "Hello?"

He doesn't move. There's no way to get down there to him, or see how badly he's injured. Thank Christ.

She clambers back down the ladder and runs around the building to the car. Bucky is going wild, pawing at the window, circling his own tail, barking. When she opens the door, he almost knocks her to the floor. While he stalks around the car, relieving himself at each wheel, Juliet plugs her phone into the car charger, and hands shaking, dials the emergency number Karen gave her.

"Stay with the dog," Karen says. "Lock yourself in the car. I'm coming out."

"We need an ambulance too," Juliet says.

"Are you hurt?"

"Not for me. For him."

CHAPTER FIFTY-TWO

A call is put through from Declan to Karen at a few minutes after seven thirty, as she's walking back into the station in Inverness, having finally dropped Juliet back at Erica's flat.

The streetlights around the carpark are starting to extinguish, although it's barely first light. In a few days, the clocks will go back. Karen can hear the tiredness, the adrenaline saturating Declan's voice. He attempts to explain everything that's happened since he and Lotta set foot in Manchester, and why they went there in the first place.

He describes Marcus's investigation into Bernhard Palmer and the Eden Club.

Karen lets him finish, although Juliet has told her much of this already during the night's questioning. While he delivers the information, in disjointed snapshots, she writes a note for her partner, Andrew Turner, and takes it to his desk.

Check Liverpool hospital admissions for Sophie West.
Female, thirty-four years old.

Turner frowns and nods.

Declan's still gabbling. "Marcus said they're untouchable. That they've got some kind of protection, high up. I didn't know who else to contact but you. I know Marcus had evidence, on his laptop. And we've got footage on a USB from one of the victims. But it's all behind a password. I don't know how to get past Marcus's security."

"That's a problem. It could take weeks to brute force our way in."

Karen opens up a national reporting screen where she can log *persons of interest* in a homicide, but stops short. Until they know what's on the laptop, she can't take that risk, not if Blythe is involved somehow, as Juliet's tale of last night suggests. They need watertight evidence, and the laptop could be the key. There's not much else to go on. Given how badly the forensics on the jacket are compromised, the irregular way she obtained it in the first place – just taking it from the hospital – could make it inadmissible. She might just get away with it, but it would be up to a judge, who could decide it should be disregarded.

Declan continues. "Look. They obviously know someone's onto them. And they've already linked it to me and to Lotta, which is why they sent their thugs to Liverpool. To Sophie. What if they've got someone else on their way? Coming after Juliet, or Erica—"

Karen steps inside a small office, and closes the door. "I need to stop you there, Declan. There's already been an incident here tonight. Juliet is fine. She's back with Erica, and I've got extra patrols in the area. I've only just finished with her... She wanted to talk to you herself, in the cold light of day, but... it looks like someone tried to seriously frighten her."

"Oh, Jesus. What happened? Karen, is she okay?"

"She's fine, Declan."

"What happened?"

"She'll tell you everything, I'm sure. I'm more concerned right now about these suspects trying to leave the country before we have enough to nail them with to be honest. The best thing you can do is—"

She's about to say, *get in the car and bring me that laptop*. Turner reappears and hands her a scribbled memo.

West admitted Liverpool three hours ago, after 999 call. Dead on arrival. Sexual assault and throat cut.

CHAPTER FIFTY-THREE

Karen arrives back at Erica's shortly after eight. Normally she wouldn't go in alone but this is no time to stand on procedure. She needs to get Erica and Juliet to a safe place, and fast. Turner waits in another car, parked beneath the cherry tree at the entrance to the driveway, with instructions to keep watch.

Erica buzzes her in and she climbs the stairs. The door is open, and she makes her way into the flat. She finds Erica still in her dressing gown, boiling water for tea and putting make-up on, mascara wand hovering for a few moments, paused, while Karen stands stiffly at the kitchen bench, explaining.

Erica concentrates on Karen properly now, for the first time. "What's going on?

Karen hesitates. "I'm really sorry about this. I know you've had a disturbed night, but I need to speak to Juliet again. And I think it would be best to take you both elsewhere. We're going to have to wake her."

"She's not here. She couldn't sleep. She took the dog for a walk. Said she was going to pick up some more things from the summerhouse."

Karen bites her lips. "Right. I'll need to get out there to her then. Turner will take you—"

"What's happened?"

Karen flinches. This was not a conversation she wanted to get into right now. Some of her colleagues seem naturals at keeping families abreast of an ongoing enquiry; knowing exactly how much to say and when; maintaining their distance while providing reassurance and comfort. She however has always found it an immensely tricky business. She hates having to explain when leads turn out to be non-starters. She hates the false hope of it. And too much information in the wrong hands of family members can be hugely problematic. But after what Juliet said about discrimination, she's reluctant to hide anything from Erica.

"Some new evidence suggests that Beth may have known something about some… organised crime. It looks like they're covering their tracks. There's been a murder in Liverpool this morning which may be related."

"Murder?"

"Yes."

Karen stomach tenses suddenly. She hopes to God Erica doesn't ask who. She doesn't know if Sophie was a close friend to all the family. This would not be a good way to break the news.

"But how – what's the link to Beth?"

"We still need to establish whether or not there was one. But—"

"So, you're saying… there's a chance Beth didn't commit suicide? Someone killed her?"

"Perhaps. Or… She may have been under some pressure that we didn't know about. Something that drove her."

Erica lights a cigarette. Her hands tremble slightly. "How long have you been investigating this?"

It's not easy to tell whether Erica is upset because this is opening up wounds, or because she feels left out of the loop, but not for the first time Karen gets some insight into Erica and Juliet. It can't have been easy, having such a high-profile, high-flying twin, and all the while being her own worst enemy.

"Look, Erica, you need to understand, this is…" Karen hesitates. It's probably better not to mention the jacket or the exchanges she's had with Juliet. "It's been quite a fast-moving enquiry and very sensitive due to the nature of the facts emerging."

"Hardly fast-moving. Beth died in June."

"We… I'm acting on a new source. It's actually a friend of Declan's. A journalist. And, well, none of this is exactly… on the record. I'm putting myself on the line here."

"Isn't that your job?"

Karen blinks. It's a fair comment and there's no point in arguing. There's no time.

"Erica. Declan's on his way here now from Liverpool, with a laptop containing information we may be able to use. In the meantime, we need to be careful about—"

"What do you mean, 'we may be able to use'?"

"It depends on the nature of the information. And we'll need to get past security on the laptop."

Erica nods. "I can help with that. Won't take long. I'll just need to pick up some things from work. What time does Declan fly in?"

"He's driving."

"From Liverpool? But that will take hours."

"Yes. Look, Erica, I really need to get out to the summerhouse—"

"Yes. Yes. You should go. Get out to Juliet. And if your colleague drives me, we can intercept Declan en route across country, can't we? It would speed things up. Halve the time it takes for them to get here? Then we'd get into the laptop more quickly?"

Although she's talking quickly, Erica sounds very practical, like a mother organising after-school pick-ups. "What time did he leave? If we leave now, we'd probably meet at… where? Gretna, somewhere like that?"

Karen stalls.

She's well aware from office gossip that Erica, having failed the competency review a couple of years ago, when the local council began developing shared online services, is frequently asked to solve bugs and bypass encryptions by her juniors – who get to take the credit.

"My priority is keeping you safe, Erica. You, Juliet—"

For the first time, Erica raises her voice a little. "I know what you're thinking, Karen. But I'm perfectly fine. You can call Cathy, my doctor, if you like. Check to see what she says. If you think I'm going to sit around here when I could be doing something to find out what happened to Beth, you must be more crazy than me. And if you have a better option for getting into the laptop, all you need to do is tell me. But, unless I'm mistaken, it sounds like you don't have that many channels open to you right now."

CHAPTER FIFTY-FOUR

Bucky runs ahead of Juliet along the beach. He likes to gather driftwood and be praised profusely for it. He trots along proudly, dipping and weaving his high forehead, holding several of the smooth, grey limbs in his mouth, all overlapping and interlocking; sometimes they're so big he can hardly keep his balance.

Juliet left Erica's as quietly as possible and headed out early. After listening again to Declan's panicky, insistent message and failing to reach him, she decided to collect a few things from the summerhouse and leave it locked up for now.

She's still wired after the night's misadventures, it feels somehow like she's escaped. The birdsong is deafening at the reserve. Geese and sandpipers clatter into the air above the mudflats, flashing their pale underwings, as Bucky runs among them. She throws more sticks far behind them both, so he's obliged to double back before charging to catch up with her again. He never seems to question this methodology, or tire of it.

"Good boy!" she says, as he flies towards her again. "Good boy." She throws another stick just as he arrives, and he looks mildly bemused, but it's just a momentary hesitation. He carefully puts down the wood he's just retrieved and goes after this new plunder.

Juliet keeps walking. About a hundred metres ahead,

coming into view around the headland is Toby, his black hoodie up against the wind. She grimaces, remembering that first day here, just a couple of weeks back, when she could hardly walk this sea path without dissolving into a quivering mess. At least she knows now, it's not the mild rise and fall of the water but the pregnancy making every step feel as though she's pushing through some chemical cloud. He grins and raises a hand in greeting, and she does the same. Why does he walk this way, every day? Is it part of their project to keep an eye on her?

Ahead, on the shore – a small pale red object – almost halfway between them.

Juliet spots it first. She changes her direction slightly to bring her towards it. Toby notices first her change of trajectory, then sees she's heading for something. He adjusts his course. When they're about twenty metres apart, Juliet realises what she's looking at.

Beth's shoe.

CHAPTER FIFTY-FIVE

Bucky doesn't hesitate. He races for the shoe. Toby starts running too and to Bucky he looks like a fun contender, but he's calling Bucky's name now, which is not in the rules. A dog is not to be distracted from his prize. Bucky barks once. *Joy? A warning?* Perhaps a bit of both. It may be just a faded deck shoe, but shoes are his favourite. And this is his most beloved game.

He reaches it with metres to spare and snatches it up in his jaws with an uncharacteristic snarl. This is not just any shoe.

He springs away, off up the sloping sand and onto the pebbles towards the treeline. Juliet and Toby stand almost side by side, both breathless. Juliet hardly dares look at Toby. He bends and puts his hands on his knees, panting.

"Shit," he says.

The little spurt of running has somehow made Juliet's nausea lift.

"Shit indeed," she says lightly. Too lightly. It's hardly the time for sarcasm, but it must be another part of her brain with a false connection.

Toby shifts his shoulders back and forth. "What do you think he's found?" he asks.

Bucky flops down near the forest edge, long tongue lolling from the side of his grinning mouth, the shoe between his front paws.

"Bucky! Stay!" Juliet shouts.

She turns to face Toby now, her face pale. Her childhood accent drips like acid through her voice. "You know exactly what he's found. That's Beth's shoe."

"God. Really?"

"You know, Toby, it's strange; it's a real wee puzzle, because… the shoes at the summerhouse fit me. And, you probably don't realise this, but Beth was not the same foot size as me."

He runs his hands through his hair. "Bizarre. Maybe they shrank."

"No. They've not shrunk. They've not shrunk at all. In fact, they look almost as good as new. And they fit me perfectly because they're a size forty, and I, I am a size forty."

"I'm sorry. You've lost me."

"I'm a size forty, in ladies' sizing." Juliet smiles. "But Beth wasn't. She took a wider fitting. She always wore a man's forty; a man's shoe."

"But—" Toby stops himself.

"Yes?"

"I've seen other pairs of her shoes. They were a forty."

Juliet nods very slowly, her eyes scanning Toby's face. He lowers his gaze.

"Why have you such an interest in her shoe size, Toby?"

"Look," he laughs again. He raises his eyes to give her the headlight treatment, but this time he can't pull it off. "I don't know. Our place was always full of boy stuff, and then suddenly there were girl things everywhere. Handbags. Shoes. It was hard not to notice them."

"Really? Because, you know what I'm thinking? I'm thinking that the shoes I have at home are not Beth's. And if they're no her shoes, then it likely wasn't Beth who placed them out on the path. And if the shoes were not hers, then the suicide note that was tucked inside them… that didn't belong to her either."

It's Toby's turn to nod. "Listen, Jet, are you sure you're okay? Because—"

"Don't be calling me Jet."

"What?"

"Don't you fucking dare call me Jet, and don't try and make it sound as if this is all in my head."

Toby ignores her now, and starts walking up the beach towards Bucky.

"Here, boy!" he calls, patting his thighs encouragingly. Bucky stands, ears pricked. He takes the shoe in his mouth again, just in case.

Juliet watches, heart thundering. She waits until Toby is almost upon Bucky and then calls the dog, urgently. Toby spreads his arms and legs as if he's about to perform a haka. Bucky dashes past him and heads for Juliet.

But he still thinks it's a game. He almost lets Juliet take the shoe from his mouth, before loping past her. He dances from foot to foot on the shoreline, a few metres away.

Juliet knows not to shout or become frustrated. Bucky doesn't respond to that. He likes to know he's getting it right. "Good boy," she murmurs. She glances back at Toby, who remains near the trees. She begins walking towards the summerhouse, casually. "Good boy. C'mon!"

She finds one of his sticks and picks it up. A decoy. It's slathered in dog dribble. "Here, boy. Look! Look, what's this?" She lowers it to Bucky's muzzle. He sniffs. He's seen this trick before.

It is almost irresistible though. He snorts a little and his eyes move back and forth, tracing the stick's movement across the leaden sky as Juliet tries to draw his attention. It's Toby's approach however that really changes his mind. He's not letting that guy have his stick. As soon Juliet throws it, he'll go after it and take it and the shoe with him.

But Juliet doesn't throw the stick.

Toby seizes it from behind as she holds it in the air and wrenches it from her hand. She cries out, grabs her twisted wrist, and spins round to find Toby standing there, the driftwood raised in the air like a war cry. He stares at her strangely.

"Toby," she says. "Toby, I really don't know what's going on but—"

He jerks the driftwood oddly, viciously. She steps back.

"Please! Toby! Listen. Please don't hurt me."

Still he doesn't move or back down. His eyes have taken on an almost silvery sheen.

"Whatever it is you're caught up in, we can talk about it."

Bucky growls.

"Toby, I've known now for some time… this must be… something way beyond you. Something that shouldn't involve you. We can talk about it. You can trust me, Toby."

His face is contorted. He's barely recognisable.

Is this what happened to Beth? Was she beaten unconscious here on the shore?

For a moment, a split second, Juliet wants to know what it felt like, as if by taking that on herself, accepting the violence of it, she'll finally understand… and the constant grief and questioning, and everything she's ever known or believed or worried about, will cease. And she'll be at peace.

Toby clenches his lower jaw, scraping his bottom teeth against his upper lip oddly, moaning. *What is wrong with him?*

"Toby?" she repeats.

It's like an incantation. People love to hear their own name. She used to coach Fiona to call journalists by their name in press conferences. Hearing their own name activates the part of the brain linked to making judgements about themselves. It distracts them from judging others.

"Toby. It's okay. Look, I don't believe you want to hurt me."

He moans again.

"Or my baby." She pauses. "I'm pregnant, Toby. I'm having a baby."

He stands there, arm still raised, and blinks once. His gaze flickers to Bucky and the shoe. Then his face seems to cave.

All the tension slackens, as if he's aging ten years all at once. His arm loosens and he drops, collapses to sit on the mud and stones, head in hands. He throws the driftwood a few pathetic feet away.

Bucky looks at him in disgust.

For a second, Juliet can't tell if Toby's angry or in distress, or both, until his shoulders begin to shake violently. "Oh, God," he moans. "Oh, Jesus Christ. Help me."

Juliet can hear him desperately trying to swallow down his sobs. She knows what that feels like. Her own eyes burn with a mix of relief and empathy.

She sits beside him. "Take your time."

CHAPTER FIFTY-SIX

Lotta, deep in shock, says nothing as Declan climbs into the driver's seat of her Golf. They abandon Marcus's car outside the quarry. With a seven-hour drive to Inverness ahead, they need the most reliable vehicle they have. Shivering uncontrollably, Lotta curls into the foetal position on the back seat and Declan covers her with a blanket. She turns her face away.

There's a border-crossing an hour into their journey, on a quiet road just south of Chester. Ishtar sits up a little and turns her head to look at the sign.

Welcome to ENGLAND, it says, beneath a figurative red rose. They pass by without incident, their only witness the bright yellow moss at the roadside.

But the border crossing is not the worry. They were at the cottage for a little over two hours. More than enough time for Sophie's killers to reach it from Liverpool, if they somehow managed to discover its location.

No one arrived – which for Declan means one of two things. Either they didn't find it and are somewhere behind; or the thugs are already ahead of them, on their way to the summerhouse.

CHAPTER FIFTY-SEVEN

Toby exhales, long and low, and glances over his shoulder along the brightening shore, in the direction of the recording studio.

"We can't stay here," he says. "They'll see us."

"Who?"

"They'll come looking for us. Max, Karlo. Or Lyall. He's arriving later. He called and said he's flying in." He's gabbling. "Coming for the boat. Says he's picking up a crew in the Netherlands. Something about Palmer's villa in St Barts. He's got fuel arriving at lunchtime. He'll be here soon."

"Just calm down. Tell me what happened to my niece. Tell me about the shoes. The note."

Toby swallows again, three or four times, then breathes out long and hard. "It's bad. It's really bad, Jet. Sorry, Juliet."

"We can walk," she says. "Let's head back to the summerhouse. Tell me on the way."

They get to their feet; Toby helps Juliet up, shooting nervous looks up and down the mudflats. A curlew ignores them, staring into the water. Bucky runs ahead, carrying both the stick and the shoe.

"Beth…" he begins. He looks over his shoulder. "Lyall…" And suddenly it's rushing out of him, like a tide. "There's… there's something you should know. It goes back years. I didn't know any of this when I got involved with them, but… Max has been dealing with it forever."

He stops and listens deeply into the woods for a few seconds, before continuing. "Karlo's got a problem." His Adam's apple rises and falls. "He's into young girls. I mean, I don't think they're even all girls. And he got caught out. I think he might have been set up, I'm not sure, but there are girls there. At the Eden Club. Not just the lapdancers in the club. I'm talking about… This is worse."

He's stopped walking and is looking at Juliet, searching her eyes, desperation in his own. He surveys the treeline again, before turning to her. "Juliet, these kids. They're underage. There are rooms. It's like… like they're on supply."

She wonders how long he's been carrying this information around. She can't give him the reassurance his looking for – that somehow this isn't as bad as it sounds.

"A couple of years ago, when we were setting up Delta Function, Max was looking at how all the contracts were set up, trying to do it differently, but from nowhere, these photos started arriving of Karlo with these kids, and I think he panicked. So he signed with EMG again."

"And Lyall ever so kindly offered to help cover up this sickness?"

Toby stares at her. He nods.

"So he's blackmailing you all?"

"When Max brought me on board, I realise now, it was his way to try and break out. You know, a new band, new material. New intellectual property. But, gradually Lyall kind of took over. He brought us all up here, to get us away from everything, to start recording the album. He said he needed to protect us."

They can see glimpses of the summerhouse now, between the pines. They turn onto the path.

"He basically used it to dictate everything. We couldn't get out of the contract with him, go it alone, because he said he was the only one who could keep Karlo's thing out of the press. I mean, he's like some kind of partner in Eden Media. And he said if anyone found out about Karlo, it would destroy us. We'd never work again."

"And this is what Beth discovered?"

"Yes." He lowers his voice. "And Lyall… he's a fucking monster. I mean, everyone knows he's a prick, but it was like he'd got a thing about Beth. Like he needed to prove something. He was always showing off, trying to impress her with his money and his lifestyle."

Juliet tries to walk steadily. She keeps her gaze fixed on the ground just in front of them.

"Anyway, Beth wasn't stupid. She could see there was something weird going on with Karlo. And she wouldn't let it go. Every time she got a bit drunk, or anything, she'd start on about it. That's when Max and Lyall said she should start designing for the band. And Lyall arranged a night at the Eden for us to play. It was a big deal. He insisted we all needed to go. I mean he treats it like his own personal gentleman's club. But…" He stops and scans the forest suddenly. "Did you hear a car?"

"No. It's okay. Carry on."

"So, Max deejayed at the club. Max is obsessed with… with getting old, irrelevant. Out of touch. And this was a big night for him, to be back at the Eden. I realise now, Lyall must have arranged it partly to keep Max sweet.

"And I don't know how Max let it happen but while he was deejaying, Lyall took Beth up to these apartments, where they have these sort of… sex parties. Like, there are escorts and stuff at the club, but in the apartments, it's different. That's where the kids are."

He takes a huge breath and glances around again.

"I shouldn't be telling you any of this. They'll kill me." He chokes up. "They'll kill us both."

He doubles over suddenly and heaves from the pit of his stomach. He spends several minutes hunched over like that, throwing up greenish bile into the stones. Juliet steps backwards, and folds her arms to stop herself from comforting him. It's as if he's purging himself, finally, of something poisonous. When the moment finally passes, he wipes his hand shakily across his mouth.

"Sorry," he stammers.

"Lyall, and Palmer. These people," she says. "They're the ones who should be afraid, Toby."

He nods, unconvinced.

"So Lyall took Beth into this... this place. Where there were kids."

Toby looks around again.

"I don't know why he took her there. The only thing I can think of is that he wanted to compromise her somehow. Make her look like she was involved. But she went ape. I mean, really mental. She stormed back into the club and Max had to interrupt his set, and they spent the rest of the night screaming at each other. She was hysterical. She wanted to go straight to the police."

"And? Why didn't she?"

"Lyall went to work on her."

"What does that mean?" Juliet is afraid of the answer already.

"His usual. Veiled threats. He said there was no point in throwing her career away before it had even started. That sort of thing. That she was already in deep. Talked about the effect on you."

"Me?"

"Yeah. How it would ruin you and PA if it got out that your family was linked to child sex and stuff. And he kept pushing. Pushing the idea that she was already a member of Delta Function."

Juliet tries to imagine Beth navigating all of this, trying to work out how much power Lyall had, deciphering how to tread the line of least harm to everyone involved. *There's some wee things I need to talk to you about,* she'd said in their last call. How many times had Beth rehearsed that line, trying to sound calm? Trying to sound in control.

"I don't believe she would have gone for that."

"Yeah, but she was crazy about Max. She didn't want to ruin him. I think she just kind of buried her head in the sand for a while. Kept on designing. I think it was a way to keep Lyall at bay. Ward him off. She just kind of immersed herself in the album covers, like it was some kind of design therapy."

Juliet wants to slap him. She holds her hands behind her back, to anchor herself. Something about this still doesn't add up. She can't get Beth's album design out of her mind: that pale, distorted face in the window of the Eden building.

"And what made this little plan go wrong?" she asks.

Toby looks confused. "What?"

"My niece is dead," she says icily. "Somewhere along the line the plan went wrong. The *design therapy* stopped working."

They've come to a standstill in the middle of the forest path. They can't be far from where the shoes and the note were found.

"I don't know. Once she started designing, I guess… I guess, it was like she couldn't go back. Like she'd gone along with it all. She was implicated. And at that point, I think Lyall felt he could do anything. Max had a massive fight with him, because apparently Lyall kept… touching her."

A chasm seems to open up inside Juliet chest. The abortion. She wonders if Toby knows. Is it possible that Lyall raped Beth?

"She just kind of withdrew more and more into herself. She got more and more…" Juliet expects him to say *depressed,* but he hesitates. "Angry. Really angry. She was a better person than I'll ever be."

He breathes in deeply, snottily, presses the cuffs of his hoodie into his eyes, which are puffy with tears. He walks to the edge of the path, facing the sea and begins to trace out a large oval in the pine needles with his right foot.

Juliet watches him. Is he thinking about his career;

possibly even her career, or PA? As if any of that matters. But when he looks up and opens his mouth, he utters something completely other.

"So finally she said she was leaving. That she couldn't live like this anymore. That's where the note came from."

"What?" The hairs on Juliet's neck stand up.

"She wrote Max a note, left it on the bedside table. *I can't live like this anymore*. And we didn't see her for about a week. Max was beside himself. He was afraid she would go public with it all. And then Lyall arrived to save the day. He said he'd talk her round. So, Max managed to get hold of her and he persuaded her to come over and we… we went on out on Lyall's boat. All of us."

He clears the centre of the shape he's drawn, flicking lichen and needles and twigs out of it with the toe of his shoe. Then he starts slowly, absently tracing patterns in the cold, dry earth. Juliet watches. He's drawing a noaidi drum. He sniffles and wipes roughly at his snotty nose again.

"He served champagne. Lyall. Acted like it was a big treat. But Beth was just… stony. She wouldn't speak to anyone. For like, an hour. And Lyall started getting angry. He called her a spoiled little bitch, and she went crazy, arguing with him. All the stuff she had bottled up. She said he was evil, a monster and she didn't want to be anywhere near him. She just kept repeating it. Like a broken record. She wanted to get off the boat, and Max grabbed her and they struggled, and she threw her shoe at Lyall, and it went overboard, into the water, and then Lyall hit her. It happened so quickly. She fell. Hit her head. There was this noise. I've never heard anything like it… and she kind of crumpled and went into the water."

He starts crying again. He crouches on the floor, huge shaky breaths wracking his body.

"And Lyall just walked round the boat calmly. At first I thought he must be getting a rope or a life ring, but he… he was bringing up the anchor, and so I jumped in. But I couldn't find her. I kept diving. And Lyall… he fucking started the engine. He just left me there. And I couldn't find her." He heaves oxygen into his lungs. "I couldn't find her."

Juliet trembles. She's been listening, eyes averted, unable to watch him painstakingly marking out shapes, while he describes Beth's last moments. But now she looks up, and there's something… some movement near the summerhouse.

Karen Sutherland.

Juliet holds her up her hand to Karen, hiding the gesture from Toby. *Wait*.

"So? How did you manage to get back?" she asks.

"I…" He gulps. "I started swimming and eventually Lyall turned around again… about two hundred metres away. I made it over to them and they pulled me up."

Karen steps closer. Toby rubs his face.

"I'd lost it. I was completely out of my mind. And they tried to settle me down. Lyall said it was all going to be okay. He kept saying she'd wanted to get off the boat. Let her swim." He's crying openly now, unashamed. "I mean, I'd heard the way she hit her head. It was obvious she was fucking unconscious. I knew… we all knew she wasn't going to be doing any swimming. And then later that night, when she hadn't come back… Lyall turned it around. Said it was our fault. We were all to blame."

He's sounds like a child, a small boy, which – thinks Juliet – he is. Just a baby really.

"He said if it came out, we were all going down; it would come out about Karlo, and that we'd all colluded. And he came up with this idea. He said we couldn't risk the publicity. And Max went along with it."

"You covered it up."

"Lyall had Beth's other shoe on the boat, and he said we could make it look… He went off and bought two shoes the same. But, I guess he never thought to get the men's fitting. He must have bought the wrong size. And they used the fucking note she'd written Max, when she'd said was leaving him."

Juliet stares at the patch of earth and repeats softly, "That she couldn't *live like this anymore*."

Toby nods. He hangs his head and stops marking out the soil. Karen stands less than three metres behind him. He still hasn't seen her.

"Who planted the shoes?"

"I did." A bubble of mucus bursts from his nose. He wipes it on his sleeve. "They said I had to do something or they couldn't trust me, and… I didn't want to burn her stuff, I couldn't do that, so Karlo did. I think he fucking enjoyed it. He dressed as her. Took her jacket and the entrance code and went to the university. And they made me put the shoes and the note…"

He taps on the ground with his foot, in the centre of the form he's created.

"Right here."

CHAPTER FIFTY-EIGHT

Shortly after lunchtime, Lotta's Golf pulls into the outskirts of Gretna, where Karen's partner, Turner, has arranged to bring Erica to meet them at a hotel. A sign at the entrance to the town declares *Welcome to Gretna: Historic Railroad Village*.

Declan slows down, finally, and rotates his shoulder blades to release the tension held there. He seeks out Lotta in the rear-view mirror. Bundled up like a Russian doll in her blanket, she gazes, unseeing, into the middle distance. The sky is white, almost completely colourless. Ishtar, in the front, glances at Declan sideways.

The Anvil Hotel is a three-star place with free wifi and a large café area where a buffet is laid out at mealtimes. A big bay window framed in brown wood looks out onto the small houses opposite. Declan enquires at the desk, pays some money and they are ushered into the dining area and given plates, although the buffet is being cleared as they walk in. Ishtar fills her plate with pasta. Declan goes straight to the coffee pot. Lotta sits in silence, her back to the window.

They wait.

Nineteen miles behind them, Paul's been keeping a leisurely pace, travelling alone. After the botch in Liverpool, he dropped Taj. He doesn't want to take any more risks. Scanning police channels, he worked out that a standard patrol car from

Inverness was on its way to an out-of-division meet in Gretna. It was too much of a coincidence not to follow up. An old police contact confirmed it for him, although he had no further explanation about the purpose of this journey. Not that the reason for anything is supposed to matter to Paul.

He switches radio stations and accelerates on a long straight section of the M6.

Declan watches Sergeant Andrew Turner pull up with Erica. He doesn't look happy, which is hardly surprising after a three-hour drive out of the North East Division. He probably thinks whatever's on this damn laptop should be handed over to a Specialist Crime unit, not hacked at some backwater hotel.

Turner goes straight to reception to ask for a meeting room, while Erica heads for the table occupied by Declan, Lotta and Ishtar in the back of the restaurant area. Although they've never met, instinctively Erica throws her arms around Lotta, who momentarily allows herself to be held.

They move to a seminar room, barely big enough for the elliptical table it contains, and the small group – Declan, Ishtar, Turner – watch awkwardly, while Erica sets up.

She removes the hard drive from Marcus's laptop and plugs it into a portable device.

While this is happening Ishtar tugs at Declan's sleeve. She jerks her head towards Lotta, who is leaning into the corner of the room, shoulders shaking.

Declan returns to reception, and has to wait several minutes while an elderly couple join the hotel's loyalty scheme before checking out. He curls and uncurls his toes impatiently inside his shoes. Finally, the clerk turns to him. Small conical lightshades hang so low over the desk that it's impossible to lean in and ask discreetly for anything. He keeps his voice as quiet as possible, books a room, and asks if a doctor can be called to the hotel.

Paul sits in the concourse, reading a paper, unnoticed by Declan. For such a big man, Paul knows how to blend in, a skill acquired over many years. His ex-wife used to claim he could make himself appear and disappear in crowds at will. She didn't like it. He turns the page.

While Erica curses at how slowly her brute-force software is running, Declan and Ishtar accompany Lotta back through the empty reception area, up to the second-floor room he's just booked. He sets the bath taps running and tells Ishtar to stand guard and not allow Lotta to lock herself in.

Declan's so tired, after the drive through the night and more time on the road today, he's tempted to curl up on the white bed linen right there and then, but he knows he wouldn't sleep anyway. Behind his eyelids, the form of Marcus's body on the tramlines is engraved. And every now and then, he hears the voice of the neighbour on the other end of Sophie's phone. The disbelief and horror ringing out.

He blinks rapidly. He must keep going. It's all he can do. He tries to smile at Ishtar, and is about to return downstairs when he remembers something.

"Do you still have the camera pen?" he whispers. "The pen Marcus gave you?"

Ishtar nods, and fishes in the little woven bag that hasn't left her shoulder. She hands it over, with some reluctance, blinking, not meeting his eye.

"It's okay," he says. "Whatever's on there, you've done nothing wrong."

Paul drags the maître d' for the evening service by the feet, and hides him behind the clothes rail in the corner of a service room just off the corridor to the left of reception. He swipes through dry-cleaned uniforms, hanging in plastic suit-bags, looking for an XL. He settles for large. Never mind. The shorter the trousers the more harmless he'll seem.

Back in the meeting room, Erica lets the brute-force software run, and plugs Ishtar's pencam into a USB slot on her own laptop. The room, already quiet, takes on a new quality of silence as the video clip, fifty-three minutes long, launches.

"Have you been a good girl since I last saw you?" a male voice asks.

Ishtar's body blocks the camera briefly. *"Yes."*

The man sitting on the bed in the film wears a white shirt, unbuttoned. His torso is portly yet sagging and yellowed like old milk. His double chin is covered in stubble, but there's no hiding who it is. Bernhard Palmer.

He beckons her with one finger and a small smile. She takes two timid steps towards him.

"I can't watch this," says Erica.

She pushes her chair away from the table violently, and goes to the door. It opens just as she reaches it. A huge hotel employee with short trousers, pushing a trolley of refreshments covered with a tablecloth, blocks the entire doorframe. She stands aside, letting the porter through. All other eyes in the room, Declan's, Turner's, are fixed on the laptop. Erica edges through the door and escapes outside for a cigarette.

"Come and kneel over here."

Turner's eyes widen.

Behind him, Paul pushes the low trolley to one side of the room. The white cloth draped surgically over the trolley's tray hides a selection of weapons. He turns to see what's on the screen.

"You know what to do. Hold it in your hand."

Paul is not stupid, but this is the first time he's come face to face with his paymasters' depravity. It feels like an age since he saw Ishtar, although it was only last night that he drove her from her tram stop to her appointment at Palmer's apartment. He somehow never imagined this. She sweeps her long dark hair to the side of her face. Palmer takes hold of it, tightly, gathering it in his fist, a gold-and-diamond ring on his little finger.

Declan's stomach heaves. He closes his eyes and draws breath slowly, trying to lose the rising nausea. Breathing out, he opens his eyes a crack and suddenly becomes aware of the porter in the room. He pauses the video and clears his throat.

"Well, it looks like the camera worked. I'm not sure there's any need to—"

He turns to the man, and frowns in recognition. Their eyes meet, just as Turner, frozen in his chair for the last couple of minutes, comes to his senses. He stands abruptly, placing himself between the image on the screen and the hotel employee. His voice shakes as he asks the porter to ensure they're not disturbed again.

The porter's hand lingers over the draped trolley.

"Please," says Turner. He takes a step forward. "We need you to leave, now. Police business."

CHAPTER FIFTY-NINE

It's early afternoon by the time Toby, standing on the rear deck of the *Favourite Daughter,* hears Lyall crossing the pontoon. His gait, that heavy stride – each step falling slightly later than expected, like Frank Sinatra keeping his own time – is unmistakeable.

"What the hell are you doing out here?" Lyall says to Toby, with no greeting.

"Just wanted some headspace."

Lyall snorts.

"Don't laugh. I come out here to think about Beth sometimes."

Lyall puts down the crate of supplies he's brought with him, and makes a show of checking the hull. He climbs on board and starts pulling at the underseat storage. He pulls out the life jackets and counts them. Although his gestures are measured, he's clearly tenser than usual.

Toby trails him, watching his movements, wishing he'd stay still.

"Going on a trip?" Toby asks.

Lyall doesn't respond.

"She should never have got involved with us."

Finally Lyall bites. "What the hell are you talking about?"

"I told you. Beth."

Lyall crouches stiffly and starts unpacking the crate.

"Maybe none of you should have got involved with her. She was clearly a fucking psycho. And it's put the album back while you lot mince about, getting over yourselves."

"She was not a psycho."

Lyall winks. "You know nothing about women, my boy. You've got a lot to learn."

"Oh, and you knew Beth, did you?"

"She was a spoiled little girl. An attention-seeker."

"Hardly. She spent all her time trying to avoid your attentions."

Lyall laughs more throatily now. "She enjoyed it. All women do. Bit of flattery. Flirtation. It's their lifeblood. Makes them tick."

Toby stares. "Oh. My. Christ. You really believe that, don't you?" He shakes his head. "You actually think that a girl like Beth—" His voice catches. "You believe a girl like that enjoyed you sliming your way around her?"

Lyall's colour rises, blood creeping slowly up his chest and neck and into his cheeks. Two raspberry blotches appear either side of his nose.

"You know what she called you, don't you?" Toby grins. "She called you Pepe. Pepe the frog."

Lyall chuckles. "There's a fine line between attraction and repulsion. When you learn that, you'll start having more success with pussy."

"What? Like you? Call that success?" Toby raises his eyebrows and nods once. "I know what you tried to do to her. Max told me."

Lyall blinks now, slowly. "That was a mix-up. I've been over this with Max. We understand each other. Most women don't even know what they want. How are we supposed to read the signals?"

"She seemed pretty clear what she wanted to me. Right up to the end. When she was screaming at you to take her back to shore or let her off the boat, she was pretty fucking loud and clear."

"She was hysterical."

"She was not hysterical. She was angry. There's a difference."

"Angry?" Lyall's voice rises now. "Angry? That little bitch had nothing to be angry about. She was working – at the highest fucking level for her first fucking job – straight in at the top. The exposure that would give her? She was no better than a whore. Fucking Max to get where she wanted."

"That's not true though, Malcolm, is it? Because you're the one who pushed her into it. Doing the album design? It was you. We may have sold our fucking souls to you, Max and I. We caved in to you. But not everyone's as weak as us. You tried to buy her silence and it didn't work."

"You need to be careful, boy."

"You think we don't know where those pictures of Karlo came from? That we don't know you're the one supplying Karlo with girls?"

"It's in everyone's interests that there's a safe space. I protect—"

"Protect?"

"You've got no idea what I do to protect you. Max. The whole band. That's what I do. That's what you pay me for, remember?"

"And just how was it protecting us to take Beth to Manchester? To Palmer's place?" Toby laughs now, a hard, disbelieving laugh. "You arrogant prick. You're unhinged. Did you really think you could do whatever you like? Taking her to that place? Did you think she'd be impressed? Excited?"

Lyall says nothing. It's like he has a radar for anything that might incriminate him.

Toby pushes on. "Or were those little girls not supposed to be there? Was that a mix-up too?"

Lyall's face is almost completely purple. His control is rapidly deserting him. "You really have no fucking idea, do you?"

Toby stares at him. "What?"

"Listen, you naïve little cunt. While you guys were falling all over yourselves at the feet of your supposed angel, I was busy protecting you. You had no idea who Beth was. Did you? None of you had thought it through. She was twenty-two. Do you really think she was going to live happily ever after with Max? She was going to bleed you all for what she could take, and Max was going to lose interest eventually as always, and then what? We'd have another situation with a little bitch running around spreading rumours and lies."

"Why would she—"

"Because she thought she was better than all of you. Her aunt is the vanguard of the fucking feminist apocalypse. How long do you think she would have waited before destroying you all?"

"What the hell are you talking about?"

"Control." Lyall smiles now, a wide, tooth-filled grin. "I'm talking about control. About not taking any risks. About covering your back. And that takes ammunition."

Toby waits. This is gathering a momentum all of its own.

"They're all the same," Lyall says. "She would have tried to screw us all. Sooner or later. She'd have come out with some bleeding-heart story about *abuse* and *the poor children*. Little snowflake. What did she fucking know? These are not your average kids. They've travelled halfway round the world some of them. They know exactly what the arrangement is. Do they ever have a gun to their heads? No. But she would have used it to destroy us. To destroy you.

His blood's up. He goes on. "And how do you stop that happening? You make sure she's got a vested interest in never letting that information out. That she's dripping in it. Up to her neck. Or at least, that's what she believes."

"What, so you arranged for those girls to be there? So you could incriminate her? How could you take that risk?"

"You've never heard of plausible deniability? It's not even my place. It's Bernie's."

"But you didn't succeed, did you? Your fucking plan? Your ammunition? She didn't care. She was going public. That's why you needed her dead."

"I didn't need her dead. She wanted to be off the boat. That's what she'd been screaming for."

This is it.

Toby's heart feels like a nest of eels. "Right." He mustn't flounder now. "Next, you'll be saying she was asking for it."

"She was fucking asking for it. Little whore. Screaming in my face like that. Stupid bitch. Wanting to be let off the boat. How was she going to swim? We were three miles out. She was fucking suicidal and she got what she wanted. I just saved her some unnecessary suffering."

He draws breath at last, magnanimously. "She didn't know what hit her."

A hundred metres away, crouched in the gap between the recording studio's smoked glass gate and the great hedge, Juliet rips off her headphones. The young police officer beside her grips Toby's shotgun mic steadily, as Toby had instructed.

"Ms MacGillivray?"

Juliet's head pounds. Something inside her has shifted. She felt it, a catastrophic change – like a plate crashing apart far inside the earth – and now pure wrath swells through her heart and veins and stomach, eviscerating all other senses. She just about swallows a violent scream. She stands, rips away the cables and equipment attached to her.

"Juliet?" asks the young officer. "Ms MacGillivray?"

She doesn't respond. She walks compulsively towards the jetty and the *Favourite Daughter.*

CHAPTER SIXTY

Juliet's footfall resounds through the alder planks. She doesn't notice or care. She's being carried by a force outside herself, as though her lungs are pumped full of burning octane. She reaches the boat.

"LYALL!" she shouts. Reflected by the disused piles of the old jetty at her side, the shade of her own voice calls back to her. She steps onto the boat's rear platform, and quickly mounts the steps.

In the midship lounge area, Toby gets to his feet as she enters. He pulls a face and holds out his hands, desperately questioning what the hell she's doing.

Lyall appears, climbing the stairs from the cabins below. His incarnadine tan glows offensively and the curls at the nape of his neck, coyly brushing his turned-up collar, seem outrageous to her now. How did she not see it before? Why is it always the way with these men? Their depravity seems so obvious after the event.

"Juliet!" He laughs with amusement, his hands on his hips. "You're still on holiday? Nice of you—"

"Shut up!" she says. "Don't. Speak. I don't want to hear your voice ever again. Don't say another fucking word."

Toby's eyes widen further. He stands uncomfortably between them.

Juliet ignores him. "I know what you did, Lyall," she

continues. "I heard everything. What you did to Beth?" Her voice drops lower as each word siphons out. "You cowardly piece of shit. What the hell kind of man are you? An entirely innocent girl? She'd done nothing to you, nothing wrong. You killed her. You knocked her into the water, and you didn't even stop to look for her? You killed her twice."

"Now, look, I—"

"I said *shut up*. You had your chance. You had the chance to go back for her, and you chose not to. But that's not all, is it? That's not even half of it. You must have some kind of special instinct for corruption. Those kids in Manchester? The children you like to rape? You're a monster. You and your cronies. You're all going down for this."

Lyall fixes his face somewhere between a smile and a grimace. He walks straight past her, climbs onto the deck and – working fast – circles the gunnel, untying lanyards and gathering in the fenders.

"What the fuck?" Toby hisses at Juliet. "What are you doing? This wasn't the plan."

Juliet stares at Toby. "I don't know. I just…"

"You heard it all? Did we get enough? Where's Karen?"

"I don't know. She should be here by now. They were blocking the roads. She was supposed to be scrambling the coastguard."

They both stiffen as Lyall jumps off the boat. He crouches on the gangplank and loosens the hawser from the cleat.

"What's he doing?"

"It looks very much like he's getting ready to leave."

Lyall jumps back aboard and casts off. He starts winding the capstan. The anchor chain grinds noisily. Toby looks edgy. He makes for the door to the aft deck, and turns.

"We should get off."

Juliet sits, deliberately. "You go. I'm not going anywhere. This is exactly what he wants. To frighten us."

"Juliet." Toby shifts uncertainly. "It's not safe. He's

capable of anything. I can't leave you here. I've never seen him like this."

"I'm staying put."

"Right." He searches her eyes imploringly. He's terrified. She needs to give him a reason, permission to leave her.

"You go. We need Karen. Go and get her."

Toby backs out of the cabin reluctantly. Juliet follows him onto the lower deck, watching as he scuttles down the steps and retreats up the jetty, glancing fearfully back at her. She remembers the first day she saw him here; his watchfulness. His clumsy dive – following Karlo – into the water. Were they looking for the shoe, even then?

Lyall starts the motor. Juliet climbs to the topside helm. Diesel fumes fill the air. She's surprised by how high above the water they are. A flicker of fear licks through her. She's not wearing a life jacket.

"What course are you setting?

Lyall's jaw works angrily.

"Some magical destination in mind, where you can escape? From yourself?"

He bites. "Well, let's just see." His voice is even but has a taut quality. "Your first cruise courtesy of Malcolm Lyall. Very gracious of you to accept my hospitality."

There's something animalistic, sadistic about the way he says this. She wonders what kind of punishment he has in mind for her. She says nothing. Taking a seat on the top deck behind him, she grits her teeth as he steers out of the small harbour. It was a stupidly dangerous decision to stay with Lyall, but there's no changing her mind now.

He glances over his shoulder at her. "Are you sure you're in for the ride? If you're certain I'm such a brute, people will be surprised you were happy to come."

"Oh, don't try that on me. I don't care what people think. I'm staying put for the satisfaction of seeing you go down. You won't get far. You know they're coming for you, don't you?"

Lyall's weak blue eyes dart across the horizon.

They pick up speed. The wind catching now in her hair, Juliet wonders how Beth felt about Lyall's boat. She loved being on the water, but up here, in such luxury, everything is so removed, disconnected somehow from the elements. Did that distancing make Beth feel invincible on that last day? Did she misjudge it? They were three miles out, Lyall said. She used to manage the swim to the Hippo and back – nearly half a mile – with ease. Three miles she could probably have handled too. If Lyall hadn't hurt her.

Juliet breathes in the briny, fume-rich air, watching the back of his neck. At starboard, they pass the summerhouse, about four hundred metres out. They'll be passing the Hippo any moment now. She scans the water for its barrel-like granite surface.

"The roads are blocked, you know. The coastguard—"

"Ha!" he spits. "We'll be long gone by the time the coastguard trundle round."

"I wouldn't be so sure."

"Just shut your fucking mouth," Lyall snaps. "For one second. Do you think that would be possible? You haven't stopped talking since I let you on my boat, you know that? Fucking lunatic bitch."

Juliet raises her eyebrows with a delighted smile. "Does it disturb you? My voice?"

Lyall looks out to the horizon. Juliet glances back to shore, taking in their position. She still can't see the Hippo, which means… they must be almost on top of it.

"Lyall," she says, her voice rising. "You need to steer hard starboard."

"Don't tell me what to do, woman."

"But—"

"NO!" He shouts over her. "MY BOAT. MY RULES."

She looks for the boat's kill cord to pull the power. Lyall's not wearing it.

"Don't be fucking stupid, Lyall. I'm trying—"

Too late.

With a terrifyingly loud roar, the boat, newly full of fuel, jumps vertically out of the water, as though riding up a wall. There's a detonation somewhere, and Juliet is aware that she's left the boat – she's being pushed through the air – and the *Favourite Daughter* is above her and all around her now, disintegrating, following its own chaotic logic, turning on an unseen axis. Somewhere nearby Lyall is screaming. And in surreal slow motion, before she hits the water, Juliet sees and hears it all.

CHAPTER SIXTY-ONE

Juliet tries to take a gulp of oxygen before she goes under but it's knocked out of her on impact with the firth's icy surface. The water roils and surges around her, tumbling her with such violence she has no idea which way is up. She holds her breath and fights the deadly urge to breathe.

Teeming, thundering sounds fill her ears. Perhaps it's her own blood? Her own heart straining. *Watch the bubbles*. Isn't that what they always say? *They rise to the surface*. But the bubbles are everywhere; a mercurial onslaught, filled with bone-like shards that rasp and chafe at Juliet's eyes and skin.

And without warning, there, sliding past her, is Lyall, eyes terror-wide, arms grappling with some unseen enemy, legs spread-eagled, cycling desperately in the drink.

Instinctively she reaches for him, and just as it seems the eddies will flush him beyond her grasp, their fingertips touch, scrabbling for purchase, and their eyes meet. His pupils are large, dark discs. Panic has taken him and he clings to her, dragging her with him like a weight.

At that moment, a huge broken section of the *Favourite Daughter* plunges into the water above them. Juliet cries out but her voice is engulfed. The wood and fibreglass shell hits Lyall in the head and chest with shocking force and speed. It cleaves his face and takes him down, down to pin to the sea floor somewhere below. As he disappears, all Juliet can see is Beth's body, unconscious, dropping through the water like a lead doll.

Her throat and lungs flood instantly as she sucks in brackish liquid and the penetrating darkness fills her, holds her, and she doesn't choke or struggle because there's no fight left to fight. The last thing she is conscious of is a sense of relief. She closes her eyes, remembering, remembering, and in that peace she remembers that she too is a shell, a protective layer and that inside her, she carries a life – swimming, floating, breathing – in the serous world she has created.

She kicks.

THE STANDARD: EDEN CEO SUPPOSED DEAD IN FATAL CRASH

2 October 2018

Bernhard Palmer, Chair of Eden Media Group, is supposed dead following a light aircraft crash yesterday morning on the Caribbean island of St Barthélemy. His two-seater plane apparently came down in windy conditions on volcanic terrain and caught fire. There are no known survivors. Local investigators examining the wreckage say identifying the human remains will take some time.

Palmer was wanted for questioning in relation to the death last year of a young female migrant and related charges to do with sex offences and indecent images – crimes allegedly committed in a private apartment behind his exclusive Eden Club development in Manchester.

Police sources say a number of other high-profile individuals are within the scope of the investigation, including Palmer's close personal friend, and well-known public relations director, Malcolm Lyall. Lyall was also killed in a boating accident in Scotland ten days ago. New information linked to the case has prompted authorities to reopen enquiries into the death of twenty-two-year-old Beth Winters.

Previously thought to have committed suicide earlier this year, Winters had been dating Lyall's long-time client, DJ Max Bolin. She was the niece of politician, Juliet MacGillivray, current favourite in the Progressive Alliance leadership race. MacGillivray has issued no comment.

CHAPTER SIXTY-TWO

The package arrives on a Tuesday morning in late October at Juliet's office in Brixton, wrapped in plain paper just like all the others. Her assistant brings it to her.

"Do you want me to open it?"

Juliet shakes her head. When the first parcel arrived here at work three weeks ago, and was opened by a junior researcher, she'd had a lot of explaining to do.

"No. That's fine. Thank you. Just... would you just put it on the side?"

But she can't concentrate with it sitting there. After a few minutes, she rises reluctantly and turns it over in her hands, examining the postmarks. Nothing indicates a sender; it carries no more information than the previous three. It's about the size of a folded newspaper.

She sighs heavily, angrily, and with bitten nails tries to pick at its strong brown tape for a few moments, before giving up; resorting to scissors. Her back to the office window, she slices through the cardboard and tips the packet onto her hand.

A soft, pale fabric drops from the packet and falls across her open palm. A babygro. It's decorated with tiny pink rabbits wearing bow ties. *Playboy* rabbits. The label says 0-3 months.

Furious, she shoves it roughly back into the package. She knows already there'll be no forensics to go on. Karen has had the other parcels examined and found nothing. But Juliet doesn't need a fingerprint, or a shaft of hair to know who sent it.

Heart racing, she calls Declan.

"Don't let this shite get to you," he says. "Hand it straight over to Karen's people, and get on with your day. Don't let them win."

She knows he's right, but she's finding it increasingly hard to put this policy into practice. "It's him," she says. "Palmer. I know it's him."

"He's dead and gone, Juliet."

"No. He's letting me know he's not."

"If that's the case then, he's doing it on purpose. To needle you. Don't give in."

"I don't understand what he's getting out of it. Surely it's in his interest to disappear? He's gone to such trouble to convince everyone that he's dead."

"If it is him, and I'm not saying it is, then you've got to think like him. He's not a politician, Juliet."

She says nothing.

"To him it'll be a bit of sport. He wants to let you know that you haven't won. And he knows you won't go public. Not with this."

Still, she's silent. Thinking.

"Do you want to?" he asks. "Go public?"

"No." She pauses. "No. This is our private life. It's no one else's business. How the hell did he even find out?"

"You know," he muses. "I've been wondering about that and there are other people it could be, sending these things. There are a lot of nutters out there. People with axes to grind. Pro-lifers maybe. You said there are staff at the hospital in Inverness who heard you talking about… you know."

He began this train of thought partly to distract her from the idea of Palmer, still out there somewhere. But now he's saying the stuff out loud, it doesn't seem like such a good idea. They argued bitterly when she finally told him about her conversation with the obstetrician and her initial uncertainties about the baby. He'd been hurt. Hurt that she'd waited so long to talk to him, even though he knew he had no right to feel that way, after all the secrets he'd kept himself.

If he keeps on about the hospital, she'll think he's raking it all up again.

"Are you sure it's no one at work? Trying to undermine you? Or maybe that journalist from the hospital. Digging for a story?"

"Of course it's not. It's Palmer. I know it's him. There's no proof he died in that plane."

"You can't expect absolute proof. Look, you've been through a nightmare. We all have. It's a natural reaction to feel afraid after all that. A bit paranoid."

A bit paranoid.

"Don't patronise me, Declan. You've seen the comments online. The threats. I've got a thick skin. I'm used to that kind of crap. What I'm not used to is receiving shredded baby bonnets through the mail."

"You're right. That came out wrong," he says, "What I meant to say was, if you hadn't seen Lyall drown with your own eyes, isn't there a part of you that would still worry he was alive? Alive, and out to get you?"

She grips the parcel tightly.

"We know Lyall's dead, but whether or not Palmer is too, there will always be others." Declan presses on, perhaps unwisely. "I mean, people out there who are just as bad, who'll keep on doing what Lyall and Palmer did. What are you going to do? Sell the flat in London as well as the summerhouse, and go into hiding? Live the rest of your life in fear that they're coming for you and your loved ones?"

Juliet blinks. She hasn't told him about her latest conversation with Erica, a late call a few nights ago. They'd been talking about the final arrangements for the sale. Erica had been sounding wistful.

"I hope you don't feel weird," Juliet had said. "About

selling the summerhouse. I just don't see how we can enjoy being there again. How we can ever disassociate it from what happened to Beth, or Lyall."

Erica had made a strange noise, not quite a laugh. "But it's always been associated with Lyall. Don't you remember?"

And suddenly it all came flooding back. The family. The neighbours with the monster hedge and impeccable lawn and ostentatious steam room where eighteen-year-old Juliet had stumbled upon Erica in flagrante with the groper, the visiting cousin, with longish dark hair, and an obscene tan. Juliet had lost it. Called him a pervert and told him to get away from her sister, or she'd report him.

After a long pause, Juliet had cleared her throat. "You're not telling me that guy was Lyall?"

Erica continued, seemingly oblivious to Juliet's disbelief. "Do you remember how angry he was? I mean, I suppose it's hardly surprising. You and Dad came just at the right time."

It was such a long time ago, and just one in a string of similar incidents with various guys. But how could she never have made the connection? A sliver of horror slid down Juliet's back as she did the maths; the question had slipped out before she thought better of it.

"He wasn't Beth's father, was he?"

"No." Juliet had listened as Erica took a drag on a cigarette. "At least, I think not. I suppose we'll never know."

"Juliet?" Declan says now. He's been waiting for a response. "You can't eliminate all the evil fucks in the universe. Are you going to hunt them all down, as if they're all out to get you?"

Juliet grips her temple.

"It's not about anyone being *out to get us,*" she manages. "It's about justice for Beth, and all those kids whose lives they ruined. And Sophie. And Marcus. Whoever is sending this stuff is letting me know they got away with it, Declan. And it's worse than that. They're telling me they'll do it again. I mean, a wee babygro with fuckbunnies on? What could be clearer than that?"

A press officer walking past her office glances in through the glass. She lowers her voice. “The symbolism is pretty blindingly obvious.”

The other ‘gifts’ – an obscene dummy; a bib with a revolting blood spatter design – flash through her mind. She listens to the silence at the other end. No matter how much Declan wants to reassure her, this time words fail him.

CHAPTER SIXTY-THREE

Dominic Palmer takes his father's call on his second SIM. He's been half expecting it for some days now. But when it arrives from Moscow it's still surprising – for a number of reasons. The preliminaries, as usual, are curt. Being in hiding hasn't brought out any paternal sentimentality then.

Conversely, his father's focus on Juliet MacGillivray is bordering on… what's the word? Not emotional exactly, but excessive, obsessive. Sure enough, it's among the first things he mentions.

"What are the polls saying?"

Dominic suppresses his irritation.

"She's still ahead of all the other progressives. Approval high."

"Un-fucking-believable."

"Not really. Not when you look at the context. I mean, she's riding all the #MeToo stuff."

"Idiots."

Fervid. That's it.

At least, Dominic supposes, it's one way of avoiding the elephant in the room. The Eden allegations. They haven't discussed them at all; his father won't divulge what his lawyers are saying. The man's ego is phenomenal. He hasn't even bothered to deny any of it.

It's quite an extraordinary performance: to be reported

dead; to be wanted for child sex offences; yet acting as if nothing's happened, as if it doesn't affect anyone else. As if it hasn't wiped thirty percent from EMG's share value. As if Dominic hasn't had to spend hours explaining to his own hysterical wife that there's no way his father had a sexual predilection for kids, and there's especially no way that, even if he did, it would have extended to his own grandchildren.

At least Mother's dead. That's one blessing.

And at least this MacGillivray fixation means his father has relaxed the whip. Predictably, there's been no acknowledgement of anyone's… efforts. Of Dominic stepping up. Not a word of thanks, or praise or pride. Well, *fuck it*. Let him stay in fucking Russia, and stay mentally deranged. To be frank, it's a welcome change not to have to rehearse every fine detail of every area of the Eden empire. To have some freedom.

"Why aren't you using the abortion angle?"

"You're not listening, Dad. I've told you" – he never used to speak to his father like this. It's invigorating, to be honest – "the timing's way off. It would be better to wait. We don't know for sure if she did abort it. Imagine the headline coming out the day after the birth. Or just before? That could be counter-productive."

"I'm not so sure."

"I'm telling you: at this juncture, the whole story would sink like a stone. It would only sharpen attention on this bloody ordeal they've been milking. She's a liberal wet-dream right now. She can do no wrong." Dominic hesitates briefly. "This entire thing, her involvement, the more details that come out about how she contributed to the fucking investigation the more it's all just playing into their hands. Her law-and-order rating is off the chart. Seriously. It's higher than any right-winger."

"Fucking nonsense." A guttural rumble, almost a growl, comes down the line. "*Law and order*. What about security? The economy? Jobs? What about twelve fucking billion in exports?"

Dominic looks at his watch.

"And... how are you? Okay?"

"I'm being well looked after. Very comfortable. A man could get used to it. The room service is, how shall I put this? Exceptional. And by that, I mean, getting your order right and on time is the exception, not the rule."

"Well, at least they get it to you. They're looking after you?"

"Of course."

They say their goodbyes. Less than effusively.

Bernhard Palmer snorts as he hangs up. Sometimes he wonders about that boy. He's a pussy, and he always has been, there's no denying it. Palmer often wishes his daughter had shown an interest in the business. She's got what it takes. Not that she's spoken to him in years.

There's movement in the lobby of his suite. That'll be the herring. At last. The dining porter knocks once, and enters, pushing a trolley covered with a white cloth into the sitting room.

Palmer rises and turns to the desk in front of the window to put down his cigar. In the blue-black frame of the window, he watches the reflection of the porter as he pauses in the middle of the room.

"By the fireplace," he says. "I've told you this before."

The guy doesn't move.

Palmer turns. But even as he does, he can see it's not the usual porter. This guy is taller... massive. He makes the trolley seem like a child's toy. Palmer squints. He should have his glasses on. This is... He recognises this guy.

It's that gofer, isn't it? How the fuck did he get here?

Well, that's mightily impressive. Palmer chuckles softly to himself. Blythe did say this guy was above average. Loyal. Ex-filth? Wasn't that it? He's outdone himself to find his way here. He must want paying, that'll be it.

Palmer clears his throat. "My God! I didn't recognise you. Come in." He walks slowly to the drinks cabinet. "Can I offer you a drink?"

There's no reply.

His vast back hiding the trolley from Palmer, Paul removes the linen cloth. Ice clinks behind him as Palmer makes a drink. Calmly, Paul threads the silencer to the P22. He loads and checks it meticulously.

When he turns, Palmer is standing – a whisky decanter in one hand, a heavy crystal tumbler in the other – in front of the art deco cocktail unit on the other side of the living room. The sunburst mirror frames him perfectly.

Paul puts a bullet neatly through the middle of his boss's boss's temple. There's no exit wound.

CHAPTER SIXTY-FOUR

Declan does a sweep of the summerhouse, and carries the last box to the car. He hears Juliet shout.

"I just… I'm going to the sea."

As she runs along the beach, she knows it's the last time she'll see the mudflats at Culbin. She can't bear to look back at the house, to search for wood smoke still unfurling into the sky like a child's drawing. She turns instead to the sea, to this stretch of Moray coast that used to bring her comfort. Ignoring the cold, she takes off her shoes and hurries towards the water's edge.

Where the sand darkens she falters, but the sea surges on, skirting around and behind her as if determined to reach the bands of driftwood and mussel shell middens at the edge of the forest. A few metres away, the waves smack and slap against a natural causeway of sandbars; droplets fling themselves upwards into the salty air, where they hang for a moment, before squirming, finally, across the map of rippled silt below her feet.

She doesn't even notice the sensation of cold water on her toes. Her eyes are fixed now on the Firth beyond: a pewter mass, rising and falling rhythmically against the white-grey sky. She can just see the Hippo, four hundred metres out.

She collects a large flat stone, which she weighs in her hand. She crouches and gathers another and another, arranging them carefully. She imagines Beth doing the same, out on Kelspie. Clever. Leaving her trace, like a needle in the air.

It's been a month since Juliet sat alongside Toby on the summerhouse deck, both of them shocked and silent while Karen made a series of phone calls. As if on autopilot, he'd begun explaining how his recording equipment worked. How he thought he could make Lyall talk.

He would have gone on, continued describing to Juliet the range and comparative recording qualities of his various mics, if she hadn't interrupted.

"Toby," she'd said. "On that last day, on the boat. Was she scared? Beth. Was she afraid?"

He'd looked at her, and a new expression came over his face, replacing the resignation and shame painted for so long on his features.

"No," he replied. He shook his head slowly. "She was furious. Defiant, right to the end."

Juliet picks up a pebble now. It's about the size of a small fig, smooth and grey, with pinkish veins running through it. The size of the life inside her. If she throws it into the water, she won't even hear the tiny sound it will make as it drops into the waves a few metres away. How long would it be before it reaches dry land again? On this shifting stretch of shore, there's no telling.

She pockets it, safely, and it bounces softly against her. She stands, stretches her toes and notes its weight in her jacket. A talisman. For good luck. For the leadership campaign. For the nursery perhaps.

Declan's watching her from the treeline. She hears his voice again, calling her name. She turns back towards him and takes a step.

EPILOGUE: CITY COURIER:
Dark Heart of Event City

1 November 2018

- **Exclusive posthumous report by Marcus Keyes, with Declan Byrne.**
- **Child exploitation and sex abuse is rife in Manchester.**
- **Despite the recent deaths of two perpetrators, others remain active at the highest levels of society.**
- **Undercover investigation exposes how the police, city funding mechanisms, and celebrity patronage have combined to hide a paedophile ring that may have been operating for nearly two decades.**

It starts with the hope of a better life.

Last year, 2,952 unaccompanied children applied for asylum in the UK, according to Home Office data. Most of these children travelled on their own to Europe from countries like Sudan, Eritrea, Vietnam, Albania, and Syria. Many became separated from their families in transit, and have experienced severe trauma and abuse. Word of Home Office hostile environment measures is out there, but desperate kids, often with no papers, keep coming.

Why? Our laws are generally in line with international

guidelines and lone child refugees are supposed to be treated in the same way as any other looked-after-child. But the UK has a history of providing sanctuary. Many British remember with pride the protection offered to evacuees and the *kindertransport* of World War Two. Perhaps this makes us seem an attractive destination.

In reality, the influx in recent years has placed a huge strain on provision. Human Rights organisations are flagging worrying failings. Lack of screening, poor mental and physical healthcare, insecure housing and inadequate safeguarding are just some of the shortfalls identified. Unicef have reported that "criminals rather than formal procedures offer the most likely route to the UK for unaccompanied children" and some Local Authorities say they have "insufficient funds to fulfill their duties to these children". There are scores of missing child refugees in the UK, and Europol has said 10,000 missing across Europe would be a conservative estimate.

At the time of these reports, I was already undercover in Manchester, investigating the reality of life for these desperate young people.

After just four days basic training, I was able to work in the canteen of a reception centre, with unrestricted access to the children there, aged twelve upwards. Boys and girls of a wide range of ages and mixed cultures were sharing accommodation, and I saw staff turn a blind eye as children and unidentified adults came and went from the site, often late at night, unrecorded. When I questioned this, I was told it was not a detention centre.

Manchester seemed like as good a place as any to start. In September, a fourteen-year-old female asylum seeker disappeared from her accommodation in an eastern suburb, and was later found dead in a city park.

The police rapidly concluded that the killing had "honour motives" within the refugee community. But during my work there, it became clear that community tensions were not the only, or even main issue. These children were extremely vulnerable to exploitation in the city, ranging from acts of pocket-money prostitution to systematic grooming by organised criminal gangs.

After months of investigation, evidence has now been obtained, thanks to the courage of one of the survivors, proving that one of these rings operated at the cultural heart of England's Event City, and involved high-ranking members of the establishment, including national law enforcement. Peter Blythe, Minister of State for Law Enforcement and Fire Services, is understood to be suspended, pending investigation.

As well as identifying a number of her abusers through photographs, the survivor was able to tape secret footage of the offences, which has now been passed to the authorities. Two of those accused, PR agent Malcolm Lyall and Eden CEO Bernhard Palmer, have died in what some say were suicides, since incontrovertible evidence of their involvement came to light.

ACKNOWLEDGEMENTS

Huge thanks go to Jemima Forrester and David Higham Associates, to Lauren Parsons at Legend Press, and to Lucy Chamberlain, Ditte Loekkegaard, Rose Cooper, and the whole Legend team. It's an honour to be among your authors.

To Beatrice Hammar and Andreas Nilsson, for the seeds: your summerhouse and the original 'Swallow'. And for your feedback, and that of other generous readers, Jane and Henry Branson, Susannah Waters, Mark Love, Jenny Ogilvie, Cat Walmsley, and Andrei Rada. Thank you all. Extra props to Andrei, an incredible musician and composer. Your *Sea of Bones* score is inspired. It's been a pleasure to collaborate.

To phenomenal woman and author, Rosie Walsh, my writing partner. For problem-solving, insight and encouragement far beyond the call of duty. Thank you is not enough. I can't wait to see your brilliant follow up to *The Man Who Didn't Call* fly off the shelves.

Knight's Forensic Pathology must have a mention. And Darren Bush's writing on blacksmithing is recommended. Many thanks to him for sharing his knowledge and for the phrase, 'heating, holding and hitting'. To the welcoming people at Loggerheads Country Park, particularly Joel Walley, Ecology Officer. And to the Winchester Writers' Festival, which I urge aspiring writers to attend.

Thank you to the friendly students and staff, especially

June Hyndman and her class, at Moray College, University of the Highlands and Islands, who welcomed me to the Fine Art Textile department and shared their work and expertise.

To everyone at the Belga where I've been treated like one of the family. A big thank you, and respect.

Alison Rendle helped me set out on this journey. As did Mrs Riddett, Ann Watts, Madame Jolly, Mrs Leech, Paul King and Brian Campbell. Teachers and story-planters. Thank you.

To Brian and Chris O'Donoghue, for a home where books were valued and language was fun. Mum, for long hours spent typing my childhood efforts. Anna and Charlie, without you, I couldn't have imagined this book. And Jane Branson, for a lifetime of sisterly wisdom. Your beautiful novel is what the world needs.

Above all, to Tom Wellings. For your fierce love, support, and challenge. Thank you.

If you enjoyed what you read, don't keep it a secret.

Review the book online and tell anyone who will listen.

Thanks for your support spreading the word about Legend Press!

Follow us on Twitter
@legend_press

Follow us on Instagram
@legendpress